HIS DECEIT FORGED
THEIR MARRIAGE.
HER MAGIC CREATED
THEIR LOVE....

HE SWEPT HER INTO HIS ARMS, AND CARRIED HER FROM THE DINING ROOM TO HER BEDROOM WITHOUT A WORD OF EXPLANATION.

"Oh," Meggie said, pressing her cheek against his hard shoulder as he started up the staircase, giggles still shaking her body. "I do not think this is at all correct. Aunt Dorelia said most specifically that you were to keep your hands to yourself tonight. I am not to be ravished until tomorrow."

"I don't give a damn what Aunt Dorelia said," Hugo replied. "Furthermore, regardless of what ideas that absurd woman might have put in your head, if you think I'm about to take you to your room and ravish you, you're very badly mistaken."

"I am?" she said. "What a shame . . . but never mind. I can wait. I've waited my whole life."

"If you're trying to tell me you're a virgin, sweetheart, I'd already reached that conclusion."

Hugo slowly lowered her to the floor, his fingers barely pressing on her flesh, and yet she felt his fingertips pulsing against her as strong as a heartbeat. She shivered under the intimacy of his touch. "We really will be married tomorrow?" she asked.

"Yes," he answered, his voice low and smooth as velvet. "We will be married tomorrow, and once we are, my lovely Meggie, then we are free to enjoy each other as we please. Exactly and as fully as we please . . ."

HIGH PRAISE FOR BESTSELLING AUTHOR
KATHERINE KINGSLEY
AND HER PREVIOUS NOVELS

ONCE UPON A DREAM

"Miss Kingsley has woven a delightful tale . . . a sparkling gem."
—*Romantic Times*

"An ardent and magical retooling of *Cinderella* . . . draws the reader in and leaves her holding her breath . . . emotionally compelling and intensely romantic."
—*Romance Forever*

IN THE WAKE OF THE WIND

"Ms. Kingsley has done an excellent job of bringing us two wonderful lovers and a cast of secondary characters you can sink your teeth into."
—*Rendezvous*

"Another dreamspun romance . . . once more Katherine Kingsley works her magic . . . in a story that lifts your heart and makes your soul sing . . . [she] continues to break new ground with her unique love stories and this heart-lifting tale is no exception."
—*Romantic Times*

Dell Books by Katherine Kingsley

In the Wake of the Wind
Once Upon a Dream
Call Down the Moon

KATHERINE KINGSLEY

Call Down The Moon

A DELL BOOK

Published by
Dell Publishing
a division of
Bantam Doubleday Dell Publishing Group, Inc.
1540 Broadway
New York, New York 10036

ISBN 0-440-22386-5

Printed in the United States of America

Published simultaneously in Canada

May 1998

10 9 8 7 6 5 4 3 2 1

OPM

To Pat Kendall

Who has guided, nurtured, and cherished me
for the larger portion
of my life, and always with great good grace.
With all my love.

Acknowledgments

Thanks go to a myriad of people who aided and abetted during the course of this book:

In Suffolk, England, thanks to Sarah and Roger Pinfold, John and Doris Fulford, and in particular, to Mandy Radice who many years ago first introduced me to Woodbridge and the glorious coastal waters. Also thanks to Tom and Jill Standon, for allowing me to use their home in Orford as my base for the two happy months that I spent researching. I would be amiss if I didn't mention Peter Hill of the Lighthouse Restaurant in Aldeburgh who provided true delight and a deep love for Suffolk through brilliant food and company.

Back at home, thanks as always to Jan Hiland, Francie Stark, and my husband Bruce for patiently reading mountains of manuscript and commenting vociferously.

Thanks to Marshelle Joseph, less formally known to me as Tis, who kept my body upright and in working order when I was ready to retire it to the glue factory. She was—is—a true saving grace.

Finally, thanks to the most wonderful and inspirational Clarissa Pinkola Estés who not only wrote the brilliant book *Women Who Run with the Wolves,* but who first taught me how to howl without reservation. I haven't stopped since. This book owes much to her insights.

To the readers: Please continue to write with your thoughts and comments. Your letters are a source of inspiration. You can reach me at P.O. Box 37, Wolcott, Colorado, 81655. I will always reply if you enclose a SASE.

Prologue

Ipswich Orphanage
Ipswich, Suffolk
August 1816

"Meggie Bloom, you are an utter disgrace to yourself and those around you," the Mother Superior announced in chilly tones.

Meggie stood before her, her pride commanding her posture into a rigorous upright position. It wasn't easy, considering that she'd just come from a caning.

The stripes on her back stung ferociously, but Meggie reckoned every one that Sister Luke of Mercy had delivered was worth the pain. At least she'd finally gotten a bit of her own back at the silly nun, who had been tormenting her for years. The temptation had been irresistible.

No matter how much Sister Luke of Mercy might deny it, it *was* true that the sister harbored lust in her heart for Father Kent. All Meggie had done was to repeat the exact words that she'd heard clear as a bell inside the sister's head when the priest had arrived to celebrate morning Mass.

That they happened to be rather explicit hadn't been Meggie's fault. That Meggie had chosen to ask Sister Luke of Mercy what "wishing I had the Father's body heaving inside me" meant, and whether it had anything to do with Holy Communion, had.

But oh, the satisfaction.

"I realize that I should not have spoken to Sister Luke

of Mercy as I did, Mother. I ask your forgiveness for my impertinence," Meggie said in the litany she'd been repeating for eight long years. She might not be a Catholic, but she knew the rituals inside out.

"For your *impertinence*? My girl, your sins go far beyond something so elementary. This latest incident has led me to decide that you are not fit to live in any level of society."

The Mother Superior folded her hands together in a beatific fashion, as if she were enrolling for sainthood, and regarded Meggie grimly. "I have therefore concluded that the only place you *are* suited for is the Woodbridge Sanitarium."

"The—the sanitarium, Mother? Do you mean the asylum for the insane?" Meggie asked faintly. She prayed that dizziness had distorted her understanding.

"Yes. The asylum for the insane," the Mother Superior agreed, her lips thinning. "There is no need to look so shocked, Miss Meggie. Consider your fate a blessing. I might have sent you to work at Bedlam, since the insane are all you're suited for. At least the Woodbridge Sanitarium is a private institution where the families of the afflicted pay well for their keep." Her lips thinned even further until they looked positively ghoulish. "Maybe the inmates are already so afflicted by the curse of Lucifer that they will not notice his handmaiden in their midst."

"You—you will not honor your agreement?" Meggie whispered, her hand at her throat, which was so constricted she could hardly breathe, let alone speak.

"Our *agreement*?" the nun said, peering down her long nose at Meggie with the utmost disdain. "We had no agreement, other than that this orphanage would feed you, clothe you, and educate you until you reached the age of eighteen. Although it is true that you are only seventeen, you are no longer welcome here. We are a

Christian institution and have suffered your depravity long enough."

Horror turned Meggie's blood cold as the nun's words sank into her numb brain. Teaching was what Meggie had always wanted to do—the Mother Superior knew that! Meggie had worked extremely hard over the years to prove herself. Academics was the one thing that she *had* done right, excelling in nearly every class.

She'd made a huge effort with her elocution, too, modeling her speech after that of Sister Prudence who had been born an earl's daughter. Even given the unfortunate circumstances of her birth, it had been Meggie's highest hope that if she spoke correctly, she might find a position as a governess in a fine family. Failing that lofty ambition, she could have been a teacher in a fine school at least. She'd had every reason to expect a good reference from the Mother Superior when the time came for her release.

It never occurred to her that the Mother Superior would be so cruel as to punish her this unjustly. To sentence her to five days of confinement in one of the outhouses to be followed by a caning was one thing—but to sentence her to life in an asylum? And a sentence it was, for the Mother Superior knew Meggie had no choice but to do as she was told. Where else could she go? She had no money, no relatives to whom she might appeal.

"I have already applied to Sister Agnes, a nun from my order who is director of the sanitarium, to take you on," the Mother Superior continued. "She has agreed, but only because she is so badly short-handed. She knows all about your wicked ways, and I can only pray that you will not torment the nuns under her charge as you have done here."

What little blood was left in Meggie's face drained out of it. Not only was she to be condemned to life in an asylum, but far worse, to an unending life with the nuns. The thought was almost more than she could bear.

She wanted to cry, to beg the Mother Superior to change her mind and give her the chance to be a teacher, but her pride wouldn't let her. She knew it wouldn't do any good, anyway. The Mother Superior had never changed her mind about anything in all the years Meggie had known her.

Meggie bowed her head in acknowledgment, refusing to give the woman the satisfaction of seeing how devastated she was.

She packed her few possessions in the same carpetbag she'd arrived with eight years before and walked out of the door of the orphanage without once looking back, her spine straight and her chin raised. Whatever life brought next, Meggie refused to be broken or bowed.

As she started down the road from Ipswich that would take her the twenty miles to Woodbridge, she told herself she would ignore the whispers that were bound to continue. She would suffer the inevitable punishments in silence. She would do whatever work was given to her without complaint.

And she would never let anyone know the bitterness she carried in her heart.

1

Woodbridge, Suffolk
March 1822

Hugo heaved a sigh of annoyance as he regarded the gray facade of the manor house. Taking another step closer, he peered at the discreet brass placard to one side of the heavy door.

Woodbridge Sanitarium it announced, as if it were some sort of benign rest home for the infirm instead of a residence for raving lunatics. He still wasn't entirely sure how he'd let his mother talk him into this thankless mission, although the sight of her streaming nose and red-rimmed eyes and the sound of her raspy voice and congested cough had certainly helped to persuade him.

Her severe cold might have prevented her from carrying out the errand, but he'd been an idiot to agree to come in her place. He loathed infirmity of any kind and paying a duty call to an establishment like this was *not* his cup of tea. He cursed himself silently for allowing himself to be put in this position.

Of course it was his own fault for mentioning that he was on his way to inspect a piece of property for sale on the Suffolk coast near Woodbridge. How was he to have known that his mother's pet charity was practically on its doorstep?

Still, there was nothing to be done; he was here now and had an obligation to carry out his duty. He lifted the door knocker, letting it fall with a loud thud.

In a matter of moments, the door opened and a pleasant-looking woman in her middle years clad in a neat gray dress, white headdress, and a starched apron peered out at him.

"May I help you, sir?" she asked, gazing at him with no more than a curious expression. No insanity there, he thought with surprise and relief.

"You may," he replied in his most imperious manner. "Please inform the matron that Lord Hugo Montagu would like a moment of her time," he said, attempting to appear perfectly calm. "You might add that I am the younger son of your patroness, the Dowager Duchess of Southwell."

"Indeed I will, your lordship," she replied equally calmly, oblivious to his discomfort. "Would you care to step inside while I inform her that you are here?"

Hugo cleared his throat. "Thank you," he said, much against his better judgment. He had no idea what to anticipate once inside the door. Wild screaming from behind heavily barred doors, a sour, noxious odor of filth and overcooked cabbage, perhaps?

In this preconception too, he was mistaken. He removed his hat and crossed the threshold into the main hall, finding it much the same as any other civilized manor house he'd ever visited. Comfortable chairs were arranged in cozy groups, and the only smell to reach his nostrils was the sweet fragrance of fresh flowers placed in strategic positions. For all outward intents and purposes, this might have been the home of a family friend.

He wondered how much his mother had to do with the pretty deception, given that she had been a patroness of this particular establishment for years—something he'd only just discovered. He didn't understand her motive for supporting this particular cause with her position and money. Why on earth had she chosen to befriend madmen when there were plenty of other worthy charities?

But that was none of his concern and his thoughts moved on to his real mission for having come to Suffolk. The area had the advantage of having one of the milder climates to be found. Also in its favor was that it was far enough from his brother's ducal seat in Leicestershire that he wouldn't be on the family doorstep where they could watch his every move.

In any case, it was time that he invested in a place of his own, now that he could afford to. He needed a nice country pile where he could entertain properly, make the right sort of impression. The address of the land agent sat in his breast pocket and he was expected this afternoon. He needed a place that would keep him busy and away from the temptations of London. He was bloody tired of living at Southwell right under his mother's nose.

He started as a door banged somewhere above him and the sound of voices came faintly, then faded away down a corridor. He sat back in his chair again and took a deep breath.

They were absurd, these nerves of his. What was he afraid of, some deranged person leaping upon him out of the blue? The inmates were carefully guarded, surely, as carefully and quietly controlled as their environment was. Yet he still couldn't shake the feeling that someone was about to pounce upon him.

Whatever had his mother been thinking to send him here? He couldn't imagine a more awful fate than not being in one's right mind.

He spun around at the sound of footsteps coming across the marble floor. It was only the woman who had opened the door, he realized with infinite relief as she came toward him.

"Your lordship, the matron will see you now. If you'll just follow me?" she said in that cool, controlled voice, inclining her head toward the far side of the hall.

The corridor down which he was led was agreeable enough, brightened by the sunlight that flooded in through the tall windows on the ground floor. No, there was nothing he'd seen so far that could be described as even remotely sinister.

Perhaps the insane were locked up elsewhere, out of the sight and sound of visiting relatives who would naturally be anxious that everything seem as normal as possible. After all, the families paid handsomely to be sure that appearances were kept up.

The woman in the gray dress abandoned him outside a paneled mahogany door, disappearing down the hallway.

Hugo watched after her, reminding himself that he had survived a handful of duels. What did he have to fear from a starched matron who had nothing better to do than look after a houseful of lunatics?

He knocked firmly.

"Please come in," intoned a brisk voice from the other side.

Hugo pushed the door open—and stared.

An elderly woman garbed in black and white robes sat behind a large desk in an equally large room, regarding him with what he could only describe as a no-nonsense expression. A *nun*? It was the last thing in the world he expected.

"Lord Hugo," she said, gesturing for him to sit on the chair facing her desk. "What a pleasant surprise this is. I am Sister Agnes. I was expecting your mother, but she has obviously sent you as her emissary."

"She did," he replied after a moment's hesitation. "She neglected to tell me this is a nunnery," he added. Nuns and lunatics didn't mix in his mind. Nuns were supposed to be holy, sacrosanct. They upheld the laws of God. Lunatics defied it.

"This is no nunnery, Lord Hugo," the matron said

with the touch of a wry smile. "I was merely called by my order to be director here and some of the other sisters fill out the staff. However, we do strive to alleviate the suffering of those in need, and those here are in great need indeed. Compassion for the mentally ill is in short supply."

Hugo regarded her in silence. He didn't need a lecture from a nun of all people, although he couldn't help wondering if she had read his mind.

"Do you doubt it, Lord Hugo? Perhaps you think, as many people do, that those who are unstable in mind and spirit should be cast to the winds, that their affliction is of their own making?"

"I think nothing of the sort, er—Sister," Hugo said, shifting uncomfortably in his chair. "Actually, I have no opinion at all. I merely came on my mother's behalf. She has a bad cold, you see."

The corners of her mouth lifted in a knowing smile. "I think I do see," she said gently. "You are not comfortable here, and there is no reason why you should be—most are not. Your mother is an exception to the rule, an exceedingly sympathetic woman to whom we will always be grateful. Without her patronage, we might have had to close our doors years ago, but she has been a staunch supporter even in our times of greatest trial."

Hugo nodded. "My mother is a staunch supporter of whatever she believes in. Although I happen to be a fortunate beneficiary of her great faith, I am not like her, Sister. When it comes to virtue, I am no example to live by."

"This is not the confessional, Lord Hugo," the nun said with a low chuckle. "Our sins are our own and only between us and our Heavenly Father. So tell me. What missive did your mother send you with?"

He didn't know why he had broached the topic of his past sins, many though they were. Feeling acutely ill at ease, he slipped his hand inside the breast pocket of his coat to retrieve his mother's letter. He proffered it to the elderly nun. "My mother sent me with this offering, Sister, and with an inquiry into the health of Lady Eunice Kincaid."

Hugo knew Eunice Kincaid only slightly and liked her even less. He had been present when Eunice had experienced her final descent into madness in Ireland six months before. That the episode had happened the same day that his brother Raphael was being married to Eunice's stepdaughter was extremely unfortunate. Hugo thanked his lucky stars that he'd been laid up in bed with an injury and had thus missed witnessing the actual breakdown. From what he'd heard of it afterward, it hadn't been a pleasant scene.

Naturally his mother had known exactly what to do and she'd had the unfortunate woman shipped off to this very place shortly thereafter. Hugo really didn't care to know much more.

"The duchess is very kind to ask after Lady Kincaid," the nun said, placing his mother's letter on the desk unread and folding her hands together in front of her. "You might tell her grace that Lady Kincaid is doing very nicely. Oh, she is mostly lost in her childhood, but I can only see that as a blessing, as it keeps her content for much of the time. She is certainly improved from the time of her arrival."

Hugo felt relieved. So far, so good. No suggestion that he pay a social call to the madwoman. "I am pleased to hear it. From what I understand, she gave little pleasure in her life in the outside world. It is good to know she is not creating problems here as well."

He rose and walked over to the elongated window behind Sister Agnes's desk, gazing out over the manicured lawns. Everything looked perfectly normal.

A frown creased his brow as his gaze wandered yet

farther. It drifted up over the tops of the bare trees to the high walls that ran around the perimeter of the property, once built to keep the public out, but whose purpose now was to keep the demented in.

"Lady Kincaid causes no trouble," the nun agreed. "Her former life is now forgotten. We do not judge our patients for their prior behavior, Lord Hugo. Many of them had no control over their actions, and those who did . . . well, as I said, we do not judge. We only seek to support and to heal where God shows us that healing is possible."

Hugo only dimly heard her. A young woman had appeared out of thin air, walking directly past the window where he stood. She was dressed all in white, her uncovered hair as fair as corn silk in midsummer, falling down her back in a loose braid. The sun, on a lowering westward arc, caught her from the far side, backlighting her profile and casting a nimbus about her head. Hugo drew in a sharp breath between his teeth.

The girl looked like a bloody angel straight out of a church frieze, complete with halo.

He raised his hand and reached out to touch her and to determine if she was flesh and blood or just a product of his fevered imagination. His fingertips met only cool glass.

The illogical disappointment that flooded through him made him feel like a fool. What had he expected? That his hand would magically pass through the windowpane? And yet he refused to lower it, pressing his palm against the glass.

At that exact moment her step slowed and she glanced to her left, as if she had sensed not only his presence but his frustration. Her eyes met his full-on.

Hugo wasn't prepared for the piercing jolt that he felt, as if God had deliberately aimed a bolt of lightning at him for presuming to stare at one of His own. Hugo was mesmerized by the young woman's astonishing eyes.

Her eyes were light gray and as translucent as starlight—so translucent that he felt they had seen straight through him and out the other side, as if he were nothing more substantial or significant than a cloud.

She held his gaze for the space of a few heartbeats, and then she calmly looked away and continued on her way. A moment later she disappeared from sight.

Hugo blinked. And blinked again, his heart pounding furiously in his chest. He wanted to call after her, tell her to return, to explain herself to him. He'd never had any experience with angels—he didn't even believe in their existence. So if she wasn't an angel, then what *was* she?

She wasn't an ordinary woman, he was certain of that. He'd never been affected by a woman in this way, nor had he ever seen a face like hers before. It was so clear and tranquil, as if the cares of this world had never touched it. It was as if *she* didn't exist in this world at all.

As if she didn't exist in this world at all . . .

Hugo's eyes widened in horror.

How could he have been so stupid? She was one of *them.* He had been exactly right, but in the worst sort of way. She didn't exist in this world in the least, but in some different world of her own making, the world that lunatics inhabited.

An angel indeed, he thought cynically. Obviously the air in the asylum was contagious, for he'd clearly caught some form of dementia for even thinking such things, even if she did resemble something out of a blasted Byzantine fresco.

It seemed a hell of a waste that Mother Nature had bestowed such bounties on a madwoman, but he supposed that couldn't be helped.

On the other hand, the tightening in his groin he most *certainly* should be able to help, he thought, infuriated with himself. The unsolicited physical reaction was utterly ridiculous, given the circumstances.

"Lord Hugo? Did you hear me?"

"Sister," he said, clearing his throat, speaking over his shoulder as he tried to suppress the evidence of his baser nature in front of the nun. "I was wondering. Is *anyone* allowed to wander freely about the grounds?"

"That entirely depends on who it is," Sister Agnes replied, her tone unconcerned. "Why do you ask?"

"Oh, I just saw someone passing by," Hugo said as casually as he could manage. "I couldn't help but wonder, not knowing what your regulations are."

"Despite what you might think, this is not Newgate Prison, Lord Hugo." The nun rose and joined him at the window, slipping on a pair of spectacles that she produced out of some hidden fold in her voluminous habit. She peered out. "I don't see anyone."

"She's gone now. She was young, dressed in white, with fair hair, no cap or veil or anything like that, and—and slim. Slim, and quite tall for a woman. Almost . . ." He'd been about to say ethereal, but decided that would be inappropriate. "Almost the height of my mother," he finished.

"Ah," Sister Agnes said, glancing over at him with an impassive expression. "That would be Meggie Bloom. She came to us from the Ipswich orphanage some six years ago."

"The orphanage?" Hugo said.

"Yes, she's had a hard life, poor child. Meggie's mother died only minutes after she was born, leaving her an orphan, and then the woman who was kind enough to take her in died only nine years later. There was no one else willing to look after Meggie once her foster mother was gone, so the orphanage it was."

Hugo wondered at what point young Meggie Bloom had lost her mind. She'd certainly had an unpleasant welcome to the world, and it didn't sound to him as if it had gotten any better along the way. He didn't wonder that the girl had become unstable.

"So the orphanage sent her here when they could no longer manage to keep her?" he asked, unable to contain his curiosity.

"Yes, it seemed the only solution. But we were happy to take her."

Of course you were, Hugo thought to himself. You positively thrive on lost souls. The more the merrier.

The nun shot him a quizzical look. "You appear surprised, Lord Hugo. Perhaps you think Meggie is very young to be with us, but she is older than she appears—twenty-three, as it happens. It is unfortunate that the outside world could not find a place for her, but we appreciate her unique qualities."

Hugo frowned. He understood that the nun had taken vows, one of them being compassion, but for Sister Agnes to describe insanity as a "unique quality" was painting it a bit too brown for his liking. "I would know nothing about it," he said, putting a quick end to the discussion. "I must be going, I'm afraid. I have an appointment in town."

"It was kind of you to spare us a small portion of your valuable time, Lord Hugo," the nun said with an undertone of something that sounded very much to Hugo like irony. "I don't expect we shall be seeing you again."

"As my mother rarely succumbs to illness of any kind, I don't imagine you will," Hugo said. "Good day, Sister Agnes."

"Good day, Lord Hugo. May God go with you," the nun said.

Hugo didn't hear the valediction, as he was already halfway down the hall before she'd finished it.

2

Meggie placed a careful stitch in the tapestry she'd been working on for the last six years and didn't expect to finish before she died. At least embroidery gave her something to do when she wasn't busy tending to the patients.

She rubbed her eyes and leaned back, examining the most recent scene she'd been toiling over. The left side of Eve's torso was coming along nicely, although her face still needed some attention. When the piece was finally done it would be Meggie's personal depiction of the Garden of Eden. Before the serpent came along, naturally, when Adam and Eve were still in accord with God and each other.

It was foolish of her to be so whimsical, perhaps, but she took a small measure of pleasure from indulging herself in the idea that there once had been perfection in the world—a time when there had been no disease, no hunger, no unhappiness, no loneliness. No madness.

Meggie wasn't at all sure what she was going to do when the time came to tackle Adam. She had next to no knowledge of how a man's unclothed anatomy looked, beyond a hazy memory of an illustration or two she had seen in a book in her foster mother's house. In that book all the men had been wearing fig leaves or carefully draped pieces of cloth. She'd better bestow a fig leaf on Adam, even if it wasn't historically accurate, or she'd really be in trouble. What she needed to concentrate on were the strong lines of the torso, the powerful musculature of the arms and legs . . .

She closed her eyes for a moment, remembering in

perfect, magnificent detail the dark-haired stranger who had gazed at her through Sister Agnes's study window that afternoon and had so deeply unsettled her. Now *he* might make the perfect model for Adam if she just stripped him of his clothes . . .

Meggie shook her head sharply, refusing to let her thoughts wander in that direction. His image had been plaguing her ever since, but to go so far as to imagine him wearing nothing but a fig leaf—that was truly wicked. One did *not* go about unclothing men, even in one's mind.

She glanced up as Sister Agnes yawned and stretched her gnarled fingers toward the warmth of the fire, her gaze focused on the flames. Meggie knew from experience that the nun was about to vanish into deep thought. Sister Agnes could either be completely alert, aware of every last detail of what happened in her small dominion, or completely lost in contemplation over what improvements she might bring to bear on it.

Meggie smiled fondly at the elderly woman. She would never forget the day she'd appeared dirty, dusty, and exhausted at the Woodbridge Sanitarium all those years ago. She had been so frightened, thinking that her life was going from miserable to unbearable, since the Mother Superior of Ipswich Orphanage had warned her Comrade-in-God about Meggie's depraved character.

Instead, she was greeted by a woman as warm as she was wise. Sister Agnes had actually embraced her upon her arrival—embraced her! Meggie had nearly keeled over with shock. She hadn't been embraced in more than eight years. She'd hardly been touched in any way, except in punishment. Touching wasn't allowed at the Ipswich Orphanage.

Sister Agnes took her inside, fed her the best meal Meggie had eaten since her foster mother had died, and allowed Meggie to nod off at the dinner table.

From that day until now, Sister Agnes had never spoken an unkind word to Meggie. She had taken Meggie under her wing and treated her with compassion and infinite understanding, a healing balm to Meggie's wounded soul.

From the beginning, Sister Agnes made it clear that she believed not one word that the Mother Superior had written about the inherent evil lurking in Meggie's heart. Instead, she accepted Meggie, and as Meggie gradually came to trust Sister Agnes, she allowed herself to open up. One day she even found herself telling the nun about the strange talent she'd been born with. She'd never admitted it before to anyone, fearing the repercussions. It was bad enough when people only suspected.

Witch. Devil. Liar.

Yet instead of condemning Meggie, Sister Agnes had told her that her talent was not God's curse, but His blessing—a true gift that could do others good if she used it wisely and carefully.

Meggie still wasn't convinced about the blessing part, although she did realize that her talent had a special function in the sanitarium, and Sister Agnes encouraged her to make use of it.

She wished she knew why she was able to hear the inner thoughts of the deeply troubled and deranged with hardly any distortion. Animals were just as clear to her, although she didn't exactly read their minds as much as sense their impressions. But, her talent was entirely unpredictable when it came to dealing with the sane.

Sometimes she'd hear the thoughts inside their heads as clear as day, and sometimes she had nothing more than a vague sense of their thoughts. And sometimes she couldn't make much out at all, although she was never without an acute sense of a person's presence.

What she'd like to have was the ability to *choose* to read the minds of those around her—or better yet, not to read them at all. As it was, she never knew when an errant blast of someone's private contemplations was going to enter her mind.

Usually she had some warning, a vague buzzing like a distant conversation that was easy enough to tune out. But when she wasn't paying attention, the buzz suddenly crystallized itself into words and images and, well . . . it could be embarrassing. This morning had been a classic example.

Jasper Oddbins had been giving her the day's gardening instructions, as if she couldn't work out what needed to be done for herself. She'd let her mind wander, much to her regret, for the next thing she knew, Jasper Oddbin's exploits of the night before were singing in her head completely uninvited.

Owd Sally Potter were a fine 'un, she were, full of daviltry, and me cherry merry. Wouldn't mind if I don't ha' another trosh tonight, e'en if it do cost me my week's wages. . . . Now liddle Miss Meggie here, waal she'd be fine enow, but I'd be a dunner if that nun got wind I ha' a fancy for the gal. . . . A nice, tidy bosom, yass sah, e'en if it be all hidden away in that sack . . .

Blushing ferociously, Meggie had belatedly snapped the mental shield into place that protected her from unwelcome knowledge, but she hadn't been able to look Jasper in the face after that.

"Goodness, it's been a long day," Sister Agnes said, returning from her reverie as suddenly as she'd gone into it.

"Has it, Sister?" Meggie replied, happy to be distracted. "What trials crossed your path today?"

"Well, first we had a disturbing incident with poor Mr. Blecksott—I did tell Peterson that he needed to keep a more careful eye on the razor when he shaved the man. It's a blessing Mr. Blecksott didn't manage to do Peterson any damage when he grabbed hold of the razor and chased poor Peterson about the room."

"I know you don't like me to speak unkindly, Sister, but what Mr. Blecksott needs is a good wallop to his backside," Meggie replied tartly. "If his mother had seen to it when he was a child, Mr. Blecksott would probably have gone through life in a much more regulated fashion," she muttered half to herself.

"Now, Meggie," Sister Agnes replied, her mouth curving in a tolerant smile that belied the sternness of her tone, "you know better than to speak like that. Mr. Blecksott cannot help his predisposition to violence. You must try a little harder to feel kindly toward him."

"Perhaps I would if I didn't believe Mr. Blecksott is with us in order to escape his creditors. This dementia he pretends to display is enough to keep him here for as long as it pleases him—and I am certain it pleases him far more than a stint in jail would. He never does any serious harm to himself or anyone else, does he?"

Meggie knew perfectly well that her words would make no difference. Mr. Blecksott would be there tomorrow and the day after that, and on and on *ad infinitum*, just as surely as she would be. They were both locked into the same humdrum routine, and she was sure Mr. Blecksott terrorized Peterson and everyone else out of sheer boredom. What else did he have to do with his time?

"He may not have harmed anyone yet, but not for lack of trying," Sister Agnes said gently. "Since you tell me that you cannot see clearly in his case, you must not make assumptions. You of all people should realize that."

Meggie just shrugged. Maybe she was hardened, too aware of the bitter realities of life to be as compassionate as Sister Agnes would like her to be. Sister Agnes had not experienced life's hard edges in the same way that Meggie had.

Sister Agnes had been brought up in a loving family. It had been *her* choice to turn her face away from the temporal aspects of life and devote herself to God and the care of the less fortunate.

Meggie'd had no such choice. Life had been dictated to her, defined by loss, shaped by helplessness. She'd learned early on that her life would never be like everyone else's, and she had long since developed a pragmatic core that concealed her loneliness.

Her dreams were of no importance in the great scheme of things, nor would they ever be. Sister Agnes had drilled into her head time and time again that she was God's servant, doing God's work for those poor souls whom God loved best. Meggie should try to be grateful and have faith that God had a plan for her.

Meggie didn't believe for a moment that God had a plan for her. Not that she had anything against God—it was just that she didn't think He interested Himself in the day-to-day problems of each of His servants, sane or otherwise. He had certainly shown no interest to date in Meggie and she didn't expect that to change.

For Sister Agnes's sake, though, Meggie did try to find a reason to be grateful for her circumstances. So far she hadn't had much success.

She looked hard for what beauty each day might hold, and she occasionally managed to find it in the small satisfactions, such as the work she did in the gardens. Sometimes she was even rewarded by a minor miracle when one of her patients found the way back to reason and was discharged to live a full and healthy life.

Meggie couldn't help wondering if she'd ever leave the sanitarium. Where would she go? What would she do? She might have been trained for teaching but between her unfortunate background and her unusual ability she doubted she'd find a respectable position. The

Mother Superior had clearly come to the same conclusion.

She supposed she should be grateful that at least here she didn't stand out as a freak. The patients didn't seem to notice that she could read their thoughts, caught up as they were in their own perverse sense of reality. Her job was to see to their needs as she perceived them, and she seemed to make a difference to their peace of mind. Sister Agnes understood that and honored her talent, telling Meggie time and time again how much she appreciated her help. Here, at least, Meggie was needed.

She bent her head back over her stitching, forcing her attention back to her work and pushing her troubled thoughts into the corner of her mind that she kept to herself.

Meggie had also tried to push thoughts of the mysterious man she had seen earlier to the same corner of her mind. What *had* he been doing in Sister Agnes's study, and why had he been staring at her with such fierce concentration, his hand pressed up against the glass?

For one foolish moment she'd thought he'd been reaching out to her . . .

"Where have you gone now, Meggie?" Sister Agnes asked, turning her head at Meggie's extended silence. "You've been unusually quiet this evening."

"I was just wondering about the man who visited you today." The words slipped out and Meggie wanted to bite her tongue. Since she couldn't take them back now, she decided that she might as well forge ahead. Her curiosity had been gnawing at her ever since their gazes had locked for those unnerving moments. She remembered breaking the contact and urging her feet along the path, resisting an impulse to glance back to see if he was still watching her with his piercing cobalt eyes and their unfathomable expression.

Perhaps that was what fascinated her most of all—that

he had been so completely unfathomable to her. Usually she sensed *something* from a person, even if she couldn't read his thoughts. In the stranger's case there had been nothing at all, no clue as to his character, his intentions. She had heard only a great, unfamiliar silence.

Instead, something else had stirred deep inside her, something equally unfamiliar and also frightening, as if she were far out of her depth. It was something that had wakened a part of herself that spoke of being a woman and left her in no doubt that he was a man.

She thought she finally understood what poor Martha Lindsay meant when she ranted about the uncontrollable physical urges of her body that had led to her downfall and to Woodbridge Sanitarium. Meggie had been hard pressed to understand what a physical urge for a man might feel like, but now she had a fair idea. She really wished she had remained in the dark.

"I—I saw him in your window," Meggie added feebly, trying her best to sound unconcerned about the incident. "Was he here to inquire about one of the patients?"

"In a roundabout way," Sister Agnes replied, snipping a thread off her own embroidery. "He came on his mother's behalf, but I do not think he was by any means comfortable stepping foot in a sanitarium."

"Who *was* he?" Meggie persisted, fascinated by this small kernel of information about the mysterious visitor.

"His name is Lord Hugo Montagu. His mother is the Dowager Duchess of Southwell, one of our patronesses. Lady Kincaid is a relation of the family's and it was the dowager who brought her to us."

"Oh . . ." Meggie said, her head spinning with this unexpected revelation. Never in a million years would she have made a connection between Eunice Kincaid, whose soul spoke to her of chaos, and this enigmatic stranger whose soul was silent, but whose physical appearance had wreaked havoc on her equilibrium.

So he was a duke's son. Maybe that explained his complete inaccessibility, she thought wryly; perhaps his thoughts and feelings were far too rarefied for the likes of her. She chewed on the end of her finger for a moment. "Did he come to see Lady Kincaid?" she finally asked. "I was with her earlier this evening, and she mentioned no visitors, not that she is fit to see anyone in her present condition."

"No. He came merely to pass on the duchess's good wishes and to deliver another bank draft, bless the woman for her great kindness. I don't know how we would carry on without her benevolence. Why do you ask, child? You are not usually interested in the comings and goings of outsiders. In fact, you go out of your way to avoid visitors."

"I don't know . . . there was something different about him," Meggie said truthfully. "I suppose you've already explained it—as you said, he wasn't comfortable here."

Sister Agnes's eyes suddenly sharpened. "Did you sense something, Meggie, something I should know about? An illness, a mental imbalance, perhaps?"

"No, Sister, nothing. Really, I only saw him for a moment," Meggie replied, pulling out the row of stitches she'd made that evening. The line had gone badly askew, not unlike her composure. She didn't want to have to explain any further. She wouldn't know how to explain in any case. *Actually, Sister, I do believe he stirred carnal desire in me.* Oh my, yes. That sentiment would thrill the sister.

"I see," Sister Agnes said. "Well, that is reassuring; these problems can run in families. If I were you I would not concern yourself any further on the issue of Lord Hugo, as I doubt very much he will ever return. His world has nothing to do with ours."

Meggie nodded. Sister Agnes was right—there was no

point concerning herself with him. Lord Hugo Montagu belonged to another world, one she would—could—never be a part of. He had nothing to do with her.

Yet a small, treacherous voice at the back of her mind badly wished that he had. This wish concerned her most of all, for Meggie knew how dangerous it was to wish for things that could never be. *Especially* when she found herself wishing for a tall, dark-haired man with eyes like daggers of blue ice that sliced right into her and opened her body up to its most primitive desires.

She was a disgrace, she really was, for entertaining such thoughts at all. Look where that path had led her mother.

"And Meggie, dear, I do wish you'd wear your hair up and covered with your cap when you are outside of your private quarters," Sister Agnes said, glancing over at her, a touch of humor crinkling her lined eyes. "You might find that it will save you from unwanted attention."

Meggie's mouth dropped open and she quickly snapped it shut again. "I will try to remember," she said dutifully. Even though Sister Agnes was not able to read people's minds, she still saw far too much.

3

Standing on the stretch of land that looked out over the river Butley, Hugo drew in a deep breath of the tangy salt air blowing off the North Sea not far beyond. The raucous cries of seagulls resounded in his ears, a wild cacophony that echoed on the wind and seduced his soul into believing it could fly just as freely as birds on the wing.

He turned and gazed back at the magnificent edifice known as Lyden Hall. It was a classic Palladian house, built in 1734, the land agent had informed him, barely drawing breath before he'd barreled on. "The Hall, which as you can see consists of the square central block and two wings, is built entirely from brick made on the estate."

He'd beamed proudly as if this gave the house extra value. As if the price of sixty thousand pounds wasn't inflated enough, Hugo thought, shoving his hands into his pockets. Then there was the troublesome matter of the two elderly spinsters, the Misses Mabey. What in the name of God was he going to do with them?

"You see, my lord, the old earl felt it best that Lyden be sold after his death," the agent had said, gingerly broaching the subject of the Mabey sisters. "His concern was that his wife's two cousins have lived here since his marriage, and he could not in good conscience remove them from what has become their home, simply because he was going to be inconsiderate enough to die. This is why he made it a provision of sale that his relations, distant though they may be, be allowed to stay on until their own deaths."

Normally, Hugo considered dryly, a house came with furniture, not relatives. He frowned. All in all, Lyden Hall was not what he'd had in mind at all. He'd been led to believe that he was going to see a fine period house, impressive, but nothing too extravagant. He was beginning to wonder what the land agent considered extravagant.

Lyden was well over the price he had in mind and far too large for his needs. Still, he could afford it—just. The house was contained in an encircling park of nearly five thousand acres, and a lovely estate it was, containing huge tracts of farmland and good hunting grounds. Surely all of that would bring in a healthy income? He could live like a king without having to expend any capital, he rationalized.

His brother Rafe did it, after all. Southwell alone provided him with an enormous income with its countless acres, despite the upkeep for a house as big as all of kingdom come.

But then his sainted brother had been slated to inherit that great pile from birth, as well as numerous other properties *and* a vast fortune to support them all. Hugo, second in line, had been left a mere three unimpressive estates that he'd quickly sold for the ready money he was always in need of.

Lord, how he regretted the follies of his youth. He'd behaved like a perfect fool, hot-headed and impetuous, not caring what anyone thought of him and forever embroiled in scandals. He spent money like water, throwing huge sums away at the gambling tables. He had never thought about the consequences—and there had been plenty of those.

He winced, not wanting to remember his three miserable years of exile in Paris where he'd slowly gambled away the little money he had left. It was only by the grace of God that the night he was at his most desperate, he'd won an enormous fortune on a single throw of the dice. Two hundred fifty thousand pounds, free and clear, enough to pay his debts and leave him the bulk to turn his life around.

He'd sworn to himself that he would never gamble again and he hadn't, as strong as the temptation was at times. He'd also sworn to prove his newly reformed character to his family and he was damned well going to do it.

Still, was this the way? He scratched the back of his neck, wondering if he was crazy even to consider buying Lyden Hall.

There was something about the property, something that kept him from dismissing it out of hand. He couldn't put his finger on what it was. Somehow the place made him think that it might actually be possible to find a measure of peace and completion here.

He couldn't remember the last time he'd felt either peaceful or complete—he hadn't even realized until this moment that either condition was something he might desire, and he couldn't have been more taken aback. Life had always been about staving off boredom. Quietude was the last thing he'd ever desired.

So why did he stand there feeling as if a part of him that had lain sleeping for most of his life had suddenly stirred and stretched, called out to him that *this* was life. *This* was what he had been missing for all of his twenty-six years without even knowing it. That here he might find real happiness.

He caught himself up short, realizing that he was being ridiculous—and worse, sentimental, an emotion he abhorred and considered the refuge of the weak. His task was to find himself a sensible place of his own. Nothing more, nothing less. Why battle so hard over what was in the end a simple decision? Surely he wasn't letting the idea of inheriting two old spinsters get in his way?

He clenched his fist and brought it down hard by his side. He'd do it. He'd buy the place. He wanted to make something of himself, and this was a way to go about it. He would settle down and become a dignified country gentleman, entertaining and enjoying the rustic life. Moderation. That was the answer.

Lyden Hall would be his salvation and would keep him on the straight and narrow. He couldn't wait to tell his mother.

He would show her and the world that he walked not in his brother's ducal shadow, but in his own footsteps.

The Dowager Duchess of Southwell gazed impassively at her son over the rim of her tea cup. Hugo suppressed a furious desire to sweep the fine porcelain straight out of her hand. Here for once he'd done something right in his life, and she didn't look the least bit impressed by the import of such an act.

"Mama? Don't you have anything to say?" Hugo asked, hurt battling with impatience. "I just informed you that I've laid out an enormous sum of money for an estate on the Suffolk coast, and you look at me as if I've said nothing more significant than I decided to invest in cattle futures."

"What would you have me say?" his mother replied, her expression remaining neutral. "You told me that you saw the property once, thought it perfect for your needs, and bought it on the spot. Did you ask about the exact income the estate brings in? Did you inquire as to the state of the tenancies, which crops thrive and which have failed over time?" She placed her cup back in its saucer. "Did you have anyone inspect the condition of the house to make sure that it is sound? You have mentioned nothing of this, which to my mind indicates that you acted without serious thought."

Hugo glared at her. "I said nothing because I did not think you would wish to be troubled with such details." In truth, he hadn't asked at all, or at least nothing beyond the obvious, but he really couldn't see why that should be an issue. He'd seen Lyden, liked it, and that was enough for him. It was none of his mother's business beyond that. "I suppose you think that as usual I should be more like my brother and examine a situation to death before making a decision. Allow me to point out, Mama, that I am not anything like Rafe, as much as you might wish me to be. I am my own man and I make my decisions according to what pleases me."

"That is my concern," his mother said calmly. "Buying a property of this size is a large commitment, darling. I would hate to see you lose your investment simply because you didn't bother to investigate it properly. Attention to detail is paramount in such matters."

"Naturally I investigated it properly. From everything I saw in the books there was no problem. Lyden manages itself, with the help of a steward, of course. Why shouldn't it?" he added, realizing belatedly that he was digging himself an ever deeper grave by prevaricating so thoroughly and had better forestall any more questions. "There are thousands of acres of arable land, good grazing grounds, and the river traffic brings an entirely separate resource. Just think of the goods that come in—and I now control one of the ports, as it is located on my property. I might even invest in overseas trading."

"I see." His mother suddenly smiled. "It seems that I owe you an apology, my dear. You have been responsible in the matter, then. I was worried only because your past behavior has not led me to have a great confidence of your judgment, but it appears I was mistaken." She leaned across the sofa and took his hand, clasping it warmly in her own. "I only wish to be proud of you. I know you told your brother and me that you had turned over a new leaf when you returned from Paris last year, and I wanted so much to believe it. But," she said, hesitating for a moment before she continued, "you must understand that given your prior behavior—the duels, the gambling debts, the unsavory women . . ."

"Mama, that is all in the past, as I've told you," Hugo said, stung to the quick that she would bring all that up now. "I came back to England having realized the errors of my ways. I don't know what more I must do to prove it to you and Rafe." He dropped his forehead into his hand, frustration seething through him. Why did he always have to *prove* himself?

"Only be responsible, darling. Show us both that you can sustain your intention. That is all that matters to me. I realize how difficult it has been for you to grow up without the guiding hand of a father. You were so young when he died, but I suppose that cannot be helped. Raphael did do his best."

"As I have done mine!" Hugo roared, fed up with hearing about his brother's eternal perfection. Rafe had never hesitated to lord it over his younger brother, as if four years' difference in their ages gave him the right of fatherhood as well as a right to criticize every move Hugo had ever made. He was sick to death of always being second best, sick of already being perceived as a failure before he'd even begun.

"I have done my best," Hugo repeated in a quieter voice. "I apologize if I have not lived up to your expectations. I am trying. Buying this property is an effort to make that clear to you; it is my way of showing you that I am serious. I only hope you can appreciate that."

His mother nodded and squeezed his hand. "I will take you at your word, Hugo. You have no idea what happiness it would give me—and your brother—to know that you have given up your wild ways for good in favor of settling down to a temperate life."

"And buying Lyden Hall is a good beginning, is it not? I regret that I lost the other holdings Papa left to me, admittedly by my own foolishness, but I cannot change that now. I do promise you that my gambling life is behind me, and I plan on making you proud of me."

"Then find yourself a wife and establish yourself and your family in the home you have chosen for yourself," his mother said, releasing his hand.

"A wife?" he said, gaping at her.

"Why not? It would be the next logical step, would it not? I cannot imagine you want to spend your time rattling around your new home all by yourself."

"Well, actually there are two elderly relatives of the previous owner, Lord Eliot, who will be living there as well. I agreed to keep them on so that they would not find themselves in distressing circumstances."

"Hugo! How very good of you," his mother said with obvious pleasure that he would be so charitable. "How very good indeed! Who might these relatives be? I knew Lord Eliot and his wife slightly. So tragic, her dying only two years after their marriage."

"They are cousins of Lady Eliot's, by the name of Mabey. I believe they must be infirm, not able to go about much, as they were confined to their quarters. I did not actually meet them when I was there."

A peculiar look crossed the dowager's face. "The Mabey sisters? Yes . . . indeed, I do recall meeting them in London many years ago. How very interesting. Goodness, I haven't thought of them in years. They must be in their eighties by now." A smile tugged at her lips. "Well. How nice that you will have some company, but I was thinking of someone of your own age."

"I will consider it, Mama, but I make no promises. After all, look how long it took Rafe to find a wife." He thought that a rather inspired defense.

"Raphael's wait was well worthwhile, for Lucy makes

him very happy. And look at your cousin Aiden and his wife Serafina—they are blissful together. I do not suggest you marry for anything less than love, my darling, only that you might start looking for the right person to give you the same happiness." Her smile broadened. "You know I am not a stickler for dynastic unions. A nice girl who suits your temperament will do well enough."

"Yes, Mama," Hugo said dutifully, hoping she would now change the subject.

She must have been satisified with his response, for she rose. "Good then. Go forward, Hugo, and demonstrate yourself to be a man of strength and character. I know that is what your father hoped you would become, and nothing would give me greater pleasure than to see you fulfill your potential."

Hugo turned his head toward the window. "I will try not to disappoint you," he said, forcing himself to speak in a neutral tone. He would rather die than let her know how deeply her words cut.

"I would prefer that you did not disappoint yourself," she replied gently. "In the end it is ourselves we have to live with. I will see you at dinner."

Hugo barely registered the swish of her skirts as she left. He felt like a man who'd had his belly ripped open and his entrails pulled out. He fully understood the instinct that caused a man to try to stuff his guts back into his body—nothing could be worse than having them hanging out where they didn't belong. Emotions were exactly the same, and they had no business being anywhere but carefully locked away.

He crossed the room to the tray of drinks and poured himself a large glass of whisky, downing it all at once. He took a sharp breath against the fire that burned in his belly and waited impatiently for the spirits to numb the pain that raged through him.

Here he'd expected to finally win his mother's approbation and had only received a qualified blessing along with a bucketful of skepticism.

Apparently it wasn't enough that he'd bought Lyden, now his mother wanted him to fill it with a wife. Was there no pleasing her?

He scowled darkly and poured himself another drink, then sank into a wing chair.

Well, maybe he should go ahead and follow her suggestion since she set so much stock in marriage. Why the hell not—a wife to go along with his fine estate, the perfect window dressing to present to his family.

The London Season was to begin shortly. There would be eager young misses enough, misses more than willing to throw their various over-embellished caps at him. He'd seen it all before. He was young, handsome, and charming, his family connections impeccable. He had a fortune and an estate. In short, he was highly desirable, despite his questionable past.

The prospect of a Season seemed endlessly dreary, but then so did the prospect of marriage. He smiled bitterly to himself, thinking that respectability carried one hell of a price. Still, if the seal of his family's approval was what he really wanted, then he was condemned.

London it was.

Meggie lay on her narrow bed, gazing up at the ceiling and dreaming of the world outside the walls of the Woodbridge Sanitarium. She'd gone into the bustling town that afternoon to buy some colored thread for her tapestry and had dawdled outside the market, watching the throngs of people going about their business.

She'd smiled from her anonymous seat on a bench as a young couple walked past her. They were deep in conversation, their fingertips occasionally reaching out to meet surreptitiously, their faces filled with private happiness, and utterly content in each other's company, completely in love.

A lovely warmth had emanated from them, washing over her like an embracing wave. After they'd disappeared, the warmth had vanished like a cloud passing over the sun, leaving a chill in her lonely heart.

Meggie rolled onto her side and reached her hand down over the side of the bed to bury her fingers in Hadrian's thick dark fur, taking comfort in the contact and Hadrian's contented sigh as she gently scratched behind his ears.

"Oh, well," she whispered, "it's no good pining for what we can't have, is it? You and I will have to make do with each other and what little comfort we can find within these walls."

The wolf grunted, and Meggie knew he agreed. Hadrian nearly always agreed with her, except on the matter of the frequency of their walks. He suffered from his confinement as much as she did, but there was little she could do about it. Long domesticated, releasing him back into the wilderness would mean his certain death, and that she couldn't bear to think about.

Hadrian had been her dear companion of five years. Meggie had rescued him from a trap in the woods, his poor tiny paw broken and bloodied by the gruesome steel teeth. Sister Agnes had reluctantly allowed her to keep him, and Meggie had nursed him back to health.

Of course, Sister Agnes hadn't realized at the time that Hadrian was a wolf pup, Meggie thought with a small smile. By the time his eyes had turned yellow and given the matter away, it was too late for Sister Agnes to object to his presence.

Hadrian was a model of perfect behavior, never threatening anyone. Meggie was careful to keep him away from visitors, though, just in case they panicked at the sight of him. The patients she never worried about, as they seemed to take comfort from his presence. Hadrian had an affinity for the sick and troubled, much as she had.

They were utterly devoted to each other, and Hadrian filled a void in Meggie's life that would otherwise have remained empty. If she was condemned to live a life without ever knowing the fullness of human love, at least she had the unwavering love of this fine animal.

They were two of a kind, both separated from their pack, both suspect in a world that didn't understand them. And they both would have given their eye teeth for freedom.

A tear trickled unbidden down Meggie's cheek. She didn't know what had come over her—she'd been unsettled for days. It wasn't like her to feel sorry for herself or to indulge in tears, for that matter. What was couldn't be changed any more than she could change the color of her hair or the circumstances of her birth.

She clutched her arms over her chest, wondering for the thousandth time what the real story behind her birth was. Dear Aunt Emily had prevaricated every time Meggie had asked, saying only that Meggie's father had died months before Meggie's arrival, and her mother had followed him after giving birth to her only child.

Meggie knew there was more to it than that. She'd gone so far as to try to use her talent to discover the truth. She would pry into Aunt Emily's head as well as the head of everyone else she came across, but had never heard anything but unintelligible garble. It was as if she wasn't supposed to know.

What she had heard were the whispers in the village when no one thought she was listening. Then later she'd overheard the nuns in the orphanage discussing her tainted origins in scandalized tones. Sadly, Meggie never heard the details, just the condemnation.

Bastard . . .

Considering that stigma, Meggie didn't understand why her foster mother had bothered with her in the first place, but then Emily Crewe had been a good woman who believed in doing her Christian duty. Meggie could only suppose that since Aunt Emily had been a childless widow, taking on an abandoned infant must have seemed the right thing to do.

Those first nine years with kind Aunt Emily had been happy, especially compared to the following eight at the orphanage. Of course anything would seem happy in comparison to the orphanage, Meggie thought with a shudder. The memories of dark, dank rooms and perpetual cold, of a stomach that constantly ached with hunger, of cries smothered in her pillow at night, of continual punishment for crimes real and imagined could not be stopped. But then everything Meggie did had been a crime except praying, and half the time she didn't do that right, either, according to the nuns.

So really, what right did she have to complain about her present lot in life? The sanitarium was bliss in comparison.

She only wished she could erase the thoughts of Lord Hugo Montagu that continued to plague her and rob her of her much-needed rest. They came uninvited, usually as she was drifting off to sleep. They were always the same—she looked over to see his tall figure standing in the window, his hand flattened against the glass as his sapphire gaze bored into her and took her very breath away.

Only she'd managed to embellish the reality beautifully. Now she heard his voice as well, deep and compelling, calling to her. *"Meggie . . . Meggie, my love. I need you, Meggie . . . please, come to me."*

"Yes," she would answer in her head, *"yes, I will come to you. Just wait, Hugo. You have to wait for me . . ."*

And her body would shake with a longing she didn't know how to control.

Meggie stuffed her face into her pillow with a groan. She really couldn't go on like this. Life had been difficult before, but at least her existence had been peaceful enough, not invaded by an absurd desire for a man who was no more than a fragment of memory that she'd turned into an overblown fantasy.

"Meggie Bloom," she whispered, "you must take after your mother—your good sense clouded by uncontrollable physical urges. If you're lusting after a man you've never met and will never see again, girl, goodness only knows what you'd do if confronted with the real thing. Maybe it is a good thing you're locked away, after all."

A tap came at the door and Meggie quickly sat up, anticipating what a summons meant at this late hour.

"Yes? Who is it?" she called, already knowing. She could feel Rose's presence through the heavy wood, driving straight into her tired head.

"Meggie?" Rose's voice came as urgently as her panic. "It's Rose—come quickly! Lady Kincaid has taken a bad turn. I'm sorry to disturb you, but you're the only one who knows how to calm her, and she's tearing her room to bits and upsetting the other patients something fierce."

"I'll be right there," Meggie called, instantly jumping to her feet and pulling her night rail over her head. She replaced it with the spare work dress she'd carefully laid over the chair. She splashed cold water over her face to bring herself to full alertness, then slipped on her shoes and threw a shawl over her shoulders. Hurrying down the passageway, she started toward the women's wing.

Rose, a young local girl who was rather dull witted met her halfway, her white cap slipping sideways on her head. "I don't know what set her off, Meggie, I really don't. I was sitting outside with everything all quiet-like and everyone sound asleep, when her ladyship suddenly set up the most frightful yelling and carrying on, flinging things across the room so's that I couldn't even get in there."

All this Rose breathlessly imparted as the two of them ran full speed down the hallway, their skirts hitched up about their knees.

Meggie could hear Lady Kincaid already, her screeches echoing down the staircase as Meggie and Rose tore up it.

"Something must have happened. Can you think of anything, anything at all? She was calm when I left her this evening," Meggie panted.

"No, not so as I could say. Oh, well, mebbe, now that I think about it. She asked for her mam, and I told her that her mam was long gone to heaven and she should settle back and get some sleep. That was two hours ago."

Meggie stopped in her tracks, thoroughly exasperated. "Rose, how many times do I have to tell you that the truth doesn't necessarily serve in these cases?"

"I cannot lie, Meggie," Rose said, her eyes wide with alarm. "It's true, her mam did die many years before."

"Yes, but Lady Kincaid doesn't know that. You have to remember she's living in the far past when her mother was still alive. All she needs is a little reassurance."

"You wanted me to tell Lady Kincaid that her mam was going to walk into the room any minute? She'd have known it for a lie in no time, Meggie! God would damn me for sure for telling such a mistruth." Her eyes filled with tears.

Meggie felt instant remorse for having snapped at Rose, who couldn't help being simple. Meggie could feel with perfect clarity Rose's confusion with a concept outside of her limited comprehension.

"Never mind. Did you summon Sister Agnes?" Meggie asked. She was already anticipating the black, wild whirlpool of the violent spells from which Lady Kincaid suffered.

"I thought it was best to come fetch you, Meggie. You know how Lady Kincaid is when she gets like this—no one else is any good at fixing her fits. Did I do the right thing in leaving her to you?"

"I suppose. There's really no point in disturbing the good sister. She needs her rest."

Meggie sighed heavily, thinking of the task ahead. It was going to be another long, trying night spent sorting through the tangled fabric of Eunice Kincaid's lost wits. Meggie's task was to find the particular thread that had unraveled this time and pull it back into place, or at least enough into place to grant the rest of them a bit of peace.

4

Hugo lurked behind one of the potted palms that decorated the wall of Lady Cumberland's ballroom, stealthily peering out at the assembled company. Respectability was deadly dull. Being on his best behavior had done nothing but depress his spirits and make him question why he'd ever conceived the notion of reforming in the first place.

He certainly questioned why he'd decided that taking a wife was a good idea. Not a single eligible miss had left anything but a sour taste in his mouth. One dreadful female in particular had made his life a living hell, pursuing him as if he were a prime piece of beef that she intended to consume with gusto. This was the main reason why he was trying to fit in with the greenery.

He ought to have pleaded the headache and sent his excuses to Lady Cumberland. Actually, he ought to have shot himself and put himself permanently out of his misery.

What had become of the Hugo he'd once known and loved—the Hugo who was gifted at having fun, being irreverent, and cared for nothing but what new diversion lay ahead? This Hugo he found a tedious bore, a man reduced to asinine behavior. Since when did he cower behind potted plants evading determined ingenues?

He batted a frond out of his face, thinking that he ought to throw the entire idea of marriage out the window and be done with it. Nothing was worth this misery.

"Ah, Montagu," said a voice from behind him. "So this

is where you have been hiding. Disguising yourself as tropical foliage, are you?"

Hugo turned around to find his old friend Michael Foxlane gazing at him with lazy amusement. "Oh, hello, Foxlane," he said uneasily. He'd deliberately avoided the man for months. Michael Foxlane had a well-developed taste for the gaming tables, and Hugo had lost his shirt to him too many times. "What are you doing here?" he asked, forcing a smile to his lips. "You loathe this sort of amusement, if it can be called by such a name."

"I am obliging my aunt Hermione," Foxlane said with a careless shrug. "She is chaperoning a cousin about town this Season. I agreed to come along and dance with the creature. Miss Amelia Langford is her name." He shot Hugo a sly look.

"Good God," Hugo said, staring at his friend who had just intoned the name of the very woman he was trying to escape. "Do you mean to say she is connected to you?"

His tormentor possessed buck teeth, bad skin, and a complete lack of brain, but she also possessed a long pedigree and a large fortune. These last two had gained her an entree into the most exclusive level of society. So everywhere Hugo went, so did Miss Amelia Langford.

He covertly looked about to see if she had spotted him.

Foxlane grinned. "She's set her cap at you, my friend. I heard all about your incredible charms on the way over here. She means to have you, make no mistake about it."

"There is no need to remind me of Miss Langford's ambitions. She has made her intentions perfectly plain," Hugo said with a rueful smile, silently cursing his bad luck that Foxlane was related to the cow. Now he'd have to be polite to her.

"Well, if you will put it about that you are hanging out for a wife, you have to expect to be pursued," Foxlane retorted. "The word is all over town. There's even a wager in White's betting book that she—or rather her fortune—will have you snared by the end of the Season." He scratched his cheek. "We are all wondering what has come over you—you've been ignoring your friends, Montagu. Is this what comes from acquiring a place in the country? If so, remind me to keep my money in my pocket."

"Oh, you've heard about that, too, have you?" Hugo tried unsuccessfully to repress a stab of guilt. As much as he enjoyed the company of his friends, they were strong reminders of his past pleasures—and past downfall. "I confess it has kept me busy," he said, even though he had not once been to Suffolk since buying Lyden Hall. Lyden could wait.

"Busier than acquiring a wife?" Foxlane raised one eyebrow in clear skepticism. "From everything I've heard, you've been in town these past two months, and still you ignore us. Perhaps your pockets are so empty that your only hope is marriage to an heiress?"

"To the contrary," Hugo said, annoyed that his friends had assumed that to be the case. "My pockets are very nicely lined, thank you. It is merely time for me to settle down and establish my nursery."

"*You?* Establish your nursery?" Foxlane nearly choked.

So did Hugo when he heard what he'd said. Starting a nursery was the least of his desires. What did he want with a bunch of sniveling brats yapping about his heels? He hadn't even considered that consequence of marriage and the thought was enough to make his blood run cold. "What I meant is that I wish to give the *appearance* of intending to establish a nursery so that my mother will cease to bother me over the issue," he said, backtracking quickly. "Surely you can understand my motives? As I recall, your own mother has been after you for years in pursuit of the same noble cause."

"Ah," Foxlane said, pressing one long finger against

the side of his equally long nose. "I believe I begin to understand. This quest for a wife is all a subterfuge then, designed to placate your dear mama. And why not?" He clapped Hugo on the back. "When you produce no bride, it will not be for lack of trying."

"Precisely," Hugo said, feeling more in accord with Foxlane by the moment.

"And Cousin Amelia is the perfect choice for such a ploy," he said, nodding thoughtfully. "No one believed you planned to marry her for anything but her fortune, but since you say you don't need it . . . well, then. You have tried admirably for all the right reasons, but in the end you won't be able to bring yourself to marry her for any of them. Or anyone else." He chuckled. "It is a very clever plan."

"Exactly," Hugo said, thinking that it *was* a clever plan. He ought to have conceived it long before instead of torturing himself for eight long weeks.

"Oh! There you are, Lord Hugo. I have been looking for you everywhere! You promised to waltz with me this evening, if you recall."

The familiar high-pitched voice made Hugo cringe. He turned to see Amelia Langford eyeing him with her usual carnivorous expression.

He *had* promised, he remembered with a sinking heart. It had been at Almack's the week before. At the time, he'd been desperate to escape her company and the promise to waltz with her seemed the only thing that might shake her off.

Naturally she'd come to claim her prize. How foolish of him to think he might avoid her. "Good evening, Miss Langford," he said with a curt bow.

She touched her fingers to her mousy curls, overdone as usual. Everything about Miss Amelia Langford was overdone, including her confidence that her money could claim her anything she wished, despite her unfortunate appearance. "I have been looking forward to the occasion all week," she said, fluttering her invisible eyelashes.

"And I," Hugo said, trying to ignore Foxlane's knowing smile. "Shall we?" He offered his arm, hearing the strains of the waltz start up. Amelia Langford had timed the situation perfectly so that he could not possibly refuse, and Hugo resented her intensely for it. He'd never known a woman so controlling, not even his mother.

He endured the waltz and her vapid conversation, answering her only when absolutely necessary. "Yes, Miss Langford, the weather has been fine. . . . No, I did not notice Lady Anne's unhappy choice in dress. . . . Indeed, did Mr. Pompheron really say such a thing. . . ." and all the while wishing himself anywhere but there.

It was Foxlane who finally rescued him. "Come along to White's," he murmured when Hugo had finally shaken off Amelia's clinging arm. "We can catch up with each other in amiable surroundings. I declare, I cannot bear another moment of this tedious nonsense myself. I have done my duty and so have you."

Hugo seized hold of the life raft offered him without another thought. Anything. Anything but another instant of torture. He claimed his hat and cloak and willingly followed Foxlane out the door.

"Deal another hand," Hugo said, wiping at the cold sweat that beaded on his brow. He didn't know how this catastrophe had come to pass, only that the hours had slipped away until dawn was breaking over the horizon.

What had started out as an evening of light enjoyment with some friends, a few hands of cards, and a few bottles of good brandy had turned into deep play. Hugo was in imminent danger of losing everything he had gained back in Paris—and more.

He took another pull from his glass with a badly shaking hand. It was his own stupidity that had brought him to this table, his arrogance that had made him believe he could gamble with the best and walk away with his pockets fuller than before. After all, he'd given up the habit, hadn't he? He'd only set out to have a bit of fun.

"Are you sure?" Arthur Waldock cast him a look of grave concern. "I have taken enough off you tonight, Hugo. Let it rest."

"Let it rest?" Foxlane interjected. "Have you ever known Hugo Montagu to back down when he is in a tight spot? Good Lord, man, I once saw him win fifty thousand on a single hand of vingt-et-un when he was in just this position. He has the luck of the devil when it comes to turning a bad situation around. Do not deny him his chance to take it all back from you and then some."

He rubbed his chin and gave Hugo a look of encouragement, his eyes flashing with excitement as if he already smelled blood. Michael Foxlane thrived on living on the edge, and he had never much cared who fell off as long as it wasn't himself.

Hugo should have remembered that before he'd allowed himself to be lured away, but it was too late now. He attempted a cocky smile in return. "Are you afraid to lose what you have gained, Waldock?" he said, trying to sound unconcerned.

"But what have you left to put up?" Waldock said, frowning. "I have enough of your markers here with which to sink a battleship and you along with it, Hugo. Why don't you go home and sleep this night's work off? You can have another try at your luck tomorrow."

As far as Hugo was concerned there would be no tomorrow, not if he didn't recoup his disastrous losses.

He really would rather shoot himself than face the inevitable scorn of his family and prove them right about his weakness of character.

He took a deep breath. "Lyden Hall," he said his heart pounding. "I'll put up Lyden, worth sixty thousand pounds. It is free and clear, and I'll risk it on one hand of vingt-et-un, winner take all. The game has brought me luck before—perhaps it will again."

Waldock shook his head, then shrugged. "Very well. Have it your way. I have nothing to lose that I didn't have before walking in here tonight."

Foxlane nodded, his teeth drawn back from his lips in an almost feral expression. His forehead too was covered in a fine film of perspiration. "You've always had the golden touch when you put your mind to it, Montagu. Let's see what you can do. With luck you can bid farewell to my cousin once and for all."

"It was never about Amelia Langford," Hugo said, running his hands over his eyes for a brief moment. If the cards came up wrong, it might be all about Amelia Langford after all, and in a way he'd never even considered.

"We'll use a fresh pack for luck," Foxlane said, snapping his fingers at one of the passing footmen. He cut the cards and dealt.

Hugo received a ten of spades down and a five of clubs showing. His heart sank—Waldock's showing card was an ace of diamonds. The odds were heavily against Hugo, but he had no choice. He nodded, and Foxlane dealt him another card, the four of hearts, bringing Hugo to nineteen.

Hugo took a long drink of brandy. He forced himself to focus. Gritting his teeth, he tried to suppress a surge of nausea as Waldock nodded at Foxlane.

Foxlane dealt. A six of spades. That gave Waldock

either seven or eighteen, depending on how he counted the ace.

Everything now hinged on what Waldock's hidden card was.

Waldock met Hugo's eyes for one brief moment before turning it over. The four of clubs.

"Twenty-one," Foxlane said, in a voice of suppressed excitement. "Montagu?"

Hugo shook his head and flipped over the ten of spades.

"Nineteen. Bad luck, Montagu. Congratulations, Waldock."

Hugo released a long hiss from between his teeth as bile rose in his throat and his world spun in a long downward spiral into blackness.

His last thought before he passed out was that he was ruined.

Again.

Hugo hazily opened his eyes and winced against the immediate stab of pain behind his forehead. His mouth tasted like the bottom of the Thames and felt as if it were coated with cat hair. He groaned and rolled over, burying his aching head in the pillow. He couldn't remember a damned thing about why he was in such an appalling condition, but he knew that whatever he'd done, it had been a bad mistake.

He hadn't felt so awful in a good year, not since the night he'd left Paris for London to forcibly terminate his exile abroad. He tried to rally his muddled thoughts, but he couldn't even remember how he'd gotten home, let alone where he'd been. The last thing he recalled was leaving Lady Cumberland's ball in fine spirits, Foxlane at his side.

Foxlane. Hugo struggled to sit up, one hand clasped

to his throbbing brow, straining for memory. White's. That was it, they'd gone to White's. But from there . . . where? On to Boodle's, that was it, he thought with triumph. They'd gone to Boodle's and met up with a group of friends he had been elated to see again.

After that it was all a blur. Nothing but a black hole and a feeling of terrible dread that lay at its center.

He wished to hell he could remember why.

A discreet knock came at the door and he mumbled for the intruder to enter.

"Good afternoon, my lord," Mallard said, quietly nudging the door open, a tray balanced in one hand. "It is gone two o'clock, and I thought you might be prepared to rise."

"Two bloody o'clock?" Hugo said, severe alarm turning his blood cold. "What time did I get in?"

"At seven this morning, my lord. Lord Waldock delivered you and left us to put you to bed. He asked that I give you this note when you woke." The valet rested the tray across Hugo's lap and handed him a folded sheet of parchment, then opened the curtains, but only partway.

Hugo was grateful for Mallard's tact, even though there wasn't a hint of sunshine to be seen in the gray, wet afternoon. Any light at all felt like a knife piercing his skull.

Hugo dismissed him with a curt nod. When Mallard had closed the door behind him, he picked up the butter knife and broke the seal, peering at the elegant script written on Southwell paper.

My dear Montagu,

We have been friends these many years, and I am deeply distressed that you find yourself in such difficult circumstances owing to the play of this night. Although I hold your markers for the sum of one hundred forty thousand pounds as well as the promise of the deed to Lyden

Hall, worth another sixty thousand, I wish to offer you every opportunity to find extra funds so that you need not lose Lyden.

Therefore I propose that I give you ninety days to come up with the total sum of two hundred thousand pounds in hope that you manage to find a way to recoup your losses. I will await your reply.

Your Obedient Servant,
Waldock

Hugo stared at the paper, sick memory flooding back in full. Vingt-et-un. Oh God. He remembered it all now. The cards, the endless play of cards, his losing at every turn, but foolishly confident that his luck would change. And then the final folly, the last bet, his judgment gone to hell by then in the bottom of a brandy bottle as he'd staked everything on Lyden. And lost.

He groaned, closing his eyes and praying with everything he was worth that it was all a bad dream.

But when he opened them again the same gray light assaulted his eyes and the same damning letter crackled between his fingers.

He could think of only one solution to rescue him from this dilemma. And it was even more unpalatable than the taste in his mouth just now.

"Lord Hugo, what a pleasure to see you again so shortly after our last meeting over your purchase of Lyden Hall." Mr. James Gostrain of the esteemed law firm of Messrs. Gostrain, Jenkins, and Waterville rose from behind his desk to shake Hugo's hand. Hugo didn't feel like shaking much of anything other than Foxlane's throat for having led him into disaster, but he obliged, forcing a smile to his dry lips.

"Mr. Gostrain. Your servant. Thank you for seeing me so readily."

"Not at all. What may I do for you, my lord?" Mr. Gostrain asked pleasantly, gesturing at the chair on the other side of the desk.

Hugo took a seat. "I am thinking about marrying," he said. "I wish to know the formalities behind drawing up a marriage contract, and how soon such a contract can be pushed through. There is a sizable dowry involved, you understand. I do not want legalities to be a cause for unnecessary delay."

Mr. Gostrain, a man in his early sixties with thinning gray hair and a sharp nose, had negotiated many a tricky deal over the years. He allowed himself a long look at Hugo. "I gather you have a reason to marry in haste?" he said, tapping the tips of his fingers together.

"I do, although not for any reason other than if I lose my nerve, I most likely won't marry at all. Therefore I desire to understand the underpinnings of such a binding contract."

Mr. Gostrain nodded. "It is wise to be thorough before the fact, if you will allow me to say, Lord Hugo."

"I couldn't agree with you more," Hugo said, wishing that Gostrain would get on with the matter. Hugo's entire life hung in the balance.

Mr. Gostrain tapped his fingertips together again, an annoying habit that Hugo wished would cease. "May I ask if you have approached the lady in question with a proposal of marriage?" Mr. Gostrain said.

"No . . . I thought it best to wait until I understood all of the ramifications." The only ramification Hugo really cared about was getting money back into his pockets as soon as possible, but he wasn't about to explain that to Gostrain.

"Ah, well. A marriage settlement is not as complicated as you might imagine, my lord. Generally speaking, the matter is conducted between the two families and afterward, their solicitors. Your obligation is to inform the parents of the young lady of exactly what your circumstances are, and their obligation is to inform you of the degree of her fortune, which will become yours upon marriage."

"All of it?" Hugo said, determined there should be no mistake.

"All of it, save for any separate property her parents might wish to set up in trust for her that would remain under a trustee's control. This, however, is not a common practice."

"I see," Hugo said, relieved to hear it. He didn't want anyone in control of her money but him. He'd really have to insist on that if the subject came up.

Gostrain cleared his throat. "As you are a younger son, there is no line of succession involved. Your wife will of course share your courtesy title, but her parents will naturally be concerned about your ability to support their daughter in suitable style. You must keep in mind your future wife's right of dower upon your death, should you predecease her. That would be something approximating one third of your income, providing you do not establish a jointure for her in the premarital contract."

"Oh," Hugo said, thoroughly bored. He tuned Gostrain out as the man droned on, not interested in the distant future. He realized he would have to lie through his teeth to convince Amelia Langford's parents that Lyden Hall still belonged to him and that he also still had substantial funds.

". . . Now. As to children. The marriage contract will specify what their portions will be."

Children? Over his dead body. Yet he would be expected to share her bed and carry out his husbandly duties. Oh, God. The very idea of marriage to Amelia made him feel ill. The more Gostrain carried on about the binding legalities involved, the more panicked he became about being condemned for life to someone he already detested and found physically revolting.

Hugo was sure he must have turned a sickly shade of green, for Gostrain suddenly stopped mid-speech. But he said only, "If you will excuse me for a moment, Lord Hugo, I see Mr. Jenkins beckoning me. This should only take a moment."

He rose and left his desk, walking into the next room to confer with his partner. Hugo pressed his hands to his eyes, wishing himself dead. There had to be another way. There just had to be . . .

The murmur of voices rose and fell through the open doorway as the two partners conferred, but Hugo paid no attention until he heard a certain name mentioned.

"A Margaret Bloom of Ramsholt, Suffolk, you say?" Mr. Gostrain repeated. "I suppose we can try to track her down, despite the passage of so many years. What do we have to go on?"

Hugo rose and quietly moved closer to listen.

"It says here that David Russell knew Margaret Bloom to be with child when he left the country for India twenty-three years ago," Mr. Jenkins replied. "His will states most specifically that he wishes the fortune he made to be left to Margaret Bloom and any lineal descendant born in the year 1799, and we have been retained to investigate the matter. Four hundred thousand pounds is no small sum. Extraordinary, really—all accumulated in India through his business in sea trade."

Hugo nearly fell over in shock. Four hundred thousand pounds? Just floating around while they looked for a descendant of a certain Margaret Bloom?

"What if we should not discover the heir? What then?" Mr. Gostrain asked.

"Then the money is to be left to charity," his partner

replied. "Again, Mr. Russell was very specific about how it is to be distributed in that event. However, he apparently had great confidence that this Margaret Bloom did give birth in the summer of 1799, which would make the child now twenty-three years of age."

Hugo pressed his cheek against the wall in disbelief.

"Mr. Russell attempted many years ago through investigators to discover the whereabouts of mother and child, but with no success. In any case, if the child is still alive—indeed if he or she ever existed at all, he or she would be Mr. Russell's only immediate relative and legally entitled to the entire sum, as he wished. The funds now sit in a London bank waiting resolution."

Hugo's mind raced a million miles a minute, landing directly at the Woodbridge Sanitarium and the image of an insane girl with the face of an angel. It couldn't be her—*could* it? Woodbridge was only a stone's throw from Ramsholt, and Meggie Bloom was just the right age to fit the story. The name . . . the name alone was nearly identical to the mother's.

He knew Meggie Bloom's mother had died in childbirth, and if he was right—and how could he be wrong—Meggie herself was now worth four hundred thousand pounds. *Four hundred thousand pounds.* He couldn't bloody well believe it! It was the most incredible coincidence he'd ever come across.

Four hundred thousand was more than enough to get him out of all his difficulties with lots to spare. It would be his for the taking. All he had to do was marry the girl before Gostrain, Jenkins, and Waterville found her. Best of all, he had the jump on them, since he already knew where she was. It would take them at least a fortnight before they could track her down, if they could manage it at all when a previous team of investigators had been unsuccessful.

Hugo suppressed a wild desire to shriek with hysterical delight. It was perfect—perfect! A fortune like that would mean nothing to someone like Meggie Bloom—what would a crazy girl do with money? She couldn't function as it was.

He sobered for a moment, realizing that this meant he'd be taking a lunatic for a wife. But then, really, didn't the situation solve all of his problems?

He could get over his little problem with lunacy. How hard could it be? The nun herself had said that Meggie was harmless enough.

The only real responsibility he'd have to her would be to install her at Lyden Hall and discreetly hire a keeper to look after her. He could always pretend that he had met and married her on impulse, if anyone asked.

Who would blame him for his rash action after they'd seen her? She was a stunning creature. Then once he was married he couldn't be expected to marry anyone else, which took care of that problem. He'd look like a martyr.

He supposed children were inevitable, since he didn't plan to keep his hands off her, and he could only pray that they wouldn't be born with her affliction.

But if they were, he'd look even more like a martyr. How much more respectable could one get?

Hugo almost started believing in the power of prayer, for this was surely deliverance.

How he was actually going to persuade the befuddled Miss Meggie Bloom to marry him was another question, but Hugo had no doubt that he could find a way. After all, she didn't have a lot of options—or sense, common or otherwise, for that matter.

He quickly resumed his seat, attempting to look lost in thought. As soon as Gostrain returned, Hugo looked up and sighed heavily.

"I must thank you for your time, sir, and your advice. For after due consideration of everything you have told me, I've decided that I cannot marry this particular woman after all. The truth is that I do not love her, and I do not think I can marry without love. The idea is far too unsavory."

Gostrain scratched his head with one finger. "Begging your pardon, Lord Hugo, but if that is the case, then why did you consider marriage to her at all?"

"I suppose because I thought it was what was expected of a man in my position," Hugo said, knowing it was essential that he set up his story now if he was to be believed later. "Her breeding, her connections are impeccable and as I said, her dowry extremely large. Nevertheless, the prospect of living out my life with someone I do not care for repels me. I think I must put aside the expectations of others and follow my heart."

He paused for a long moment as if hesitant to continue, and then he lowered his voice. "The real truth of the matter is that I am in love with someone else, although I have hesitated to propose marriage to her."

"Ah. Is this other young lady perhaps not as well connected as the first?" Mr. Gostrain asked, his tone infinitely tactful.

"My dear Mr. Gostrain, as far as I know she is not connected at all. She is an orphan, utterly penniless, and without protection in this world."

Mr. Gostrain's mouth dropped open.

"Yet she is the sweetest, most gentle of creatures, kind and good," Hugo continued blithely. "My mother recently encouraged me to marry for love—nay, practically insisted on it. And so I shall. So I shall! My good man, I cannot thank you enough for preventing me from making a terrible mistake."

"But I—"

"Good day, sir. I hope to speak with her shortly and can only pray she will accept me. Naturally I shall notify you when the happy event occurs. It will be a quiet wedding, of course. I think that best under the circumstances."

Hugo made his bow, collected his hat and cane, and left, fully enjoying the expression of blank astonishment on Mr. Gostrain's usually composed face.

5

Oh God. Oh God, oh God, oh God. Hugo didn't actually know what he was praying for, unless it was divine protection. He couldn't believe that he was back at the asylum, a place he'd sworn never to go again.

But he was desperate, and desperation had a way of urging one forward no matter how fiercely the body and mind resisted.

He clutched his hat in his hands as he waited for the summons to Sister Agnes's office, silently rehearsing what he intended to say, all of it untrue.

Still, he was an expert at appearing to be sincere. He'd been doing it for as long as he could remember and usually successfully. In any case, he doubted a nun would know the difference between truth and fiction when it came to affairs of the heart.

As before, he was led to Sister Agnes's office by way of the long corridor. He drew in a deep, steadying breath, then knocked lightly and pushed the door open.

"Lord Hugo," the nun said, looking up at him over her spectacles as he entered. "This *is* a surprise. What brings you back to us so soon? I was under the impression that you had no interest in our activities here at the sanitarium." She arranged the papers in front of her into a tidy pile, regarding him with obvious speculation.

Hugo graced her with his most charming smile. "I can understand your confusion, Sister. I was confused myself, most confused indeed, to discover that my thoughts kept returning to this place. Indeed, not so much to this place as to one person in particular."

Sister Agnes's steady gaze did not waver. "What person would that be, Lord Hugo? As I recall, you showed little interest in visiting Lady Kincaid."

"It is not Lady Kincaid who has been occupying my thoughts. This might sound strange, but it is Meggie Bloom who has weighed heavily on my mind—"

Sister Agnes sat up very straight, her eyes boring sharply into his in a manner that Hugo found disconcerting. "Meggie Bloom? Why would Meggie Bloom weigh on your mind? Forgive me, my lord, but you do not even know the girl."

"No, Sister, I do not. And yet she left a profound impression on me."

"A profound impression. What type of profound impression, might I ask?"

Hugo arranged his features into an expression of a man earnest in his intent, leaning slightly forward as he lowered his voice. "The story you told me of her tragic past touched me deeply. I have not been able to rid myself of thoughts of her ever since. Even in my sleep, she is there." He sighed, but with only the slightest exhalation of breath, intended to convey wistful longing. "I would give my very soul to change her life."

"Just how would you go about that, Lord Hugo?" the nun said, sounding as worldly and skeptical as his own mother might, had he made the same pronouncement to her. "Perhaps you intend to offer her your protection?"

"Sister, I believe you misunderstand me." Hugo forced muted moral outrage into his voice. "If you think that I have come here to make a dishonorable proposition . . ."

"I have no idea what sort of a proposition you have in mind," the nun said succinctly. "I would find it rather odd for you to be coming to me with a suggestion of anything inappropriate. Therefore, I assume that you mean only the best for Meggie."

"Yes, of course," he lied. "My intention is solely honorable."

"That is good, Lord Hugo. Then what is it you wish to do for Meggie that would change her life? She has everything she needs here. An offer of money would not affect her circumstances, as she has nothing to spend it on. Her needs are very simple."

"This has nothing to do with money," Hugo said, annoyed that the nun was not behaving with the gratitude he'd expected. He was, after all, offering to take one of her charges off her hands. He bowed his head to conceal his frustration. "Or at least not in the way you might imagine."

"Ah. Then perhaps you wish to employ Meggie in some capacity in your household? I heard that you bought Lyden Hall not long ago. I assume you will be needing staff."

"Yes, that is true, but it isn't that either. You see, the truth of the matter is that I—I wish to marry Miss Bloom."

He waited for the burst of indignation, the stream of protests, for which he had all sorts of arguments prepared.

"You wish to marry Meggie Bloom," the nun said without any show of emotion. "What makes you think Meggie might wish to marry you?"

Hugo was taken aback. This conversation was definitely not going as he had anticipated. "Why, I can offer her my position, for one," he said indignantly, as if that wasn't obvious. "She would bear my name, as well as becoming mistress of Lyden Hall. I realize she is not like other women, but this does not worry me," he added when the nun still didn't reply. "I want only for Meggie to have the happiness she has been deprived of for so long. I am capable of looking after her very well, Sister." He clasped his hands together. "Indeed, I would make it my life's work to see to her contentment, her peace of mind."

Sister Agnes gazed thoughtfully at a point somewhere over his right shoulder. Then she placed her palms flat on her desk, meeting his gaze squarely. "You say that you understand Meggie is not like other women. What do you mean by that?"

Hugo stared at the nun, dumbfounded. How could the woman be so obtuse? "Is it not obvious, Sister? She is unique," he said, using the nun's coded language for the mentally incompetent. "Special. I feel a need to shelter her from the harshness of life. I have been fortunate in my birth, my privileged circumstances, and I would like to share those with her. In all honesty, Sister, no one has ever struck such a spark in me as Meggie did when I first saw her."

He frowned. Oddly enough, that one statement really was true, although he knew perfectly well what sort of spark he was referring to, and it had nothing to do with Meggie's being "special."

"I see. Yet you know next to nothing about her."

"But I do," Hugo protested. "Naturally I made inquiries before making up my mind on the matter. For example, I know that Meggie's mother was a Margaret Bloom and she hailed from Ramsholt." Hugo waited with baited breath for confirmation.

The nun nodded slowly. "Yes. Yes, it is true."

He practically leapt out of his chair with delight, although he was already as certain of his facts as he could be. "It was a tragic story," he said, taking a shot in the dark, but then it was fairly safe to venture that particular assumption.

"Indeed. Very tragic. And yet you still wish to marry Meggie, knowing what you do about her?"

Hugo nodded. "Her background may be troubled, but it is nothing that cannot be overcome."

"You are most broad-minded to say so, but I wonder if even a man in your position can afford to take as wife a woman whose background is . . . troubled, as you say. Have you bothered to think about the repercussions?"

Hugo was ready for that question. "Meggie should not be held responsible for what she cannot help," he said, pretending a supreme confidence he didn't really feel. Taking on an addle-brained wife was not a choice he would have made in any other circumstances. "I feel confident that I can protect her and guide her through whatever difficulties she might encounter."

"Including the censure of society?" the nun asked. "Your elevated position is one thing, Lord Hugo, but I am not sure even you can shield Meggie from the whispers and innuendoes that are bound to occur when those of your circle discover the truth about her. It has been hard enough for her to endure the contempt of the outside world. At least in this place she is protected from scorn, for as I told you once before, here we do not judge."

Hugo scratched his cheek, trying to think of an argument to counter the nun's. "I thought long and hard about what you said, Sister," he replied. "Why can I not look after Meggie at least as well as you have done? She will live a quiet life at Lyden Hall, much as she has done here, but she will have a far larger degree of freedom and the protection of my name."

"Perhaps. You nevertheless will place her in a position where she will be expected to take on responsibilities that she is not prepared for. You have already said that she will be mistress of Lyden Hall. How can you expect her to fulfill that role when she has no idea of all that it entails?"

"Meggie will have no responsibilities in that regard," Hugo countered. "I will hire a competent housekeeper, and there are already two elderly women in residence who have lived at Lyden for most of their lives. They can assist her. If Meggie should need any extra help in, . . . coping, then I shall arrange for that as well. Would you really rather see her condemned to living out the rest of her life here?" he added, playing his trump card. "I repeat, I care only for her happiness, which I feel sure I can provide."

"I too care only for Meggie's happiness. I am very fond of the child. It is only that your proposal is so unexpected. I never imagined that anyone might actually—well. Suffice it to say that I never expected Meggie to be leaving us." She treated him to another of her piercing looks. "You spoke of wanting her happiness. Why is her happiness *really* so important to you that you are willing to make such an enormous sacrifice?"

"I—I hesitated to speak to you of this, Sister, fearing you would think me foolish," he said, "but . . ." He allowed himself to trail off for just a moment, then cleared his throat. "I realize you are a woman of religion and so not given to these feelings, but do you believe in the phenomenon of love at first sight?"

He lowered his gaze to his hands as if embarrassed by being forced to admit the emotion. "I myself never thought it possible, but here I am as proof that the condition must exist. When I saw Meggie, I was hit by a bolt of lightning, a *coup de foudre,* as the French say."

That too was true enough. He'd never forget the paralyzing sensation—and had stayed well out of thunderstorms ever since.

"Yes, Lord Hugo. I do know what the French say. Yet you ask me to believe that you actually fell in love with Meggie while you were looking at her through a window?"

"I know it is preposterous. And yet the instant I saw her I felt as if I had been wandering in the world alone, and suddenly my salvation was at hand." He thought that a rather inspired touch and decided to push the point a little further. "It seems absurd even to my own mind, but I do not know how else to put it. I felt as if I had seen an angel, a being not entirely of this world, and yet the world suddenly made more sense than it ever had before. I have not been the same since."

Sister Agnes stayed silent for a few long moments, which made Hugo nervous. When she spoke again, her voice was suddenly softer. "I admit, you have greatly surprised me, Lord Hugo. I did not expect to find this degree of understanding in you, but I learned long ago that the Lord truly does work in mysterious ways, and it is not for us to question His methods."

A sudden jolt of excitement ran through Hugo's body. "Then you believe me?" he asked earnestly. "You do not think me mad?" He colored as he heard what he'd inadvertently said. "I mean—you do not think me foolish to feel as I do?"

Sister Agnes smiled. "How can I? If you have not only perceived Meggie's true nature but also accepted her for who she is, then who am I to stand in your way? There are few people who have ever done either—I am grateful for your perspicacity."

"I don't know about my perspicacity, Sister, but I would be grateful for your blessing, as there doesn't seem to be anyone else to bestow upon me Meggie's hand in marriage."

The nun folded her hands together. "If it is my blessing you are asking for, then you have it. For Meggie's sake, you have it."

"Thank you, Sister," he said with utmost sincerity.

She stood and walked over to the window, looking out, with her back to him. "Do not thank me yet," she replied quietly. "It is not my place to make such a decision for Meggie. I am not her keeper, and these walls were not built to confine, but rather to protect. Meggie is free to do as she wishes; you will have to speak to her. She must use her own judgment."

"Yes, of course," Hugo said, before the nun could change her mind. "If you will just tell me where I can find Meggie, I shall put my proposal to her personally."

"I think it might be best if I spoke to Meggie first in order to prepare her," Sister Agnes said firmly.

"If you don't mind, Sister, I would rather approach her myself," he replied. For all he knew she would fill Meggie's scrambled head with misguided information about what marriage actually involved, for Meggie couldn't be expected to understand it herself. "I know it is not entirely proper, but I believe there are things only I can say that will convince her of the sincerity of my cause, things she might understand better if they come directly from me. I give you my word that I will not frighten her."

Sister Agnes turned and regarded him severely. "My concern is not that you will frighten her. However, it is essential that you understand Meggie is a complete innocent. Furthermore, she is not accustomed to the company of people from the outside world. If I agree to let you see her, then you must promise me that you will be utterly circumspect in your behavior."

"Naturally," Hugo replied, trying to conceal his impatience. "I will do and say nothing untoward. I only wish to make my offer. If she refuses me, I will not press her further." He didn't mean it for a moment. He'd do whatever it took to snare Meggie Bloom and her four hundred thousand pounds.

The nun nodded, but Hugo saw her lingering reluctance. "I swear I will be careful with her," he said. "I care for her far too much to do or say anything that might alarm her."

"Very well. I take your word on the matter only because I know and respect your mother and trust that she raised you as a gentleman." "Which brings me to ask you—have you consulted your mother on this matter?"

He hadn't even thought about his mother's reaction and shuddered to think what it might be when she heard the news. "My mother? No, I saw no reason to speak until I had something to tell her." He shrugged as if it was of no importance. "As you must know, my mother is exceptionally progressive in her thinking. She has always encouraged me to be the same. I believe she will accept my choice of wife and will come to love Meggie as I do."

A likely story. But he would deal with his mother when the time came. She had gone to Rafe's estate in Ireland to be present at the birth of her first grandchild. When she eventually returned from Ireland he'd have solved all of his financial problems and she'd never be the wiser. A lunatic wife was a small price to pay.

"As you say, Lord Hugo. You surely know your mother better than I, although I pray you are correct in anticipating her reaction." Sister Agnes released a sharp breath as if she still wondered whether she was doing the right thing. "Meggie usually works in the vegetable garden at this time of day. If you go out the front door and turn right, you will find a path that leads around the building to the back. Follow it as far as it goes. You will see the garden directly in front of you."

Hugo jumped to his feet. "Thank you, Sister. I thank you from the bottom of my heart."

"Do not disappoint me. Should you upset the girl in any way, I can promise you that you will have me to answer to."

Hugo hoped to hell that wouldn't be the case. His sole intention was to get Meggie Bloom to say "I will" as quickly as possible.

* * *

Meggie dug her hoe into the side of the row of lettuce, carefully cultivating the soil and freeing it of weeds. She always looked forward to her gardening chores. They freed her to think her thoughts, rather than constantly trying to screen out the random thoughts of others.

Meggie untied her apron and spread it on the ground. She wished Sister Agnes didn't insist she wear white, the most impractical color on earth, but at least it separated her from the nuns and the novitiates, who wore black and gray respectively. Still, since Sister Agnes considered primary colors overstimulating to the patients, Meggie had no choice. White it was.

Kneeling, she carefully spread the dirt evenly around each little burgeoning plant, patting it into place with an encouraging word. It was essential to let each one know it was important, valued. She'd seen the results over the years, the part of the garden that was her responsibility bursting with health and double the produce.

She found it so satisfying to watch the earth come alive in the spring, bringing forth new growth. Spring was her favorite time of year, although summer did give her enormous satisfaction, wielding its generous bounties. But summer was easy. Summer only had to reap what spring had sown. Spring had to conquer the small, cold death of winter, and that took real strength.

She loved the autumn almost as much, the brilliant colors of the trees and shrubs a last magnificent showing before winter again claimed its price. Now *that* was bravery, she decided, rising to fetch the watering can. Each cell in each fauna and flora knew this was its final goodbye before dying away.

Really, it took even greater bravery to stir anew and start the cycle all over again. This was the essential nature of life itself.

It had often occurred to her that the patients under her care went through much of the same process. When they arrived, most of them were living in the long, dark winter of the soul. Only the luckiest, most determined ones found the strength to renew themselves, to stretch out and make the journey back into the world, rediscovering the joy of life the way the plants of God's earth did every year.

"Oh, you really are lovely lettuces," she murmured, standing back, hands on her hips, surveying her crop with pleasure.

She glanced up in surprise as Hadrian, who had been basking in the sunshine, emitted a low growl from his throat. Hadrian only growled in such a manner when a stranger approached, but she hadn't sensed anyone coming and she always felt a person's presence. No, she was absolutely sure they were alone.

Hadrian did not agree. His growl deepened and his body tensed, shifting from the lazy position he'd assumed alongside the fence into a half-crouch, his ears pricking back, his legs stiffening.

Alarmed, Meggie rose, turning and shielding her eyes against the rays of the slanting sun.

She was surprised when she saw that Hadrian hadn't been mistaken after all. A man walked down the path toward her, but she couldn't make out who, only that his figure was tall and imposing. His face was obscured by the brim of his hat, leaving his features in shadow.

She stretched out her mind, trying to read something, anything at all from the stranger, but nothing came. Nothing at all . . . except a sudden awareness of something dangerous and indefinable that struck not at her mind, but at her body. She'd experienced this sense of physical chaos from only one other person before, and that was over two months ago. The memory would be burned into her brain for all time.

She pressed a shaking hand to her mouth. It *couldn't*

be. Oh, dear gracious Lord in heaven, not Hugo Montagu? Impossible.

And yet she knew it was, and not just because every nerve ending in her body vibrated with heightened awareness. She also experienced the same absolute silence in him that she had before, a total blank that left her without any point of reference.

It was only now, without the benefit of her talent, that she realized how much she relied on it. For the first time in her life she felt completely alone in the presence of another person, with not even the vaguest of whispers to guide her.

As unfamiliar as the experience was, in a way it was an enormous relief. Or it would have been if she hadn't been shaken to the core of her being.

Hadrian growled again as Hugo approached the garden gate.

"Lie down, there's a good boy," she murmured, knowing that Hadrian must sense her alarm, and so he should: her knees threatened to give out at any moment. "All is well," she lied, feeling a complete fraud, which Hadrian must also know. But he still lowered from his wary position to one of quiet watchfulness.

Meggie's heart filled with gratitude, realizing that she wasn't entirely without protection—although she wasn't sure that this was the sort of situation that Hadrian could really protect her from.

She closed her eyes, trying to collect herself, which was impossible as the creak of the garden gate opening sounded a thousand times exaggerated. She finally dared to look, allowing herself only the slightest of squints.

Oh, dear, *dear* Lord in heaven. It really was. In the flesh. In the all-too-real flesh, flesh she'd spent an indecent amount of time fantasizing about.

"Miss Bloom?"

His voice was deep, yet melodic at the same time, and

hearing it turned Meggie's blood to water. She had imagined how he might sound, never expecting to find out. What alarmed her more than anything was that he sounded exactly as she'd expected. She would have found the situation far easier to bear if only he'd come out with a cracked falsetto.

"Yes?" she managed to say. Her legs shook so uncontrollably that she thought she might blow over in the tempest he'd brought in with him.

"Allow me to present myself. I am Hugo Montagu. Will you be so kind as to sit with me for a few moments? There is a pressing matter I wish to discuss with you."

Meggie swallowed hard. She knew she must look frightful, all disheveled with dirt covering her face. She turned her head sideways and opened her eyes a touch wider, taking him in peripherally, as if that might save her from the full blast of his presence.

Oh, no. He was even more beautiful up close, surpassing her wildest imaginings, and she'd thought she'd imagined him rather well. His eyes blazed like the finest of sapphires, so clear that they seemed to reflect the sun itself. His full, well-sculpted mouth curved in the slightest of smiles as he looked down at her.

She squeezed her eyes shut again, just for a moment, wondering if she hadn't finally caught the inmates' disease of fantasizing so clearly that she could make anything seem real.

When she opened her eyes again he was still there.

Meggie couldn't help herself. Her mouth dropped open and she turned to face him, staring for all she was worth.

"Oh," she couldn't help but utter. "Oh, my."

"I beg your pardon," he said, his voice quiet and soothing, as if he were speaking to a frightened animal. "I did not mean to alarm you."

"You did not alarm me," she said, trying to gather her addled wits about her. "It is only that I did not expect anyone. I was talking to—I mean, I was thinking about the lettuce."

"Yes. The lettuce. Why not? I am sure the lettuce is worthy of all the attention you can give it."

He smiled, and Meggie felt as if the sun had come out and brightened over half a lifetime of gray skies.

He might as easily have been a god descending from Mount Olympus to grace a mortal with a moment of his divine presence.

"It helps," she said, feeling so nervous she wasn't even sure what she was talking about anymore.

"You are . . . fond of lettuce?"

Meggie nodded. She couldn't believe they were standing there speaking of something so mundane. She couldn't believe they were speaking at all.

Fumbling for something to do, she bent down and gently uprooted one of the more mature plants. "Are you fond of lettuce yourself? If you are, this might suit you nicely. You need only to dress it simply. Lettuce doesn't take well to showy treatment at a tender age."

He looked down at the tightly folded plant she handed him. "Thank you; it is very lovely. I will dress it with care. As carefully as an ingenue in her first Season. Nothing but the most pristine of colors." He tucked it inside his coat.

Meggie passed a shaking hand over her brow, feeling as if she were surely dreaming. "Lemon," she babbled. "You had best dress it in lemon. Lemon does not overwhelm."

"Indeed not. I will be sure to choose exactly the right shade. And what would you have me top this magnificent lettuce with? Surely it needs a fine bonnet?"

A faint image came back to Meggie of a wonderful

salad her aunt Emily had once made. "Er . . . a mushroom? Peeled, and with the stem removed. It would make a very fine presentation." She'd never felt so tongue-tied in all her life. If this was the best she could do, she might as well disappear into the lettuce bed itself.

"A mushroom bonnet. Indeed. I will take that into consideration," he said with a twitch of his lips. "I am sure it will make a most original impression."

Meggie stared down at the ground, feeling like a complete fool. "As you say. I am no hand in these matters."

"Miss Bloom." The touch of his hand on her arm burned through her sleeve, and she shivered as his heat imprinted itself on her flesh.

"Mmm?" she mumbled through a sudden dizziness.

"I wonder if you remember back some two months ago when you and I first spotted each other. You were walking along the path as I was standing at Sister Agnes's window. Our eyes met—and you turned away very suddenly. Too suddenly. I have wondered why ever since."

Meggie colored furiously as if she'd been caught out in an indecent activity. "I—I do not recall," she lied. "But then my memory is short—not reliable."

"Is it, my dear? Never mind, for that is of no importance. What is important is that I have not forgotten the moment, not for one instant. That is why I am here with you now, why I have come all this way to speak with you."

Meggie's eyes shot open in alarm. She had assumed that the only reason he had reappeared was because he had a continuing interest in Eunice Kincaid's condition and had been told Meggie was the person to whom to apply for details.

"You have come to speak to *me*? But—but why?" she stammered. "I have nothing to say."

"Oh, but you do. You can say 'I will.' "

"Say 'I will?' I will what?" Meggie replied, confused.

His voice dropped very low, soft as pure velvet. "Say you will marry me, Meggie Bloom."

6

Meggie stared at him, certain she could not have heard correctly. People didn't just waltz up a garden path and demand to marry someone they'd never met before—especially dukes' sons who surely had better things to do than playing at proposing to orphan girls with absolutely no prospects. Even she knew that much.

Meggie, my love . . . please come to me . . .

She shook her head hard, forcing herself back to reality. That was her private fantasy—nothing more. If she had learned anything in her life, it was that she could not afford to indulge herself in dreams. She was sensible to the core.

She had to be missing something in this absurd offer of marriage that had come out of the blue.

And then with a sudden flash of insight she realized what Hugo Montagu had *really* come for. Marriage, her foot. Her mouth dropped open in horror.

"Do you still have nothing to say?" he asked, looking down at her with a wide smile, revealing two long, tantalizing creases in his lean cheeks.

Meggie's own cheeks burned with anger. So, he thought he could lead her astray with primrose promises and take what he wanted before abandoning her, did he? Well, she would give him what for. She knew all about rogues. She may never have actually met one before now, but she knew all about what they liked to get up to. She was a product of that particular activity.

"I think you must be mad," she said, sorely tempted to give him a swift kick in the shin for his impertinence. What was it about her that made men think she was there for the taking? All they ever had was one thing on their minds, and she'd read enough of those minds to know. "Or maybe you're perfectly sane, which would be an even greater pity."

"What the . . . my dear girl, did you not hear me?" he said, looking at her as if she was the one who was mad. "Surely you do not receive proposals of marriage every day? Or did you not comprehend me?"

"I comprehended you perfectly," Meggie said darkly. "And I think that you should go away before I box your ears. I think you should please go away, that is," she amended politely. "Your lordship."

"Ah . . . so you do know who I am. I wonder how, if you have no memory of me." He cocked his head to one side.

"It—it came back. Just now," she said, embarrassed that he'd caught her out in a bald-faced lie. "Sister Agnes mentioned you when you were last here. She said that you came to ask after Lady Kincaid."

"Yes, that is right, and I asked Sister Agnes to tell me all about you at the same time."

"You did? Why?" Meggie said, astonished that Sister Agnes hadn't said a word about it.

"Because Meggie . . . may I call you Meggie?"

She shrugged. "Everyone else does. Why should you stand on ceremony?"

"Indeed. Ceremony can be so tedious. But to answer your question, I asked about you because I was taken by you from the moment I saw you. Do you understand what that means?"

Meggie swallowed hard. She knew exactly what it meant, far too well for her comfort. "I—I really don't think it is at all proper for you to speak of such things."

To her surprise, he burst into laughter. "Maybe it is not proper, but considering what I am asking of you, I don't see the harm. Again, perhaps you did not understand my proposal. Would you like me to clarify it for you?"

Meggie's blood began to boil. He obviously not only thought her an easy mark, he thought her stupid to boot. Fine. She would give him a taste of his own medicine and see how he liked being treated like an imbecile.

"I *believe* what you were trying to say is that you want to take me away from this, my home, and you want me to sleep with you. In your bed. Is that not right? Or did you mean something else entirely?"

It was his turn to stare at her. He cleared his throat with an obvious effort. "I . . . well. Yes, that is part of it," he said, "but sleeping in my bed is not *all* there is to it."

"Oh. I suppose you mean the part about the baby that usually comes afterward," Meggie retorted, starting to enjoy herself. "You do know about that?"

"Yes." He cleared his throat. "Yes, I do know about that. I have no trouble with the idea of your having a baby, though. Have you?"

"Why ever should I?" Meggie said, thinking him perfectly shameless. She wondered how many bastard children he had already spawned, or if he'd even bothered to count. "However, I have no interest in sleeping in your bed. I am perfectly happy in my own."

He reached out and picked up one of her hands, looking down at it with an unreadable expression. Meggie assumed he was trying to hide his revulsion at the soil encrusted under her fingernails and the mud that coated her palm. He certainly was persistent if he was willing to dirty himself, she thought, knowing she should pull her hand away, but enjoying the touch of his fingers around hers far too much to break the contact.

It was only for just a moment, after all. She might not feel her hand in his ever again, and he did have a very nice hand, large and warm and firm. An inadvertent sigh escaped her lips.

"Forgive me," he said softly. "I think I have frightened you, and that was not my intention. Perhaps I should not have approached the subject so abruptly."

"Oh? How else would you have approached it?" Meggie really could not believe she was even participating in this conversation.

"I should have told you first that I am in love with you, that I have felt this way for weeks now. In all sincerity I couldn't stay away any longer. I had to come, Meggie, I really did."

I need you, Meggie . . .

Meggie firmly shut the treacherous refrain out of her head, gazing at him with no expression. Oh, he was a clever one. He'd say anything to achieve his goal: promise marriage, plead love—she doubted he had any conscience at all. "You are in love with me?" she said, deliberately puckering her brow. "Very deeply?"

"Painfully so," he said, gazing earnestly into her eyes.

She gazed earnestly back at him, although it was harder to do than she'd anticipated. His eyes really were the most extraordinary color—an azure that made her think of the deep blue of cloudless summer skies. "Does it hurt very much?" she asked, forcing her attention back to the absurd conversation.

"It hurts more than I can say," he replied, lightly squeezing her fingers. "My heart fell to you in that split second I saw you through the window, and it has ached terribly ever since."

She smiled brightly at him, even though she badly wanted to kick his shins. "Perhaps you need a bandage. I can fetch you one if you like."

His mouth tightened. "What I need is for you to say you will be mine. Please. I will be good to you, Meggie. Very good."

"Good to me?" she said, resting the forefinger of her free hand on her lower lip, hoping she looked like a complete naif. "You have to forgive me—my understanding is limited. What does 'good to me' mean?"

"It means you will have everything your heart desires. All you have to do is agree. Sister Agnes would be so pleased if you did."

Meggie narrowed her eyes, abandoning her game. "Sister Agnes would have your hide if she knew what you were suggesting," she said with cold fury. "She'd have your hide if she knew you were out here at all."

"Sister Agnes does know," he replied, running his thumb over the back of her hand and sending shivers down her poor defenseless spine. "I spoke to her before coming to you and she gave me her full blessing. Who do you think sent me out here?"

Meggie jerked her hand from his grasp and clutched it to her chest. "Oooh—you really are despicable," she cried, outraged to her core. "Sister Agnes would *never* agree to anything so wicked! Will you stop at nothing to further your disgraceful cause? Do you think me so completely addle-brained that I would believe you?"

He actually colored, and she saw with satisfaction that she'd hit a mark of some sort, although she couldn't be sure what it was. Oh, *what* she'd give to be able to read his thoughts—or even just his nature.

"Meggie," he said, looking extremely uncomfortable, "I don't know what the nuns have told you, but I swear to you, there is nothing wrong with the physical union between a man and a woman. God Himself decreed it should be so."

Meggie was so amazed at this further piece of audacity that her mouth fell open wide enough to catch flies. First he invoked the blessing of nuns, and now of God Himself, to put a stamp of approval on seduction? "Did He," she said weakly. "How extraordinarily openhanded of Him. Did Sister Agnes tell you that, too?"

He groaned, looking frustrated and annoyed. She felt deliciously pleased that she'd managed to knock him off his self-satisfied pedestal for one small moment.

He released a long breath and stared down at the lettuce bed. When he raised his eyes to her he looked entirely different, smiling at her as if she were his favorite person on earth.

"If you agree to marry me," he said in treacle tones, "you will have lots and lots of pretty clothes, and a nice soft bed all of your very own. You may get up from that bed whenever you please and go to sleep in it whenever you please and—and you may have as many chocolates as you can eat. Day in and day out. Lots of *big* chocolates. Wouldn't you like that?"

He nodded rapidly, up and down, up and down, the way some of the patients did.

Meggie's eyes widened with dawning comprehension. Could it be that Lord Hugo Montagu was short a few sheets?

"*Big* chocolates?" she repeated, instantly reformatting their entire conversation to see if it fit this new framework. It did—all too well. She might not be able to read his thoughts, but she certainly knew how to read all the signs of instability. She couldn't believe she'd missed them earlier. Sister Agnes had even asked her two months ago if Meggie had noticed anything amiss about him. She had said that he is a relation of Eunice Kincaid's and that mental illness ran in families.

"Oh, my goodness," she murmured, one hand creeping to her throat in real dismay. She wanted to cry. Hugo Montagu, the magnificent man she'd been pining after for a full two months, was as mad as a hatter, just like his relative. *That* was why he was here. How could she have been so stupid not to realize, given his preposterous remarks?

"Barrows full of chocolates," he said, nodding even harder in that peculiar fashion. "Wagonloads. And a garden of your very own, so that you are never without heads of lettuce, which you may dress in anything you please."

"Thank you," she said politely, finally knowing how to handle him. This was second nature to her after all her years at the sanitarium. "You are very generous."

He looked vastly relieved, as if they were finally speaking the same language, and she supposed they finally were. "Ribbons too, lovely lemon ribbons for your hair, as many as you like. How does that sound?"

Meggie bestowed a matching smile on him, deciding that he must have just arrived and somehow contrived to wander away when no one was looking.

Poor man. He really did need help. "I am sure lemon ribbons would be lovely," she said, trying to think how to coax him back to the building without alarming him.

"Barrows full of those, too. Just say you'll marry me and you may have anything you like."

Meggie tilted her head to one side, sure of her ground now. "Anything?"

"Indeed. Anything at all. Whatever your heart desires."

"My heart desires that you come back to the house with me and speak to Sister Agnes."

"I've already spoken with her," he said, his expression returning to one of thorough exasperation. "I told you, she gave me her blessing. You are free to leave this very afternoon. I have a special license, so there will be no impropriety."

"I'm sure you have," she said in her most reassuring voice, her heart aching to see how delusional he really was. A special license to abduct young women? Oh, well—at least he was original. "I still think we had better go see Sister Agnes," she urged.

"Oh, for God's sake, Meggie, just marry me and you won't have to think about Sister Agnes or this place ever again. Furthermore, if you don't want me to come near your bed until you're more comfortable with the idea, then that is fine, too. Whatever you wish—just be sensible and say you'll be my wife, will you?"

Meggie chewed on her lip. She did have an obligation to return him as quickly as possible before the alarm was raised. There couldn't be any harm in playing along with him just a little in order to achieve her goal. "Very well," she replied, placing her hand on his coat sleeve. "I'll be sensible."

"You will?" He peered at her closely. "Do you mean you really will?"

"Of course I will, but you have to be sensible, too, and do as I've asked." There, that wasn't entirely a lie. She was being sensible, after all, and returning him to where he belonged.

His handsome face lit up as if she'd just told him it was Christmas morning. He raised both hands to the sky and threw his head back with a shout. "Oh, thank You, God! Thank you—I'll never doubt You again!"

"Lord Hugo, I don't think you should excite yourself so," Meggie said. "It's really not good for you."

He looked at her with a huge grin. "It's extremely good for me—*you* are good for me, Meggie Bloom, best girl in the world. You have no idea how happy you've made me!"

Before she had a chance to react, he grasped her by the waist and swept her off her feet, whirling her around in wide circles. She gasped and clutched at his shoulders, feeling as if she were flying. It was not an entirely unpleasant sensation, especially since he was holding her so tightly.

A low, menacing growl broke through the air and Meggie suddenly remembered Hadrian. He'd been so quiet that she'd forgotten he was there, but this unorthodox treatment of her by a sheer stranger was clearly too much for his protective instincts.

Hugo froze with Meggie still mid-air. "Good God," he whispered. "Don't move. Don't move a muscle."

"Actually, I think you'd better put me down," Meggie said, feeling positively light-headed. Trust her to be carnally attracted to a madman whose thoughts she couldn't even access.

Life was going to be hell with him on the same premises, she could see that now.

"I don't think you understand," he said, his voice so low it was barely audible. "I don't want you to panic or scream, but there's a—never mind. Just stay calm and I'll try to get us out of here in one piece."

Meggie gazed down at him, her hands still resting on his broad shoulders. He was the most handsome man she'd ever seen. Really, it was a shame that his interior wasn't as well put together as his exterior. "There, now," she said in soothing tones. "That's just my dog. If you put me down he'll stop."

Hugo nearly dropped her in his haste to release her. "Your *dog*?" he repeated. "My dear girl, I hate to disenchant you, but that's no dog. That's a bloody wolf! He's liable to attack us at any moment."

"Don't be absurd," Meggie said. "Hadrian is perfectly harmless."

"Funny—Hadrian doesn't *look* harmless," Hugo replied tightly, carefully backing away from her, his gaze glued to the wolf the entire time. "Does your dog usually behave like this?"

"I don't think he liked your manhandling me." She went to Hadrian and bent down, stroking his head. "It's all right, darling, Lord Hugo isn't going to hurt me. He's just a little . . . energetic."

Hadrian's ears pricked forward and he licked her hand obligingly enough, but he still looked dubious. "That's a good boy." She glanced up at Hugo. "You see? Harmless."

"Meggie . . . please," he said, his face white as a sheet. "Get away from him. You may think he can be trusted, but he's a wild creature. He could turn on you at any moment."

"Nonsense. I'm his closest friend. He'd never harm a hair on my head." She nuzzled her face in the warm, sweet-smelling fur on Hadrian's neck to prove her point.

"Oh, God. I think I'm going to be sick," Hugo said, slipping one hand over his eyes.

"You are being very silly," Meggie said sternly, but then an interesting thought crossed her mind and she softened her tone. "Is it just Hadrian who frightens you, my lord, or are you afraid of all animals?"

"No, I am not afraid of all animals," he said, glaring at her. "I'm just afraid of the wild ones with sharp fangs who threaten to attack me."

"Hadrian has no intention of attacking anyone," she replied indignantly. "He is a most sensitive and understanding creature. You'll get to be friends soon enough."

"No," he said, putting both hands out in front of him. "No, no, and no. If you think you're dragging a savage animal along with you, you're ma—er, you'll have to think again. Hadrian can go right back into the forest from whence he skulked."

Meggie turned and glared at Hugo over her shoulder. "He most certainly will not, and he doesn't skulk. He is my faithful companion, and you will simply have to become accustomed to him, just as everyone else has done."

"Are you trying to tell me that beast wanders freely

about the grounds?" Hugo said, looking appalled. "My God, does Sister Agnes know about this?"

"Sister Agnes knows everything that goes on here. I really can't see why you're kicking up such a fuss. All he did was warn you away from me, which he has every right to do."

Meggie frowned. So far no patient had objected to Hadrian's presence. But Sister Agnes had made it very clear that if anyone did, steps would have to be taken because their first obligation was to the patients' peace of mind. If Hugo raised enough of a fuss, Hadrian would be banished.

"You're not *really* afraid of him, are you?" she asked, nervously.

"Are you suggesting that I put my hand in his mouth to show you what a brave man I am? I value the use of my limbs—all of them."

Meggie had to smile. Hugo Montagu might be demented, but despite that, she couldn't help truly liking him. Even if he was afraid of animals.

She walked over to him and slipped her hand through the crook of his elbow. "Come along," she said with a little tug. "We've tarried long enough. However, as a favor to you, my lord, I will leave Hadrian in the garden. He won't mind, and I'm sure you'll feel more comfortable."

"You're so thoughtful," he said dryly.

"I do try to be," Meggie said, relishing the feel of his well-muscled arm through the fine fabric of his coat.

Really, having Hugo Montagu around might not be so bad after all, she thought, suddenly feeling happier than she had in a long while.

Hugo allowed Meggie to pull him along, not that he wasn't in a damned hurry himself. The sooner he got

Meggie Bloom out of Woodbridge Sanitarium and installed under his own roof, the better he'd feel. Then it was only a matter of putting a ring on her finger. They could be married as early as tomorrow and would be, if he had anything to say about it.

He was pleased that she now seemed enthusiastic about the idea of marriage. For a time there he'd been sincerely worried that he was going to leave empty-handed. Logic hadn't worked with her—but he'd been an idiot to assume that it would. Nor had flowery language, although she'd seemed more responsive to that than logic.

However, coaxing her with promises of trinkets and sweets as if she were a child of five had worked like a charm. He would file that piece of useful information away in the back of his head for future reference on how to manage Meggie.

Glancing down at the top of her flaxen head, he decided that she wasn't really insane, just a little . . . confused. Fey. Off with the fairies. Perfectly harmless, really. He just had to remember that she didn't occupy the same world as everyone else and they'd get along famously.

She looked up at him and smiled sweetly, her gray eyes calm and clear, completely trusting. He felt like a man stealing candy from a baby and knew he should be ashamed of himself. On the other hand, he was giving her a far better life than the one she had, he reminded himself. She ought to be grateful to him.

"Here we are, my lord," she said as they approached the house.

He nodded, suddenly feeling oppressed at the thought of having to enter the asylum. "Why don't I wait for you out here?" he suggested. "You can tell Sister Agnes your decision and gather your things."

"No, I'm afraid that won't do. I need for you to come inside with me."

"Why, Meggie? I'll only be in the way." He knew he sounded ridiculous, but he couldn't help himself. He loathed the place. "Anyway, it seems a pity to waste a beautiful afternoon sitting inside with nothing to do."

"Oh, but there is lots to do," she said, practically dragging him to the door and pushing him inside. "There is nothing to be afraid of, really there isn't."

"Did I say I was afraid?" Hugo retorted sharply. "I said I preferred to sit in the sunshine."

"Then the place I have in mind is perfect. You can wait in the solarium while I sort everything out," she said cheerfully. "There are books to read and games to play."

Hugo rolled his eyes. He was just wasting time arguing with her. "Very well. Take me to the solarium, but don't be long."

"Not long at all," she promised, leading him down an unfamiliar hallway in the opposite direction of Sister Agnes's office.

She opened another door and took him into a room that was large and comfortable enough, filled with sofas and chairs and bookshelves. Sun did indeed stream through the long windows. The only problem with the picture was that every single window was covered with steel bars.

Hugo shuddered involuntarily and turned his back on them.

Meggie gave him a look he couldn't decipher, then took his hand and squeezed it lightly. "Everything is going to be all right," she said solemnly. "You will see. It's only a matter of getting used to a new situation."

Hugo couldn't think what the hell she was talking about, but that came as no surprise. "Just get on with it, Meggie," he said curtly, already longing for escape.

"I'll be back in no time," she said, softly closing the door behind her.

The next thing Hugo heard was the scrape of a key in the lock and a loud click. And then another scrape, slightly below the first and a second click.

His heart froze in his chest.

He strode across the room and turned the brass handle, jerking it toward him. The thick mahogany door didn't budge. He turned the handle the other way and jerked again. It still didn't budge.

He bent down and examined the door. Two separate keyholes. Both made of heavy brass. Both tumblers turned.

He couldn't believe it. Meggie had locked him in.

"Meggie? Meggie Bloody Bloom, let me out of here at once!" he shouted, banging on the door with his fists. Nothing happened. He pressed his ear against the door and listened, but he couldn't hear a thing. Which meant no one could hear him either.

Hugo unleashed a furious volley of curses.

He was going to kill her. As soon as he got out of his temporary prison, he was definitely going to kill her.

Unfortunately, he was going to have to marry her first.

7

Meggie paused a moment to collect herself before tapping lightly on Sister Agnes's door. She hoped to heaven that she'd done the right thing by leaving Hugo Montagu in the solarium all by himself. There hadn't been anyone else within calling distance to keep an eye on him, and she had felt that time was of the essence in seeing that he would be taken safely to quarters of his own.

"Meggie!" Sister Agnes said, looking up as Meggie entered. "Here you are at last. Sit down, child," she said, gesturing to a chair. "I've been expecting you."

"I thought you might be," Meggie said, perching on the edge of the seat. "You were waiting to hear about Lord Hugo, weren't you?" She knew that much, since his name was going around and around in Sister Agnes's head, coupled with anxiety.

"I did hope he had found you . . ."

"Yes, he found me in the garden. He gave me quite a shock, I can tell you that."

Sister Agnes nodded sympathetically. "I can imagine he did. I do hope I was not wrong in sending him to you, though."

"Oh," Meggie said, her hand slipping to her mouth in dismay. Hugo Montagu had told her Sister Agnes had sent him, but without her talent to guide her, she had not believed him. "Did you intend for me to say something particular to him?"

The two ingrained furrows between Sister Agnes's eyebrows deepened. "I intended only for you to speak as you saw fit." She lightly touched a hand to her cross.

"Perhaps I should have prepared you first, but I thought that with your ability, you would know better than I how to judge."

Meggie shifted nervously in the chair, not knowing how to explain the unprecedented failure of that ability. "Oh, Sister. I am so sorry, but I have to be absolutely honest with you."

"You have always been honest with me, Meggie. Whatever you have decided, you can tell me. There is no need to hide anything."

Meggie blushed, since there was one thing she did need to hide—the ridiculous havoc Hugo Montagu wreaked on her body. Sister Agnes would be deeply alarmed to hear about that and would probably see to it that Meggie was kept as far away from him as possible. Probably not a bad idea, all things considered.

"Why do you hesitate, child?" Sister Agnes asked. "You are usually more forthcoming than this, sure of your intuition."

Meggie shook her head in bewilderment. "That's just it. Lord Hugo was a complete mystery to me. I cannot tell you anything about him that you do not already know for yourself."

Sister Agnes regarded Meggie with considerable surprise. "You are saying that you could read nothing at *all* of his character, of his thoughts?"

"Nothing." Meggie bowed her head. "I am sorry if I have disappointed you. I don't know what to make of it myself—I've never been so completely at a loss."

To Meggie's astonishment, Sister Agnes chuckled, then chuckled again. "Well, well," she said. "Miracles never cease, and you haven't disappointed me in the least."

"I haven't? But—but you said you relied on my ability, that it helped you immeasurably in our work here. Why would you now change your mind?"

"I haven't changed my mind, child. I still have the utmost faith in your gift and its infinite benefits to those in need. However, in this instance I cannot help but feel it is best that you cannot divine Lord Hugo's every thought."

"But isn't that why you sent him? Because you wanted me to assess his state of mind as thoroughly as I could?"

"I sent him because I trusted in your ability to assess your own mind—and your heart. I assumed that you would also be able to see inside his, but that is apparently not the case, and that is why, despite my surprise, I rejoice." She leaned back in her chair, her hands tucked beneath the folds of her habit. "It is better, I think, that two people living under the same roof have a little distance between each other. Don't you agree?"

Meggie rubbed her forehead, acutely embarrassed. She might have known that Sister Agnes would somehow manage to perceive the one thing Meggie didn't want her to know. "Yes," she murmured, knowing there was no point in prevaricating now. "A little distance. I suppose it is for the best, given the circumstances."

"Does that mean you have reached a decision then? Will you accept Lord Hugo? It means taking on an enormous responsibility and a challenge, but I believe you are capable of both."

"I—I don't understand," Meggie said, now completely confused. "Why would you want me to take responsibility for Lord Hugo when his thoughts are inaccessible to me?"

"Take responsibility for him? I'm not sure what you mean, my dear. Surely Lord Hugo will be taking responsibility for you. That is usually the case in a marriage."

Meggie nearly fell off her chair in shock. "M-marriage?" she gasped, gripping the edge of the seat with her fingers. No. Oh, no . . . she couldn't have been so badly mistaken. Could she have?

"Yes, of course marriage. What else did you think I was referring to?"

"But he's insane! He's here to be admitted, isn't he? Oh, Sister Agnes, tell me I'm right. Please, please tell me I'm right?" Meggie wanted to curl up into a little ball and die from mortification.

"Insane? Here to be . . . what on earth? Meggie, surely he did not tell you anything of the sort? Did he not explain why he came?"

"Yes, but—but I didn't believe him! I mean, only someone who was a full-fledged lunatic would want to marry me. I don't even know him—he doesn't know me. Why, *why* would he want to marry me of all people? Don't you see, he *must* be mad!"

"My dear child," the nun said, her face wreathed in a broad smile, "he is certainly not mad, I can tell you that. Goodness, your gift really did fail you." She looked positively gleeful.

"Oh, please do not tease me now, Sister. I truly don't understand! How can he be anything close to sane if he honestly meant to propose?"

"Do you really think I would have sent him to speak to you on such a serious subject if I thought him even slightly deranged?"

Meggie squeezed her hands together so hard that they turned white. His words echoed in her head in all too vivid detail, only this time with an entirely different significance.

Sister Agnes does know . . . I spoke to her before coming to you and she gave me her full blessing . . .

"Then you believe he truly meant it?" she whispered.

"Yes," Sister Agnes said, her expression sobering. "I did believe he meant everything he said. He pleaded his case eloquently. Did he not do so with you?"

I am in love with you . . . I have felt this way for weeks now . . . I had to come, Meggie, I really did . . .

The words rang silently in her ears, embarrassing her to her very core. How could she have behaved so badly? She buried her face in her hands.

"Oh, Sister, I have made a terrible mess of everything. I thought at first that he only said he wanted to marry me so that he could—" She cut herself off abruptly. "You know," she mumbled. "Like what happened to my mother."

"Dear me," Sister Agnes said, her brow creasing. "I didn't think you knew anything about your mother's predicament. I am sorry, child. I had hoped to protect you from the pain of that truth."

Meggie looked up, feeling weary to the bone. "It doesn't matter, Sister. Really it doesn't. I accepted my illegitimacy long ago. What puzzles me is why Lord Hugo Montagu would have any intention of marrying someone of my low birth—or maybe he doesn't know about that particular part of it."

"He has made it his business to learn a great deal about you, Meggie, and he made it clear that although he knows about the circumstances of your birth, he doesn't care in the least. Furthermore, and I don't know how, he seems to understand about . . ." She trailed off and was silent for a brief moment before continuing. "He seems to understand that you are different."

Meggie nearly choked. "That I am *different*? What is that supposed to mean? That I have no named father or that I have two horns and a forked tongue?"

"Actually, he said that he thought of you as an angel, not entirely of this world," Sister Agnes retorted. "I thought that a remarkable perception, given everything."

"He actually said that?" That was too much even for Meggie to believe. An angel? He really was deluded.

"He did. He also said some other things that made his meaning clear enough, although those are for him to tell you if and when you are prepared to listen. I have to believe that he spoke the truth."

Meggie knew Sister Agnes meant every word. She could feel the nun's sincerity in her heart, but something still didn't ring true to her. She couldn't put her finger on what it was, exactly. Sister Agnes was no fool—the exact opposite was true. She had a well-developed ability to judge character. If she said that Hugo Montagu was in his right mind, then he must be, and if she said that Hugo Montagu genuinely wanted to marry her, then he must do.

The question was, why? Unless . . . Meggie sat up very straight as an astonishing idea occurred to her. Unless he was afflicted by as strong a physical attraction to her as she was to him—and *oh,* how attracted she was.

Meggie shivered at the thought that his attraction to her was strong enough to make him want to marry an ill-bred nobody, and if she was to be honest with herself, she couldn't deny that the idea of marrying him had appeal. A great deal of appeal. Sleeping in his bed every night, being held in his strong arms, having him make love to her . . .

Meggie nearly melted in her chair at the wanton images that flooded her brain. She blushed profusely, ashamed of herself for thinking anything of the sort in front of Sister Agnes. In any case, that wasn't the point. If she was even going to consider the idea of marriage, it had to be for the right reasons—but what were they?

She stared down at her hands, thinking hard.

Marriage would give her freedom, for one. Hugo had said that he would give her everything her heart desired. All she really desired was a simple life with a bit of breathing space and some time to call her own. No bells to rise to, none to tell her it was time to put down her book and turn off her light. Not one bell to call her to a meal or morning prayers or evening vespers. Real freedom.

And she liked Hugo Montagu. She really did, even if she couldn't see a thing beyond his handsome face.

"Sister," she said, trying to collect her thoughts into a semblance of order, "I know you are not opposed to the idea of this marriage, but it doesn't seem right to me to accept Lord Hugo's offer, as attractive as it is."

"Does it not, child? Why is that?"

"Don't you see, I would be taking advantage of him in order to gain the freedom I want so very much." She clutched her hands together. "Oh, Sister, forgive me, but I *do* want it—I want it so badly that I can almost taste it. Yet surely it would be wrong to accept him simply because he could grant it to me?"

"Meggie, do you really think I do not know that you have longed for your freedom—and longed for it before you stepped inside these walls? You have never stopped pining. This is your opportunity to gain that very thing."

"That is not taking advantage?" Meggie asked, greatly surprised that Sister Agnes was so pragmatic about holy matrimony.

"Meggie, dearest, do you not believe that God hears our prayers and sends us what we need when the time is right?"

Meggie shook her head helplessly. "Yes, but God also trusts that we act in accordance with His commandments. Would it be right for me to marry Lord Hugo when I do not love him?" Except in my fantasies, she added to herself.

"You might not love Lord Hugo, but that will grow in time. There are other things to consider. In any case, where in God's commandments, may I ask, does it say that you must be in love with your husband when you marry him?"

"Yes, but you see, Sister, he insists that he loves me, even though I don't understand why."

"Perhaps Lord Hugo's idea of love is not altogether grounded in the spiritual," Sister Agnes said, her eyes twinkling in what Meggie thought an exceedingly worldly fashion. "Men are often confused on the subject."

Meggie's face broke into a smile. She hadn't expected Sister Agnes's candor. "So I have gathered," she said. "I must confess, I thought that might be his motivation."

"Well, then. Is that so terrible a reason to refuse an offer he seems to mean sincerely? What other chance will you have to make a life for yourself?"

"I am so tempted, Sister. If I did accept him, I would do everything I could to be a good wife, but marriage to a duke's son . . . I am not of his world," she insisted, trying to be brutally honest with herself and the good sister. "He is of such high birth, and I am—I am no one. No one at all."

"You are your own lovely self, Meggie, and he is a man like every other, with the same hopes, the same fears, the same needs. It is that with which you should concern yourself, not the disparity between your worldly ranks. The point is whether you think you can be happy with him, as he clearly thinks he can be with you."

Meggie felt as if God had reached down from heaven with her dream cupped in His hands and held it out to her for the taking. All she had to do was to reach out and accept it. Her hands shook with desire to do just that, but she could not until her conscience felt completely clear.

"I—I do want happiness," she said, "but suppose it comes at Lord Hugo's expense? Suppose he changes his mind after we're married, and he realizes what he's really taken on?"

Sister Agnes leaned across the desk and covered Meggie's shaking hands with her own. "You mustn't forget that this is his choice. He came to you, and he came with full knowledge of your situation."

"What about his family, his friends?" she persisted. "What will *they* think when they meet me? I am not only illegitimate, I don't even know who my father was! I cannot imagine any family, let alone such an aristocratic one, being pleased about that."

"You are overly harsh with yourself," Sister Agnes said sternly. "You are not responsible for your parents' mistakes. We make of ourselves what we can in this world with the gifts we were born with and the opportunities we are given by God. Is it really for you to question why God has opened this door for you?"

Meggie colored hotly. "No," she whispered. "I suppose not."

"That is more like it," Sister Agnes said, her severe expression relaxing. "I believe that God has always had a special plan for you, Meggie Bloom. Do not turn your back on this opportunity simply because you do not understand *why* it has been offered."

"Oh, Sister, I do not want to turn my back on it. I want to open my arms and embrace it more than I can say."

"Then I think you should go to Lord Hugo and tell him just that," the nun said, ever logical.

With her words something swelled in Meggie's breast, something bright and beautiful, the real possibility that she could have a life outside of these walls, and best of all, a life with Hugo Montagu.

Yes, I will come to you . . .

"Yes," she said very softly. "Yes, I will. I will."

"Excellent," the nun said, clapping her hands together with pleasure. "Where did you leave him waiting?"

Meggie paled, belatedly recalling exactly where she'd

left him and under what circumstances. "In the um . . . in the solarium, Sister," she said, swallowing hard.

"The solarium—but that is no place for visitors! You know perfectly well it is only for those who are waiting to be admitted." Sister Agnes's eyes shot wide open in horror. "Oh, Meggie. Meggie Bloom. You didn't. You couldn't have."

"I'm afraid I did," Meggie said miserably.

She reached into the pocket of her apron and held up the key.

"Five thousand one hundred six, five thousand one hundred seven," Hugo muttered, fiercely concentrating on each step he paced off, trying to ignore the cold sweat that trickled down the back of his collar.

"Five thousand one hundred eight, five thousand one hundred nine . . ." He reckoned by the time he reached four hundred thousand, he would have earned every last penny that marriage to Meggie Bloom would bring him.

But by God, if he wasn't released long before that, there would be hell to pay. He didn't know how he'd kept a handle on his sanity this long. He'd never experienced such torture.

Hugo paused, bending over and squeezing his eyes shut to keep the walls from closing in on him yet again. He knew logically that shrinking walls were just an illusion. Unfortunately the logical part of his brain had shrunk to the size of a very small pea, and the section that had supplied him with highly detailed nightmares as a child had taken over as if it had never been away.

"Meggie Bloom, you will marry me if I have to drag you by the hair kicking and screaming all the way," he hissed from between his teeth, his breath coming hard and fast. "And then I will lock you up as surely as you have me and see how *you* like it. I—I will withhold chocolates and ribbons and even your bloody asinine lettuces from you. And then, when I am forgiving enough to let you out of your torture chamber after a number of excruciating months, you can damned well go and sleep in the kennels with the hounds, since you're so bloody bird-witted that you can't even tell the difference between a dog and a bleeding wolf!"

He drew in a deep, shuddering breath. "Oh God. Oh God, please take mercy on me. Please. I'll do anything you ask, I swear it, *just let me out of here*!"

He straightened in disbelief as he heard the unmistakable sound of a key turning in the first lock. God couldn't possibly have heard him so quickly.

His first impulse was to fling himself at his liberator, but some remnant of pride took over. He quickly mopped at his face and neck and pulled on his coat faster than he'd ever managed in his life.

Dignity, he told himself, stuffing his neckcloth into his pocket, since there was no time to do anything else with it. Dignity and mastery of the situation. Revenge could wait.

He stood perfectly still as the heavy door creaked open. The first thing he saw was the top of a flaxen head lowered in his direction.

"Miss Bloom?" he said in as calm a voice as he could manage. "I see you have chosen to return. How courteous of you."

"Lord Hugo." She stepped through the door, leaving it wide open. He was infinitely grateful. "I have a very great apology to make to you." She raised her translucent eyes to his, which only unsettled him further.

"An apology?" he said, forcing himself to maintain the righteous indignation that threatened to melt away in the force of her penetrating gaze. "Would that be for leaving me locked in this godforsaken room for the last forty-five minutes with no explanation?"

"Yes. I made a terrible mistake. You see, I thought you had come to stay."

"You thought I had come to stay." Hugo gazed at her with a horrible fascination. Dear Lord, but what was he letting himself in for? "You mean that you thought this was where we'd be living after we were married? I do have a home of my own, you know." He inched toward the open door as he spoke.

"I know," Meggie said. "Or at least I assumed you had. What I meant was that I thought you had escaped, and so I was returning you. When Sister Agnes reassured me that was not the case at all, naturally I was sorry. I am very sorry."

Hugo only nodded, since he had absolutely nothing to say to that piece of foolishness.

"So if you'd still like to marry me, I really would like that very much, even if I didn't understand until Sister Agnes explained everything to me. Or at least everything that she could."

"Did she. I am most obliged to her." He walked into the hallway and took a deep breath. Only about a hundred paces more and he'd be at the front door.

Meggie followed him. "Lord Hugo, don't you think we should discuss this properly? After all, as Sister Agnes pointed out, you are taking on a big responsibility, and so am I. Well, that is to say, I really have no idea what is involved, but I am sure that I will have responsibilities. Won't I?" she asked, trailing off uncertainly.

Hugo paused only long enough to glance over his shoulder. "I do not wish to discuss this now."

"Oh . . . I see. Have I made you so angry that you would rather not marry me after all?"

She sounded so disappointed that Hugo nearly laughed. He stopped and turned. "Meggie. Listen to me carefully. I still want to marry you. However, I have no intention of standing here in this—this hellhole and having an involved conversation with you on the subject."

Her brow drew down. "You do intend to discuss this at some point?" she asked. "Or do you mean to keep me so stuffed with chocolates that conversation will be impossible?"

Hugo prayed for patience, then reached out and grasped her hand, thinking that the first thing he was going to do with her when he got her out of the asylum was to throw her into a bath. He hauled her down the corridor, through the entrance hall, and directly to the front door.

"Go and collect your belongings and be quick about it," he said, taking her by the shoulders. "I will be outside. When you have finished packing and saying whatever goodbyes you have to make, meet me out front."

"You really *do* mean to take me away this very afternoon," she said, gazing at him with an odd expression he couldn't interpret, but he hoped to God it didn't mean she was suddenly having second thoughts.

He instantly switched to the persuasive tactic he knew worked best with her. "I intend to do exactly that, and this very minute could not be soon enough to leave. I have a fine carriage waiting outside with two pretty white horses to pull it."

Meggie scratched her nose. "A fine carriage with two pretty white horses?"

"Yes, and it is only a half hour's journey to my nice big house. It is by the sea, or close enough to it. Do you like the sea, Meggie?"

"I imagine I do," she said, "but then I have never seen the sea." She scratched her nose again, looking as if she was about to sneeze. "Is it also very big?"

"Not so big as to be troublesome. Now be a good girl and run along, or we will be late for supper."

"Supper," she said with a dreamy smile. "What a

heavenly thought. On Fridays we usually only have gruel and bread for both meals. It's something to do with penance, but I've never been very clear about why—of course, there is so much I am not clear on. I was hoping you could explain these things to me."

"I wouldn't worry yourself over explanations. I am sure we can do much better than bread and gruel for supper. With a little luck we will have a feast. A *magical* feast, if you but hurry," he said desperately, envisioning standing there for another two hours while Meggie's mind wandered all over kingdom come.

"A magical feast? In that case, I will use my flying carpet to carry me upstairs."

Hugo watched her scamper away up the main staircase, wincing as a volley of giggles erupted from her throat about halfway up the first flight and didn't stop until she was out of earshot.

He pressed his hands flat against his forehead, then walked out into the fresh air. It was a damned good thing Meggie Bloom was as beautiful as she was, or even his financial desperation would not have been enough to keep him from fleeing.

But now he was as close to a *fait accompli* as he could get, and there was no turning back. He would just have to find a way to manage her—or rather, manage to keep his own sanity while around her.

Maybe if he kept her mouth stuffed with chocolates, as she had suggested, he'd be able to admire the extraordinary physical bounties God had given her in place of a brain.

Thinking of chocolates, he wasn't at all sure where this magical supper he'd just invoked was going to come from.

True, he'd written a letter to the Misses Mabey, informing them of his intention to arrive that day with his bride-to-be and requesting two bedrooms to be aired and a simple evening meal to be made ready.

However, since he didn't know whether the Misses Mabey could even see well enough to read, let alone function well enough to organize a supper, it was anyone's guess as to what he might find upon his arrival.

He'd considered sending his valet ahead from London to organize the place, but had reconsidered. He realized that it was just as important to keep Mallard in the dark about Meggie's origins as everyone else. Word always spread faster than wildfire from the servants' quarters all the way up into the finest drawing rooms, and the truth flying around the finest drawing rooms was the last thing he needed.

Mallard could bloody well arrive when Hugo had Meggie better in hand, and if he didn't manage to get her in hand, well, he could always claim that the shock of their wedding night had completely unhinged her.

Hugo grinned. Now *there* was a brilliant idea.

He could just see Meggie unhinged by excessive passion. He wouldn't mind giving it a try—not that she wasn't unhinged already, but it was the excessive passion part that appealed to him. Meggie, lying in his bed with that dreamy look in her eyes that she'd bestowed on him only minutes before, her hair floating around her shoulders in a golden cloud. There was a truly appealing image.

Granted, she'd bestowed that particular look on him only when he'd promised her a fine supper, but there was more than one way to satisfy an appetite.

She just didn't know it yet.

Hugo suddenly felt infinitely more cheerful.

8

Meggie reached her room and collapsed on her hard little bed in fits of laughter. The irony was too much for her. Hugo Montagu was completely in his right mind after all, and that news had come as the most wonderful relief. But it now appeared that he thought her some kind of a simpleton. Why else would he speak to her in such a peculiar fashion?

She sat up, grinning broadly. She had to admit, as silly as it was, his mistaken assumption did make a nice change. Where most people thought she perceived far too much, her soon-to-be husband apparently thought she perceived far too little.

He might as well have been addressing Rose.

She supposed that was what he must have meant by her not being entirely of this world. What was it Sister Agnes had said? Oh, yes. *He thinks of you as an angel . . .*

Meggie shook her head. She didn't see how he could think her much of an angel when he'd made such an obvious point of wanting her in his bed, but what did she know about men and what lay behind their desires?

She found it hard to believe that he wanted a dimwitted angel for a wife, but she supposed she ought to indulge him as best she could. After all, he was being kind enough to marry her.

He'd figure out the truth eventually, and with luck he'd realize that it wasn't such a terrible thing to have a wife who was not only entirely earthbound, but sensible as well.

For the moment, her only objective was to escape from the sanitarium before anything could go wrong.

She stripped off her dress, thinking that it was a shame it was only Friday. On Saturdays she was allowed the weekly luxury of a pitcher of hot water to bathe with. By tomorrow she'd be a married woman with a home of her own. Maybe she could even have a pitcher of hot water every day. Oh, the luxury . . .

She shivered as she washed in her little basin, scrubbing herself clean as best she could with a sliver of lye soap, then rubbed herself dry on the threadbare towel that hung on a nail next to the washstand.

A clean dress—that was a good idea. She'd pack the one she'd been wearing and wash it later. The wardrobe held only her spare white work dress and her best dress for Sunday church, black with a plain white collar. She laid them both out on the bed and looked down at them, wondering which would be more suitable.

A scratch came at the door and Meggie sighed, already knowing it was Rose.

"Come in," she called, still trying to decide which dress to wear.

"Oh, Meggie!" Rose cried as she exploded into the room. "Sister Agnes sent me along to help you pack—she said you was leaving today to be married! Is it true? That is, it has to be if Sister Agnes said it was, but I cannot understand how such a thing came to pass. Did you meet him in town? You said nowt of it. . . . Is he a fine one? He must be, oh so very fine. Is it a grand passion? Oooh, this is so romantic I can scarcely bear it."

Meggie glanced at Rose over her shoulder with dry amusement. "Actually I met him right here. He is the son of one of the patronesses."

"Meggie," Rose gasped, her mouth gaping. "Is he quality, then? A proper gentleman?"

"Not just a gentleman, he's a proper lord. Amazing, isn't it?"

Rose shook her head, her eyes looking as if they were going to pop right out of her head. "Then you will be a proper lady?"

"I suppose I will be," Meggie said, genuinely startled. That hadn't even occurred to her. Meggie Bloom, who had all her life been nothing more than an unfortunate stain on the blotter of social respectability would be transformed into Lady Hugo Montagu, wife of an aristocrat. It didn't seem possible—and it probably wouldn't be unless the truth was kept quiet.

"A proper lady," she repeated, wondering how she was going to pull that performance off. It was a good thing she had an education and decent elocution, but the rest really would be a challenge.

Rose stuck one finger in her mouth. "I was just wondering . . . since you are to be a fine lady and all, you'll be needing a lady's maid to dress you up, won't you now?"

Meggie shrugged. "I don't know what for. It's not as if I haven't been dressing myself my entire life. It seems a little silly to have someone do it for me now."

"Oh, but Meggie—my sister, she was in service up at Wickham Market in the big house till they closed it down not six months ago. Mind you, she weren't no lady's maid, just a chambermaid, but she learned all about how to go about it from the Frenchie who looked after the mistress. It's been Daisy's heart's desire to work as a lady's maid ever since, but she's had no luck in finding a position." Rose sucked in a quick breath of air. "So if you should find yourself in need, well, Daisy's a good girl and hard working, and we'd all be ever so grateful. She's right there in Snape, helping Mam with the young 'uns, now that I've come to work here. Anyone can tell you where to find the Kersey cottage. I know

Daisy'll be as pleased as punch. She'll go anywhere you ask."

Meggie went to Rose and took her hand, giving it a squeeze. "I'll do what I can once I see what my new circumstances are," she said, her heart going out to the girl. For all of Rose's simpleness, she had a kind nature and only the best of intentions. "In the meantime, maybe you could help me. Which dress do you think most suitable for me to wear to arrive at Lord Hugo's house in? The black or the white?"

"Oh," Rose said, frowning hard in concentration. "It's a pity you don't have summat with a bit more color. You don't want his lordship to think you a nun like some of the others around here—but he must know better than that, or he wouldn't be taking you away with him, now would he?" She chortled merrily at her joke. "Still, why not the black? It won't stain with travel like the white will. I always did wonder why Sister Agnes thinks white a suitable color for our work clothes . . .

Meggie, who was paying only the slightest amount of attention to Rose's patter, nodded absently. She'd already put on the black dress and was busy taking the rest of her belongings out of the wardrobe and folding them neatly on her bed.

When she'd finished that task, she pulled out the carpetbag that had been gathering dust in the bottom of the wardrobe. She'd never thought she would use it again for anything other than storing her spare threads and needles, and she'd certainly never imagined she'd be using it to carry a meager trousseau.

She plunked the open bag onto the bed next to her pile of clothes and pushed the skeins to one side. Two homespun nightgowns went in first, followed by one cotton shift and her spare cap and apron. The dirty dress and apron she'd been wearing worked well enough to wrap her work shoes in, and she laid that bundle on top.

There was nothing more to add than her toothbrush, her hairbrush, and Aunt Emily's Bible.

Finally, she fetched the large satchel that contained the tapestry she'd been working on for so many years. It was the only thing she possessed that was truly *hers.*

She had thought that when she was finally done with the tapestry, it would represent the sum of her experience. Day by day. Stitch by stitch. Until her life was at an end, and she was buried in the far field where everyone without a family was given a place.

And now everything had changed in the blink of an eye.

Meggie gazed down at the satchel that contained her precious work, swearing silently to herself that no matter what came, she would not abandon her touchstone. It would always be with her to feed her truth, to reflect back to her those things she couldn't express in words. Memory was the only legacy she had.

Pulling the tapestry out, she looked over the needlework, feeling as if she was reading through a personal journal. Each segment represented a portion of the time she'd spent at the sanitarium, her memories defined by every stitch.

She traced her fingertip over the section of lush trees, with brightly colored fantastical birds roosting in their branches. She'd embroidered that during the winter six years before when Mrs. Beatrice Collins had been recovering from her terrible grief over the fifth loss of a child. Meggie showed her each panel as it progressed, speaking incessantly of God's love and wisdom, and of the joy of heaven where surely all of Mrs. Collins's children were now at peace with the angels.

Mrs. Collins had gone home to her husband just as the first buds showed on the trees, her troubled spirit finally at peace.

And here, she remembered, moving her finger along,

was the section she'd worked on the following year when Sister Agnes had been so ill with influenza that they'd all worried for her life. Meggie had sat by her bed, hour after hour, caring for her fevered body, stitching away when Sister Agnes dozed fitfully.

That month, Meggie's final defenses had fallen. She had allowed herself to trust Sister Agnes. Hadrian had begun to trust her at the same time. Hence his image embroidered into the scene.

His dear face looked out at Meggie, reminding her of how small he'd been then.

"Hadrian!" she gasped, dropping the tapestry back into the bag. "Oh, Rose—how could I have forgotten? Will you be a dear and fetch him for me? He's still in the garden where I left him, poor fellow."

"Aye, that I will, Meggie," Rose said, her smile instantly vanishing. "I hadn't thought that he'll be leaving us as well. I don't know who I'll miss more, you or that dear doggie of yours." She hung her head, tears welling up in her eyes, and in another second she was sniffling hard into her hands. "It didn't seem real till just now," she explained.

Meggie quickly moved to Rose's side and put her arm around her broad shoulders. "I'll miss you, too, but don't you worry, I'll be back to visit, I promise."

She did mean it, most sincerely. Meggie had no intention of abandoning those patients who had been benefiting from her care. She couldn't just disappear without a trace, and why should she? From everything Hugo had said, his house was only a half hour away.

She should find it easy enough to get away every now and then.

"Do you promise?" Rose asked. "You will bring the doggie with you, too?"

"If I can," Meggie said, wondering how she was going to get Hadrian out of the sanitarium in the first place, given Hugo's unfortunate aversion to animals. She supposed she'd just have to be adamant. If he wanted to marry her so very much, then he would have to accept the consequences—all of them—including life with a wolf.

Hugo lounged impatiently against the side of his curricle, wishing Meggie would get on with it. He couldn't imagine what was taking her so long.

He caught a movement from the corner of his eye, someone coming down the path that led from the garden. He instantly straightened, all muscles tensing as the figure vanished behind a copse of trees, then reappeared only yards away.

It was a girl, dressed all in white as Meggie had been, a cap hanging askew from her head. She was large boned and round, with a face like pudding. She stopped dead in her tracks when she saw him and stared. Her jaw dropped until it practically rested on the ample bosom that her hands were fanning wildly.

Hugo swallowed hard, wondering what she might do next, for she was clearly another one of *them*.

She suddenly tore her gaze away from him, looking around as if expecting something to appear out of thin air. Then she spun on her heels, put her fingers to her mouth, emitted a piercing whistle, and started flapping her arms like a chicken.

Hugo winced, wishing a keeper would come and take her away. It pained him to watch her pathetic antics.

Just as that thought crossed his mind a huge dark shape came bounding out of the copse of trees, aiming straight toward her at a lightning clip.

Hugo's knees nearly buckled with fear.

"Watch out!" he cried, instinctively leaping into action. The girl might be crazed, but that didn't mean she deserved to be devoured by a wolf.

He tore down the path toward her, intending to throw himself on her and shield her body with his own while he tried to fend off the wolf.

But the wolf reached her before Hugo could. He jumped upon her, his paws resting on her shoulders. Instead of knocking her down and mauling her, he proceeded to wash her face with his tongue while she giggled and rubbed his head.

Hugo ground to a halt, his heart pounding furiously in delayed reaction. He ran a hand over his face. Nothing in this place had any rhyme or reason to it, including the wild animals.

The wolf was as crazy as the rest of them—everyone knew that wolves couldn't be tamed. Their sole purpose in life was to eat livestock and people, and not necessarily in that order.

"You must be his lordship who's come to marry our Meggie," the girl said with another giggle, pushing the wolf down. It sat at her heels, a huge pink tongue lolling from a mouth in which sharp white fangs gleamed menacingly. "I'm Rose Kersey, and this here is Hadrian, Meggie's dear little doggie. I was just telling Meggie not ten minutes ago how we're going to miss them both ever so much, but then one can't do without t'other, so we'll just have to make do ourselves. Without them, I mean."

Hugo cleared his throat with an effort and said, "If you are so fond of Meggie's dear little doggie, Miss Kersey, you may keep him for your very own."

"Oh, no, sir, I couldn't do that," Rose said, her eyes popping wide open. "He'd pine so for Meggie, and she for him. I dunno what they'd do at night for company without each other."

She clapped her hand to her mouth and giggled wildly, rolling her eyes. "It'll be the three of you now, won't it? I reckon Hadrian's going to have to make room in the bed."

A violent protest emerged from Hugo's throat, but it came out sounding more like a strangled sob. Meggie couldn't possibly sleep with a wolf in her bed . . . could she? Then he remembered that of course this poor girl was not to be taken seriously any more than Meggie was.

"I imagine we will all manage nicely," he said in a soothing voice. "Isn't there someplace you're supposed to be?"

She wrinkled her forehead. "I don't think so, sir. Let me see. Sister Agnes asked me to help Meggie pack, and Meggie asked me to get the doggie from the garden, and . . . it's not time for supper yet, so I reckon I should be waiting for Meggie right here."

"Here I am, Rose," Meggie said from behind Hugo. "Thank you for your trouble."

Hugo turned abruptly, ready to grab Meggie by the arm, throw her in the carriage, and haul down the drive at double time.

His hand paused in midair as he adjusted to yet another shock. He hardly recognized the woman standing before him.

A shapeless black garment enfolded Meggie, its high white collar covering her throat, and an equally shapeless white cap covered her head. Everything of Meggie was covered including her flaxen hair, which no longer fell down her back but was tucked up in a tight bun under the dreadful cap.

She looked like a bloody pilgrim.

"Is something wrong, Lord Hugo?" she asked, not appearing the least disconcerted by his appalled scrutiny.

"Nothing that can't be fixed," he said, determining that the very first thing he was going to do after marrying her was to see to a decent wardrobe that uncovered as much of her as possible.

"Is it my dress that meets with your disapproval, my lord?" she asked.

"You look like Sister Agnes," he said. "What did you do, alter one of her habits?"

Meggie gazed at him serenely, his sarcasm going right over her head. "No, my lord. This is my best Sunday dress." She raised the shabby carpetbag that she held in one hand and the satchel she held in the other. "In here are the rest of my worldly possessions. I thought I'd save my clean white dress for our wedding."

Wedding. The word was enough to jolt him out of his temporary paralysis. Why was he worrying about an ugly black dress when he'd soon have her out of her clothes altogether?

"Indeed," he said. "What a nice idea. Look, here is my fine carriage and my two pretty white horses to take us away. Are you ready?"

"First we must say goodbye to Sister Agnes who is coming out directly, and I must introduce Hadrian to the horses so that they will not be afraid of him."

"Introduce? My dear girl, you are not bringing that wolf anywhere near my horses!" he said, ready to throttle her.

"You mustn't worry, Lord Hugo. Hadrian is very good with other animals. It is only a matter of letting them know they have nothing to fear. Of course I must introduce myself first."

She handed him her bags and walked over to the carriage before he had a chance to stop her or warn her that his two prize geldings were skittish.

To his great surprise, instead of rolling their eyes and snorting as they usually did when strangers approached, the horses put their heads down and snuffled at the front of Meggie's hideous dress. Their ears pricked back and forth as she spoke softly to them, stroking their muzzles.

Baffled, Hugo shook his head, then strode over to the curricle and arranged the bags under the seat. He was careful to turn his back only for a moment, but it was a moment too long. When he turned around again, his heart nearly stopped.

The damned wolf was at Meggie's side, sniffing with great interest at the extremely vulnerable legs of his extremely expensive Thoroughbreds.

What he couldn't believe was that the horses were sniffing right back, not looking at all perturbed. By all rights they should have bolted in terror.

His hand closed carefully on the reins, just in case his beasts came to their senses.

"Ah, here you are, Lord Hugo, Meggie." Sister Agnes came up next to him. "I see that Hadrian is already making friends with his new companions. How nice. You will find him a most useful addition to Lyden Hall, for he is excellent at guarding not only the house but also the livestock." Hugo's heart sank as she smiled fondly at the wolf. "He has saved us many chicken and sheep from intruders down at our little farm. We shall miss him."

Hugo smiled weakly. "Is that so, Sister?" he said. "In that case, why don't you keep him?"

Sister Agnes looked at him in surprise. "Surely Meggie has told you that he belongs to her? I wouldn't dream of separating them. She's raised him from a pup."

Hugo dropped the reins and taking Sister Agnes by the arm, he walked a few paces away with her. "Sister, surely you must—it cannot have escaped your attention—you do *realize* that Meggie's pet is a wolf?"

"Naturally," she said, regarding him with even more surprise. "I am not blind, Lord Hugo. He is also a highly intelligent and sweet-natured animal. We are all exceedingly fond of him, but it is to Meggie that he is attached."

Hugo gave up and tossed Sister Agnes into the same category as the rest of her charges. "I am afraid that is unfortunate, Sister," he said, loud enough to be sure Meggie would hear. "I cannot possibly allow a wolf to reside at my home." He looked firmly in Meggie's direction to show her he meant what he said.

Meggie didn't reply. She simply met his glance with her usual serene expression, her eyes performing that unnerving trick of looking straight through him. Then she nodded and abandoned the horses and her wolf, walking straight past Hugo to the door of the curricle.

She lifted her skirts and, unaided, hoisted herself inside. Hugo breathed a sigh of relief. Now that she was to be his wife, she had decided to obey him instead of crossing him at every turn.

He turned back to Sister Agnes. "Thank you, Sister, for all you have done. As I said, I will do my best to make Meggie happy. Naturally, I shall write to—"

"Ah, Lord Hugo?" The nun nodded in the direction of the carriage.

Hugo glanced over his shoulder only to see Meggie pulling her carpetbag and then her satchel out from underneath the seat. She straightened and looked at him with absolutely no expression.

"Just what do you think you're doing?" he asked, folding his arms across his chest. He didn't have the time or the patience for any more nonsense.

"I am staying with Hadrian, my lord. He is my responsibility, and I will not abandon him, not even for you. I am sorry if I disappoint you, but my mind will not be changed." She dropped the bags over the side of the carriage and stepped down.

With a surge of panic, Hugo realized that she was completely serious. She was prepared to give up marriage to him for the sake of a mangy wolf. If he had ever needed confirmation that she was completely mad, he had it now.

Pride should have compelled him to leave the ungrateful baggage standing there. He should damned well leap into his curricle and drive back into the land of the sane, with a trail of dust obscuring the whole dreadful place.

But the image of four hundred thousand pounds vanishing into thin air was too much for him—that, and the thought of never having Meggie Bloom gracing his bed. He'd become equally attached to that image as well.

Reluctantly acquiescing, he blew out a sharp breath. "If it means so much to you," he muttered, the words sticking in his throat, "then bring the blasted animal. However, he will *not* ride in my carriage, and he will *not* sleep in my bed. Do you fully understand me?"

"Sleep in your bed?" Meggie repeated, looking at him as if he was the one with a mental disturbance. "I should think not. As for riding in your carriage, Hadrian would much prefer the excercise and the fun of running alongside."

She smiled sweetly at him and picked up her bags again. "I think you must love me very much indeed to overcome your fear of animals for my sake."

"I am not afraid of—oh, never mind!" Hugo cried, grabbing the bags from her and throwing them willy-nilly into the carriage where they landed in an untidy heap. "Just get in, for the love of God!"

Meggie ignored him and turned to Rose. She embraced her fellow inmate who promptly burst into loud sobs. Meggie quickly whispered something into Rose's ear that instantly turned her sobs into uncontrollable giggles.

Hugo had to turn his head away. They really were too pathetic to watch.

Then Meggie turned to Sister Agnes who, to Hugo's

surprise, had genuine tears in her eyes. "Meggie, child," she said, sketching the sign of the cross on Meggie's forehead. "May God go with you and watch over you. May He grant you wisdom in all your endeavors."

Amen, Hugo thought silently, although it seemed to him the nun was asking for a huge miracle.

"Thank you, my dear friend," Meggie said. "I thank you for your every kindness over the years, and for your own wisdom. I'll try to keep your words in my head *and* my heart. I imagine there will be many times that I will need them." She bowed her head. "God keep you. You will be ever in my thoughts until we meet again."

"And you in mine, child." The nun took Meggie's face between her two old hands and kissed Meggie's forehead in the same spot that she'd made the cross. "Do your best. It is all God ever expects of us."

"I will, Sister." Meggie dropped a curtsy, mightily surprising Hugo that she even knew what one was. Then she moved past him and once again climbed into the curricle before he had a chance to help her inside.

He was going to have to break her of that habit. But since he imagined she'd never been in a curricle before, she couldn't have known the etiquette involved.

Thinking about it, he realized that she would need to be instructed in myriad points of etiquette. He could only pray that she was capable of learning at least some of these points if he was going to attempt to present her as his wife.

There were, in fact, a lot of habits he was going to have to break her of. Like a stubborn refusal to listen to him. His docile, angelic creature was beginning to appear suspiciously hard-headed. That, coupled with dementia, spelled nothing but trouble.

He quickly took his leave of Sister Agnes, then climbed up next to Meggie and picked up the reins, giving them a subtle shake.

The horses obediently responded, moving forward in a quick walk.

Hugo scowled sourly as the wolf moved along right at their side.

9

As the carriage turned onto the main road and picked up speed, Meggie allowed herself to breathe again. For a bad moment, she'd thought that all was lost. It was odd how frightened she'd been that her bright future was about to be snatched away from her, considering that she'd only *had* a bright future for a matter of two hours.

She hadn't realized how much it meant to her until she'd taken a stand about Hadrian. Facing the very real possibility that she might disappear back into the depths of the asylum, she would never have tasted freedom—and almost worse, she would never have seen Hugo Montagu again.

Still, a principle was a principle, and she couldn't have lived with herself if she'd let Hadrian down.

She glanced over the side of the carriage where Hadrian loped. His tongue was hanging out of his mouth, an expression of pure bliss on his face. He *knew* he was free.

Meggie smiled down at him, then sneaked a peek over at Hugo who had been silent from the time that he'd leapt into the carriage. His gaze was focused on the road ahead, his brow slightly drawn. He didn't appear to be the least bit aware of her presence.

That suited Meggie just fine. It gave her a chance to study his profile with its high-bridged nose and a mouth that was wide and nicely defined.

Her gaze wandered down over the firm line of jaw to where his dark hair curled at his disheveled collar, his neckcloth all askew. She grinned to herself, thinking of poor Hugo as he'd emerged from the solarium. He had looked as if all the hounds of hell had been at his heels.

She knew she shouldn't be amused, but she couldn't help herself. He obviously didn't like confinement any more than he liked animals, and there was something about Hugo in a frantic state that did make her want to laugh. Of course, she supposed that he was accustomed to his freedom and hadn't taken kindly to having it suspended, even briefly.

They really hadn't gotten off to the best of starts, considering how she'd treated him in the vegetable garden. She had jumped to conclusions because of not only her own history, but also how she'd been fantasizing about him in the most unsettling and improper way.

Strangely, though, now that he was with her in reality, she found his presence not at all alarming. He wasn't at all like the man she'd imagined, formidable in his physical power. Not that Hugo wasn't physically powerful, for he certainly was, all six extremely desirable feet of him. It was just that he didn't terrify her. Even with all his strength and breadth and height she felt safe, protected.

Indeed, she felt as comfortable at his side as if she'd known him forever, yet she knew him less than she'd ever known anyone. Very peculiar, but everything about her connection with Hugo was peculiar.

"What are you staring at?" he said, turning his head and glaring at her.

"I—I was just familiarizing myself with your face," she said, coloring. "After all, I am going to be seeing a lot of it"

"Hmm," he murmured in reply, and looked back at the road.

Meggie frowned. "Lord Hugo, do you think we might have that discussion now? About our marriage? What you expect of me aside from the part about sleeping in your bed?"

His head shot around again. "For God's sake, Meggie, can you not be a little more delicate?"

"If delicacy is what you want, then you should have picked someone else to marry." She drew in a deep breath, summoning up her courage. "You came to me with a single-minded purpose, pleading both your love and your desire for me, but you have said nothing about what my role is to be in your life—aside from being your wife, which could mean anything."

He shot her a sidelong glance that she couldn't read. "Why do we not take things one day at a time? All I require of you for the moment is to do as I tell you and to speak as little as possible."

"To speak as little as possible?" Meggie repeated slowly, suddenly feeling uneasy. Maybe he really *did* want a dimwit for a wife. A nice angelic dimwit who warmed his bed and smiled blankly at everything he said.

She winced, knowing that the price of her freedom was to try to be what he expected, but it had all seemed a bit different in the sanitarium. Now that she was actually facing reality, she wasn't sure it was going to be so easy.

She swallowed hard. "As you say, my lord. Is there anything else?"

"Yes. Stop calling me 'my lord.' My name is Hugo to you. Furthermore, so that no annoying questions are asked of us, you are to agree with me when I say that we have been well acquainted for some time."

Meggie nodded. She could see the sense in that. "You have been visiting the sanitarium the last two months?" she asked.

"No," he said, looking exasperated. "I do not wish the sanitarium to come into it. We will say that we met in

Woodbridge. There is no need to elaborate further. Do you understand me, Meggie?"

"I believe so," she replied, although she wasn't sure she did. Why would he want to hide the truth to such a degree? Unless he thought the sanitarium beneath his regard, which did seem odd when his mother was a patroness.

His mother . . . Meggie sat up very straight as she considered this new problem. "Hugo," she said, "isn't your mother going to wonder why we're lying?"

"My mother?" he asked. "What does my mother have to do with anything?"

"She will surely hear the truth from Sister Agnes, won't she? They are in close contact, after all."

Hugo paled. "Damnation," he snapped. "I hadn't thought of that. Oh, well—I suppose I'll have to tell my mother the actual facts, but she'll keep them to herself if I ask her. After all, she believes in the virtue of true love," he said absently, as if he'd forgotten Meggie was there. "She never has thought that I have any common sense, so why should she question me? No, I should be safe enough in that regard, and Sister Agnes will always back up my story."

Meggie thought that for a man who had been felled by true love, Hugo was not showing any signs of it. Indeed, he appeared more aggravated with her than anything else. Maybe he was finally beginning to understand the consequences of his rash action.

"Is it really so important what other people think?" she asked in a small voice, assailed by a fresh wave of doubt.

"Naturally it's important what other people think," he said curtly. "Vitally important. You will realize that soon enough. However, people will think what I tell them to think, unless you do or say something to contradict me. I warn you now that if you make any mistakes in that direction, there will be a great deal of trouble for both of us."

Meggie nodded despondently, only now beginning to see the full scope of consequences herself. "It is not too late to take me back," she said, fighting back tears of disappointment. "Maybe it would be for the best. I know what I am, and I can only be a trial to you."

She wiped her eyes on the back of her sleeve.

Hugo glanced over at her, then reached out a hand and covered one of hers. His touch was warm and steadying, all the more so for being unexpected.

"Forgive me. I did not mean to frighten you, only to caution you," he said, his voice more gentle than she'd ever heard it. "I will do my best to help you adjust, Meggie, and I will try not to put more on your shoulders than you can carry."

She stared down at his large masculine hand, gulping back a sob. The protectiveness of his touch was almost more than she could bear. It was always she who assumed the role of protector, she who gave tenderness rather than receiving it.

Even Sister Agnes in all her kindness had relied on Meggie to be self-sufficient, to know what needed to be done and to do it without complaining or thinking of her own needs.

She felt an enormous relief that someone was actually willing to look after her—someone who did not expect her to solve everyone's problems or even to understand them.

Maybe there was a certain beauty in being regarded as a dimwit, after all.

Hugo had previously considered the wide sweep of drive that led up to Lyden Hall beautiful, lined symmetrically by great oak trees on both sides.

He drank in the sight with particular appreciation as he turned from the main road through the great stone gates of the entryway. The last time he had been to Lyden, the trees had still been bare. Now, in full leaf, they lent the approach to the Hall a proper dignity, as if heralding that one was nearing a place of importance.

He hoped that the marginal staff were watching in appreciation as their new master approached in his fancy curricle pulled by his high-stepping Thoroughbreds.

He wished to make exactly the right impression expected of a man of his position. That had been the entire point of purchasing Lyden, after all. He chose to forget about the damned wolf still running alongside, praying that if anyone did see it, they would assume it was a very large hunting dog.

Of course, he didn't even know if the Misses Mabey had informed the staff as to his wishes, let alone his intended's arrival.

Anyway, God only knew what the staff would think when they laid eyes on his wife-to-be. Maybe it would be best if they were all in a part of the house that faced toward the sea so that he could smuggle Meggie in and cover her up in bedsheets.

Given the way she looked right now, no one would think Hugo had fallen in love with her charms, let alone believe that she'd come from the local town.

He was certain that the townspeople hadn't dressed like pilgrims for at least a century, if ever.

Then there was the matter of Meggie's opening her mouth. He wasn't worried about her accent. Indeed, it had occurred to him only during the drive that Meggie's accent was perfectly acceptable, when it should have been more like the accent of that dreadful girl Rose. He could only assume that Meggie had picked up the speech patterns of the more illustrious of the inmates.

For the small favor of decent speech he could only be

grateful, for it constituted one less stumbling block to have to contend with.

No, what worried him was what Meggie might actually say when she did open her mouth, before he had a chance to coach her more thoroughly. The trick was clearly to keep her as isolated as possible for as long as possible. He wasn't sure how long that might be, but he could always pretend that their passion was such that it precluded any public appearances outside of the immediate vicinity of their bedroom.

Hugo grinned to himself. That was not such a bad idea all the way around. He would have no problem spending his time in bed with Miss Meggie Bloom. He could coach her dear deranged mind from the comfort of his pillow, rewarding her with bouts of lovemaking when she got something right and maybe giving her an occasional chocolate if necessary.

Oh, he'd see to it that she got a lot of things right. Yes, he would.

He'd never felt so motivated in all his life.

I can't. It's not possible. God has made a terrible mistake. This was meant for someone else. Never for me.

Meggie's hands gripped both sides of her temples as Hugo's house came into sight.

She thought she might faint from shock. She'd never seen anything so enormous, so magnificent in her entire life, never even imagined anything like it.

At least five times the size of the asylum, which she'd always considered huge, Lyden Hall commanded a piece of land that looked over a vast lawn to the south, another vast lawn with a river to the north, and an entire forest to the west. More water glimmered to the east and Meggie could only assume that was the sea. Hugo probably owned that, too.

This was to be her new home?

As Hugo pulled the carriage to a halt Meggie could only soundlessly shake her head back and forth, overwhelmed. She felt numb inside, unable to grasp the enormity of what she had taken on, the enormity of what had been handed to her along with Hugo.

When she'd been packing she'd had comforting visions of a gable-roofed manor by the sea, grand by her standards, where she might have the garden that Hugo had promised her, a small and tidy plot of land to dig up and perhaps expand.

The reality, like Hugo, was beyond understanding, a fantasy gone awry.

She really didn't know what she was going to do now. Except, in sheer desperation, follow Hugo's orders and keep very quiet.

Many years before she'd learned the one skill that had allowed her to survive and continue. All she had to do, she told herself firmly as she tried to steady her badly shaking hands, was to apply that skill.

Adaptability was everything.

She would manage. Somehow she would manage.

As Hugo swung down from the carriage, the huge front door of the house abruptly opened and a tiny wizened creature appeared. She hopped up and down, with her enormous arrangement of white hair bouncing with her.

"They're here! Sister, they're here!" she cried. "Hellooooo!" She waved her arm wildly at them.

Meggie had no idea who the woman was, but she liked her immediately. She sensed nothing but genuine welcome in her, and something else, something wonderfully carefree and full of the joys of life, as if she'd never known a moment's constraint.

"Oh, dear," Hugo said under his voice, offering Meggie his hand. "This might be worse than I thought. She doesn't look the least bit infirm to me."

"Infirm?" Meggie said, allowing him to support her as she climbed down. "Stay, Hadrian," she said, knowing he would obey without question. "Whatever gave you that idea? Don't you know her, Hugo? She is standing in your doorway, after all."

"I've never met her in my life, but I'll explain later," he said. "For now just say how-do-you-do and nothing more."

Meggie shrugged. "As you wish," she said, in what was fast becoming a litany. He slipped her arm into the crook of his elbow and led her forward.

"Lord Hugo?" the woman said, an enormous smile on her face as she dashed down the steps toward them. "You have no idea how *thrilling* this moment is—we have been on tenterhooks, anticipating your arrival. I am Ottoline Mabey. You must call me Aunt Ottoline, I think, as we are to be family, and I will call you Hugo. And this is your bride-to-be? Oh, my dear, how charming you are. What is your name, child?"

Meggie opened her mouth to answer, but Hugo got there first.

"May I present Meggie Bloom?" he said, with a bow. "It is a pleasure to make your acquaintance, Miss—er, Aunt Ottoline."

"How do you do?" Meggie said, dropping a curtsy. She supposed that was the end of her participation in the conversation.

"Exceptionally well, thank you," Ottoline said, patting her stomach. "A good dose of salts goes a long way toward keeping me regulated."

Meggie grinned, liking Ottoline Mabey more by the moment. Hugo didn't look anywhere near as pleased, Meggie saw, glancing over at him.

"I am happy to hear it," he said, a bald-faced lie, if the

frown on his face was anything to go by. "I take it you received my letter, then?"

"Oh, indeed, just yesterday, and Dorelia and I have been busy as can be, preparing everything for your arrival." She looked over her shoulder at the empty door. "Sister!" she screeched, then turned back to Hugo and Meggie. "She's probably in the kitchen keeping an eye on Cookie. We found him at the Orford quay yesterday. He'd come off a merchant ship and we snatched him right up, seeing as he'd just been dismissed. So lucky we were, even if he is a bit of a crusty fellow, though I suspect he will be mellow once he settles in."

"Dismissed for what, exactly?" Hugo asked, his eyes narrowing.

"Stealing, dear, stealing, but Dorelia will have him sorted out in no time. He *says* he was only taking the extra rations that would otherwise have gone to waste, and I thought that sounded so thrifty. Still, it doesn't hurt to keep an eye out to ensure that he gets off on the right foot."

Hugo closed his eyes for a brief moment. "Never mind. Never mind. As long as he can cook."

"Well, naturally I tried him out before hiring him," Ottoline said in injured tones. "*I* thought he was frightfully clever, and so did Dorelia *and* Mr. Coldsnap. We dined very well indeed last night."

"Who is Mr. Coldsnap?" Hugo asked, rubbing one finger over the bridge of his nose.

"Why, your steward, dear. Heavens, didn't that silly man Peasenhall tell you anything when he sold you the property? Reginald Coldsnap has been running Lyden for years."

Meggie was getting the distinct impression that she was not the only one new to these premises. Hugo appeared to know absolutely nothing about his house or the people connected to it. She wondered if he'd ever even stepped inside the door.

"Mr. Peasenhall mentioned only that the estate was well managed," Hugo said, looking more annoyed by the moment. "But let us not stand out here. Miss Bloom will want to wash and change before dinner. You have prepared two bedrooms as I requested?"

"Only the best, and side by side, just as it was in our dear cousin Lally's time. Oh, she was so happy when she married Linus—that's Lord Eliot, dear, or was. Such a great tragedy when he lost her, although we did our best to make it up to him. My, but Dorelia and I have missed the old boy. We were a happy family."

Meggie's eyes widened as she caught the faintest whisper of remembered bliss—and physical bliss, if she wasn't mistaken. Her hand crept to her cheek in wonder. Was it possible that Ottoline and her sister had actually—she blushed furiously and pushed the thought away.

Ottoline shot Meggie a sharp look, almost as if she knew what Meggie was thinking, then clapped her hands together. "Ah, well, this is no time to be reminiscing, not when there's a wedding to plan," she said, steering them toward the door. "Now, I stopped by to see the vicar this morning, and he is waiting to hear from you, happy to oblige you anytime you please, although you must remember that he has Sunday morning services, so tomorrow or Monday would be best for the ceremony."

Hugo nodded as he led Meggie through the open door. "Tomorrow, I think. There is no point in delay."

Meggie barely heard him, hanging on to his arm for dear life. It was a miracle that her legs didn't collapse under her in shock.

The hall they'd entered was vast—so vast it could easily have housed an entire family. She gazed up to see that the pale blue walls were topped by a high white plastered and vaulted ceiling. Dizzy, she looked down only to see that the floor beneath her feet was a patterned marble. And on every inch of wall hung enormous paintings of biblical scenes and battle scenes and bucolic scenes of men with dogs and guns.

Meggie shut her eyes, unable to take in anything more, her head spinning. Too much. It was all too much.

"Meggie? Meggie, are you unwell?"

Meggie dimly heard Hugo's voice coming to her, and she made an effort to open her eyes and smile up at him. "I'm perfectly well," she replied brightly, then fainted dead away.

10

"Open your eyes, dear, there's a good girl. Come along, open wide. Do it for your nice auntie, won't you?"

Meggie stirred, dimly aware that she was lying on the softest bed she'd ever known, with a linen sheet loosely draped over her body. The soothing scent of lavender drifted from a cool cloth pressed against her brow.

She was sure she was dreaming. The last time anyone had cared for her in such a tender way was when she'd had the mumps at the age of seven. Aunt Emily had sat by her bedside, reading her stories and feeding her soup. But Aunt Emily was long dead and she didn't have any other aunts—she had no family at all. And nothing was wrong with her other than a sharp gnawing in the pit of her stomach.

She groaned, thinking she must have slept through supper. No wonder—it was Friday, and she loathed gruel, so she hadn't missed anything. Except lunch, she remembered. Never mind. That would have been gruel, too. Drift . . . keep drifting . . .

"Come along, child," the same voice murmured. "Poor dear Hugo is pacing up and down outside, thinking you're about to expire. He's not to know that brides have nerves, now is he?"

Hugo . . . brides.

The words tugged at Meggie through her daze. That was it—Lyden Hall. She was at Lyden Hall, and funny little Ottoline Mabey was urging her to wake up.

She slowly opened her eyes, only to find Ottoline's gaze boring straight into hers. Yet Meggie sensed none of the same giddy effervescence that had come from Ottoline before. Instead she felt a deep calm . . . and far beneath the calm, a great dark void, the place of deepest knowing.

Meggie stared transfixed into those ageless eyes for a long moment as if she might absorb strength from the giver before she responded to the call to awakening.

As she did, she heard a silent humming, a deep, strong primitive song that vibrated in her bones and echoed in her heart. A nameless song, it was one so instinctive that Meggie knew it for the song of the soul, emanating from the very depths of this woman.

She sat up abruptly. "Who are you?" she demanded. "You're not Ottoline—you can't be!"

"Just as I thought," the Ottoline-who-wasn't said with satisfaction. "You have the Blessed Gift, haven't you, child? Ottoline thought it might be so."

Meggie gaped at her with sudden understanding. Identical twins—she'd never come across a pair before. No wonder she'd been confused. However alike they might be on the surface, their inner natures were their own, and in this case as different as night and day. "You are Dorelia," she said with certainty.

"I am Dorelia," the little woman agreed, "and you are Meggie Bloom, a child of Sight. You are welcome here. You are most welcome here." Tears shone in her bright little brown eyes and she patted Meggie's hand with great affection.

Meggie didn't for a moment think to deny Dorelia's blunt statement. She could scarcely believe it, but she recognized something of herself in this woman. "You—you have it, too," she whispered. "You have, haven't you?" She wanted to cry with profound relief that she'd found someone else who had been born with the same aberration of nature as she.

"I have, dear, I do have, although I do not think my Blessed Gift behaves in the same way as yours does,"

Dorelia answered cheerfully. "You see, the Blessed Gift comes in all shapes and sizes, just as we do."

"It does?" Meggie said, wondering if here at last might be some answers to the questions she'd had for a very long time.

"Oh, indeed. There are those who can see the future, for instance. I am not one of them, thank goodness, for heaven only knows what I'd try to discover. I nose around in everyone's business enough as it is."

Meggie chuckled with true appreciation. "I know just what you mean."

"Do you?" Dorelia looked at her speculatively. "How is that, child? How does your B.G. manifest, exactly?"

Meggie wanted to laugh. Her B.G. Somehow hearing it put like that made it almost normal, like a part of her body. "Well . . ." she said, "I cannot foresee the future or anything like that, but I can—well, I can hear other people's thoughts. Only sometimes and not always when I want. Then sometimes when I do want to, I can't hear anything at all. Or so I've just discovered."

She could scarcely believe that she was talking in such a casual way about the talent that had plagued her all her life.

"Yes . . . it is irksome, isn't it?" Dorelia said just as comfortably. "Now, I have the healing touch, but I cannot produce any sort of guaranteed outcome, simply a brilliant diagnosis. After that I can only give the treatment I think proper and hope for the best."

She pursed her lips together. "I'd *far* prefer to have it the other way around, a terrible diagnosis and a perfect result, but there you are. One must do the best with one's B.G. as one can. Speaking of which," she said, gently pressing Meggie back down upon the bed. "Lie still for just a moment, while I see to you."

"There's nothing wrong with me," Meggie protested. "I just forgot to eat at noon."

"I'll be the judge of what's wrong with you and what isn't," Dorelia said, proceeding to press her hands in various places on Meggie's body, sighing and humming to herself as she did so.

"Mmm," she said when she finished. "You'll do. Hungry, as you said, and tired, too, but we'll soon have that fixed. More to the point, you're frightened and confused and your emotions are all in a tizzy, but it doesn't take the B.G. to know that. Love will do that to you."

Meggie turned her head to one side, deeply ashamed, knowing she couldn't lie, certainly not to this woman. "It's not love," she whispered. "I'm not supposed to say anything, but Hugo and I don't even know each other. He just *thinks* it's love—but that's because his baser nature has taken control of his good sense."

Dorelia stared at her, then threw her head back and shrieked with laughter. She howled from her belly until she bent over sideways on the bed, her little head bobbing back and forth, tears streaming down her cheeks.

Meggie had never in her life seen anyone laugh in such an unrestrained fashion, and although she thoroughly enjoyed the sight, she wasn't at all sure what Dorelia found so wildly amusing.

As much as she longed to know, there was no divining Dorelia's thoughts or feelings, but really, what need did Meggie have to divine anything? Dorelia's hilarity said it all. Meggie was nothing but a silly girl.

She waited until Dorelia had straightened and wiped her eyes and nose on a scrap of handkerchief she produced from her sleeve.

"You really do only see so far, don't you?" Dorelia cackled. "Never mind. You are young still."

"I realize that the situation must sound ridiculous," Meggie said, swallowing the last remnant of pride she had left, "but I have told you the truth. I accepted an offer of marriage from Hugo so that I might gain my freedom. There is nothing more to it."

Dorelia's face crumpled up again and she buried it in her handkerchief. "Your freedom," she said, when she finally looked up, vigorously wiping her nose. "Indeed? Freedom is a relative term, child. There is freedom of the mind, freedom of the body, freedom of the spirit, and each of those is qualified by the conditions you choose to impose on yourself and on others. I wonder which type of freedom you think you have attained?"

Meggie frowned. She knew that she was free of walls, free of rules and regulations that had for countless years defined every waking hour of her life, but she had a feeling that she'd just taken on another set of rules and regulations that she hadn't begun to understand. Dorelia in her own way must be giving her fair warning.

Dorelia hopped up from the bed and opened the door of the hugest wardrobe Meggie had ever seen. "I aired and pressed a dinner dress for you last night in anticipation of your arrival—just in case you were not prepared. Ottoline thought that might be a possibility. That is Ottoline's B.G., you see. She gets ideas about the future, and it's usually best to listen."

Meggie blinked. Ottoline had a B.G., too? "Oh," she said. "Oh, my."

Dorelia ignored her. "The dress is not in the latest fashion, of course, belonging as it did to my dear Lally who died many years before, but the material is still good." She nodded, looking pleased with herself. "As soon as Lally passed away I packed it in mothballs and lavender. Ah, lavender—yes, indeed, an infinite variety of uses for the darling. Where *would* we be without it?"

She reached into the wardrobe and pulled the dress from somewhere inside the great interior, holding it up to the light that streamed through the window. "Now that I see you, I think the color a good choice, suited to your complexion. There are many whose skin is made sallow by green, but Ottoline had an idea about that, too. I modified the style as best I could without a pattern."

"Oh—it's lovely," Meggie said in awe. She'd only seen such elegant clothing from a distance, worn by the grand ladies who occasionally came to visit relatives in the sanitarium. She'd never thought she'd ever wear anything so fine herself. "Are you sure?" she said, hesitating. "It doesn't seem right to be wearing your cousin's dress."

"Don't be absurd. Lally doesn't need it anymore, does she? Off with that awful black thing you're wearing." She shook the dress out and pressed it against Meggie's shoulders. "Lally was tall, as you are, so I do not think the hem will need taking up. I can make any necessary alterations in a pinch, but your figures are similar to my eye, much too slim. And just like Lally's, your bosom could do with some filling out, but that will have to come in time, I suppose. Cleavage is such an advantage."

Meggie had never given any consideration to her figure or its shape. She had certainly never spent any time dwelling on the size of her bosom. It was merely there, serving no other purpose than to earn licentious thoughts from Jasper Oddbins and others like him.

Apparently her bosom now had another function. It was there to fill out the front of clothes. She was obviously going to have to readjust her thinking about a great many things.

"Yes, Aunt Dorelia," Meggie said obediently, wondering just how her bosom was going to fill out in time. It hadn't changed one iota in eight years, and she didn't anticipate it suddenly leaping forward and producing cleavage now.

"That's better, as there's an entire trunk of Lally's clothes that have been going to waste—and if there's one thing I cannot abide, it's waste." She cocked her head and regarded Meggie with a challenging gleam in her eye. "Well, you do need a trousseau, don't you? All brides need a trousseau, and now you have one, so let's hear no more about it."

"Thank you," Meggie said gratefully, slipping out of her own dress that had served her since her arrival at the sanitarium. "I have nothing suitable of my own to wear."

"That much I do know, as I unpacked your bag. Between what I found in there and that hideous garment," she said gesturing disdainfully at it, "it looks to me as if you've come straight from some kind of institution."

Meggie colored furiously. "I—it is true," she said, looking at the floor. "I worked at the Woodbridge Sanitarium. But please, say nothing to Hugo. He would rather no one knows, and I promised I wouldn't tell. I'm supposed to say I met him in the village."

Dorelia leveled a no-nonsense gaze at Meggie. "No one will hear it from me, but young Hugo sounds as if he needs some sense knocked into his head. Where's your family, girl?"

"I have none," Meggie said with a shrug. "My mother died giving birth to me, and my father died before that." She couldn't believe how easy that admission was. She couldn't believe how easy she found it to talk to Dorelia, as if she'd known her all her life. She felt the same with Ottoline, as if communication was effortless. The experience was rare.

"Hmm. Orphaned, were you? No living relatives, not even an aunt or uncle? What about brothers and sisters?"

"I have no one," Meggie repeated.

"So before you went to the nuns at the sanitarium, you were at an orphanage. Ipswich Orphanage, right? It's the only one in the area. And it's run by nuns." Dorelia snorted. "No wonder you wanted your freedom. Well, never mind that now—you can tell me all about it some other time when there's nothing better to do. We need to get you ready for dinner. We must make a good impression on Cookie, or he's bound to bolt," she said, shaking her head. "You have no idea how difficult it is to find a good cook, let alone keep one, and I don't intend to let this one get away. We've been making do on our own for too long."

Meggie sensed that Dorelia had just firmly shut the door on the past and just as firmly opened another—this one to Meggie's future, which evidently began now.

An infuriated bellow sounded from the hallway. "Get away, you damned bloody beast! My God, has your mistress taught you no manners at all? I will *not* tolerate your insufferable attitude—let me past this minute!"

A low, familiar growl came from just outside the door.

Meggie jumped to her feet. "Hadrian? Oh, dear, he shouldn't be in the house. I left him outside."

"Oh, is that the name of your dear wolf?" Dorelia asked, shoving Meggie right back onto the bed with a surprisingly strong hand. "He came bounding inside the moment you went flat out and hasn't left off guarding your door since. A lovely fellow—and unusual to see any of their kind out in the open these days. Wolves have been badly misunderstood, don't you think?"

"Yes, but before he's even more badly misunderstood, I must go to him," Meggie said, alarm racing through every nerve in her body. Given Hugo's fear of Hadrian, he might do something truly dreadful like kick him, or even shoot him.

"Don't be silly, child," Dorelia said, brandishing Meggie's brush that she'd produced from the dressing table against the wall. "Darling Hugo must come to terms with your Hadrian, and the sooner the better. You *do* realize they are fighting over their territorial rights?"

Meggie frowned. "The house is more than big enough for both of them. This isn't even Hadrian's territory, not yet."

"I didn't mean the house; I was referring to you," Dorelia said, letting Meggie's hair down and starting to brush it with even strokes. "You are, of course, Hadrian's family, his pack, as he sees it. This much I *can* divine—the beast is devoted to you. I know animals' minds as well as I know my own. They know it, too."

"Do they?" Meggie said with a smile. It was another thing they had in common.

"Of course they do. Now here is how it is: Your Hadrian is going to have to accept Hugo as your mate and Hugo, poor boy, is going to have to accept Hadrian as your brother. Share and share alike, I always say. They will learn to tolerate each other in time, but you must allow them to come to terms without your interference."

"But Hugo doesn't like—"

"What Hugo likes and doesn't like is of no interest to me. He'll learn how things work around here soon enough."

Meggie closed her mouth on her next protest. She could see that there was no point in arguing with Dorelia. It occurred to her that Hugo was going to have to come to territorial terms with more than Hadrian.

That was going to be interesting to watch. So far Hugo hadn't struck her as the most flexible of men.

Humming, Dorelia pulled the brush through Meggie's hair with another long, rhythmic stroke. Meggie sighed, so enjoying the pleasure of the contact that she forgot all about Hadrian and Hugo, abandoning herself to the luxury of being nurtured, floating off to a place of peace where she thought of nothing at all . . .

No time seemed to have passed when Dorelia dropped the brush and uttered an exclamation.

"Dinner!" she cried. "I completely forgot about the hour. We mustn't keep Cookie and his feast waiting. You must dress instantly—quickly, girl, quickly! I do *not* know what I was thinking."

Before Meggie could register what was happening, Dorelia had twisted Meggie's hair into a loose chignon and fastened it. She produced a basin of warm water from somewhere and scrubbed Meggie's hands and face as if she were a child, dried her off with a soft, fluffy towel, and stood her upright.

The next thing Meggie knew, Dorelia had poured the dress over her head and efficiently settled it into place.

"There," Dorelia said triumphantly, whipping Meggie toward a long mirror and facing her forward. "That's perfect, don't you agree?"

Stunned, Meggie regarded herself in the mirror. She could hardly believe her eyes. The dress, a gossamer concoction of the palest green silk, looked as if it had been spun directly onto her body. Which was exactly the problem.

"Isn't it a bit—well, a bit indecent?" Meggie said, pulling at the low neckline that revealed a great deal of her small bosom. She felt practically naked.

"Nonsense. I am sure this is all the rage. I modified the design, as I told you."

"I—I've never had my neck uncovered in all my life," Meggie stammered, wondering what Sister Agnes would say if she could see her now. Not three hours out of the sanitarium, and Meggie looked like a light-skirt. "Or my arms," she added.

"If you object, you can always put a shawl around your shoulders, but I really do *not* see the necessity." Dorelia scowled. "Hmm, I think I understand. It's those nuns, isn't it? What do they know, may I ask, all dressed up fit to suffocate? You're about to become a married woman, and you can take my word for it, gentlemen don't take kindly to having their wives swaddled in shapeless packages."

Meggie couldn't help herself. "Here I thought I was trying to please Cookie," she said tartly.

Dorelia's little eyes narrowed for a moment and then she chortled, clapping her hands together. "So, the nuns didn't manage to beat all the spirit out of you after all."

"The nuns weren't *all* bad," Meggie started to say, about to explain about Sister Agnes, but Dorelia cut her off with an impatient wave of the hand.

"Yes, yes, dear. Later." She plucked a white rose from the vase on the dressing table and slipped it into Meggie's hair. "There. Perfect. Now, since you've had no mother to instruct you in these matters, I will instruct you myself. You are to concentrate fully on your husband-to-be tonight, whether you know him from Adam or not."

Meggie nearly choked at the reference. She could just see herself concentrating fully on Hugo in the context of Adam. She'd never get a bite down her throat. "Yes, Aunt Dorelia," she said in a strangled voice.

"Smile often, agree with everything he says, and for heaven's sake, keep your opinions to yourself. You will soon find that men are interested in nobody's opinion but their own. A pretty face and a pleasing manner will go a long way in keeping the waters calm. Men do not like women to be clever."

Meggie felt something inside her stomach curl up into a tight ball. Was *every* married woman expected to be a hopeless dimwit? Did all men speak to their wives in painfully short and childish sentences, as if any sort of understanding was beyond them? From what Dorelia had just said, she gathered that had to be the case.

Meggie had lived so long only in the company of women that she'd assumed that the sort of intelligent, lively conversation she shared with Sister Agnes would be the same sort of conversation she'd have with anyone with a decent brain, regardless of sex. Even her teachers in the orphanage, despite their ingrained animosity toward her, had grudgingly encouraged her to learn as much as she could and to excel at her work.

What was the use of all her fine education if from now on she was to bury it under a layer of pretended idiocy, just so she could be admired by her husband? What use was there in any woman being educated?

She'd never realized that men wanted women to be nothing more than decorative objects. Yet Hugo had clearly indicated to her on more than one occasion that this was the very thing he expected. She had been so ignorant about the standard state of affairs between men and women.

"My dear, you are very quiet. Have you been attending me?" Dorelia demanded.

"Yes," Meggie said, her voice very low. "I have attended you well. I am to be amenable in every way to Hugo's wishes."

"Well, not to all his wishes," Dorelia said, her eyes sparkling mischievously. "Some of those wishes can wait until tomorrow, and it is up to you to see that they do. Once the ring is on your finger, then it is a different matter." She peered at Meggie. "You do understand me? The nuns didn't keep you completely in the dark?"

Meggie lowered her gaze. "If you mean about the consecrated act of marriage," she said, "I have no need for instruction. It is what comes after that concerns me."

Dorelia's expression abruptly sobered. "Oh, my dear child, I was forgetting about your own arrival in this world. Naturally you would be fearful, but with luck, what comes after is a healthy child and a healthy mother."

"Oh . . ." Meggie said. She hadn't even considered the possibility of dying in childbirth, or for that matter becoming pregnant. "Is it common for mothers to die when they have a baby?" she asked nervously.

"Not *so* very common, no, especially if the birth is

handled correctly." Her face darkened. "Like your own poor mother, Lally was not so fortunate. She and her dear baby boy expired together. There was nothing I could do for either of them, curse the idiot doctor who kept me from Lally's side—but never mind that," she said, her hand sweeping through the air as if to banish the memory. "He won't be coming to this house again, I can promise you that. Any other questions?"

"Actually, what I really meant was what my duties would be. Other than producing children," Meggie said.

"Oh, that's easy. You manage your husband's house and affairs, look after his tenants, and see to the general well-being of everyone under your care."

"All of this when I am meant to be monumentally stupid, a walking epergne?" Meggie asked.

Dorelia's wizened face split into a grin. "So you do understand me after all. Good. You will need to understand as much about men as possible, my dear girl, if you're to keep your husband in hand. We will talk more about all of this, but there is no time now."

She took Meggie by the shoulders and turned her toward the door, then released her. "Go now. Do as I've told you. You are not the only woman who has walked into marriage not knowing her husband, and you certainly will not be the last. It is up to you to make this work, Meggie Bloom. I count on you. We all count on you."

Meggie twisted her head to ask Dorelia what she meant by that peculiar statement, but Dorelia had mysteriously vanished like a puff of smoke.

Meggie scanned the room for a hidden exit, but with no success. She'd have to look for it later. In the meantime, Dorelia was right.

She needed to focus her attention on her husband, discover what she could about his expectations.

And try to remember to behave like a moron.

11

Hugo glared at Meggie's bedroom door one last time, then down at the blasted wolf who kept him from ensuring that his four hundred thousand pounds was going to survive.

"Bloody damned cur," he muttered blackly. "You should be shot."

The cur turned up the corner of one lip at him and growled.

Hugo turned up the corner of his own lip in reply, then headed for the room next door that one of the two Mabey sisters had indicated was to be his.

The Mabey sisters. They were typical of his luck, he thought glumly, sitting on the bed and pulling his boots off. Not only were Lord Eliot's leavings batty old maids, they were batty twin old maids. He'd thought for an instant that he'd lost his mind when Meggie swooned and Ottoline instantly vanished, only to reappear in duplicate. As if one garrulous old maid wasn't enough, her sister twittered away just as ceaselessly.

Furthermore, neither seemed to care that he might be concerned about Meggie's welfare. He'd been banished from her room the moment he laid her on the bed as if he were of absolutely no importance. He, the owner of Lyden Hall, tossed out as if he were a schoolboy.

Damn Meggie anyway for giving him such a shock—if she was suddenly going to develop ill health, she could at least have had the courtesy to wait until tomorrow afternoon when he'd had a chance to marry her.

Hugo rubbed his feet, then looked around and located the washstand in the corner of the room. Anxious to wash the dust of travel off, he felt as if he'd been on the road for a week instead of just since this morning.

At least the man who seemed to serve as groom, footman, and chambermaid had not only brought his bags upstairs but hot water as well. It was a beginning, although hardly an auspicious one.

To date there seemed to be only the man-of-all-purpose, a dark-complexioned fellow who looked suspiciously like a Gypsy, and a thief called Cookie under employment. He had no idea how the Mabey women had been coping on their own, especially given their age, but that was none of his concern.

How he was going to cope was more to the point. He was *not* accustomed to doing without Mallard, who had been with him from the time he was twelve. Mallard had stuck with Hugo through thick and thin, even during the tedious and often impoverished years of exile in Paris. He never complained and always ensured that no matter what Hugo's condition—wounded in a duel, battered and bruised from an encounter with an irate husband, or hopelessly inebriated after a full night of carousing—at least he was always impeccably turned out.

Hugo shrugged off his coat, shirt, and mangled neckcloth and tromped over to the basin. He splashed water over his chest and face, then located clean linens and a coat and somehow managed to dress himself.

He examined his appearance in the mirror, decided it would have to do, and marched back out into the hallway, ready to renew his battle with Meggie's mongrel and the Mabey sisters.

To his surprise, the door was open and neither Meggie, mongrel, nor Mabeys were anywhere in sight.

Which meant either Meggie was dead and had been carried away by the Mabey sisters for a swift burial, or, more likely, she was fully recovered and had gone downstairs to the drawing room.

Hugo took the steps two at a time, anxious to reassure himself that he was correct about the latter presumption. He had to stop abruptly at the bottom as he tried to remember in which direction the drawing room lay.

He located it correctly, but unfortunately no Meggie graced its interior, and he had to wonder if Meggie even knew what a drawing room was and what it was used for. He tried the library across the hall, with the same unsatisfactory result. He tried the conservatory, the morning room, the breakfast room, and finally the dining room itself.

Still no sign of Meggie, but two place settings and three lit candelabras graced the long, oval cherry table. Four more candelabras blazed from the sideboards on each side of the room, casting a warm, intimate glow over the room.

Hugo was relieved that the Mabey sisters had had the sense to leave him alone with Meggie on their first night together. He could make a beginning at showing her how he meant her to go on.

If he ever managed to locate her. For all he knew, she had wandered off and fallen into the river.

Just as that alarming thought occurred, his ear caught the unmistakable sound of Meggie's laugh from the other side of the swinging door that led to the kitchen.

Hugo crossed the room in an instant and pushed the door open.

Sure enough, there stood Meggie, wrapped in a huge white apron, surrounded by the Mabey sisters, the swarthy Gypsy, and an extremely burly and rather intimidating specimen of masculinity, whom Hugo assumed was Cookie. They were all bent over a large pot, talking a mile a minute so that he could make out not one word.

The mongrel sat watching at their feet, eyebrows twitching as if it understood every word Hugo could not. It cast one indifferent glance at him, then turned its attention back to the pot as if Hugo was not worthy of any more of its time.

"Excuse me," Hugo said, with no result. He cleared his throat. *"Excuse me,"* he repeated loudly, his annoyance growing by the moment. He was not accustomed to being ignored.

They all looked up.

"Hugo, dear," one of the Mabey sister chirped. "There you are at last. Do come and look at your dinner. Clever Cookie located lobsters just this afternoon straight off a fishing boat. Oh—but you haven't been introduced. To Cookie that is, not your dinner." She smiled at him as graciously as if she were presenting a king. "Lord Hugo, allow me to present Cookie Crumpton, your splendid new chef."

After the day Hugo had just had, nothing would have surprised him. A formal introduction to a man who looked more like a pugilist than a chef seemed perfectly normal. He inclined his head. "Delighted."

Cookie grinned, showing a mouthful of brown teeth, half of which were missing. " 'Ere's to hew, yer lordship. These lobsters, now they'll goo down nice with a bit o' my sherry sauce. Hope hew've an edge on yer appetite, since a nice tender leg o' lamb's to follow with a mint jelly fo't, and—"

"Indeed," Hugo replied, in no mood to engage in conversation with a bloody cook. He'd never done so before and he wasn't about to start now. "Meggie, my dear, I am happy to see you are feeling better. Would you come with me, please, and be so kind as to leave your, er, dog behind?"

"Of course," she said, smiling sweetly at him as she removed the apron she'd been wrapped in.

Hugo's irritation instantly melted away. He could hardly be annoyed when faced with the sun itself. Here was the angel he'd first spotted from Sister Agnes's window, only infinitely more beautiful. Her slender figure was artfully revealed beneath the sheer material of her dress. In all his imaginings, he'd never pictured such perfection.

He drank in her delicate features, her swanlike neck, her graceful arms and shoulders, and the lovely swell of her small bosom. Realizing he was staring in a most blatant fashion, he forced his gaze back to her eyes; a bad mistake, since they gazed straight back at him in that translucent, ethereal fashion that threatened to undo him.

And where the hell had she gotten that dress from? For that matter, who cared? It worked its magic well enough, erasing the image of that ghastly black garment.

He held out his arm. "Let us sit down for dinner," he said, fighting the tightening in his groin. "Whenever it chooses to appear," he added as a parting shot at the others.

"Hadrian, stay with Cookie, there's a sweetheart," Meggie said, gliding toward Hugo as if she'd been gliding toward him all her life. "He'll feed you anything your heart desires, won't you, Cookie?"

"Thass the truth, Miss," Cookie said. "Owd dog and I, we be of like mind, we be. I miss me own liddle Coxswain, I called him. Went overboard in a gale, he did. Broke this owd heart, and thass saying much." He pounded his chest and squeezed a tear out of his eye.

"Oh, how sad," Meggie said with great sympathy. "I'm sure Coxswain was a fine little dog, full of mischief and yet always listening to you when it was important."

"Yass he did, miss, though I dunno how hew be knowin' it."

"I suppose because Hadrian is just the same way," Meggie said, slipping her fingers through Hugo's arm. "A good, loving animal who trusts without condition doesn't come along just every day. You have to build that trust from the very beginning, don't you, Cookie, using patience and a firm hand to train them."

"Aye, Miss, and hew've done it sure enough with owd doggie of yers here. He be a fine lad, he be." Cookie bent down and scratched Hadrian between the ears.

The cur had the gall to close its eyes and lick its chops in satisfaction.

"Oh, look at that, Cookie. He does like you," Meggie said, beaming at the man as if he were her new best friend.

Enough was enough. Hugo literally propelled Meggie out of the kitchen, telling himself that patience and a firm hand would also go a long way toward training her.

Meggie allowed herself to be driven along, feeling like an errant sheep. She cast a brief backward glance at Ottoline and Dorelia, who smiled in tandem, bobbing their heads up and down in encouragement.

"Here," Hugo said on the other side of the door, leading her to her chair. "This is your proper place."

Meggie turned her gaze on him in question. "My proper place?" she repeated, not sure if he was referring to the physical or the metaphorical.

"Yes, my dear. Where you sit at the table. With me. When we are to have dinner. You do not belong in the kitchen. That is where the hired staff spends its time."

So, he was referring to both places. Meggie did her best to keep a straight face, keeping in mind what Dorelia had said about not contradicting him.

"Yes, Hugo," she said obediently, eyeing the vast quantity of silverware and crystal on the table. Two glasses, two knives, two forks, two spoons—she couldn't think why so much was needed, when it would only create more washing.

Hugo nodded. "Very good, Meggie. I only require two

things of you, remember. That you keep silent, and that you do as I tell you. And I am telling you to stay out of the way of the servants. They will do their jobs far better without your presence to distract them."

Meggie nodded in return. "I am to stay out of the way." She put her napkin in her lap and sat up straight, shoulders back, as the nuns had drilled into her.

"Yes, that is it exactly," Hugo said, regarding her with an odd expression.

"As you say, Hugo." Meggie smiled again, although her heart wasn't in it. She could already see that she was going to have to exert an enormous effort to be dim-witted and docile in all things.

Her reward would be his approval, she told herself. His approval and the gift of his love, although she wondered how much his love would mean to her since he was bestowing it on a person who didn't really exist.

She heaved a sigh. At least there was always the prospect of the other part of their marriage—the part that happened in the bedroom. She hadn't forgotten about that for a minute.

She surreptitiously glanced over at Hugo from under her lashes, a little frisson of anticipation running through her. Oh, he really was very appealing to look at, with his wide, strong shoulders filling out the material of his coat, and his broad chest tapering to a narrow waist.

She'd already experienced firsthand the power of his arms when they'd lifted her in the air and spun her around. . . . And, my, how wonderful his touch had felt on her waist. She had only to wait until tomorrow night to discover how wonderful his touch would feel on other parts of her body. Just the thought of lying naked against him, her flesh pressed to his, made her go hot from head to toe.

Meggie jerked her gaze away, blushing furiously. She *must* be wanton to be having these fevered thoughts, and at the dinner table, of all places! Clearly she had inherited her mother's carnal inclinations, but unlike her mother, at least, Meggie would be married when she went into a man's bed.

She did hope she wasn't supposed to be dim-witted and docile there as well.

A slight movement of the kitchen door distracted her from her disgraceful train of thought, and she looked up to see one of Dorelia's little eyes peeking out from the crack. The eye winked, then disappeared.

Meggie, reminded of her duty, beamed again. "Do you enjoy your room, Hugo?" she asked. "I like mine so very much. It offers a view of the river. It even has a large four-poster bed."

"As does mine," he replied, fiddling with his knife.

"I had a pitcher of hot water in my washstand."

"Yes. I had the same," he said, scratching his ear.

"The rest of the furniture is lovely, too. I have never seen anything so lovely in my life. In my room at the sanitarium I had only a small iron bedstand and a bureau. Oh, and a small wardrobe, but then it didn't need to be very large."

"Meggie, I think it best if you do not mention the sanitarium again, even to me." He still fiddled with his knife, not looking at her.

"Oh. I beg your pardon. May I mention the orphanage? My room there was much the same, only I shared it with three other girls. At least in the—um, the *other* place I had some privacy."

"Enough chattering, Meggie," Hugo said.

Meggie clasped her fingers in her lap. "I beg your pardon," she said, trying to sound contrite.

"Not at all," he replied, still not looking at her. "But it has been a long day and I am tired. I think I'd prefer to sit here quietly and admire you in your pretty dress."

Oh, dear, Meggie thought. Dorelia did have the right

of it. She really was supposed to be nothing more than a display piece. Still, she'd better get used to it.

"Where did your dress come from?" he asked. "I thought you said you had brought nothing else with you."

"From Lally," she replied, wondering what was taking Cookie so long with the lobsters. Her stomach felt as if it had grown a hole in the middle.

"From *Lally*?" he said, his eyes shooting up to meet hers. "Do you mean Lord Eliot's deceased wife?"

Meggie nodded. "I think it indecent, but Aunt Dorelia insisted."

"Indecent?" he asked with a little frown. "Why? Because she's dead?"

"No—because there's hardly any bodice," Meggie said, thinking that he should have noticed that for himself, "and the sleeves are nothing but little puffs, and I might as well be wearing my chemise for all the coverage I have!"

"Meggie—for God's sake," Hugo said, his voice suddenly tight. "Do *not* talk about such things at the table. Indeed, you shouldn't talk about them at all. It's not—it's not proper."

"Oh, it's not proper for me to talk about, but it's perfectly acceptable for me to appear this way? I think you live in a very strange world, Hugo Montagu," she shot back without thinking.

"Oh, and the world you live in is normal?" he retorted sharply. "I hardly think so."

Meggie stared at him aghast, feeling as if he'd slapped her. He *knew*. He kenw about her ability, and he thought her a freak of nature.

He has made it his business to learn a great deal about you . . .

Someone must have told him. That was what he'd meant when he'd told Sister Agnes that he knew she was different. She pressed her hand to her cheek, wanting to die from mortification. "If you think me so abnormal, I wonder that you want to marry me at all," she whispered.

He flushed a dark red. "I do not think you . . . that is, I—I meant only that you are not . . . that you are not familiar with the world."

Meggie stared down at her hands. "Do you refer to my being shut away for most of my life," she said, her voice infuriatingly shaky, "or do you refer to some oddity about me that leaves you with misgivings?"

He blinked. "Not—not at all. I was referring only to your isolation, Meggie. Forgive me if I sounded harsh."

"Please, do not trouble yourself," she said, about to burst into tears. "You only said what you meant."

"No, I didn't. What I meant to say is that you are not to know what is proper and what is not, given your lack of experience. As I said, it has been a long and tiring day, and I wasn't thinking when I spoke."

Meggie's gaze flew to his face. She saw only genuine remorse in it—certainly no fear that she could read his mind. Thinking back, she realized he had given no indication at any time that he suspected her of any such thing.

Relief washed through Meggie, leaving her weak. He was telling the truth. He thought her no more than an ignorant girl. An ignorant girl he wanted to marry because she was decorative and he fancied himself in love with her.

"We are both tired," she said, bestowing a genuine smile on him. "And I am very hungry," she added, determined to change the subject. "You must be also. Have you ever eaten a lobster before?"

"Many times," he replied, looking as relieved as she to drop the matter. "However, I wonder if this is to be a new experience for you. You seemed engrossed in their cooking."

"I have never seen a lobster, let alone tasted one. Cookie assured me they were a great delicacy, and as you must have gathered, I am not accustomed to delicacies."

"Then it is high time that you do become accustomed to them," he said. "I promised you treats, and treats you shall have, starting tonight."

As if on cue, the door swung open and Cookie appeared with the lobsters on a great platter, beautifully dressed and garnished.

He placed them on the sideboard, and Roberto the footman, who had lived at Lyden Hall for all of his thirty years, came in behind Cookie. Roberto portioned the lobsters out, then laid the plates on the table. Meggie nearly swooned at the delicious smell that wafted up from them.

"Wine," Hugo commanded, raising an eyebrow imperiously at Roberto.

Roberto instantly produced a bottle from a bucket, pouring out the pale yellow liquid with great care before quietly vanishing again.

Meggie impatiently waited for Hugo to say grace, but when he picked up his glass and tasted his wine, she realized no grace was forthcoming. So she bowed her head and murmured to herself a prayer of thanks, then lifted the first fork that came to hand and dived into her plate without another word.

As the first taste touched her tongue her eyes closed in ecstasy. She had never sampled anything so delicious in her life; she'd never even imagined anything could taste so wonderful, so rich in flavor and yet so smooth and delicate all at the same time.

God be praised, she thought, taking another bite, for having been so kind as to put lobsters on the earth and for being even more kind for putting one in front of her to eat. God should also be praised for having produced Cookie to make the lobster so superbly good, and also for producing Hugo so that he could bring her to this very table where she might devour this extraordinary treat.

She looked up to find Hugo watching her with a slight smile curving his lips. "Mmmm," she said through a mouthful, " 's wonderful. Sup'rb."

"You made your opinion obvious from the way you attacked it," he said dryly, wiping the corner of his mouth with his napkin. "Although I must say that I agree. Cookie did a fine job."

Meggie swallowed the very last bite, then nodded vigorously. "Cookie should be canonized."

Hugo laughed. "Cookie should probably be jailed, but we'll let the matter go, considering his skill. Try a little of your wine. You'll find that it complements the flavor nicely."

Meggie, who had never had wine in her life, picked up her glass and took a large swallow. "It's very nice," she said in surprise, choking a little on the unexpected strength, but also enjoying the warmth the liquid created as it slipped smoothly down her throat.

"Easy there." Hugo reached out a hand and stayed her hand before she could take another swallow. "You must sip your wine, Meggie, not gulp it. Drink it slowly, or you'll be falling off your chair in no time."

Meggie shook her head in wonder. "All these new pleasures. You must forgive my ignorance. I've never even had wine at Communion. Well, I couldn't, but I didn't think I was missing anything."

"Oh," Hugo said, a slight frown creasing his brow. "I hadn't even thought about the question of your religion. You *were* baptized at some point?"

Meggie nodded. "My aunt Emily had me christened when I was a baby."

"Your aunt Emily?" he said, his frown deepening. "I thought you had no relatives."

"I haven't. Emily Crewe was my foster mother. I thought you knew about my past," she said, suddenly worried that maybe Sister Agnes had misunderstood him. She'd be devastated if she had to explain her status to him and he changed his mind about marrying her.

"Ah, yes, I remember now," he said, tapping his finger against his glass. "She died when you were—what, nine? That's when you went to the orphanage, I believe."

Meggie breathed again. He did know everything after all. "Yes. She was a wonderful woman and kind. I loved her very much," Meggie said simply.

"Did she have you christened in the Catholic or the Anglican Church?" Hugo said. "I only ask because I am Anglican, and your being Catholic might complicate matters."

Meggie wondered why Hugo looked so nervous. Perhaps his religion was important to him after all, even if he didn't bother to say grace. "I was baptized an Anglican," she said. "Would it matter very much if I were Catholic?"

"It wouldn't matter in the least to me," he said, his frown replaced by an expression of relief. "I'm not a religious man. I was only concerned that our marriage might become complicated."

"Why?" Meggie asked, genuinely curious.

"I really don't know, Meggie," he said impatiently. "I've never been married before and therefore have never paid any attention to the ins and outs of the various legalities. Who knows if there isn't some inconvenient Catholic directive about marrying outside the faith? The point is that I do not want anything getting in the way of tomorrow's ceremony."

"Really?" she asked softly, a warm glow spreading

through her at the thought that Hugo was so anxious to marry her, even if it was just to get her into bed.

"Really. However, the way I see it, as long as you are a member of the Church of England, as I am, and above the age of consent, as I am, and we have a valid license, which we do, there is nothing to stop us. Nothing at all."

"Where will we be married?" Meggie asked, excitement blossoming in her breast at the prospect of standing at the altar with Hugo. "Is there a parish church? Aunt Emily and I used to go to our parish church every Sunday, and I so liked the simplicity of the services. Catholic services are so much more . . . tedious."

"Yes, I can imagine that you must have found them tedious," Hugo replied. "I, too, would be bored if I couldn't understand what was being said."

Meggie bit her tongue. She understood Latin well enough to have read Virgil in the original, although Hugo wouldn't want to know that. What she'd actually meant was that she preferred the lack of pomp and circumstance of the Anglican church, but Hugo probably didn't want to know that, either. "You didn't answer my question," she said instead. "Is there a parish church?"

"I imagine there must be, Meggie, since there's a vicar," Hugo said, rubbing his cheek with his fingertip. "However, I will ask the vicar to come here to Lyden to marry us. It is less vulgar to be married at home, I think, than in a local church where neither of us has ever set foot before."

"Surely we have to be married in a church?" Meggie said in considerable surprise.

"No, we don't," he replied patiently. "The special license I told you about, which I obtained at great expense and for this very reason, allows us to be married wherever we please, whenever we please, without waiting for the reading of banns or the need for a church."

"Oh," she said, trying to hide her disappointment. In

the rare fantasies she'd had about marrying someday, she'd always seen herself in a simple little church with a wreath of flowers on her head, saying her vows before a kind-faced vicar.

But this was no time for indulging herself in fantasies, as much as a church ceremony would have meant to her. Hugo obviously was not on comfortable terms with God, which seemed a great shame, but none of her business. So she smiled and recited her pat reply. "As you wish, Hugo."

"Exactly," he said. "The drawing room should suit well enough. I will write to the vicar first thing in the morning and ask him to come after luncheon. That way, he won't expect to be asked to stay for a meal." He looked at her sternly. "I cannot abide a fuss."

Meggie had never heard of anything so unromantic, but she held her tongue. Roberto cleared away the plates—and the first set of knives and forks—and refilled the glass of wine that Hugo had already emptied.

Moments later Cookie marched in with a platter containing an entire leg of lamb. The delicious aroma distracted Meggie from her gloomy visions of tomorrow's wedding. Nothing was going to keep her from enjoying her meal, not even the thought of being married in a drawing room.

She watched in fascination as Cookie expertly carved the joint at the sideboard, producing paper-thin slices of juicy pink meat unlike anything Meggie had seen before. In her experience, lamb was gray and greasy and appeared in sinewy chunks well-laced with fat.

Cookie really could work miracles.

In the mealtime, and much to Meggie's astonishment, Roberto produced another bottle of wine, this time red, and poured it into the larger glasses on the table.

So that was what they were for, she realized, but why

two types of wine with dinner? It did seem excessive, rather like all the knives and forks.

Oh, well, the ways of the aristocracy were not for her to question. Her task was to learn about them as quickly as possible, so that she wouldn't disgrace Hugo or herself.

Roberto slipped a plate heaped with lamb and vegetables and crisp roast potatoes smothered in gravy in front of her, and Meggie gave herself over to the sheer pleasure of eating. This wasn't just food, it was ambrosia. As much as Meggie had loved her Aunt Emily, she'd been no cook. To her food was meant solely to nurture the body, not inspire the spirit.

Meggie had never realized that food could be a form of art—every bit as much as a painting or a tapestry or a beautiful piece of music. Edible art. She smiled to herself. Apparently artists came in all shapes and sizes, too. Cookie was a shining example of that.

Hugo didn't speak a single word during the second course, or the third, a delectable fruit pudding in a meringue crust. His gaze remained firmly fixed on his plate.

Meggie prayed that the reason for his silence was an equal appreciation for Cookie's talent. Meggie didn't think she could bear Hugo's dismissing him, not after she'd just discovered the true joy of food.

Anyway, she liked Cookie. She knew he had a warm heart and a wonderfully sentimental nature despite his appearance to the contrary. So far he hadn't invaded her head with unwelcome thoughts—always a good sign.

She looked up as Roberto magically reappeared yet again and refilled her glass of claret, which had gone down so smoothly she'd hardly realized she'd finished it.

Roberto then poured the last of the wine into Hugo's glass. Meggie gaped, realizing somehow during the course of the meal, Hugo had managed to consume almost the entire bottle on his own.

Sipping from her goblet, she waited in fascination to see if he'd fall off his chair, but the wine didn't seem to have had any effect on him. Hugo stayed perfectly upright, not even slumping a little.

She was impressed by his stamina. She'd had only two glasses—well, three if one counted the glass of white—and just those alone had left her feeling light-headed. Positively giddy, she realized, leaning back in her chair, feeling as if she might just float away. Her head felt completely disassociated from her body, but in the nicest possible way.

Her body. Yes, there was that serious matter to consider. She clasped her hands over her stomach, wondering how she was going to manage to waddle out of the dining room and all the way upstairs without bursting at the seams. All that food had to go somewhere.

She put her hand over her mouth and giggled as a ridiculous vision came dancing into her head of great alabaster orbs, swollen over time by enormous helpings of food and more food.

"What, may I ask, is so amusing?" Hugo tossed his napkin onto the table, barely sparing her a glance.

"Oh—I just . . . I just realized how Aunt Dorelia plans to fill my bosom out," she said, smothering a hiccup of laughter.

"I beg your pardon?" His startled gaze met hers. "You just realized *what*?"

"It's very simple," she said, wiping her eyes with her napkin. "All Aunt Dorelia has to do is feed me like this every day and I'll have cleavage pouring out of my bodice in no time at all." She collapsed into gales of laughter. "Oh, what *would* the nuns say? A sure sign of excessive sins of the flesh, no doubt."

The next thing Meggie knew, Hugo had hauled to her feet, swept her into his arms, and carried her from the dining room without a word of explanation.

"Oh," she said, pressing her cheek against his hard shoulder as he started up the staircase, giggles still shaking her body. "I do not think this is at all correct. Aunt Dorelia said most specifically that you were to keep your hands to yourself tonight. I am not to be ravished until tomorrow."

Hugo paused mid-step and looked down at her, his eyes narrowed. "I don't give a damn what Aunt Dorelia said," he said, biting out the words. "Furthermore, regardless of what ideas that absurd woman might have put in your head, if you think I'm about to take you to your room and ravish you, you're very badly mistaken." He started up the stairs again.

"I am?" she said with infinite disappointment. "What a shame." She smiled up at him. "But never mind. I can wait. I've waited all my life."

The storm clouds instantly vanished from Hugo's face, replaced by vast amusement. "If you're trying to tell me you're a virgin, sweetheart, I'd already reached that conclusion. When would you ever have had a chance to be otherwise?"

Meggie vaguely registered the thought that Hugo's moods were as changeable as the weather. "I suppose that is true," she said. "Not that I would have been wicked even if I'd had the chance. Or at least I don't think I would have been, since the thought of being wicked never crossed my mind until you came along, although I have to confess that once it did cross my mind, it wouldn't go away."

Hugo burst into laughter. "Is that so?" he said lazily, brushing a strand of hair off her cheek with one finger.

She nodded earnestly. "Ever since I saw you in Sister Agnes's window I couldn't stop thinking about you, but since I never imagined I'd see you again, I suppose I felt a *little* less wicked—that is to say, I wasn't actually in the path of temptation. It is a good thing I'm not a Catholic though, or I would have been obliged to confess all my lustful thoughts to the priest, and what on earth would he have thought of me?"

"I shudder to think," Hugo said, reaching her door. He didn't hesitate for a moment, pushing it wide and carrying her inside.

Meggie gazed at him in breathless anticipation, wondering what he was going to do next. She hoped he really might ravish her, even though she knew she shouldn't wish any such thing, at least not tonight. She found the heavy throbbing between her legs and the sudden flood of moisture that dampened the secret place between her thighs hard to ignore as he stared down at her, his breath coming rough and fast.

Every nerve in her body felt on fire.

Hugo's eyes shone dark as midnight, glittering as if he knew all about it.

"Hugo?" she asked, catching her bottom lip between her teeth.

He slowly, so very slowly lowered her until her feet rested on the floor, his hands sliding sensually down over her rib cage, coming to rest on her hips. "Hmm?" he replied. His fingers were barely pressing on her flesh, and yet she felt his fingertips pulsing against her as strong as a heartbeat.

She shivered under the intimacy of his touch, nearly forgetting what she'd been about to ask. "We really will be married tomorrow?" she said, forcibly pulling her thoughts together.

"Yes," he answered, his voice low and smooth as velvet. "We will be married tomorrow, and once we are, my lovely Meggie, then we are free to enjoy each other as we please. Exactly and as fully as we please. Do you like that idea?"

She swallowed through a dry throat, her heart pounding ferociously. "I like it very much," she whispered, the heavy pulsing between her legs almost unbearable. She stifled the urge to grab his hand and place it just there. "Very much," she choked.

"Good. Because I have been thinking about you every bit as much as you have me, and with all the same longing." He lifted his hands and ran his fingers down the sides of her face. "I am pleased to hear that you are so willing to be my wife. Earlier today I thought you might be averse to the idea of sharing my bed."

"Oh," she sighed, tremors shaking her body. "That was only because I didn't believe you meant to actually marry me. Now it is different."

"How different?" he asked, his voice a low whisper.

"Very different," she whispered back. Her legs were threatening to give way, an alarming tendency they'd developed in his presence.

Her breath caught hard in her throat as he moved one warm hand down her neck, slipping it behind her nape, pulling her close.

"Show me, Meggie," he murmured, bending his head, his mouth now only inches from hers. "Show me that you mean it. Kiss me, sweetheart, so that I have something to remember you by this night."

Meggie could not resist his request any more than she could resist her own desire.

Her eyes fluttered shut as she raised her face to his, her lips parting instinctively to meet his, her heart pounding ferociously in her chest.

His mouth closed on hers, hot and demanding. Meggie melted against him, her hands reaching up to twine through his thick hair as she abandoned herself to his kiss. Opening her mouth fully to his insistent pressure, the sensations that coursed through her beyond any previous imagining.

She couldn't help pressing herself against him, her legs slightly parting against the thrust of his hips, only to meet the steel length of his arousal. This only served to inflame her further. He felt so right, so good. She wanted more, so much more—her instincts urging her to press herself against him even harder as if she could satisfy her craving—but all that did was to feed the flame of her desire.

The contact inflamed him equally. He abandoned all control as his tongue swept against hers, delving even deeper, exploring the secret recesses of her mouth, running along the inner rim of her teeth, evoking such overwhelming sensations that she cried out in intense pleasure.

The sound of her own voice snapped her back to reason. She tore herself away with a strangled sob, a deep intuition telling her that she would not be able to stop herself if she let him carry on his erotic play for one more second. "No," she gasped, summoning every last vestige of will she possessed. "Not now. Not yet. We must be married."

Hugo buried his face briefly in her neck, then raised his head and looked down at her with blazing eyes. "I'm sorry. That was perhaps a little foolish on my part," he said between deep, ragged breaths. "Although very encouraging. Very encouraging indeed."

He ran his hands down her arms, then turned away and moved quickly toward the door, glancing only briefly over his shoulder as he pulled it open. "Tomorrow," he said, smiling at her. "We will both have to survive until then."

The door closed softly after him.

Dazed, Meggie stood frozen, not at all sure what had just happened to her, but knowing with certainty that it was going to happen again.

She felt nothing but delight at the prospect.

12

Blinding sunlight assaulted Hugo's eyes and he threw an arm over his face, wondering with annoyance why Mallard had opened the draperies without any warning.

Cautiously opening one eye, he squinted toward the offending windows. Both eyes shot open as he realized that he was not in his usual bed and Mallard was nowhere in sight. Furthermore, he sported an extremely large and painful erection, and it had nothing to do with a full bladder and everything to do with something he'd been dreaming about. No, someone.

Hugo shot bolt upright. Meggie Bloom. He'd been dreaming about Meggie Bloom. She was in the next room where he'd left her the night before, nobly taking the same very large and painful erection to bed with him.

This was his wedding day.

Rubbing a hand over his face, he tried to bring his thoughts into order. He had to summon the vicar. That was it. A quick letter to the man with a request to appear at Lyden that day, and Hugo would be wed to his four hundred thousand pounds.

Staggering over to the bell pull, he yanked it hard, hoping against hope that the Gypsy would realize that meant a demand for a pot of steaming coffee. Some buttered toast would not go amiss, either, and hot water would be extremely useful.

Lord, last night had taxed his endurance. He'd first thought he might die of physical shock as Meggie had sat down at the table and whipped her shoulders back, presenting her bosom as if it were to be the first course.

He had done everything in his power to keep from diving in.

But Meggie being Meggie, she'd naturally had to draw his attention back to her lovely breasts, pointing out just how unclothed they were. This was after talking about her bed and how large it was. In between all of that, as if that wasn't enough, she'd secretly regarded him with a heated gaze that had nearly set his trousers on fire.

And later . . . oh, dear *God,* later, after Meggie'd had a glass too many of wine and let loose the full force of her sensuality—he really thought he might expire from wanting.

He'd never exerted such physical restraint in his life. He deserved a medal of valor. He might be marrying a lunatic, but by God, lunacy began to look very fine if Meggie's sort of sensual abandon was part of the picture.

Really, the payoff was not so bad, he reasoned. He could put up with her hopeless conversation, her non sequiturs, her blank smile. He could even put up with hearing a constant stream of "as you wish, Hugo," as if she were a trained parrot. He could probably put up with anything if he could just have her body. Often. Very often.

Maybe lunatics had a deliciously well-developed sense of the erotic that made up for their addled brains. In which case he was not taking advantage of Meggie by marrying her, he reasoned, but rather giving her what she understood and could appreciate.

The thought fortified him hugely. He really ought to be grateful for her condition. How many normal wives returned their husbands' lust in full measure?

He was about to retreat to his bed when the corner of a piece of paper caught his eye, poking out from underneath the doorsill. Bending down, he picked it up and turned it over.

Lord Hugo Montagu it announced in spidery writing.

He unfolded the page and peered down at the same spidery script, trying to make out what it said. After a few minutes of reading and rereading it, he finally managed to decipher the whole thing:

Hugo, my dear boy,

If you are not up by ten o'clock, I shall come and summon you myself, but I do hope you are not so lacking in discipline as to lie abed any later than nine o'clock.

Now. Here is your schedule for today: You must dress, of course, and come downstairs for breakfast, which Cookie will naturally have prepared brilliantly.

You are then to spend the morning with your steward, Mr. Reginald Coldsnap (you do *remember my telling you about him?), who will keep your mind off your forthcoming nuptials by plaguing you with pressing problems about your estate.*

I have already been to see the vicar, who is happy to perform your wedding in the Lyden chapel at two o'clock this afternoon. All family weddings have been conducted at this chapel for the past eighty years. He is not available any earlier, I am sorry to say, so you will simply have to wait as patiently as you can.

Regarding the ceremoney: Mr. Coldsnap has agreed to stand up for you, that is, unless you would prefer Cookie. My sister and I will naturally support the bride.

Until then you will leave darling Meggie in peace. Dorelia and I shall look after her perfectly well. That means absolutely no interference on your part, and you will also leave her dear animal in peace, for he will only bite you if you persist in aggravating him. I cannot say I would blame him.

What you do with yourself and Meggie after *your wed-*

ding is entirely up to you. Dorelia and I do not expect to see hide nor hair of you, so please feel no obligation toward us. We are perfectly content to entertain ourselves.
Your loving aunt,
Ottoline

Hugo snorted. His loving aunt? Crazy old bat. She didn't really think she was going to dictate to him? He'd set her straight and her bossy sister, too.

He crumpled the letter up and tossed it in the direction of the fireplace, then pushed both hands through his hair, desperate for his coffee.

Fortunately for the Gypsy, he knocked at the door just as Hugo finished with the water closet, thereby sparing himself a serious tongue-lashing.

"It is Roberto, your lordship."

"I would hope so. Enter," Hugo called, flopping back on the bed in full expectation of a tray.

"Good morning, your lordship," Roberto said as he walked in bearing nothing more than a steaming pitcher of water.

"Where is my coffee?" Hugo demanded.

"Your coffee? I believe it is downstairs on the sideboard, your lordship. Miss Ottoline made certain Cookie brewed a fresh pot not an hour ago. It is nearly ten o'clock."

"Do you think to reprove me?" Hugo snapped.

"Indeed not, my lord, but you should know that Mr. Coldsnap has been waiting this last hour for you. He was so pleased that you had finally appeared at Lyden, but then it is not my place to speak for him," Roberto added, regarding Hugo with a wary eye. "Your water," he said, placing the pitcher on the washstand and disappearing before Hugo could say another word.

Instead of raising holy hell, Hugo decided to make use of the water before it went cold. He washed himself thoroughly, his temper becoming more frayed by the moment as he struggled, unaided yet again, into his clothes. Then, he attempted to tame his hair into some sort of order without much success.

He opened his door and glanced down the hallway, only to see that the damned mongrel was back outside Meggie's door. He wondered blackly at what point it had skulked back upstairs.

His temper wasn't improved by his arrival in the breakfast room where a chinless, needle-nosed man in thick spectacles sat at the table. Hunched over an enormous pile of papers, the man alternately poked and prodded at the papers and then at his forehead.

"Good morning," Hugo said coolly. "May I help you?"

"Lord Hugo," the man said, leaping to his feet. "At last! Ah, my good sir, I have been looking forward to this occasion for many weeks now."

"Have you?" Hugo replied, looking him up and down. Reginald Coldsnap was *not* his idea of what a steward should look like. Stewards were meant to be hardy-looking fellows who ran about fields all day, not weedy, pasty specimens who looked as if they'd never stepped outside of an accounting office.

"I have, indeed I have," the steward said enthusiastically. "And now we finally meet, and on such an auspicious day!" He grabbed Hugo's hand and shook it vigorously. "May I extend to you my most heartfelt welcome to Lyden Hall, as well as my congratulations on your imminent nuptials?"

"Thank you," Hugo said, thinking that this man would stand up for him at his wedding only over his dead body. "Now if you do not mind, I would like to enjoy my breakfast in quiet. After that, we will speak."

Reginald Coldsnap's face fell. "I beg your pardon," he said, clasping his bony, oversized hands at his equally bony chest. "I did not mean to intrude on your privacy.

It is only that Lord Eliot and I always began the morning together in this room going over the accounts. I suppose I fell prey to force of habit."

"There is not need to look so downcast, Coldsnap," Hugo said, relenting slightly. "I am not accustomed to going without my morning coffee in my bedchamber, and I certainly never confront accounts of any kind until *after* my breakfast."

"I understand, my lord. Would you be agreeable to meeting me in the study in a half hour's time? I would not press, but there are matters which simply will not wait—accounts long overdue, wages left unpaid, that sort of thing."

"What do you mean by 'that sort of thing'?" Hugo asked with a frown as he helped himself to a cup of coffee and took his seat. He didn't like the sound of Coldsnap's tone at all. Not one bit.

"You would like me to tell you now?" Coldsnap asked nervously, adjusting his glasses.

"Given that you've just sounded such a loud alarm, you cannot seriously think I will breakfast in peace?" Hugo shot him a cold look. "Get on with it, man. What is the damage?"

Reginald Coldsnap looked down at the table. "This has nothing to do with damage per se, my lord. Lord Eliot ran Lyden competently, very competently indeed. The trouble comes from the interim period since his death."

"Yes?" Hugo said impatiently. "And?"

"The trustees of Lord Eliot's estate were reluctant to extend any monies on the property, so my hands have been largely tied."

"Tied?" Hugo said, draining his cup and going to refill it. Now that the coffee had fortified him, he was willing to look at the various covered dishes that littered the sideboard. He filled a plate with kidneys, boiled eggs, and kippers. "Why have your hands been tied?" he asked, settling himself back in his chair. "You are the steward. Surely you acted as you saw fit?"

"No, my lord. The trustees refused to authorize any expenditure over what they considered absolutely necessary. Therefore, the various improvements that Lord Eliot and I had planned did not take place."

"What sort of improvements? Everything looks just fine to me."

"Perhaps around and about the house, but tenants' cottages have not been mended, drainage ditches have not gone in, cattle have not been moved to the appropriate fields to allow for crop rotation. Virtually everything was put on hold." He shrugged. "As I said, my hands were tied. I prayed for a buyer, one who would be willing to see to the necessary work, and as quickly as possible. After two long years of frustration you came along, my lord, the answer to my prayers. I do hope I was not mistaken?"

He peered at Hugo through his glasses, his eyes so distorted through the thick lenses that they looked twice the normal size. Hugo felt as if he were being pinned by the gaze of a very large bug.

"What do you expect me to do, Mr. Coldsnap?" Hugo asked, looking around for some sign of buttered toast.

"Well, my lord. It is up to you to bring the estate back to its previously flourishing condition." Reginald Coldsnap pulled out a handkerchief and mopped his brow. "It will take money and a good bit of it. Lord Eliot never begrudged pouring a large percentage of his profits back into the estate, but the trustees have allowed only a tiny portion of the estate's income to be released."

"Why is that, Mr. Coldsnap? Surely the trustees of Lord Eliot's estate would have wished to see it thrive?"

"No, my lord. They had no interest in anything but milking as much as they could from Lyden so as to increase the value of the trust—and therefore their commissions, I suspect. You see, Lord Eliot's will stipulated that Lyden be put on the market at the time of his death, and the trustees reasoned that any improvements should be the responsibility of the new owner, not of the trust."

"Oh," Hugo said, not really caring about the late Lord Eliot's trust or his trustees.

"So you see, we have fallen far behind, and as a result, income has dropped terribly, although the percentage of income allotted by the trustees has remained the same. Every last penny of what we do have has been used just to keep our heads above water."

"Mmm hmm," Hugo said, annoyed in the extreme. He had bought Lyden Hall to support him, not the other way around.

"It is not just the estate that is in trouble," Coldsnap persisted. "Good people who have long lived under the care and protection of Lyden have been struggling to make ends meet. We have yet to evict a family—I have managed to find ways to prevent that to date. However, without your help . . ." He trailed off, then pushed his glasses up on his nose and stubbornly resumed his attack. "These people are dependent on you, my lord."

Hugo felt an unfamiliar twinge of conscience. He'd never been responsible for anyone in his life save for himself, and he hadn't done a very good job even at that. He *had,* after all, bought Lyden with the intention of proving his reformed character first to his family and then to the world. What better way than to save some struggling tenants who happened to be his very own?

"How much money is this going to take, precisely?" he asked cautiously.

"A good fifty thousand pounds, my lord." Coldsnap mopped his brow again.

"Fifty thousand pounds?" Hugo nearly choked.

"I realize that fifty thousand sounds a very great deal.

But you did get the estate at a very reasonable price, everyone knowing what the troubles were after Lord Eliot died."

Hugo rubbed his hands over his face. Why didn't his brother ever have these troubles?

With an inward groan, Hugo belatedly remembered his mother's warning about acting without thoroughly investigating the situation.

"Let me see if I have this right: You are telling me, Mr. Coldsnap, that not only can I not reap any profits from my own estate, but now I have to dig heavily into my pockets to shore it up?"

"Yes, that is what I am saying, my lord. However, if you make the investment, I can nearly guarantee that Lyden will pay back double your money in a bit of time—perhaps even within the year. The income from the estate would also be vastly increased as a result."

Double his money? Hugo rather liked the sound of that. Once he married Meggie, he'd have four hundred thousand pounds—well, two hundred thousand, anyway, after paying Waldock. Fifty thousand wasn't so very much to put out, not if he'd see the return within a year.

"Yes," he said slowly. "It wouldn't do to let the tenants suffer or to let Lyden slip any further downhill. Double my money, you say, as well as increase my income?"

"Indeed, my lord," Coldsnap said, leaning forward with an eager expression.

"Well, I do believe in wise investments, and I have the money at hand. I am always interested in building my financial holdings."

"Ah," Coldsnap said, nodding with satisfaction. "So you are a man of business. I am pleased to hear it. Forgive me, my lord, but so often men of your . . . status, shall I say, are interested only in spending money, not in making it. I have seen more cases of lives wasted, if not ruined, by self-indulgence."

Hugo colored, feeling as if Coldsnap had somehow seen through him. "That is not the case here," he replied tightly.

"Indeed not, my lord. You are clearly a man who understands the meaning of responsibility. My heart is gladdened to say that you take after Lord Eliot, and I cannot say enough fine things about him, God rest his soul."

Alarmed to see a mist forming behind Reginald Coldsnap's spectacles, Hugo smiled weakly. "I am complimented by your good faith."

"Lyden is indeed fortunate to have you," Coldsnap continued, moving his handkerchief to his nose and sniffing loudly. "It will be a joy to have you and your wife here, Lord Hugo, it will indeed."

"Thank you," he said dryly. "You are very kind. I hope my wife and I will prove ourselves worthy of your confidence."

Oh, *God.* What had he gotten himself into? Not only had he inherited two batty spinsters, he'd also inherited a myopic steward overflowing with sentiment. And that wasn't even taking into consideration the lunatic—though extremely desirable—wife he was about to acquire.

Coldsnap leaned a little closer, his needle nose positively twitching. "Speaking of confidence, my lord, tell me. Do you ever invest on the 'Change?"

Hugo had never invested in anything but pleasure before buying Lyden Hall, but he saw no reason for Coldsnap to know that. He rather liked being regarded as a man of business. "On occasion," he lied. "Why do you ask?"

Coldsnap lowered his voice to a near whisper. "If you are interested in lucrative investments, then I would advise you to listen to Ottoline and Dorelia Mabey. Lord Eliot told me they have a genius for the 'Change."

"You cannot be serious," Hugo said, hiding a derogatory smirk in his napkin. The Mabey sisters couldn't hold two thoughts together, let alone know a sensible investment from a hat pin.

"I am perfectly serious," Coldsnap said. "Lord Eliot followed their every suggestion."

"Did he?" Hugo replied, wondering if Linus Eliot had possessed any common sense at all. If Eliot really had allowed the Mabey sisters to rule the roost, let alone been mad enough to listen to their advice on finances, it was little wonder that Lyden was now in trouble.

The whole truth became obvious to Hugo: The real reason for the trustees' hard line was that they'd been trying to salvage what they could from what Eliot had left behind, not that they were greedy, as Coldsnap had implied. No wonder the price of Lyden had been severely reduced. Eliot had left no money to support it.

Oh, well. No need for *him* to worry. He'd be a rich man in a matter of hours. All in all, he'd done very well for himself, the small matter of Lyden's present financial difficulties aside. He would show everyone what a clever man of business he really was by bringing Lyden back from the brink of collapse. With a little effort, he could make it one of England's showplaces.

He wiped his mouth and tossed his napkin aside, feeling much better, even magnanimous, now that he'd eaten. "When do you need this money?" he asked.

"As soon as humanly possible," Coldsnap said. "That is, when you can, my lord. May I make expenditures based on your promise, then?"

"Naturally," Hugo said. "What is the use of having money if not to put it to some good use? Forge ahead, my good man. Let us reclaim Lyden's former glory, shall we?"

Coldsnap actually leapt to his feet. "Let us indeed, my

lord. We will meet the challenge and we will emerge victorious!" he cried, as if he were Henry the Fifth about to launch the battle of Agincourt. "You have a few hours to spare until your marriage—why do we not make a beginning at surveying the property? I will introduce you to some of those whose lives you are about to restore. What more worthy a gift to your tenants on your wedding day than this news? They will forever be grateful, not to mention forever loyal to you!"

"Yes," Hugo said, seeing a pleasing image of himself riding about in style, heaping beneficence on his tenants. It *was* a worthy gesture. He could more than make up for his undignified arrival yesterday with such a gesture. This would be his proper homecoming.

Yes. That was it. He would take one of his perfect white geldings and prance elegantly about, accepting his tenants' homage most graciously on this, the day of his wedding.

He couldn't have choreographed anything more perfect himself. "Do let us get started," he said to Coldsnap. "We haven't all that much time."

"Indeed not, my lord." He beamed at Hugo. "You will give great happiness, I assure you."

Hugo, by this time feeling so filled with happy visions of his future along with *bonhomie* toward Reginald Coldsnap for having provided the means for a triumphant arrival, stood and merrily slung his arm around the older man's gaunt shoulder.

"Proceed, Coldsnap," he proclaimed. "We shall announce the good news to all concerned that they have a new lord, one who will return them to prosperity. Organize some kind of celebration in the village tonight for my tenants so that they know it for truth—a feast, perhaps. Say it is in honor of my wedding."

"A splendid idea," Coldsnap said with satisfaction. "I

will confer with Cookie and the Misses Mabey about what can be put together at such short notice, then meet you outside. Oh, it is a fine day, sir, a fine day indeed."

Hugo rather agreed with him.

13

"Lift them up, Ottoline, lift them up," Dorelia mumbled through a mouth full of pins.

Ottoline obliged her sister, yanking Meggie's arms above her head while Dorelia fiddled with the side seam of the white lace and satin dress she was attempting to fit to Meggie's body.

"Mmmph," Dorelia said. "Down again."

Ottoline yanked Meggie's arms back to her side.

Meggie didn't mind being pushed and pulled about, and talked about as if she were not there. She was too busy thinking about what would happen once the dress came off again. If she could stay awake, that was.

She'd hardly slept the night before, not very surprising considering what had happened to her in only a few short hours. One minute she'd been plain old Meggie Bloom going about her daily chores as usual. The next minute she found herself affianced to a duke's son, swept away to his grand estate, dressed in silk, and fed lobster and meringues. Not to mention being kissed good night as if she were the most beautiful, desirable creature on earth.

And she'd thought such things only happened in fairy tales.

Meggie smiled to herself. At some point in her life she must have been very, very good for God to be rewarding her so, although she couldn't recall when that might have been.

"Lovely, lovely," Dorelia said, hopping up from her knees and admiring her handiwork. "Oh, the memories this brings back of darling Lally's wedding day. She looked so charming in this dress, do you remember, Ottoline?"

"Really, Sister, do you think I am losing my wits? Naturally I remember. I also remember how pale and nervous she was, unlike our dear Meggie here." Ottoline regarded Meggie thoughtfully. "Of course it was little wonder, Lally having been sheltered all her life," she added with the raise of an eyebrow. "The dear was a complete innocent. She even swooned before entering the chapel. If *you* remember, Sister."

Meggie blushed furiously, wondering if Ottoline somehow knew about the fevered kiss Meggie had exchanged with Hugo.

"Ottoline!" her sister said in a reproving tone. "Not all brides swoon before their wedding. In any case, Lally's nerves were always delicate. Meggie has not enjoyed a life where she could indulge in the same delicacy of disposition."

That was true enough, Meggie thought to herself. Heaven forbid if the nuns had ever caught her displaying anything but fortitude.

"*I* consider Meggie's demeanor to be suitably serene," Dorelia continued. "Why should she be nervous when she knows she has made a wise choice?"

Meggie prayed that was the case. She'd spent a portion of her sleepless night quaking with fear that she didn't have the first idea what she was doing.

Ottoline took the slippers Dorelia handed her and brushed the toes with her sleeve. "Did I tell you, I saw dear Hugo leaving the house with Reginald. He gave every appearance of being cheerful, so perhaps I was mistaken about a certain surliness of temperament."

She put the slippers on the ground and nodded toward Meggie, which Meggie assumed meant she was to step into them. Fortunately they just fit. Meggie envisioned Ottoline happily removing a toe or two if they'd proved too tight.

"Cheerful? It *is* dear Hugo's wedding day," Dorelia pointed out to her sister. "He has every reason to be cheerful. We shall have to wait and see about his temperament. Time will tell, time will tell."

Meggie had wondered about Hugo's temperament herself. She had noticed a tendency toward moodiness, but she had attributed his bouts of irritation to exhaustion. Oh, she did wish she could tell at least a little something about what went on inside his head.

Still, she'd learn about him soon enough, and in the normal way that people went about discovering each other's nature. She supposed her failure to read him really was for the best, maybe even the blessing Sister Agnes seemed to think it was.

"Now for the finishing touch," Ottoline said, pushing Meggie down into a chair without ceremony. She placed a delicate lace veil on Meggie's head, arranging it so that it trailed down Meggie's back.

Dorelia clapped her hands together in delight. "Perfect. Where is the wreath of flowers I made, Ottoline?"

"Outside on the balcony where you put it yourself not an hour ago," her sister replied impatiently. "Ha! You worry about *my* wits going wandering?"

"There's no need to be rude," Dorelia snapped, retrieving the wreath and securing Meggie's veil with it. "Yes," she said, regarding the effect with pleasure. "Very nice indeed. I *am* clever, even if I do say so myself."

"What about me, may I ask?" Ottoline said, scowling. "I had every bit as much to do with the final result as you. Really, Dorelia, sometimes I think you should have taken to the stage where you could have stood in the spotlight all day and night."

Meggie ignored their squabbling, standing up and

walking to the cheval glass that stood against the far wall.

A woman gazed back at her who bore almost no resemblance to the Meggie Bloom she knew. Which was just as well. The Meggie Bloom she knew would have been digging in the asylum garden just about now, or calming a distressed patient, or cleaning food off the walls where the same distressed patient had just finished flinging it.

On the other hand, the woman who looked back at Meggie was someone she knew not at all. This woman had lived a life of refinement. She knew all about table settings, calling cards, and what dresses to wear at what time of day, had servants to put those dresses on and take them off and clean them and press them and put them away again. This woman was an aristocrat.

Yet there was something oddly familiar about her . . .

Meggie suddenly realized what it was. Ottoline and Dorelia had done their best to recreate history. Meggie knew because she'd noticed a portrait hanging on the wall as she'd gone down to dinner the night before. It was a painting of a young fair-haired woman in exactly this dress, gazing into the distance as if she was dreaming about the most blissful—and private—things.

Meggie looked just like Lally Eliot in the portrait painted a good thirty years before, complete with the wreath on her head.

She smothered a laugh. Dorelia and Ottoline Mabey were too dear for words. They had loved their younger cousin, that much was obvious, and in their own way they honored Meggie by trying to cast her in Lally's exact image, or as close to it as they could get.

Meggie could only be honored in return.

"Thank you," she said, turning from the glass. "You have been very kind."

"Ah, child." Dorelia's wrinkled face broke into a great smile. "You are our family now, and we are so pleased to stand at your side on this great occasion. It is a shame you do not have a mother to be here with you, but that cannot be helped."

"Who *was* your mother, dear?" Ottoline asked, her brow crinkling. "I have been putting my mind to the question, taking into account your being orphaned, but there are so many Blooms running about this part of Suffolk that sorting one out from the other becomes impossible."

Meggie looked down at her hands. The last subject she wished to discuss on this happy day was her mother. "Her name was Margaret," she said reluctantly, her voice low.

"Margaret?" Ottoline's fingers fluttered on her chest. "Is that so? What was your father's Christian name, child? Which branch of the Blooms did he come from?"

"I don't know his given name," Meggie said simply. "I don't know anything about him except that he died before I was born. I don't really know anything about either of them."

She declined to say that not only did she not know her father's Christian name, she didn't even know his surname.

"Dear me," Dorelia said. "How very unfortunate. You know nothing? Nothing at all?"

Meggie sensed alarm from both of them, which she supposed was understandable. "Only that my mother was all alone in the world after my father died," she replied. "No one told me anything else."

"How extraordinary," Ottoline said, exchanging a quick, glance with her sister.

"I don't suppose *you* know anything about her?" Meggie asked, wondering why they both looked so uncomfortable.

"Know something?" Ottoline said, twisting a finger in her hair.

"*I* never knew a Margaret Bloom, did you?" Dorelia said, glaring at her sister.

"Never did, never did," Ottoline agreed. "Well, never mind. As I said, the region abounds with Blooms. Always has. Yes indeed, it always has."

"Please," Meggie said, looking back and forth between them. "If you do know something about my mother, will you tell me? I can't help but feel you are keeping something from me."

"What you feel are nerves, dear," Dorelia replied brusquely. "I didn't think you would display them, but there they are, and little wonder, since it is time for the ceremony to begin."

Meggie, effectively distracted, clenched her hands at her side, her mouth going dry. "Now?" she asked. "Right now?"

"Yes. The chapel is only a short distance away, but we really ought to make our way."

"The chapel?" Meggie repeated in confusion. "Are you sure? Hugo told me last night that we were to be married in the drawing room."

"The drawing room indeed," Dorelia said, waving her hand as if a bad smell had violated the air. "It is time you begin to disregard most of what your husband tells you and start listening to those who know better." She sniffed loudly. "You are being married in the family chapel. *Now,* dear. We really should be going, as it doesn't do to keep the vicar waiting."

Meggie's heart overflowed with gratitude. She would be married in a church, after all. Her vows would be sanctified at an altar. On top of all that, she actually wore a white dress and veil and a wreath of flowers on her head.

She couldn't have asked for anything more. All her dreams had come true at last.

It wasn't as easy as he'd thought, Hugo realized as he stood at the altar.

He wished he were still out playing indulgent lord to his needy tenants. *That* had been satisfying. He had received enormous gratification without having to expend any effort, other than making promises for the future. His tenants had applauded him, made him feel important, practically kissed his hand as he'd rode along.

No wonder Rafe enjoyed his estates so much. He obviously reaped the same sort of adulation ten or twenty times over if one took in the measure of his properties and multiplied the number of adoring tenants.

Standing here in this chapel, on the other hand, did not feel so fine. Not only was there not an adoring person in sight, but the bloody Mabey sisters had arranged his wedding in a church. Very well, a chapel, he amended sourly. It was the same damned thing in the end.

Taking meaningless vows in front of a God he didn't take much note of and had even less faith in was like blasphemy. Well, if not blasphemy, at the very least a church wedding seemed absurd, a charade. He was marrying strictly for practicality. Nothing more came into it. Meggie—well, Meggie herself he could handle.

Oh, and he'd handle her well, he thought with a lazy grin, and when that ceased to be interesting, then he'd see to it that she lived a life of comfort tucked away in a corner of Lyden with a caretaker to see to all of her needs.

Where the devil was she, anyway? Trust Meggie to forget her own wedding. She'd probably forget her own lovely head if it wasn't attached to her equally lovely shoulders. He drifted off into a daydream about Meggie's shoulders and what lay immediately below them.

Reginald Coldsnap cleared his throat and nudged Hugo in the side.

Hugo looked back at the door. His heart nearly ceased beating in his chest.

Meggie stood there, an angelic vision in white again. Only this time the nimbus about her head revealed itself as a backlit wreath of flowers; the ethereal effect heightened by the veil that fell from her head and about her shoulders. Her dress, fashioned from some diaphanous material, caught the same light streaming in from the open door of the chapel.

But Hugo now knew that although Meggie Bloom might look like an angel, there was absolutely nothing angelic about her. He really didn't know how he'd gotten so lucky—a few vows and Meggie would be all his to take to bed and educate. That would be one sort of education that Meggie Bloom would absorb readily, he was sure of it.

He smiled as he stepped forward to meet her, holding his hand out to her.

She took it easily, handing her posy to one of the two Mabey sisters who had appeared out of nowhere. He supposed they'd been hiding behind Meggie's veil as she walked up the aisle. And then she smiled at him in return. This time it was not one of her empty, mindless smiles that made him think no one was home behind her pretty face, but a smile of real joy that shone through her eyes and sent a jolt straight through him, leaving him breathless and off-balance. Just like being struck by lightning, he thought uneasily, and struck not for the first time, but for the second.

If he'd had more faith in God he might have taken it as an omen, but instead he put the experience down to nerves. Forcing his gaze from Meggie, he fixed it firmly on the vicar.

As soon as the man started his drone, Hugo forgot all about Meggie and her smile and her eyes and her body. All he could think of was the permanence of what he was about to do.

Meggie might be lovely to him now, but what happened when the physical attraction wore off, as it always did with time? What happened when he grew weary of her tiresome prattle—or even worse, what happened when her brain disorder became obvious not just to him, but to everyone else? Suppose her condition deteriorated? He might end up with a dribbling, screaming full-fledged lunatic on his hands. He might have to lock her in the west wing and throw away the key. He might even have to lock his children away with her if they turned out the same way.

A sweat broke out on his brow. Four hundred thousand pounds, he reminded himself. Salvation from ruin. Yes, that was it. Much better.

"Lord Hugo?"

He looked at the vicar blankly. "Yes?"

"I said, wilt thou, Hugo Philip Michael George, have this woman to be thy wedded wife, and so on, finishing with loving her, comforting her, honoring her, and keeping her in sickness and in health—and forsaking all others, so long as ye both shall live? Did you not hear me, my lord?"

"Oh. Beg your pardon. I didn't. I mean, I will. I will do all of those things." Hugo thought he might be sick on the spot.

"Very good," the vicar said, nodding at him in encouragement. "And Meggie, wilt thou have this man to be thy wedded husband—"

"Madrigal," she said.

Hugo shut his eyes. It had already begun. "Meggie," he murmured, "just say you will."

"I will not," she said indignantly. "It wouldn't be right."

"Oh, for the love of God, this is no time for one of your fits!" he said impatiently. "We're in the middle of our wedding!"

"I do realize that," she said, glaring at him. "I am only asking that I be addressed by my proper name, which is Madrigal, when I take my vows. And I do not see how asking to be called by my proper name constitutes a fit."

"Madrigal? What sort of a name is that?" Hugo demanded, nonplussed.

"Madrigal is the name I was given by my mother at birth, and the name I was baptized with," she retorted. "I am sorry if you don't like it, my lord, but there it is. And I would like to be married using it, if you don't mind."

"Meggie, I wouldn't care if your name was Jezebel. Just get on with it, will you?"

"It is actually Madrigal Anna," she said. "The full usage would not go amiss, given that you've just had your own roster of names trotted out. And there's no need to be rude."

The vicar cleared his throat. "Might I suggest you have this discussion later? You are in the middle of your vows, after all."

Hugo nodded curtly, ready to strangle Meggie. "Proceed, vicar."

"Wilt thou, er, Madrigal Anna, have this man to be thy wedded husband . . ."

The rest of the service went without interruption.

Meggie blinked as she emerged into the sunlight. A married woman—she was actually a married woman. She could hardly believe it.

She could also hardly believe Hugo's performance in the chapel, daydreaming in the middle of his vows, interrupting the vicar, and taking umbrage at her request to be addressed by her full name. This after he had greeted her in the chapel with a smile of such warmth and welcome that it had made her heart sing with happiness.

What sort of man *was* he? She looked down at the shiny gold band on the fourth finger of her left hand, knowing that it tied her to him for life, and began to wonder just what she had done.

If she didn't know better, she'd think he really was a madman. His moods swung back and forth like a pendulum, but not in any predictable fashion.

At the moment he was perfectly affable, shaking hands with the vicar and Mr. Coldsnap and heartily accepting their congratulations as if he'd never had a moment's disagreeableness inside. Indeed, he was behaving as if he were the only one who had been married.

She might have been a piece of statuary for all the attention he was paying her.

"My dear child," Ottoline cooed, patting her arm, "it's so very thrilling, don't you think? Fancy your given name being Madrigal—why, you could have knocked me over with a feather, and Sister, too."

Dorelia glared at Ottoline. "Nothing knocks me over with a feather. I will, however, allow that yours is an original name. And the ring it has: Madrigal Montagu. Lovely. Simply lovely. It's a pity you must be called Lady Hugo, not nearly as melodic. Do you play the pianoforte, dearest? You should, with a musical name like yours."

"I do, but not very well," Meggie said, forgetting how annoyed she was with Hugo. At least *someone* liked her name. And she could hardly help but get caught up in the twins' excitement; it burst from them like fireworks. "Sister Prudence at the orphanage taught me a little, not because of my name, but because she thought I might end up being a governess and would need the skill."

"A governess? Goodness, no. How very unsuitable that would have been," Dorelia said.

"Unsuitable?" Meggie repeated uncertainly, worried that Dorelia had worked out the truth about her parentage after all.

"That is what I said. You were destined to be mistress of Lyden Hall, child, not to work for some second-rate family who would look down their noses at you."

Meggie laughed. Apparently Dorelia had simply decided to elevate Meggie's standing now that she'd married Hugo. "You are very kind, Aunt Dorelia, but I'm afraid that I was destined for nothing more than a life of servitude, one way or another. My being here is a complete accident."

"Ha!" Ottoline poked her finger into Meggie's shoulder. "Do you mean to tell me you don't believe in fate? You with your B.G.? Sometimes I have to wonder about the young, I really do. They have no common sense, none at all, isn't that right, Sister?"

"It is only lack of experience," Dorelia said tartly. "You can't really blame Madrigal for not recognizing destiny when she sees it. That's more in the line of your B.G., Ottoline. In any case, the child's modesty is pleasing."

"True," Ottoline agreed. "Madrigal's modesty is one of the first things I noticed about her. Very pretty behavior, I said to myself. She will suit well."

Meggie wondered if they always spoke about other people as if they weren't there beside them, or if it was just she whom they treated in this fashion.

Mr. Coldsnap appeared at Meggie's side, his narrow face wreathed in a smile. "Lady Hugo, this is an honor," he said, bowing over her hand. "Reginald Coldsnap, steward of Lyden Hall, at your service. Allow me to welcome you to your new home and wish you every happiness."

Since no one had ever bowed over her hand before, Meggie felt rather foolish, but Reginald Coldsnap's genuine pleasure warmed her heart. So far the only person at Lyden who had been in any way disagreeable to her was Hugo.

Everyone else had been kindness itself.

"How do you do," she said, smiling back at him. "Thank you for your welcome and your good wishes. This is all very new to me." She felt a concentrated gaze boring into her and realized that Hugo stood only three feet away. He was not listening to the vicar, who was talking a blue streak at him, but to her. "Lyden is so very large, and I am only accustomed to living in a simple manor house," she added for his benefit.

Hugo could make of that what he would, and he could also answer any questions that might arise from her statement. He'd only told her not to mention the sanitarium, and she hadn't, but she wasn't going to lie, either.

"Lyden is large indeed, my lady. I have rattled about it for going on forty years now. I must say, it will be a pleasure to have a young mistress about the place. We have been nothing but old bones here for far too long." He waggled his eyebrows at her. "Perhaps with luck we will be soon be hearing the patter of little footsteps in the nursery."

Meggie blushed, not sure what the polite response was to that pointed statement. "I will do my best to oblige you as quickly as possible," she said, taking a shot in the dark.

Hugo choked.

"That is to say, I love children myself," she quickly amended, thinking she was never going to please Hugo. "I hope to be blessed with many, God willing."

"A very pretty sentiment," Dorelia said, taking Meggie by the arm. "Now say your farewells to dear Reginald, child."

"Are we going somewhere?" Meggie asked, managing a quick curtsy to Reginald Coldsnap before Dorelia tugged her over to Hugo and the vicar.

"Don't ask silly questions," she hissed. "Vicar, what a nice service you performed, despite Lord Hugo's unorthodox approach to the marriage service. Madrigal, dearest, don't you think the vicar did a nice job?"

"I do, and I thank you, sir, for using my baptismal name. I haven't heard it in years." Hugo slipped his hand under her elbow and squeezed it in some sort of warning. "I imagine my husband hasn't heard the full force of his very grand name unleashed in years either," she added, resisting the temptation to yank her arm away.

"I understand completely, my dear," the vicar said. "Had I known your full name beforehand, naturally I would have used it. It *is* customary." He glowered at Hugo.

"Oh, you mustn't blame Hugo," Meggie said quickly. "He's never known me as anything but Meggie. I should have thought to say something to him, but I've been called by my familiar name for so long that I didn't even think about my other one until the moment."

"It is of no matter," the vicar said. "Well, I must be on my way and you must be on yours. Do you go abroad for your wedding trip?"

Meggie's mouth fell open and she gaped at the vicar. "A-abroad?" she stammered. "Oh, no. I've never even been outside of Suffolk."

Hugo pinched Meggie's elbow again, this time hard, and she snapped her mouth shut obediently, thinking she was going to be black and blue by the time he finished muzzling her.

"For the moment we plan only to settle in our new

home," Hugo said smoothly. "My presence is needed here, and my wife will want to make the house her own. Later, perhaps, we will travel."

"If you will allow me to say, Lord Hugo, I think you very wise to turn your immediate attention to Lyden and postpone your personal pleasure for later. I applaud your attention to duty."

"Not at all, Vicar. The well-being of my tenants must be my first priority. I will not have peace of mind until they do. With luck and hard work, the time should not be long before they are prosperous again, and when that time does come, then I shall take my wife on a wedding trip. Not before."

The vicar shook Hugo's hand vigorously. "Thank you, my lord. You ease my own mind, which has been sore with worry these last two years. You will have many grateful souls singing your praises."

"I do not know about that, sir, but I can tell you that when I rode out today to speak to my people, they seemed relieved indeed to know that things will be changing. I intend to hasten those changes by infusing a large amount of capital into the estate . . ."

Meggie listened carefully to the exchange, astonished to learn that Hugo cared so much about people he'd never even met. She felt the strength of the vicar's gratitude and his respect for her new husband. She'd felt the same respect in Reginald Coldsnap as well.

A man who put his responsibility to those who depended on him above his own desires truly was a man to be respected. Just when she'd been questioning the strength of his character, he'd proved her wrong. She felt ashamed that she'd ever doubted him. Clearly his erratic behavior had been caused by nothing more than the strain of taking on so many new burdens, herself included.

All the reservations that had plagued her for the last

eighteen hours melted away in the face of Hugo's obvious goodness.

She was fortunate indeed to be married to such a man.

Overcome by a wave of remorse at her own unsteadiness of character, Meggie covered the hand that gripped her elbow with her own and lightly squeezed his fingers. She was trying to let him know that she was sorry for her earlier temper.

Hugo stopped dead in the middle of a sentence and glanced down at her coolly. The coolness vanished the instant he met her gaze, turning to brilliant blue fire.

Meggie caught her breath. She knew that look. She'd seen it only three times before—the first through Sister Agnes's window, again last night in her room, and again briefly in the chapel when she had first stepped to his side.

It was the look of Hugo Montagu's naked soul.

"Will you excuse us, Vicar?" he said. "You and I will meet again soon to discuss the situation in more detail. I shall write to arrange an appointment."

"Yes. Yes, indeed," the vicar said, his cheeks coloring like two ripe cherries, as if he'd divined the nature of Hugo's thoughts. "Indeed. Good day, Lord Hugo, Lady Hugo. Lovely day. Do enjoy it."

He vanished around the corner.

Meggie looked around to find that she and Hugo were completely alone. "Oh," she said, turning her gaze back to his. "This *is* nice. What shall we do now?"

"That depends entirely on you," Hugo replied, running a finger down her cheek. "You no longer look as if you wish to claw my eyes out, which is helpful."

"Hugo—forgive me," Meggie said, staring at the ground, cursing herself for the quick temper she'd been plagued by all her life.

Even the nuns at the orphanage had been unable to

tame it, despite the myriad punishments they'd inflicted on her. Sister Agnes had been far more gentle with her, but had not failed to point out the same flaw each time Meggie transgressed. "I did not mean to be so difficult. I sometimes act without thinking. I do try to control myself, but I do not always succeed."

His finger slipped under her jaw and he gently raised her face to his. "You must not chastise yourself, sweetheart. You are what you are, and at least you know your limitations. What is important is making an effort to improve, to become better."

"I will," she said earnestly, utterly lost in his gaze. "Truly I will."

He bent his head and touched his mouth to hers, his lips moving softly on hers in the lightest of caresses.

Meggie trembled at his touch, wanting nothing more than to throw her arms around his neck and drag him back into the kiss they'd shared the night before.

She managed to restrain herself. If Hugo had thought that the proper thing to do, he would have done it. Daylight hours were clearly reserved for circumspect behavior among the socially correct.

It did seem a pity, she thought as she reluctantly pulled her mouth away.

"Meggie," he whispered against her temple. "Meggie, what am I to do with you?" The words came out on a long sigh of what sounded like a mixture of longing and regret.

She understood both sentiments completely: the sun still burned high in the sky, and they had what seemed like an eternity to fill before it finally set.

"Shall we go look at the sea?" She reached her hands up, cupping his face between her palms, relishing the slight scratch of beard, the finely honed planes of cheek and jaw. "There are hours left before dusk, and I would be so happy to spend them there. If you don't mind, that is. I have never seen the sea."

"No . . . no, that would be fine," he replied with a strained smile. "You said as much yesterday, and I should show it to you. Why not now?"

"Why not?" she said cheerfully, lowering her hands, since her touch seemed to pain him. Hugo obviously felt as frustrated by their wait as she did, and that made her feel much better—at least she wasn't the only one ready to melt with wanting. "Hugo . . . since Hadrian has never seen the sea either, may we bring him along?" she asked in a small voice, already anticipating his reaction.

He surprised her. Instead of the expected outburst, he shrugged one shoulder. "If it will give you pleasure, why not," he said. "It is your wedding day, after all. I want you to be happy."

"Oh, thank you!" she cried in surprise and delight, thinking all over again what a good, kind man he was. "I am happy—very happy."

"Good. Do you ride?"

"Horses? Well, when I was little, Aunt Emily gave me a pony of my own and I rode him all the time. Then she died and I went to the orphanage, and I haven't been on a horse since. So I suppose the answer is maybe."

Hugo smiled down at her. "Would you like to try? The sea is not very far from here, and I spotted a mare in the stables this morning that might suit you. Coldsnap said she was gentle."

"I would love to try," Meggie said. "You will have to be patient with me, though. I will probably bounce around like a sack of potatoes before ending up on my head."

"I won't let that happen," Hugo replied, taking her hand and squeezing it lightly. "Let's go on up to the house and see if one of those ridiculous women can't find you one of Lally's old riding habits. I'll ask Roberto to saddle up the horses and bring them around front."

Meggie beamed. "It will be an adventure. A perfect, wonderful adventure."

"Something tells me, my dear Meggie," he said, lifting her hand to his mouth and kissing her fingertips one by one, "that life with you will always be an adventure."

"Oh, I do hope so," she replied with a laugh. "I'd so hate to be boring."

14

The mare, a pretty bay with the unimaginative name of Star, stood patiently while Meggie mounted the unfamiliar sidesaddle with the help of Hugo's hand under her foot.

Hadrian intently watched the process, his head tilted and his ears pricked, and Meggie had to laugh. She knew perfectly well what Hadrian thought of Hugo, and the wolf could not be pleased that the man who had already so rudely appropriated his mistress was now putting her in possible danger.

"We're going to the sea, Hadrian," she crowed, picking up the reins. "Just you wait. You can run along the sand—there *is* sand, isn't there, Hugo?"

"I would hope so," he said, swinging up onto his own mount, one of the white geldings.

"Oh, good. You can chase crabs, too—there are crabs, aren't there, Hugo?"

"I will do my best to locate a crab for you," he said, looking amused. "I haven't actually been to this part of the seaside myself."

"Oh. Well, I'm sure there will be lots of things for Hadrian to chase, even if there aren't any crabs. May we go now?"

"Absolutely. As soon as Roberto lets go of her head all you have to do is nudge her with your heel and she ought to walk on. Don't be frightened."

"Frightened? Heavens, whatever for? Star might be surprised to have someone on her back after all this time, but she's perfectly happy to be going out for some exercise, aren't you, poor darling? She's been bored to tears."

"Oh, and I suppose she told you so when you were whispering in her ear?" Hugo said dryly.

Meggie bit her lip. In her excitement she'd spoken far too freely. She would have to be more careful if she was to keep the truth about her gift from Hugo. "It only makes sense," she retorted. "Wouldn't you be bored if you were penned in all the time?"

"I wouldn't know, as it's never happened to me. All right, Roberto, let her head go."

"Be careful, dear!" Ottoline and Dorelia cried in tandem from their vantage point on the steps.

"I will," Meggie said with a wave. "We'll be back before dark."

"No hurry, no hurry. Have a lovely time and mind the high tide." They waved their handkerchiefs wildly as if Hugo and Meggie were going off for a month instead of a few hours.

Hugo turned the gelding's head toward the east and moved off. Meggie urged Star forward, quietly asking her rather than using her heel, which seemed rude. The mare was happy to oblige, taking her place on Hugo's right as if she'd always done so.

"That's another thing," Meggie said to him, after whistling for Hadrian to follow. "I cannot possibly call this dear horse Star."

"You can't?" Hugo said, the corner of his mouth twitching. "Why is that?"

"Because it doesn't suit her. She needs a prettier name, something more lyrical."

"Like Madrigal, perhaps?" he said, casting a sidelong glance over at her, his sapphire eyes dancing wickedly.

"Hugo, do not start up with that again. You needn't call me anything but Meggie, but it's very unkind of you to make fun of the name my mother chose for me. Aunt

Emily told me my mother's last request was that I be called Madrigal Anna. In a way, my name is the only gift I have from her, other than my life, of course, and since she gave her own for mine, I owe her a special honor."

"I beg your pardon," he said quietly, the expression in his eyes sincere. "I didn't mean to upset you. Actually, I think Madrigal a very nice name, just—unusual. How did it come to be shortened to Meggie?"

"I don't remember," she replied. "I suppose Meggie was easier for people, so that's what they called me. It's not so unusual for people to have their names shortened, is it?"

"Not at all. As a matter of fact, my brother's name is Raphael, but his good friends and his family call him Rafe. Everyone else calls him Your Grace," he added with a short laugh.

"Then he's the duke," Meggie said, trying to imagine Hugo's brother, wondering if they looked anything alike. "He must be very grand."

"Rafe? No, not really. He can be annoyingly high-handed, but he doesn't have time or tolerance for airs and graces."

"Are you and Rafe close?" she asked, wishing she'd had a brother or sister to share her joys and sorrows with.

"No, I wouldn't say we were close, exactly," he replied, glancing over at her. "Our natures are very different. For a long time we weren't even friends, but we've ironed out the worst of our difficulties, which I think is a relief to us both."

"Well, that's good. It would be a great pity to have a brother and not be friends. Are there any more of you? Brothers and sisters, I mean?" Meggie knew she was plaguing him with questions, but she knew almost nothing about Hugo beyond what little he'd chosen to tell her.

"No," he said patiently enough, "just Rafe and myself. I suppose there might have been more of us, but my father died when I was a small child, and my mother never remarried."

"I'm so sorry," Meggie said, her heart going out to him. "Losing your father at such a young age must have been very hard. What happened?"

"An accident. I don't remember much about it," he replied curtly. "But let's not think about anything unhappy, Meggie. Today is about the future, not the past. It is a chance for us both to make a new beginning."

Meggie nodded. She liked the sound of that, although she didn't see why Hugo needed to make a new beginning. It seemed to her that he was already doing very well. To her, Hugo was a man who knew his own mind and acted on it without hesitation.

Take her for example. He'd seen her once, decided he'd fallen in love with her and wanted her for his wife, despite her background. Now here she was, riding at his side with a wedding ring on her finger and a brand new name.

It was the same with Lyden Hall. He'd only just arrived to take charge of it, but he'd wasted no time in discovering what needed to be done and how to improve the situation.

Maybe for Hugo a new beginning only meant moving into a new home with a new wife, but for her, life itself had completely changed. Nothing would ever be the same again, and all thanks to him.

"Wave," he said.

"Pardon me?" Meggie asked, startled from her thoughts. "Wave at what?"

Hugo looked at her as if she were an imbecile. "At the people, Meggie, what did you think? You do see the people on my left, just up ahead? Well, those are Lyden tenants. You are their new mistress, so wave at them."

Meggie looked where Hugo had directed, spotting a group of men and women in work clothes standing on the side of the road. The women were bobbing curtsies, the men were respectfully touching the brims of their caps.

Tears started to Meggie's eyes as a flood of goodwill and enthusiasm rushed directly from them to her, filling her with surprise.

She was accustomed to being ignored in the outside world, being invisible. To be welcomed so, as if she was of real importance, as if she actually *mattered,* overwhelmed and awed her. For the first time she realized just how great her responsibilities as Hugo's wife would be. These people were now her people, just as they were Hugo's.

She waved at them with a huge smile, her heart overflowing with gratitude for their unquestioning acceptance of her.

"Enough," Hugo murmured, lowering his own hand. "You need only be gracious. Save your energy for tonight."

Meggie stared at him, then burst into laughter. "Are you afraid I will prematurely tire myself, my lord? I assure you, I am no wilting flower, even if I did faint yesterday. However, that was an aberration, due largely to lack of food and too many shocks, and is not likely to occur again."

"The point," he said, raising his eyebrow, "is that you are a lady now. A lady does not wave like a circus performer. She simply raises a hand and moves it slightly and briefly from the wrist. You may apply the same principle to any physical activ . One wants to appear graceful and restrained at all times."

"Oh?" Meggie said, unable to suppress her laughter. "Are you absolutely sure?"

"Naturally I am sure. Why do you ask?"

"Well, you just told me to save my energy for tonight, although I cannot think what I will need it for if I am to be restrained. But as you wish, Hugo."

He ran a finger back and forth over his eyebrow. "You needn't interpret everything I say quite so literally, Meggie. I was referring to your behavior in front of others."

"That *is* a relief," Meggie said, thinking that sometimes Hugo's sense of humor went entirely missing. Maybe he just didn't like being teased. Or maybe he didn't like to be reminded of her background and how ignorant she was of his way of life. She sighed. Oh, well. Maybe with time she'd learn and he'd forget.

"Meggie—look," he said as they topped the rise of a hill. "There it is. Your sea." He pulled his horse to a halt and pointed.

She stopped alongside him, gazing at the dark, shining water that seemed to stretch forever, then closed her eyes, drawing in a deep breath. So this was how the sea smelled—rich with brine and a myriad of other unfamiliar aromas. The sharp, exuberant scent filled not only her nose, but her head, her heart, her very being, with joy.

She looked down at Hadrian, whose own nose twitched back and forth, his yellow eyes half-closed as he drank in all the delicious permutations she could only begin to guess at with her own limited sense of smell.

She fancied she saw a smile on his face, and she understood why. She could feel the joy running through his blood.

"May we go quickly, Hugo?" she asked, unable to contain her excitement.

"Do you really think you can stay on if we pick up the pace?" he asked, looking dubious.

"Don't be silly. If I've stayed on this long, I don't think I'll fall now. Anyway, I don't have time to fall. Hadrian and I are in a terrible hurry."

Hugo regarded her with absolutely no expression. "Whatever you say, Meggie. I must confess, if nothing else, your confidence is staggering, but I suppose I shouldn't be surprised. Caution only comes with common sense."

"Are you saying I have no common sense?" Meggie said indignantly. "All I asked was to go a little faster."

He released a quick breath. "Very well. Lean slightly forward and keep your hands steady. Try to move with the natural rhythm of the gait, not unlike being on a rocking horse. Perhaps you remember that much from your childhood."

Meggie, who remembered very little but trusted completely in the ability of her mare to keep her safe, just nodded impatiently.

"Stay next to me, and for heaven's sake, whatever you do, don't let the horse get away from you. If she does, sit back, then draw on the reins, which will grind the bit against the sensitive corners of her mouth."

Not on your life, Meggie thought. She couldn't believe anyone would do such a horrible thing to an animal. "Don't worry," she said out loud. "We'll both do very nicely. Let's just go, Hugo. I'm about to jump out of my skin with impatience."

He gave her one last look, then moved forward into a canter.

Meggie instantly followed, finding the mare's gait smooth and easy. She glanced over her shoulder to check on Hadrian who loped just behind, mouth open and tongue hanging out, not in exhaustion but in sheer delight.

Laughing, Meggie leaned forward over the mare's neck. "Go on, girl, run as fast as you please. Give yourself some real pleasure."

The horse tossed her head with a whinny and obliged,

stretching her neck out and lengthening her stride until the road streaked by in a blur.

The wind whipped about Meggie's face, flicking loose strands of hair against her cheeks. She raised her face to the sun, thanking God for giving them all such a perfect moment.

This was freedom, this wild rush to the sea, no boundaries to stop them, no rules or regulations to hold them back. Nothing existed but the sun beating down and the wind blowing hard, the coast only a heartbeat away now.

She glanced over at Hugo to see if he was enjoying himself as much as she, only to find him watching her at that very moment with a smile of amazed approval on his face. She supposed he was thrilled that he hadn't had to scrape her up off the ground just yet.

She grinned at him, then turned her focus back to the fast-approaching beach, her heart pounding with anticipation.

Minutes later they arrived.

"You, my dear girl, are entirely unpredictable," Hugo said, reaching up to help Meggie dismount. "I never know what to expect from you. You say you haven't ridden since you were a little girl, and yet you behave as if riding a horse at breakneck speed is second nature." He parked her on firm ground.

Meggie looked up at him, her hands still resting on his shoulders. Her clear gray eyes filled with her own brand of amusement that he was only just beginning to recognize. "Why shouldn't it be?" she asked. "The mare and I have no argument with each other."

"It has nothing to do with argument, Meggie," he said as patiently as he could manage. "Generally speaking, a certain level of skill is involved in sitting a horse at a gallop."

"Oh," Meggie said, waving her hand in a dismissive fashion. "Well, that may be, but I don't think skill always applies. She happens to be a very sensible animal who knows exactly what needs to be done, which makes up for my own lack of expertise. I've decided her name should be Aria, Greek for the wind, since she runs like it."

"How on *earth* would you know the Greek word for the wind?" Hugo asked, taken aback by her casual statement.

"Oh. I—I suppose I heard it somewhere," she said, her hand slipping to her cheek, coloring as if she'd said something wrong. "All those years of Catholic liturgy must have left their mark." She bent down and began to strip off her boots and stockings, her face hidden from him.

"I imagine so," Hugo said faintly, trying to ignore the tantalizing sight of Meggie's slender ankles. It wasn't beyond reason that a few words might have unwittingly slipped into her head, although by all rights they should have been Latin, not Greek. What other explanation could there be? But why on earth had she looked so mortified, as if she thought it a sin to have a bit of knowledge?

Meggie was becoming more of a mystery by the moment.

For example, take her ability to sit a horse as if she'd not only been born to it but had ridden every day of her life. Yet, she hadn't been on a horse in sixteen years.

It had to be coincidence—perhaps the mare was one of those rare horses who instinctively knew how to carry anyone, no matter their ignorance. Although he had to admit, Meggie had looked completely at ease. Her lithe body moved in perfect conformity with the mare's strides, not a touch of fear on her face even at a full-out gallop.

So perhaps, instead, Meggie was one of the rare naturals who instinctively knew how to ride no matter her inexperience.

Whatever the case was, Meggie was all inconsistency.

One moment she seemed as lost as could be, making no sense, and in the next, she appeared to possess a razor-sharp awareness. If he dared to think it at all, there were times when she actually seemed perfectly normal . . .

Hugo ran a hand over his eyes, knowing that was wishful thinking on his part. He supposed some mentally confused people had their moments of clarity before they became lost again. Anyway, he *knew* she wasn't normal. He'd plucked her from a lunatic asylum, hadn't he?

He watched as Meggie took off toward the water, her long flaxen braid flying behind her, her riding habit hitched up around her knees, exposing shapely calves.

Swallowing hard, Hugo tried not to think about how the flesh of those exquisite legs would feel under his hands. He'd find out soon enough, but first he had to get through the rest of this day. All he wanted was to take her here and now.

He released a slow breath of longing, telling himself to focus on nothing more than a lazy afternoon at the beach.

Meggie's wolf ran at her heels, kicking up small tufts of sand, nudging at her hip, then dancing a circle around her as if to draw her faster toward the sea. Meggie danced with him, laughing and teasing, running forward and back again, then racing away down the beach. Hadrian crouched, then took up the chase, springing at Meggie as he reached her, but careful to miss her by inches.

As he watched them play, Hugo wondered why he'd ever thought the animal dangerous. Hadrian behaved exactly like the most loyal of dogs, perhaps a touch overpossessive of Meggie. He really couldn't be faulted for that, though, Meggie being what she was and helpless to understand danger.

Maybe Sister Agnes had known what she was talking about after all, when she'd said that he was sweet-natured, intelligent, and good at guarding livestock. He obviously didn't worry the horses, nor did he seem to worry the people who came into contact with him. To be honest, the only person whom Hadrian had worried was Hugo himself.

Well. Now that he'd had time to assess the situation in a thorough and logical manner, he could now see that Hadrian was no more threatening than a large dog.

Meggie bent down and picked up a seashell, examining it carefully, rubbing it between her fingers. She lifted it to her face and smelled it, then held it out for Hadrain to smell.

Hugo smiled. Meggie was like a child, exploring the world with all of her senses, eager to share her findings. She took such delight in the simplest things—things he took so much for granted. The taste of lobster, the first drop of wine on her tongue, even the smell and texture of a seashell she rejoiced over.

Hugo hadn't examined a seashell in years.

An irresistible impulse took hold of him, and he pulled off his own boots and stockings and rolled up his trousers.

He walked across the sand toward her, drawn by her enthusiasm. A dim memory stirred in him of the days long ago when life had still been vivid and exciting, a new discovery around every corner. The days before the world had assumed a sameness, a gray dullness that permeated everything. A sameness that brought nothing but weariness and boredom and an urge to find ever-increasing thrills in dangerous exploits and physical excesses.

Emotional numbness could be attained from large quantities of drink.

"Hugo, look," she said, holding out something else she'd found. "It is a crab skeleton, I'm almost sure of it. Isn't it? It has claws with tiny pearly teeth and see here, ridging on the sides of the flat shell." She gently placed it in the palm of his hand.

Twenty-four hours before Hugo might have scoffed at such foolishness. Now he held the little skeleton as if it were the most precious of treasures. "It is indeed," he said. "Which means that there must be crabs scurrying around somewhere. Let's go see if we can find a tidal pool. That would be the most likely place to find a crab." For some reason suddenly nothing seemed more important than finding Meggie a crab.

They spent the next hour or so walking along the beach, poking among the rocks, discovering all sorts of wonders: sea urchins, their glistening round black bodies covered with sharp spikes; fossils of sponges; periwinkles glued to rock faces; and in one pool, a wriggling eel, patiently waiting for high tide to sweep it back out to sea.

Meggie exclaimed over everything, poking and prodding, smelling and stroking. Meggie proclaimed seaweed, which Hugo had previously viewed as slimy and unattractive and to be avoided at all costs, to be beautiful. She pointed out the silky texture it assumed underwater, the graceful sway of the fronds, the rich green hue that only became dark and dull when exposed to air and sunlight.

Hadrian, equally curious, poked his nose into everything, which only served to get his nose nipped by a crab when they finally came across one. He yelped in surprise, then swatted a paw at the crab, sending it flying. When it righted itself, it scurried away in indignation.

Meggie laughed until she cried, and Hugo joined in,

wiping tears from his eyes. The wolf vanished behind a tussock on the dune to lick his imaginary wounds and recover his dignity in private.

Hugo smiled in supreme satisfaction. He'd found Meggie her crab. He felt as if he'd given her the most enormous gift.

They wandered some more, Meggie unearthing a spent seagull egg, a piece of green glass polished smooth by the sand and wind and sea, and a curiously shaped piece of driftwood that made Hugo think of a snake he'd once captured and tried to tame—unsuccessfully.

All these ended up in the coat that Hugo had removed to act as a bundle for Meggie's fast-growing collection. He doubted his coat would ever smell the same again, but he found that he didn't mind in the least.

Finally, when the sunlight began to soften to deep gold and lower steeply toward the west, and the shadows lengthened on the beach, and the tide began to creep up the shore, they found a sheltered place against the dunes. Sitting with their backs resting on the rise of sand, they watched the seagulls flying and screeching overhead, diving into the sea to feed and emerging with wriggling fish in their bills.

Meggie, who hadn't stopped talking in hours, became silent. Her gaze followed the seagulls' swoops until her eyelids grew heavy, finally closing altogether.

Hugo slipped his arm around her shoulders, nestling her in the protective curve of his arm, drawing her head down to rest against his chest as she dozed.

Hadrian lay quietly off to one side, his head resting on his huge paws, but his eyes ever watchful of Meggie.

Hugo released a long breath of contentment, his gaze traveling out over the water as his thoughts traveled inward into the unfamiliar quietude of his soul. Toward peace. Toward Meggie.

He couldn't remember an afternoon that he'd enjoyed

so much, and it had required nothing more than a beach and the company of this woman. Amazing.

Somehow Meggie made everything seem fresh and vibrant to him, as if he were seeing the world through new eyes, Meggie's eyes. Eyes that were clear and untroubled, eyes that made him think of angels. Now he knew that the quality he'd first perceived as ethereal was really nothing more than simple innocence.

Maybe that was what he needed in his life: a good dose of innocence. He'd been so jaded for so long that he'd almost forgotten what innocence was.

This afternoon had reminded him how precious a gift innocence was. He'd known enough women in his time, all of them full of affectations and endless manipulations, to realize that Meggie was a rarity. She had not a trace of pretentiousness in her, no studied mannerisms, no feminine wiles.

God knew, she didn't need any. He desired her to the point of distraction exactly as she was.

His hand stroked over her hair as he thought back to the moment when he'd first stood on Lyden land. Hearing the cries of the gulls from the sea, he had believed that he might actually find happiness here. That his own wings, so long lame, might stretch and take flight. That he might actually find a measure of peace. Of completion.

And here he was, two months later, sitting on a patch of sand with a sleeping wife in his arms, feeling an extraordinary sense of satisfaction.

Granted, he didn't really know her, and she wasn't exactly the sort of wife he had expected to end up with, but he could find nothing to regret. Or at least not at this point, despite her unfortunate mental limitations. Yet without those, would she be the sweet, unaffected girl she was?

The truth was that despite all of her shortcomings,

Meggie made him feel more alive than he had in years. She made him *feel,* period.

Oh, those feelings as often consisted of frustration or annoyance as they did of amusement, but that didn't trouble him. Nor was he bothered by the way he bounced back and forth between these sensations as if he were as demented as she. The point was that he made no effort to suppress any of his emotions.

That alone was astonishing, really, considering that he'd spent his life concealing his feelings from everyone, including himself.

Something about Meggie most definitely touched him, and in a way and place no one had ever touched him before. He only knew it felt good, even familiar in the oddest sort of way.

Maybe he simply felt accepted. Completely accepted. He didn't have to pretend to Meggie. He had no need. She had no expectations of him, and therefore for the first time in his life he was not required to meet any. Meggie was happy simply to be, and as a result she liberated him to do the same. Just to be. It was a unique experience.

Hugo, who'd had little sleep the night before, closed his eyes. The pounding of the surf, the distant cries of the gulls, and the sound of Meggie's soft breathing just beneath his ear provided a gentle, soothing backdrop.

The last thing that occurred to him before drifting off was that he hadn't thought of money in hours.

It was another first.

15

A contentment she had never felt before filled Meggie as she and Hugo slowly rode home. They occasionally exchanged a comment about the passing scenery, but otherwise they preserved a companionable silence. Meggie was glad for it; she needed time to gather her thoughts, to absorb everything that had happened to her in the last few hours. As if the last twenty-four hadn't been startling enough.

But this afternoon had been the first time she'd felt a real sense of connection to Hugo. This afternoon had shown her a side of him that she had only hoped for. He had revealed a capacity for merriment as well as tenderness.

Tenderness . . . she'd thought she was still dreaming when she awoke to find herself in his arms—his temple resting on the top of her head as if he had always held her that way, his chest rising and falling against her cheek in the soft, even rhythm of sleep, and his heartbeat strong and steady beneath her ear.

Drowsily savoring his closeness, she drank in his warm, masculine scent and relished the shape of the hard, sculpted muscles beneath his shirt. The weight of one arm rested loosely across her waist; his other arm draped around her shoulder, with his hand lightly cupping her arm.

He had given her an afternoon she would cherish for the rest of her life, simply because she'd asked.

He, a sophisticated man of the world, had run about in the sand with bare feet, waded in the surf, explored puddles and pools, poked in rocks and dug in holes, all to please her.

She had laughed harder than she could ever remember, reveled in every last moment. And in the process she had lost her heart.

Meggie shook her head in wonder.

She'd actually fallen in love with her husband, just like that. A deep, singing happiness filled her very being, for she hadn't expected God to give her such a gift. It was enough that He'd given her Hugo at all. Now her conscience was clear because she could return Hugo's feelings fully and honestly as he so richly deserved.

She wished she could tell him so.

The trouble was that she didn't know the first thing about how to go about it—she didn't really know the first thing about love, when it came to that. She had loved her aunt Emily, of course, and Sister Agnes, too, but that was a different sort of affection, nothing to do with the love between a man and a woman.

Perhaps if she'd had a mother and a father to learn from, or married friends, or sisters with husbands, she might have felt more confident about how to behave. Instead, she had been raised by an elderly widow and nuns. Men hadn't been any part of her experience, except for the random thoughts she happened to intercept in the few she had come in contact with. And those interior musings *certainly* didn't have anything to do with love.

She was getting the impression that love was not something men liked to speak about. Hugo hadn't said a word about it since his proposal, and even then he'd only mentioned the subject reluctantly. At first all he'd said was that he was "taken" with her.

So maybe speaking of love was incorrect. Maybe ladies and gentlemen considered the subject vulgar, overly sentimental. On the other hand, Hugo had no trouble speaking about lust, so that was obviously perfectly correct.

She sighed, her head aching with confusion. She didn't want to do or say anything wrong, especially not on so important a topic. Oh, well. Hugo was bound to know enough about the proper behavior for both of them. He would show her the way. He would teach her. All she had to do was follow his lead, be silent about those things that he was.

Fortunately, tonight she wouldn't have to say a thing. She could demonstrate what was in her heart with no words at all.

Meggie shivered with anticipation. The sun had nearly set and nightfall was just around the corner.

She looked around, realizing that while her thoughts had been wandering they had changed course, and she didn't have the first idea where they were. This route was different from the one they'd taken going out. It skirted around toward the west, following the river from a deep bend it made along its course, and then wound east again.

Scented pines lined the path they'd turned onto, a liquid wash of rich golden light filtering through their boughs and dappling the ground. Just as Meggie wondered whether she'd entirely lost her bearings, the house came into sight. Her hands froze on the reins.

Lyden Hall was ablaze, brilliant orange flames illuminating all the windows of the west wing.

"Hugo!" she cried in panic. "Hugo, we're on fire!"

He looked over at her and laughed. Their beautiful home was about to burn to the ground and he actually laughed.

"Hugo, for heaven's sake, *do* something," she said, appalled by his indifference.

"What would you have me do, Meggie? Extinguish the sun?"

"The—the sun?" she stammered.

"The sun," he repeated. "Look again."

She did. Of course. The reflection of the sun, setting in the west, had caught in all the hundreds of panes of glass and gave the illusion of fire. "Oh. How silly of me. I should have realized."

"Why? You've probably never seen a house with so many windows. It is an amazing sight, isn't it? This happens at Southwell, too, whenever we have a good sunset. The whole bloody place looks as if it's about to go up."

"Does Southwell have as many windows as Lyden?" she asked, trying to imagine what Hugo's family home looked like.

"Even more," he said. "I'll take you there one day soon and you can see for yourself. It's one of the larger houses in the country."

Meggie's eyes widened. "Really?" she whispered, terribly impressed.

"Really. That tends to be the case with ducal seats. Southwell has been in the family for generations, and every now and then when one of my ancestors developed an urge to build onto the structure, build he would. You could get lost in it for days."

"I could easily get lost in Lyden," she said. "Oh, Hugo, how am I ever going to adjust to being married to you? First I thought I was going to live in a sweet little house, only to discover all of this." She made a sweeping gesture that included not just the huge house but the land as well. "Now you tell me that Lyden is nothing compared to Southwell." She shook her head. "I don't know how I will manage. How does your mother look after it all?"

"She doesn't. There's an enormous staff who looks after it. She merely keeps an eye on them, especially in my brother's absence. Now that Rafe is married he and his wife spend much of their time at their home in Ireland."

"I suppose they have an enormous staff there as well?"

"Large enough to keep everything running smoothly. That is how it will be here, Meggie, once I hire a housekeeper and butler and a proper complement of servants. Were you worried that you would be all on your own?"

"Well, not as worried as I was yesterday," she said honestly. "I realized very quickly that Aunt Dorelia and Aunt Ottoline know everything about running Lyden. Why do we need to hire a housekeeper when we have them? Isn't that a terrible waste of money?"

Hugo snorted. "Dorelia and Ottoline do not run a house, they run a carnival from everything I've seen so far. We have a Gypsy for a footman, a criminal for a cook, and God only knows who else lurks in the bowels of the house. I wouldn't be surprised to discover the laundry woman has two bearded heads. I will know for certain when I discover whiskers in my small clothes."

"Hugo," Meggie said, laughing at his foolishness. "You must be kinder about Aunt Dorelia and Aunt Ottoline. I think them very dear, and they are so thrilled to have us here." She frowned. "That reminds me—I've been meaning to ask you. I gathered from everything I've heard that you only recently bought Lyden Hall."

"Yes, that's true," he said. "I bought it two months ago. Actually, I bought it the same day I saw you for the first time, an interesting coincidence." He flashed a smile at her that made her heart turn over. "I must have known even then that I was going to marry you, and I'd need a house in which to install you. Why do you ask?"

"Only because I wondered how it all works, why the aunties are still living at Lyden when it has been sold away from the original family," she said. "Are you related to them in some way? I was not sure on the point, since you are so rude about them."

"*Related?* Good God, no. I told you, I'd never laid eyes on them before. They came with Lyden like a twin pair of horsehair sofas, all prickle and annoyance and no comfort."

Meggie grinned. "You do have a way with words, even if they are unkind."

"It's called irony, my dear, but I wouldn't expect you to understand. Nor should you."

Meggie refrained from answering. Irony? The true irony was that for an entire afternoon she'd forgotten she was meant to be a dimwit, and Hugo hadn't even noticed her lapse.

Not that they'd touched on subjects that had evoked any exhibition of intelligence on her part—that slip about Aria had been the worst of her mistakes—but she hadn't remembered to be overtly stupid, either.

Maybe if she was careful to keep her exemplary education to herself, she could simply be herself. Wouldn't that be a blessing? Really, all she wanted was to enjoy Hugo's company and to have him enjoy hers, to be in perfect accord with each other just as they had been on the beach. Surely that couldn't be so difficult, even if she wasn't supposed to understand what irony meant or a host of other things.

The bigger challenge was going to be keeping her gift from him, she thought with an inward wince. If he ever found out about that, he'd surely take a disgust of her, and that she didn't think she could bear. He might be wonderfully generous but his generosity would never stretch so far as to accept a wife who divined other people's thoughts. He was bound to see her as just another carnival freak.

"Meggie, why are you looking at me as if I'm a fly on the wall that you intend to swat?" Hugo asked as they pulled up the horses in front of the steps.

"A *fly*?" she said, summoning up a smile. "I did not think men of your station compared themselves to anything less than lions and dragons and such," she teased.

"Surely no fly has ever flown on a ducal standard? Or perhaps I am too ignorant to know any better."

Hugo's face went very still. "Perhaps," he said, dismounting and tossing his reins over the post by the steps. He helped her down and let go of her quickly.

Baffled by his sudden coolness, Meggie wondered what she'd said wrong this time, and then she remembered that he didn't like to be reminded about the differences in their breeding and upbringing. "I'll take Hadrian to the kitchen and see to his supper," she said, trying not to be hurt by his change of attitude.

"Meggie—leave Hadrian there tonight, will you? I'd rather not have him skulking about."

"You're not still afraid of him?" she asked, astonished. "You seemed to get along so well this afternoon."

"Oh, for the love of God," he snapped. "I've never been afraid of the damned beast, as I've repeatedly told you. I'd just like some privacy in the bedroom. You *can* understand that much, can you not?"

"Yes, of course," she said in a thin voice, fighting back tears. "I beg your pardon. I didn't take your meaning at first."

"Never mind," he said more gently. "I forget sometimes that you do not always grasp the point."

"It would help if you tried to be more direct," she said, looking down at the ground, not wanting him to see that he'd upset her. "You can't expect me to read your mind."

The words slipped unbidden out of her mouth, and Meggie choked in horror as she heard them. "I—I didn't mean that," she stammered, her face flushing with heat. "I only meant to say that I—that I . . . oh, never mind!"

She turned and fled into the house, her composure in shreds.

* * *

Hugo watched her go, perplexed by her sudden show of emotion. Here she'd been happy as a lark the afternoon long, as pleasant company as could be, and in the blink of an eye she'd turned into a tearful, jabbering wreck.

He supposed that was what came of mental instability, although to be fair, in his experience women often behaved in this illogical manner. He just hadn't expected it of Meggie. She'd seemed so full of fun on the beach, easy to get along with. So . . . comfortable.

Hugo raked both hands through his hair with a muttered curse. All he'd done was ask her to put her damned wolf in the kitchen, for God's sake. He didn't see what was so unreasonable about that. Anyone would think he'd behaved like an ogre.

Still, he supposed he'd have to make it up to her or she'd be sulking for days, if past experience with the female sex was anything to go by.

Damn. He didn't even have any trinkets on hand to cheer her up with. Baubles always worked well with women, and with Meggie they needn't even be expensive, since she'd never know the difference.

Maybe some nice chocolates would do the trick. With luck there'd be some stored in the pantry. He'd have to lower himself to ask one of the wretched Mabey sisters or the even more wretched Cookie, but he supposed a small lowering of himself was worth the price. He wanted Meggie eager and willing in his bed tonight.

Lord—he'd die if he didn't have her in his bed tonight.

At least he had the solace of knowing that the tears that had threatened were genuine, and not some clever ploy to wring an unwilling concession from him or to make him feel guilty for a real or imagined crime.

If there was one thing he hated, it was a woman who tried to manipulate him by withholding sexual favors. The beauty of Meggie was that she wasn't capable of manipulating her own mind, let alone his.

"Roberto," he bellowed, not accustomed to waiting for a footman to take his horse away.

Roberto did not appear. Naturally Roberto didn't appear, Hugo thought blackly. Why should he? No one paid any attention to Hugo's wishes. No one would even know he was lord of the manor, given the way they summarily ignored him.

Well, tomorrow he'd set things straight. Indeed he would. He and Reginald Coldsnap would sit down and see to the hiring of a proper staff, a staff who showed some respect, not to mention some credentials.

In the meantime, he had to attend to stabling the blasted horses since there was no one else around to do it.

Meggie managed to fight back her tears, diligently taking Hadrian to the kitchen. "Would you mind feeding him and looking after him, Cookie?" she asked. "His lordship doesn't want Hadrian upstairs, you see." She made a feeble attempt at a smile. "I know Hadrian likes you, so I feel comfortable leaving him with you. If you really don't mind, that is."

Cookie patted her shoulder. "Owd doggie and I, we be fine. Leave Cookie to it. I'll fix a nice suffin' for his dinner, and make a bed by the stove. Go on, get along and look after yer man, as it should be."

"Thank you, Cookie," she said, giving Hadrian a hug and whispering instructions in his ear. He licked her cheek, so she supposed he didn't mind being left in the kitchen *too* much with Cookie and all those nice smells.

Once she had reached the privacy of her room,

though, she abandoned all pretense at composure and threw herself on her bed, crying her eyes out, her heart aching with hurt and humiliation.

How could Hugo be so changeable, dear and sweet one minute, and cold and curt the next? He really was awful. He said he loved her, and yet he treated her like—like a silly child who had no sense.

After a few minutes, Meggie sniffed. On the other hand, he'd treated her like that from the beginning, so what was she getting so upset about now? She thought that over for a minute. Really, she *was* being silly. She had only herself to blame for letting her feelings be hurt, only herself to blame for blurting out that piece of idiocy about reading minds.

It was just that Hugo had an uncanny way of cutting straight past her defenses to her very core. She supposed her inability to read him gave him an advantage she was unaccustomed to, for he forever caught her off-guard. And that wasn't his fault, either.

Ashamed of herself, Meggie sat up and dried her eyes, blowing her nose hard. She'd just discovered the first drawback to loving Hugo. No one had made her cry in years, no matter how miserable she'd felt, but he could turn her inside out in moments.

She would have to get used to him, she told herself firmly, or she'd find herself watering everything in sight. Hugo did not mince his words or hide his displeasure. If she was going to love him, then she'd just have to develop a thicker skin. She couldn't take everything he said to heart.

Still, she'd found him a great deal easier to cope with when she'd merely liked him.

A tap came at the door and she wiped her eyes and nose again and forced a smile to her lips. "Yes?" she called.

The door flew open and Dorelia and Ottoline skipped

in, beaming. "Here you are, home at last, dearest," Dorelia chirped. "We have a lovely treat for you, and you're to . . . oh. What is this we have here? Tears, beloved?"

"Horsehair," Meggie said, rubbing at her eyes.

"Absolute nonsense," Ottoline said. "You've been crying, and I wonder why. That silly boy hasn't done anything untoward, has he? If he bedded you in the sand, I shall wring his neck. A girl needs her first experience to be conducted in a considerate manner."

Meggie gulped back a laugh. Ottoline and Dorelia had absolutely no shame about intruding on her privacy. "Nothing like that happened. We had a very nice time," she said. "I'm just tired. I didn't sleep much last night."

"Ha!" Dorelia crowed, bending over to light a fire in the grate of the fireplace. "Don't think you'll make up the lack this night. Pull yourself together, girl. You have a husband to attend to, and I'll tell you this much: He'll expect some satisfaction, not a snoring bride in his bed, and no tears either, if that's what this is all about."

Meggie blushed. "I have no fear of Hugo," she said, raising her chin, "and I have no intention of falling asleep. I just need a little time to myself."

"Then you shall have it, you shall have it," Ottoline said with a self-satisfied smile, clapping her hands. "Roberto, in you come," she called through the open door. "Quickly, quickly, before the buckets go entirely cold."

Roberto instantly appeared, dragging a huge copper hip bath that he placed in the middle of the room. He instantly dashed out again, returning with two buckets of steaming water that he splashed into the tub. Ottoline and Dorelia fetched two more each, and so they all continued until the bath was full.

Meggie stared speechlessly. This was for *her*? For her, Meggie Bloom, who had not experienced anything more than a sponge bath in more years than she could count, and those mostly in cold, if not freezing water?

"Well, child? What are you gaping at now? Clothes off."

Meggie looked pointedly at Roberto who was going around the room lighting candles.

"Oh," Dorelia said. "Yes, of course. All right, Roberto, thank you. You may go now. I will finish that."

He bowed and vanished, closing the door behind him.

Within moments, Ottoline had Meggie stripped naked, while Dorelia took a bottle from her pocket and poured the contents into the tub. The most delicious fragrance drifted up from the water, making Meggie think of a flower garden in midsummer.

"My own decoction that I blended just for you," Dorelia said, taking a deep sniff from the bottle. "It will relax you, dear. Pelargonium to steady the nerves, helichrysum for acceptance, lavender to calm apprehension, and rose, the queen of flowers, for purification—and of course love. In you get, child."

Meggie slipped down into the silky water. "Oh," she breathed, immersing herself up to her shoulders. "Oh, this is pure heaven." She closed her eyes and exhaled, all of her muscles relaxing in the delicious warmth.

"Here's the soap, dear. Rose-scented, naturally. I'll put it just here on the side. Come along, Ottoline, let us leave the girl to her ablutions and her thoughts. She has a big night ahead of her."

"Thank you so much, aunties. You are very dear."

She heard the rustle of their skirts as they tiptoed out, softly shutting the door behind them.

Meggie smiled, feeling infinitely better already. They really couldn't be any sweeter to her, she thought, just the way she imagined proper aunts might behave toward a favorite niece. Or a great-great niece.

And my, weren't they free with their advice? Although Meggie was beginning to think she was not only wanton, she was positively unnatural. From what she'd gathered from the aunties, all brides should be nervous wrecks on their wedding night.

She, on the other hand, couldn't wait. Hardly surprising, she supposed, considering her tainted bloodline. That wasn't all she looked forward to, either. She knew that afterward, when they had spent their passion, they would lie quietly in each other's arms. She with her head resting against his chest, his heartbeat strong and steady against her ear, just as it had been earlier.

Meggie slipped down even farther in the bath and daydreamed about Hugo holding her tight against him, keeping her safe against the night.

Oh, it was nice not to be alone anymore . . .

16

Deciding against chocolates after all, Hugo picked Meggie a bouquet of flowers from the garden. She liked gardens; she seemed to like anything to do with nature. His coat bore testimony to that.

He cursed as he pricked his finger on a particularly vicious rose thorn. The things he did for Meggie . . .

At least he felt sure that she'd be pleased with his offering. Bunching the flowers together, he carried them and the bundle that had once been a perfectly good jacket back to the house and marched upstairs. He managed to avoid the two old bats—fortunate, since he was in no mood to put up with any of their nonsense.

Roberto was still nowhere in sight, but at least a fresh pitcher of water stood next to the washbasin. He tested it with his finger. Lukewarm. What else had he expected?

Hugo blew out his cheeks in frustration, but decided there was no point in making a fuss. The chances of anything coming of it were slim to none. He quickly stripped before the water cooled altogether and gave himself as thorough a bath as he could manage in the small bowl.

When he'd finished washing and shaving and dressing, he stuck Meggie's flowers in the pitcher, then fetched his coat, and deposited her treasures in the soapy bowl of water to soak. As an afterthought, he opened the French doors to the balcony and took the bowl outside so that his room wouldn't be permeated with the smell of rotting fish.

The things he did for Meggie, he thought again, leaning his elbows on the balustrade and gazing down over the inky black expanse of lawn that ran down to the river. He glanced up at the indigo sky, streaked by fingers of vermilion. No moon yet, although it would certainly rise later and light up the water with silver, he thought idly. That would be nice.

Somewhere in the distance an owl hooted—a long, hollow series of notes that caused a chill to run up and down his spine.

He didn't know why the call of the owl always disturbed him, only that it made him think of love and loss, of emptiness and regret.

Something rustled in the tangled vine of wisteria that climbed up the stone wall behind him. He turned to see a blue tit busily adjusting its nest, four tiny heads poking out of the weaving. He'd have to show Meggie, he thought with a smile.

Oh, it was nice not to be alone anymore . . .

The words came out of nowhere, as clear in his head as if they'd been spoken aloud.

"What the devil?" he muttered, spinning around to see if someone stood near the balcony doors. No one was there. Of course no one was there. He knew that.

Hugo scratched his head. He didn't think lunacy was contagious, but Meggie seemed to be having all sorts of strange effects on him. It was just the sort of absurd thing she might say.

Meggie . . . what an idiot he'd been. Of course. Her room shared the same balcony. If he'd thought of that last night when the damned wolf had been keeping him from her door, he'd have saved himself a great deal of aggravation.

As he walked over to her own French doors, he realized that even if she had spoken, he wouldn't have heard her. The doors were closed against the night.

He couldn't resist peeking inside, since the draperies weren't drawn. His eyes took a moment to adjust, for at first all he could make out was the flicker of candles and the soft golden glow they cast.

It was then that he saw her. She sat in a hip bath in front of a gently blazing fireplace, her head resting against the copper back, her knees drawn up, her eyes closed, her wet hair streaming down over her shoulders into the water and drifting about her sides like a mermaid's.

Her mouth curved up in a half-smile as if she were dreaming something particularly lovely.

Hugo groaned. Whatever she dreamed about couldn't possibly be as lovely as she was in that moment. If there was a heaven on earth, he was looking directly at it.

His fingertips reached out, pressing against the glass as if he might touch her through it. He might caress that creamy flesh, the delicate swell of her breasts that floated on the surface of the water—twin spheres of alabaster tipped by pale pink nipples. And oh, to move his hand over her flat belly down to the triangle of darker hair that he could just barely glimpse, to let his fingers slip through those silken curls to the heart of her feminine flesh.

Meggie. Unbelievably, perfectly feminine. Unbearably desirable.

His groin tightened painfully, his penis swelling and hardening with need. It strained against his trousers so powerfully that he thought the size and thrust of his erection might shred the material. He felt like an adolescent looking at his first woman.

He felt like a Peeping Tom.

Forcibly tearing his gaze away, he stared blindly down at the hand that had flattened against the windowpane, trying to control his desperate, ragged breathing. She was his *wife,* he told himself. He had every right to want her this much, every right to take her there and then if he so chose. Then why did he feel so guilty to be thinking about it at all? Why didn't he simply walk in and have his way with her as he'd done countless times before with countless other women?

His hand came into focus, a sharp recollection forming in his brain of the last time he'd made that same gesture. The only time. It had been to Meggie then, too, through Sister Agnes's window.

Meggie. He shook his head. Why did she cast such an unnerving spell over him, stir his hardened heart, and waken a conscience he'd never paid any attention to before? He'd married her for one reason and one reason only, hadn't he?

Well, all right then, he conceded, gazing up at the sky where the first evening star had made its appearance. Two reasons. He desired her body as much as her money.

But now a different desire had entered the equation, a genuine wish to protect her, to ensure her happiness and her peace of mind. He couldn't put his finger on the exact moment when tenderness had replaced cool pragmatism, when he'd started to put her needs above his own. He knew that their time on the beach had a great deal to do with it, but not everything. Not everything . . .

He had the most peculiar and unsettling sense that this had all begun long before and he was only now realizing it.

His brow knotted and he dropped his arm, turning away from the window and the disturbing direction of his thoughts, away from Meggie and temptation. He'd not take her like a rutting stallion with no mind to anything but his own lustful needs and a quick release from his torment. She deserved far better than that.

He'd take his time, slowly awaken the passion that he knew burned like a slow fire in her blood. He'd had a taste of it last night—oh, how he'd had a taste. She'd sent him reeling with a kiss alone.

But Meggie was a virgin. Untouched and inexperienced. His job as her husband was to introduce her to the pleasures of lovemaking as gently as possible. Later on in their marriage would come the wild lovemaking that he sensed her capable of.

With a regretful sigh, he walked back to his own room, wishing he'd kept the cold bowl of water to dunk his head in.

Finally forced by the cooling water to finish her blissful bath, Meggie stepped out of the tub. She discovered soft, large towels immediately at hand on a stool and tucked one around her torso, using a second towel to rub her freshly washed hair dry in front of the fire. Such unbelievable luxury . . . she might as well be a pampered princess in a castle.

But despite her contentment, she couldn't escape the feeling that something very strange had just occurred. As hard as she tried, she couldn't define the sensation better than that.

Meggie stared into the fire, concentrating fiercely. Still nothing came, not even a glimmer. If she couldn't define the feeling, then surely it had to be connected to Hugo, since he was the only person she'd ever come across who eluded her so completely.

A slow smile crossed her face. Whatever the mystery, she knew no threat came from it. She would wait and see if it didn't unfold by itself. Not knowing things had ceased to bother her and become yet another luxury she'd never experienced. She had every intention of savoring it.

As soon as her hair was dry, she loosely braided it, then went to the wardrobe and pulled out the green dinner dress she'd worn the night before. She noticed with amusement that the black dress she'd arrived in yesterday had disappeared, along with her two white work dresses. Dorelia and Ottoline really hadn't approved.

Struggling with the back buttons, she finally managed to make herself look presentable. The clothes she'd worn in the orphanage or sanitarium had been designed to be put on without assistance, made of rough, serviceable materials such as nankeen or calico, shaped more like sacks with ties than dresses.

A tap came at the door, and she expected Ottoline or Dorelia had come to help her dress. Wouldn't they be surprised to see that she'd coped all by herself? The way they treated her, anyone would think she was a helpless infant.

She ran over to the door. "Look, I'm clean and dry and dressed," she crowed, pulling it open. "Oh! It's you," she finished lamely, looking up at Hugo. "I thought you were the aunties."

"I am relieved I am not," he said, producing a water pitcher stuffed full of flowers from behind his back. "I picked these for you, Meggie. As an apology of sorts."

"An apology for what?" she asked, gazing at them in delight.

"For having been curt with you earlier. I'm sorry, sweetheart. I know I upset you, as much as you tried not to show it."

"Oh, Hugo, I'd forgotten all about it," she said with perfect truth. "Did you really pick them yourself? They're beautiful! No one has ever given me flowers before." She smiled at him blissfully. "I really do feel spoiled."

"I told you, it is my mission in life to spoil you. Where would you like me to put them? If I may come in, that is."

"Of course you may," she said, standing back. "It is your house, you know."

"It is your room," he said with a queer expression in his eyes. "And it is your right to be private, if you wish."

"Hugo—we are married now. Surely you should feel free to come and go as you please?"

He placed the pitcher on a side table and took her hands in his. "I will come and go as I am invited to," he said, his voice very low. He bent and gently kissed her cheek. "Invite me again later. I think we'd best go down for dinner before we miss it altogether."

"You don't really think Cookie would deprive us of our dinner if we were late?" she asked, wishing he'd kiss her again and do it properly this time.

"That wasn't what I meant," he replied, looking down at her, his eyes flickering.

"Oh—I see," she said, blushing, not from embarrassment, but from pure physical reaction to his heated expression. "How silly of me."

"Not at all, but I have learned that you need regular feeding to keep up your strength." He tucked her hand into the crook of his elbow. "And you *will* need your strength."

Meggie smiled happily. "Then feed me without delay, my lord. I am famished, and for more than mere food."

"I am pleased to hear it," he said with a soft chuckle. "You are refreshing in your lack of inhibition, my love. Later we will see how far it stretches."

His love.

Meggie shivered at his gentle reminder that he felt more for her than mere desire. Perhaps this was how one expressed emotion in the aristocracy, couched in small endearments rather than declared in sweeping statements.

She would have to keep that in mind, she told herself

as she descended the staircase at his side, just like a proper aristocratic wife.

"Then to top it all off, I had the loveliest bath," Meggie continued in her exuberant recitation of the joys of the day, between mouthfuls of roast pigeon. "You must have seen the hip bath in front of the fire, though. It is too huge to miss."

"Yes, I saw it," Hugo managed to reply. Oh, indeed I saw it and a great deal more.

A cold sweat broke out on his brow as every last beautiful, erotic detail came back to him. He'd been having a hard enough time keeping himself under control without this ruthless reminder of what waited for him later.

"Aunt Dorelia scented the water with a mixture of flower essences. I thought I'd died and gone to heaven."

So did I, he silently agreed, taking a long drink from his wineglass. "Did you?" he said out loud.

"I did—oh, Hugo, I haven't had a proper bath in forever! I can't tell you what a treat it was—and that after all the other treats today that I've just thanked you for. I should thank you again for my beautiful flowers, too. *That's* how my bath smelled—just like your bouquet."

"Meggie," he said, baldly determined to head off any further discussion of Meggie and her bath. His nerves couldn't take it any more than his groin could. "Instead of telling me about today, most of which I am aware of, why don't you tell me about your previous life?"

He'd been meaning to ask her anyway, with the intention of getting as much background information as possible. Tomorrow he had to write to Messrs. Gostrain, Jenkins, and Waterville to announce his marriage, and it was imperative that he say all the right things. The more details about Meggie's origins that he had, the better.

This way he'd be ready when the solicitors inevitably put the pieces together and decided to inquire further about his wife's pedigree—or lack thereof—before handing over her inheritance.

This morning he'd had no problem with the idea. Why, then, did he now feel so guilty, as if he were a thief stealing not only an inheritance he had no right to, but also a private part of her history?

"My previous life?" she echoed, the smile vanishing from her face to be replaced by a look of hesitation.

"Yes," he said uncomfortably, feeling even worse that he'd wiped the happiness from her eyes. "I begin to think from the delight you take in the simplest, most commonplace things that you had an austere upbringing."

"Orphanages are not meant to be places of luxury," she said, shrugging. "Nor are asylums."

Hugo sighed, remembering about her mental difficulty. "Yes, Meggie. I do realize. I meant before that. When you were with Emily Crewe."

"With Aunt Emily?" she asked, pushing a mound of peas about on her plate. "I told you. I was happy there. She didn't have very much money, but we made do."

"So you were not actually poor. Did your aunt Emily perhaps have a little money from your own family that helped to contribute to your support?"

Meggie gazed at him, her expression puzzled. "But you said . . . you said only yesterday that you understood. About the situation, I mean. That there was no one, no one at all."

"Yes, of course," he said. Damn, it was hard work, pretending to know what he was talking about when he didn't have anything but the vaguest idea. "I only wondered if your aunt Emily was not a distant relation of some sort. After all, she took you in when your mother died. She must have had a reason."

Meggie stared down at her plate, not even bothering to fiddle with her peas now. "She was a good woman. That was her reason."

"Meggie. I'm sorry—I don't mean to upset you by reminding you of your past. But as your husband, surely you can understand that there are details I'd like to know, to better comprehend the nature of your previous life? To better comprehend you?"

"You were so good to marry me at all that I would be churlish not to answer your questions, but I'm afraid that I know very few details myself," she replied, carefully placing her fork and knife on the side of her plate. "What I do know, I will tell you, though."

She took a deep breath and laced her fingers together, resting the fist she'd made directly in front of her on the table. Her face suddenly looked pale in the candlelight.

Hugo could hardly bear to look at her, to see the pain he'd caused her by his selfish demands. "Meggie, wait. If you'd rather not go on, then we'll leave it."

"No," she said, looking up and meeting his eyes. "You are right. You should know everything before you truly take me as your wife. That is only fair."

"Fair? I begin to wonder if anything is fair here," he said. "Nothing in your life to date sounds as if that word can be applied to it." And what I am doing to you right now isn't fair either, he thought. He hated himself for having brought the subject up.

"No, that's not true," she protested. "Aunt Emily was wonderful to me, and so was Sister Agnes, but you have been even more than wonderful, Hugo. Look at what you have given me: your name, your home, and your—your friendship. There have been bad times, but I have had good ones as well, and now . . ." She smiled and simply lifted a shoulder, as if she was trying to convey something to him that she had no words for.

"Now?" he asked, suddenly longing to know just what that something was.

"Now I feel the luckiest of women. Who could ask for more?"

The sweet, trusting expression on her face as she gazed at him made Hugo want to forget about everything—his stupid questions, her answers, certainly their dinner. He'd hardly tasted a bite as it was. "Meggie, sweetheart, maybe we should talk about this another time," he said, about to propose that they skip the next course and immediately retire upstairs.

"No, Hugo. Thinking about it, I believe it really is best that I answer your questions now. Otherwise I would worry that I had not informed you properly. I wouldn't want you to discover anything about me later that would make you think I had held something back."

He scratched his ear. For someone who had been burning to know the details of Meggie's limited life, he couldn't now have cared less about a single one. But he'd asked, so he'd bloody well have to listen to the reply, as much as he wished to be doing other things.

"Very well," he said, forcing encouragement into his voice. "Tell me everything you think I should know."

"Well, Sister Agnes already said that you knew the important details, which means that you already know about my mother—and my father."

Hugo moved his hand to the side of his mouth and scratched that as well. "That your father died before your birth?" he said, making a logical guess. Given the little he did know, that would have to be the case since her mother's death had orphaned Meggie. "And we've already discussed your mother's death upon your arrival."

"Yes," Meggie said, looking back down at her hands. "Althought I should tell you what little I do know about her from my aunt Emily. She told me that my mother was all alone in the world after my father died, and when the vicar of our parish heard about her predicament, he hired her to work as his housekeeper so that she would have food and shelter. And then, as you know, she died, and the vicar appealed to Aunt Emily to foster me, since no one else in Bury St. Edmunds was willing."

"Bury St. Edmunds. That's quite a distance inland, isn't it," Hugo said, storing away this one useful piece of information. "So that is why you'd never been to the sea before."

"I'd never even been close," Meggie said, fiddling with the stem of her wineglass, her gaze distant, the sea obviously the last thing from her mind. "Or at least no closer than Woodbridge. The Ipswich orphanage didn't take us on outings, and when I was at the sanitarium . . . oh. But I'm not to speak of that. It is my life with Aunt Emily that you want to know about."

"Yes, but just the bare facts," he said, trying to speed her along. He didn't really need any more details; what he needed was Meggie in bed, in his arms. Naked.

She nodded, clearly unaware of the erotic direction his thoughts had once again taken. "Well, Aunt Emily was a childless widow," she said, "and she had no family close by. Her only brother had emigrated to Canada and her husband's relatives lived up in Yorkshire."

"Crewe . . . I seem to remember something about Yorkshire Crewes," Hugo said, straining to think. Unlike his mother, he was not a walking genealogy chart, but he had unwittingly absorbed a great deal of vital information as he'd grown up. "Are they landed gentry?"

"Aunt Emily said they were landowners of respectable stock, although not of any real social importance, and her own family, the Stoddards, were simple farmers. But Aunt Emily said that she considered character much more important than breeding, and that what was in one's heart counted more than anything else."

Meggie spoke with a dignity that touched Hugo's

heart. He understood what she was trying to ask in her own roundabout way, for she'd expressed a similar doubt the day before in the carriage. Now, however, he heard it differently, and his response came from an equally different place.

"My own mother has often said the same," Hugo replied gently. "Indeed, her actual words to me on the subject of marriage were that she was not a stickler for dynastic unions, if that reassures you, Meggie. She told me to find a nice girl who would suit my temperament, and so I have."

Meggie peeped a look at him from under her lashes. "I think you may have stretched her meaning a bit far by marrying me."

He grinned. "Maybe just a bit. But if she does bring up the matter of pedigrees, I shall remind her of her own words. Anyway, I am not concerned. She will like you, I am sure of it."

"I only pray that you are right, Hugo."

So did he. He couldn't begin to imagine what his mother was going to say when she received the news. "Look at it this way, sweetheart. By the time you actually meet her, you will have all the manners of a lady. You already speak like a lady, so you needn't worry about that. In everything but blood you will be a lady."

"Do you *really* think I speak like a lady, Hugo?" Meggie chewed on her lovely, full bottom lip, regarding him anxiously.

Hugo had to force himself to concentrate. "I do," he replied. "I also have to confess to surprise. Did your aunt Emily teach you?"

"Oh, no—she did place an emphasis on proper grammar, but Aunt Emily's accent was more . . . country than county, if you know what I mean." The corners of her mouth turned up mischievously.

Hugo, caught off-guard by Meggie's extraordinary but

uncannily accurate description of the difference between social classes, couldn't help wondering if somewhere inside her muddled brain, Meggie wasn't sharp as a tack.

"Er, yes, I suppose I do," he said, clearing his throat. "And so where *did* you learn to speak as you do, given that you grew up as a country girl?"

"I learned from Sister Prudence."

"Sister Prudence?" he said, trying to make sense out of this statement. "Who the devil was Sister Prudence?"

"She was a nun at the orphanage. But before she converted and joined the order she was an earl's daughter."

"Ah . . . well, that explains it. My dear girl, you speak as if you were an earl's daughter yourself," Hugo said, with the utmost sincerity, happy to have the phenomenon of Meggie's perfect accent explained.

She smiled at him, her translucent eyes shining with pleasure. "Thank you," she said, suddenly looking shy. "I did my best to learn. I didn't like Sister Prudence one bit, but I must admit that she did make an effort in my direction, even if she loathed every moment of it."

"It sounds to me as if Sister Prudence didn't like you, either," he observed dryly.

"Oh, she didn't. I was a terrible trial to her."

"Then why did she bother teaching you?"

Meggie hesitated. "Well, I suppose she felt it her duty to improve me," she said after a long pause. "Or maybe she simply thought banging her lessons over my head was yet another way of imposing her rules on me. All the nuns were like that, though. They had rules for absolutely everything, and if you didn't obey instantly and perfectly, whop! Down came the ruler or the cane, right on the palms of your hands!"

Hugo winced. "That doesn't sound very charitable," he said.

"*Charitable?* The nuns at the orphanage were tyrants," Meggie replied with a grimace. "When I was *really* bad, I was caned on my bottom. Sister Luke of Mercy—she was the worst. I knew she enjoyed every moment of every stroke. Sister Prudence, on the other hand, used her tongue for the whippings, and oh, but she was cruel. I often wondered how she ever got into the nunnery at all. Maybe the earl paid the order to take her off his hands."

"Let us speak no more of Sister Prudence," he said. "I am sure that however she became a nun, her father, whichever earl he was, was delighted to be rid of her. She sounds perfectly poisonous."

"She was. Goodness, I haven't thought about her in ages."

"Good, and you needn't think about her ever again, or about any of the others nuns who ruled your life for so long. You are here with me now, mine to rule and mine alone."

"And what do you rule, my lord?" she asked, leaning her chin on her hand, regarding him dreamily through half-closed eyes.

"I rule that your life should be filled with pleasure," he said, captivated by the way the candlelight caught on the tips of her sooty eyelashes and turned them to gold.

"The sisters would be shocked by your hedonistic attitude," Meggie retorted, finishing her glass of wine. "You ought to be lecturing me on my wifely duties and how I must submit to you with eyes closed and prayers sent up to heaven to endure what God has ordained as my lot in life."

Hugo didn't bother to wait for Roberto to appear, but rose to fetch the wine bottle and refilled Meggie's glass himself. A little wine seemed to bring out a side of Meggie that was most promising. "Your *lot* in life? Is that what the nuns told you? Actually, I'm surprised they instructed you on the subject at all."

"No, no. The nuns implied rather than instructed," Meggie said, obligingly taking a sip from her glass. "Although what they implied was not very encouraging—actually, what they implied was rather horrific. I learned the real truth about lovemaking from a woman at the sanitarium. Mrs. Lindsay spoke long and often about it, and in fairly explicit detail."

Hugo nearly choked. Marvelous. Meggie had been given the details of the sexual act from another lunatic. "Did she," he murmured.

"Yes. She thought it the most wonderful thing in the world. But the problem was that she had to indulge herself so often that her husband could no longer keep up with her, and neither could anyone else. Eventually she wore everyone out and had to be committed." She peeped a smile up at him. "Not that it stopped her. I happen to know she's been secretly cavorting with Mr. Carlyle—and although she might not be getting better, it's done Mr. Carlyle a world of good, I can tell you that."

Hugo smothered a hoot of laughter in his hands. He had to admit that when Meggie wasn't infuriating him, or inciting nearly uncontrollable desire in him, she amused him more than anyone he'd ever known.

She certainly gave him an entirely new perspective on life. Only Meggie would speak of such things so openly and with such gustol Since she talked about them with such gusto, goodness only knew how much she'd bring to the act itself.

He couldn't wait another moment to find out.

"Well, then," he said, pushing back his chair, "if you don't mind skipping the pudding, why don't we go upstairs and put Mrs. Lindsay's theory about the wonders of lovemaking to the test?" He held out his hand to her.

She took it without another word.

17

"Do listen, Ottoline, I believe I hear them coming up now." Dorelia lowered her knitting into her lap and cocked her head to one side. "Happy days, happy days." She hummed a little tune.

Ottoline lowered her own knitting and cocked her head in exact imitation of her sister. "I believe you are right, and coming up so early—a good sign to be sure. Heavens me, does this not bring back memories?" She rested her head against the back of her chair, a faraway smile on her face. "We did have a lovely time of it, did we not? Linus never lacked for company after poor Lally's death."

Dorelia chuckled. "Dear Linus, and vigorous to the end. Such a pity there weren't two of him to go around—still, we always have shared nicely. But never mind traipsing down memory lane. Those days are gone and there are far more important matters afoot." She placed her knitting on the table beside her, peering out the window of their sitting room. "The moon will be up soon."

"The *full* moon," Ottoline said pointedly. "A good omen, I believe. Fertility, Sister, fertility. Maybe we will be doubly blessed, given the family proclivity for twins."

"We can but hope. What is more important is how this night goes for the darling girl. She did look a little peaky to my eyes."

Ottoline sniffed. "It's those nuns and their unnatural ideas, I tell you. They've probably scared her half to death, although there is nothing wrong with Madrigal's natural instincts—that much I do know. It's what her husband does with them that counts."

"Oh, he looks virile enough to me, and from the way he comes to attention when she's about, I don't foresee any trouble there. No, it's all transpiring just as you said it would, Ottoline."

"I don't know why you sound so surprised. Have I ever been wrong?" Ottoline pushed herself to her feet with a loud grunt and went to poke the fire.

"Not wrong, but I do wish you'd learn to interpret your B.G. better." She cast her sister a reproving look. "What you *said* was that if we encouraged Linus to have Lyden sold after he died instead of leaving it to us, and to make it a stipulation that we be allowed to stay on, that we would be sent a family to cherish us in our old age."

"And? Was I not exactly right? Did not dear Hugo arrive on the doorstep with Madrigal? Is that not family enough for you?"

"That's my point," Dorelia said, jabbing her finger in the air. "You didn't say anything about it being our *real* family, now did you?"

"I can't be expected to see everything, Dorelia, and I don't know what you're complaining about—we have exactly what we wanted and more to boot. Lally would be so pleased."

"Lally is insignificant. It is Madrigal I am concerned about. We are in an exceedingly awkward position." Dorelia shook her head. "If you had paid a little more attention to the exact wording of the B.G., then we would have had time to prepare. As things stand, we have no idea how much of the truth Madrigal knows, and if you ask me, she doesn't know much of anything, the angel."

"I know, I know," Ottoline grumbled. "I was there this morning, remember? But it's not *my* fault she wasn't told about her father, and it's not my fault that the silly boy didn't get around to marrying Margaret Bloom either, so you can stop glaring at me. The point is, do we tell her the truth, or do we keep our mouths shut?"

"Hmm. Hmmm. This is the crux of the matter, is it not? Suppose she doesn't know she was born on the wrong side of the blanket? Just imagine what a shock that would be to her—not to mention what a shock it would be to dear Hugo."

Ottoline thumped back down into her chair. "We are in a tricky spot to be sure, Sister. I cannot help but feel we should keep our silence for the time being, or at least until we see which way the wind blows."

"That's all well and fine, but what are we going to do about giving Madrigal her dowry?" Dorelia drummed her fingers on her lap. "We agreed that we should transfer our trust to her, since we have no use for it, and for that we will need a solicitor. If I'm not mistaken, a solicitor will want to know why we wish to give Meggie our inheritance, and if we explain that we feel it is hers by right, then we'll have to explain why."

"Solicitors are honor-bound to keep their silence," Ottoline said. "Furthermore, there's no law against our giving our money to anyone we choose. I do not see why we have to explain anything."

"Not even to Madrigal?" Dorelia asked.

"Least of all to Madrigal."

Dorelia scowled darkly. "The far larger problem is going to be getting rid of those idiot trustees Linus chose, who have hardly let a tuppence leave their greedy fingers, even to us, who have every right to the income. What good is giving the girl a dowry if her husband can't touch it? I suppose we could just will it to her, but we might live for another fifty years."

"Oh, dear. I do hope not. My bones are creaky enough as it is." Ottoline's brow crinkled in thought. "Well. We could go to Hugo directly and ask his advice.

Surely he has a solicitor under retainer who could take care of the matter for us? I cannot imagine Hugo would be averse to receiving a dowry on Madrigal's behalf."

"I should think he'd be exceedingly pleased. Remember, too, that not only is he a man, but he is the son of a duke. He ought not to have any trouble replacing those wicked creatures who think they can take advantage of old ladies."

"Yes . . . yes, that might be a solution, but do you not worry that Hugo will see our decision to give all of our money to Madrigal as highly eccentric?"

"I've been ruminating on that very point since our earlier discussion. He already thinks us eccentric, Dorelia. So why would he think it so peculiar that we wish to dispose of our assets in his favor? The arrangement is equitable, after all."

"Yes," Dorelia replied, slowly nodding. "I suppose he would see that we have no one else to give our money to, and since he has kindly agreed to look after us until our deaths, the settlement would seem fair, would it not? Oh, you are clever, Sister. I think this might be the very answer."

"Answers enough for the moment. I am not so sure that the truth will not come out eventually. For heaven's sake, how long do you think they will both manage to ignore Madrigal's likeness to Lally's in the portrait right there on the staircase wall? Or the girl's Christian name, for that matter—it *is* written in Lally's own Bible in the library."

Dorelia sighed. "It's such a pity that David didn't marry the poor girl—just think how different everything would have been. He was a silly boy."

"But they loved, Sister, they loved, and even though it all ended in tragedy and tears, at least David had the *intention* of marrying his Meg. Look what their love for each other has brought us after all this time—a dear, sweet girl for us to adore."

"And children to lavish our affection upon," Dorelia said happily. "You do remember seeing children, don't you?"

"Will you stop treating me as if I am becoming feeble-minded?" Ottoline snapped. "I've already told you a dozen times that there will be children."

"If dear Hugo does his job right. I do hope he's not one of those inconsiderate sorts who cares only about his own pleasure; Madrigal won't take kindly to being poked and prodded and shoved about. However, if he's anything at all like Linus," she said, sighing gustily, "then she'll be among the most satisfied women on earth. He certainly has the physique for it."

"What happens between Madrigal and her husband in the bedroom is none of my affair," Ottoline said with a sniff. "Really, Sister, sometimes I think the nature of your B.G. casts you too much into the physical plane. Look how you sneaked into dear Hugo's room tonight through the old portal, with the sole purpose of ogling him. You should be ashamed of yourself."

Dorelia drew herself up indignantly. "I wasn't ogling him, I was merely trying to see if the boy had good color and tone under his clothes—these things are important in determining a man's health and prowess. For all we knew, what appeared to be mighty shoulders and thighs could have been padding sewn into his clothing by his tailor in order to deceive the gullible. It is a common practice, you know."

"Common practice or not, I do *not* think you should have been in dear Hugo's bedchamber uninvited and unannounced. Using the portal to access Linus was one thing, but this is going too far, in my opinion."

"Don't be silly, Sister. It's not as if dear Hugo even knew I was there. I was quiet as a mouse on my way out and he was too busy splashing about and making a mess to notice. I saw what I needed to see and I left."

"That had better be all you see and the last time you see it," Ottoline said, heaving herself to her feet. "I am going to bed. If you wish to sit up half the night worrying about dear Hugo's prowess, that is your business, but I warn you, you will only end up with the headache and indigestion and be none the wiser for your troubles." She cast her sister a parting scowl over her shoulder. "And I strongly suggest that no matter your curiosity, you keep your head out of the wardrobe."

Hugo paused in front of Meggie's door, his hand on the brass knob. He gazed down at her, his eyes dark as the night and filled with a question she couldn't begin to divine.

Meggie waited silently, her heart hammering like a caged thing in her chest, every nerve ending alert, acutely aware of his nearness, and of what was to come.

He reached his free hand out and traced his fingertips down her cheek. "Meggie, tell me . . ." he whispered, then stopped.

She turned her cheek against his touch and softly pressed her lips against the side of his warm hand. "What shall I tell you?" she murmured, then tilted her head back to look up into his shaded eyes.

Oh, ask me. Ask me if I love you and I will tell you truly.

"That you trust me," he said raggedly. "That you know I will not harm you. That you truly are not afraid."

Meggie's lips curved up in a soft smile, her heart aching with love for him, for his generosity. "I trust you," she answered quietly, "and I am not afraid. How could I be afraid of someone with such a gentle, caring heart as yours?"

He closed his eyes for a brief moment, as if what she had said pained him. "I think perhaps you are too trusting," he said, the pad of his thumb brushing lightly over her mouth. "But I am not going to argue with you. I am far too selfish."

"The last thing in the world you are is selfish, Hugo Montagu, and I am not going to argue with you, either. However, I would ask that you open the door without further ado."

Hugo flashed a grin down at her, the shadow vanishing from his face. "Your wish is my command," he said, turning the handle and pushing the door open. "After you, my lady." He stood back to let Meggie in, closing the door behind them.

As she crossed the threshold she gasped, her eyes taking a moment to adjust to the sudden flood of light.

The room blazed with candles. Not a corner, a tabletop, an inch of space on the mantelpiece had been left uncovered.

"Good God," Hugo murmured from behind her. "Is this supposed to be heaven or hell?"

"Heaven to be sure," she said, trying to catch her breath. "Hugo, do look at the bed."

"Oh, dear Lord above," he muttered. "Is nothing safe from those women?"

Every last inch of the bed was thickly spread with rose petals. They adorned the counterpane and pillows, and tumbled off the sides of the mattress, drifting in a haphazard fashion across the floor.

Hugo pulled her back against his hard body, his arms crossing over her waist as if to protect her. "I think we should retire to my room," he said. "We might very well suffocate in here."

"What, and let the aunties' Herculean efforts go to waste? Oh, Hugo, you wouldn't be so cruel." She wiped away tears of laughter from her eyes. "This is obviously their idea of high romance. We can't disappoint them."

"Disappoint the aunties? No, how could we—I beg your pardon for even considering it."

She turned in his arms and leaned her face against his chest, slipping her hands down to his lean waist. "Hugo?" she asked, her voice muffled against his coat, trying to still the shaking of her shoulders. "Do you really mind so much? They were rather sweet to have gone to such trouble."

Hugo's arms tightened around her back. "I don't think I mind much of anything as long as you keep doing what you're doing," he answered, his hands sliding down to cup the curve of her buttocks, pulling her full against him.

The outline of his stiff arousal pressed against her, hard and insistent, caused her knees to tremble and her blood to pound even more violently. She breathlessly clung to him for dear life, afraid that if she let go she'd collapse.

He bent his head and covered her mouth—his lips lightly grazing over hers, tasting, testing, urging a response. There was no need; Meggie sighed, her lips parting against his, hunger swirling through her body, deep and hot and pulsing.

Hugo instantly deepened the kiss, burying his fingers in her hair. His thumbs stroked against the angle of her jaw; his tongue thrust restlessly into the warm depths of her mouth.

Meggie moaned, meeting and returning his intimate touch. Her hands moved on his back, kneading the strong, corded muscles that shifted under her fingers, savoring every sensation. This . . . this was what she had been waiting for, longing for ever since she had first laid eyes on him. And now he was hers and she his, and she could give all of herself to him without reservation.

Her arms slipped around his neck. She poured herself into his kiss, drinking in his taste, tinged with the flavor of wine and something else that was sweet and salty and uniquely his.

His touch was all she'd remembered and more. More, because now there was no stopping, no need to hold any part of herself in check. Desire ran like liquid heat through her body, pooling in her very center just where that deep pulse beat.

"Meggie. Meggie, my sweet," Hugo murmured, moving his mouth to her neck, trailing kisses down to the hollow of her collarbone as his fingers found the buttons and tapes of her dress.

In a moment he had them undone, and he slipped the fabric off her shoulders and down her arms until the silk fell to her waist and glided over her hips, landing in a puddle around her ankles.

She shivered, not with the cold, but with fevered excitement as his gaze traveled from her face down over her naked body. She felt her nipples contract and grow hard as his blazing sapphire eyes took in every detail of her unclothed form.

Shameless. She was shameless, and she didn't care one bit. She *wanted* him to look at her with fierce, unrestrained need.

"Meggie," he breathed. "You are so lovely. So very lovely, so alive. So responsive. So desirable." His hands grazed lightly up her rib cage, his thumbs stroking the underswell of her breasts.

She trembled with longing, her eyes closing, her head falling back, and yearned for the fullness of his touch on her aching flesh. But instead of giving her the satisfaction she craved, he bent down and effortlessly swept her up in his arms, cradling her against his chest.

"Oh," she said in disappointment. "That felt so nice. I wish you hadn't stopped."

"I am delighted to hear it," Hugo said with a low chuckle. "However, do try to curb your impatience. I shock easily." He brushed his mouth over her forehead and she felt the smile that curved his lips.

She wrapped her arms back around his neck and sighed, drinking in his heady scent. "I can't help desiring you," she whispered, stroking her fingers through his silky hair. "Am I terribly unladylike?"

"Delightfully so," he replied, carrying her over to the bed as if she weighed no more than a feather. "But there is much to come, and I want you to enjoy every moment of this night, Meggie. And you will enjoy it, I promise."

"Oh, you needn't worry about that," she said, nuzzling her nose into the side of his throat, his skin hot and slightly damp. "I told you I'm not afraid."

"*You* might not be afraid, but I'm terrified," he said dryly.

Meggie, taken aback by the absurdity of that statement, raised her head and stared up at him. "What could you possibly be terrified of? It's not as if you haven't done this a hundred times before."

Hugo smiled, caressing a strand of her hair. "Not with my wife I haven't. What I'm terrified of is wanting you so badly that I go too quickly. You wouldn't thank me for it, and I would hate myself." Bending down, he kissed the very tip of her nose. "So as much as I may desire you, I am determined to take my time. You, my greedy darling, will just have to put up with me."

He stripped back the counterpane, cursing as a flurry of rose petals rose from the bed, swirling everywhere.

Meggie burst into laughter as fragile pink blossoms drifted down over them, covering them both from head to toe. "You look like a flower shop," she said, brushing her fingers through his hair and dislodging another shower.

"Damned old bats," Hugo said, plucking a petal out of

his mouth. He laid her down on the bed and stepped back, his gaze sweeping over her in admiration. "On the other hand, I must say, you look rather charming dressed in nothing but rose petals."

Meggie pushed herself up on one elbow. "I wish I could say the same for you," she replied, her lips trembling with mischief.

"Ah. A hint, and I do believe a rather broad hint at that," he said, stripping off his coat and undoing the buttons on his shirt. "I think I can oblige the lady."

Meggie's breath caught in her throat as he removed the fine linen. Firelight flickered like gold over his smooth skin, revealing every last magnificently chiseled muscle of his broad chest, from the flat planes of his pectorals to the sculpted ridges that ran over the top of each rib.

Bending, he pulled off his shoes and stripped off his trousers. He straightened then, as naked as she was, and looked straight at her, his expression unreadable.

Meggie stared, drinking in the absolute beauty and raw power of the male body. Of Hugo's body.

Her awed gaze traveled from broad shoulders and chest over his lean waist and muscular hips, down toward his powerful thighs. Her widened eyes arrested just at the juncture of his thighs where his manhood jutted stiff and ready toward her from its thatch of dark hair. So that's what Adam was hiding under the fig leaf.

Just the sight made the secret, feminine place between her thighs throb with renewed longing. A deep intuitive knowing stirred in her, every instinct wanting—needing—to take that masculine part of him into her, to be filled with his length, to embrace him with her body, to make his flesh one with hers.

"Oh . . ." Meggie whispered. "Oh, Hugo. I had no idea. I've always wondered, but I never even imagined anything so perfectly wonderful. . . . You are beautiful."

Hugo reached the bed in two strides and drew her up into his arms. "Meggie," he groaned, his mouth pressed against her cheek. "How do you do this to me, undo me to such a degree that I no longer know myself? Dear *God,* how I want you."

He gently took her face between his warm hands and fitted his mouth to hers, kissing her until her senses swam and she cried out in mindless need.

Pressing her back against the bed, Hugo trailed his hands down over her throat. His palms slipped over the rise of her breasts, softly cupping them, while his thumbs stroked over her nipples. Meggie's back arched in pleasure and she strained toward him as he circled the sensitive tips, lightly pinching and rolling them between his fingers.

Her heart pounded so hard she thought it might give out altogether. She'd never felt anything so glorious in her life—until he lowered his mouth and took one nipple into it, nipping and pulling. She thought that not only would her heart give out, but she'd have to be carted off to the asylum like Martha Lindsay.

"Hugo," she gasped as he inflicted the same intense bliss on her other breast. "Hugo, she was right."

"Who was right?" he murmured, his hands tracing lazily down her spine and drawing a line over her hips to her belly.

"Mrs. Lindsay," she said through the dreamlike haze that had overcome her. "She knew just what she was talking about." She caressed his back, her fingers traveling down to the carved hollow of his buttocks and exploring their shape. So hard. So beautiful. So very masculine.

Hugo raised his head and looked down at her, breathing hard. "Meggie, my girl, somehow I do not believe

Mrs. Lindsay told you the half of it. You will just have to see for yourself."

He kissed her again, hard, then lightly bit her throat. His fingers splayed low over her abdomen, reaching into her soft, damp curls, gently tugging.

Meggie gasped, writhing, with her hips twisting against the pressure of the masculine thigh that had somehow inserted itself between her own. His hard arousal pressed against her belly, and she cupped her hands around his buttocks, pulling him even closer. She wanted him so desperately that she nearly died with longing.

"Oh—oh, please," she begged, not entirely sure what she was begging for, but certain he would know exactly. Hugo knew everything.

He did. Of course he did. His fingers slipped even lower, sliding against her parted cleft, stroking that most secret of places languidly, as if he understood perfectly what she needed.

She arched up to his touch, a low cry escaping her throat. Her hips undulated against his fingers as they gently, insistently parted her yielding, willing flesh. His fingers slipped inside, rocking rhythmically, stoking the fire that burned bright and fierce—a fire that spread from her most intimate of places and flashed through every last nerve ending in her body until her entire being shook with exquisite sensation.

She gathered the fire, carrying the brilliant blue-white center back to its origin where it focused like sunlight concentrated through a fragment of glass.

"Hugo," she cried, the center of the flame transforming into an explosion of sensation bright and intense. It took her in pulsating waves that she thought might never end.

He stayed with her, his fingers moving in subtle but exact rhythm with her body's inner spasms.

And when they finally died down he was still with her, kissing her hair, her wet cheeks, her mouth, her throat, even the palms of her hands.

"Meggie," he whispered. "Meggie, I never imagined you would be . . . Will you have me? Will you take me inside you?"

She opened her eyes, gazing up at him with all the love in the world, her heart about to burst with it. "Yes—oh yes, and quickly, please?" she managed to say, her voice shaking badly.

He seemed to laugh, but she couldn't be entirely sure, since his head dropped down into the space between her breasts. She couldn't tell if it was his shoulders that shook or her fingers resting on them that trembled so badly.

She only knew that his hips rose and centered over hers. The blunt tip of his manhood pressed against her swollen, moistened flesh, seeking entrance.

Meggie embraced him with her thighs and raised her hips in invitation. Pressing her face against his chest, she cradled his back with her arms. Martha Lindsay had so far been correct in her details of the joys of lovemaking, and what she'd described as coming next Meggie could barely wait for.

Hugo shifted very slightly and pushed into her, stretching her with his rigid width and only the beginning of his length. Despite her desire, Meggie winced at the unexpected burning.

"Meggie? Meggie, love?" Hugo stroked her face, her neck, her breasts as he stayed very still just inside her entrance. "Do I hurt you?"

"Not—not enough for me to ask you to stop," she said, forcibly thrusting her hips up against his, then crying out in pain. This was the last thing she'd anticipated. Martha Lindsay hadn't mentioned this part, if indeed it was natural.

"Meggie—Meggie, my sweet girl, let me—please let me. I am sorry to hurt you so, but you are very tight, and it's best done quickly."

"What is best done quickly?" she said, frowning up at him. "I thought you said you liked to take your time. And I distinctly remember your saying I'd enjoy this."

"I do. You will. But I refer to your maidenhead, which has to be broken before you can enjoy my being inside you. It will hurt only this one time, I promise." He stroked the damp hair back off her forehead. "It's what happens when you lose your virginity—some brief pain and a little bleeding afterward."

"Oh," she said, hugely relieved that there was nothing wrong with her. "If that is all it is, then do what you must, Hugo. I'll try to be brave."

He cradled her face between his hands and gazed down into her eyes. His own eyes were filled with such tenderness that she would have done anything for him, including accepting his manhood that pressed painfully and insistently against her.

She told herself that something truly magical must lie beyond, maybe even something glorious. But, she found it hard to imagine how there could be anything glorious at all when she felt as if she were being skewered.

Hugo took her hands in his, folding his fingers through hers. He covered her mouth with his own, kissing her deeply, then thrust his hips hard.

Meggie gasped at the explosion of pain that ripped through her as Hugo broke through her barrier and drove deep into her passage. Tears stung at her eyes and she buried her face in his shoulder, her fingers clutching his in a death grip, her breath coming in rapid, shallow pants.

"Meggie, sweet, it's done now," he whispered against her hair. "All finished, my brave girl. I suppose your Mrs. Lindsay forgot about her own deflowering once she realized what came after. She obviously didn't tell you what to expect, and neither did anyone else."

Meggie turned her head and looked up at him through wet lashes. "No . . ." she admitted, dimly aware that the throbbing pain was slowly subsiding and she was gradually adjusting to his hard length inside her. Really, he didn't feel so *very* awful. "At least now I know why I wasn't a nervous bride," she said, summoning up a smile. She didn't have the heart to tell him that she really didn't like this part at all.

"Lovely Meggie," he said, releasing one of her hands and gliding his fingers down her throat to her breast, tracing its outline, circling the nipple until she shivered. He touched his tongue to it, then delicately took the hardened bud between his teeth and lightly bit.

Meggie sighed, and he moved his mouth to her other breast and did the same. She looped her arms around his neck as he continued to work his sensual magic. Little cries escaped from her throat as he drove her upward, back to that place of intense sensation where she lost herself in his sweet caresses, where nothing existed but his touch and taste. She felt the moist heat of his body against hers, the low moan against her cheek that told her his pleasure was as great as hers, the powerful thudding of his heart in his chest, the blood that beat hard in her ears so that she could no longer tell whose heartbeat she heard.

His hand slipped down to the place where their bodies joined. His fingers stroked her, finding the sensitive little nub at the apex of her tender flesh. She gasped as every nerve ending sparked with a desperate joy, his touch fanning smoldering desire into white-hot flame.

"Sweet girl, you like that, don't you?" he murmured, his fingertips circling, circling, until she writhed against him. Her fingers clutched his hair, her head tossed on the pillow. "I like it, too. Dear God, but you are beautiful, my Meggie. Let me love you. Let me show you how good it can be."

He shifted very slightly, his rock-hard length sliding higher inside her and she gasped, but this time in blissful pleasure.

Her thighs fell open, her hips tentatively swayed up toward him, seeking more of the same, and Hugo obliged her. He rocked his hips in the gentlest of rhythms, a soft undulation that slowly, slowly built in strength until he stroked her with the full length of his manhood, thrusting into her hot center. Her body opened and yielded to his in wondrous acceptance.

He reached around her, cupped her hips, and showed her how to move with him, how to open even wider, how to take him deeper still.

Her hands explored over the length of his back, down to the curve of his buttocks, up over his straining muscles. She found the rhythm he had set, her body flowing with him, against him as if they were point and counterpoint, a harmony that blended perfectly and resonated in her very soul.

And as it did, she reached once more toward the bright fire that he'd brought down from heaven to her. Her soft cries became sharp gasps that mingled with his as heaven's flames blazed and exploded in her body's heart, the racking spasms shaking her until she sobbed.

She dimly heard him call her name, felt him hold hard and deep. His muscles gathered and released in a great shudder as he poured into her, a warm flood, his life merging with hers.

The pieces of Meggie's fragmented consciousness slowly gathered together as she drifted back to the world, to herself. She had no sense of the passage of time, knew only that her heart had finally steadied and that her breath had returned to her body. She felt formless, anchored only by Hugo's weight against her.

He lay still and heavy in her arms. His own arms wrapped around her, his forehead resting on her shoulder, his heart beating against her, slow and hard. She ran her fingers over his slick skin, dreamily tracing the outline of muscle and sinew.

His hands moved on her back, slow and lazy. "Meggie," he murmured, his voice drowsy, so low she could hardly hear it. "Meggie, tell me you are happy."

"I am happy," she answered, pressing her lips to the top of his dark head, his hair so soft, so fine, still damp from exertion. He shifted to his side and leaned up on one elbow, looking down at her. His other hand reached out, gently drawing a line from temple to cheek.

"Good," he said, his fingers moving to the nape of her neck and stroking there. "As am I. I will not lie to you and tell you there haven't been other women—there have been many. But none has touched me as you have, my sweet Meggie. Not a one."

He lightly wrapped his hand around one of her wrists and carried it to his mouth. The tip of his tongue delicately caressed the sensitive flesh on the underside and stroked up to her palm.

"You are trying to be kind," she said, suddenly shy. "I know that I still have much to learn, but perhaps next time you will show me how you would really like me to touch you. I—well, you know I haven't had any experience."

He drew in a deep breath, releasing it slowly. "No. That's not what I meant. I don't know how to make you properly understand, but you must believe me when I tell you that I have never . . ." He paused as if carefully measuring his words. "Never felt such completion."

"Oh." She ran a finger down his chest, over the soft patch of hair that bisected his pectoral muscles. "I am glad. I felt the same. May we do it again soon?"

Hugo dropped his forehead against her neck,

smothering a snort of laughter. "Mmm," he said, nipping at her earlobe. "Very soon and all night long if I can manage to keep up my strength. I can see that you are going to tax it."

Meggie smiled happily. "I will do my best," she said, thinking Hugo had found a very nice, albeit subtle, way of telling her that he loved her.

Completion. She'd have to file that euphemism away for her own future use.

18

"What the bloody hell?"

Hugo, who had just rolled over in order to devote his full concentration to Meggie's sweet and responsive mouth before devoting himself to Meggie's other sweet and responsive body parts, jerked his head up. His attention snapped to the French doors through which came the muted but unmistakable shouts and howls of a rowdy mob.

He didn't bother to question who they were or what they wanted: every finely honed, ingrained instinct for survival that he'd developed over the years told him to act immediately and without conscious thought. He instantly pushed himself upright, swung his legs over the side of the bed, and dived for his discarded clothes.

They can't be here to lynch you for sleeping with someone else's wife, since this one is mine, his brain insisted through his panic as he scrambled into his trousers. You know you haven't gotten any of the local girls pregnant, either, so what the devil do they want you for? It has to be something.

At that moment, Meggie sat up, pulling the sheet across her breasts, watching him with a huge grin on her face. "Why, I do believe we have visitors," she said. "It looks as if you heard them, too."

"I don't know what you're smiling for," he said curtly, thinking Meggie was a real danger to herself if she didn't have the good sense to be terrified. "For all we know, they've come to burn the house down or murder us in our bed—although God only knows why. I haven't been in residence long enough to do anything objectionable."

"Don't be ridiculous," Meggie replied, looking highly amused. "They've come to cheer you."

"What the blazes makes you think that?" he said, buttoning his flaps and shrugging into his wrinkled shirt. The damned wolf. Maybe that was it. They'd come to demand Hadrian's instant dispatch—yes, that made sense, or better sense than anything he'd come up with so far.

"Well, it is your wedding night, and you are lord of the manor," Meggie said, as if this was the obvious explanation.

"Exactly, it's my wedding night, and they know I'm busy with—with wedding business, so you'd think they'd leave me alone. Where is Roberto, anyway? It's his job to keep uninvited mobs off the grounds."

"Hugo," Meggie said gently, "they are not a mob, they are your tenants. Go out onto the balcony and greet them, and they'll soon be on their way. They only want to wish you well and thank you."

"Thank me? For what?" he said, frowning. And then he remembered. He'd ordered Coldsnap to arrange a celebration for the tenants that evening, which had obviously gone off as planned.

From the raucous sound of the crowd below, a great quantity of good food and an even larger quantity of wine and ale had been consumed. "Oh," he said, feeling like a fool for having automatically assumed they intended the worst. Force of habit, he supposed—he wasn't accustomed to being regarded as a hero. "I forgot about the feast."

"Clearly," she said with a chuckle. "Go on, then. The longer you keep them waiting, the noisier they're going to get. Oh, and just so you know, you have rose petals stuck in your hair."

Hugo ran his fingers over his head, thinking that his life bore absolutely no resemblance to the one he'd been leading only thirty hours before—the perfectly *normal* life he'd been leading before stepping into the insane asylum and taking Meggie out.

He seemed to have taken not just Meggie, but the entire asylum away with him.

Although . . . although as hard as he tried, he couldn't really complain.

He opened the glass doors and stepped out onto the balcony, looking down over the balustrade to the crowd of boisterous people singing and shouting on the moon-washed lawn below.

The moment they spotted him, an ear-splitting roar went up.

"Lord Hugo, Lord Hugo," they changed, waving mugs in the air. Their faces were one huge communal grin.

Scores of men, women, children had gathered, as well as Reginald Coldsnap, Roberto, Cookie, and . . . and he nearly choked. Cookie, in some misguided fit of solidarity, had dragged along the damned wolf who howled away like the rest of them. Incredibly, no one seemed to care.

They actually had come to wish him well, just as Meggie had said, for those were the sentiments being shouted up at him, or at least the ones he could actually make out.

"Bless hew, yer lordship! May the Good Lord Hisself rain blessings on yer head!"

"Thank'ee, sah, thank'ee! The feasting were grand!"

"An' now you're married we wish ye joy an' every year a gal or a boy!" said another.

"All good wishes, Lord Hugo, for a happy and prosperous future. Your celebration was a great success and much appreciated, as you can see." That from Coldsnap, whom at least Hugo could understand clearly.

"Whoop, yer lordship, what a night we are havin' thanks to ye, and I'll give ye a proper Suffolk toast," cried someone else. "Here's to my wife's husband, and down goo the rest o' the ale."

The man drained his mug, swayed and rocked, then fell forward to his knees and over onto his side.

"And down goo owd Jimmy," snorted a grizzled man who looked to Hugo as if he'd been on the high seas all his life. "He *should* o' said, here's to the new husband's wife, and down goo the husband."

He laughed uproariously at his own joke, then attempted to sober, raising his own mug toward the balcony. "Thank ye, sah. Thank ye for me and mine. The future do look master fine agin, and all our bellies full wi'it."

A shared cry of " 'ear, 'ear," followed.

Hugo couldn't believe his ears. In his entire twenty-six years, no one had ever cheered him—or at least not for anything honorable. A hard lump formed in his throat, and he cursed himself for being a sentimental fool.

Still, he couldn't seem to help himself. He was touched, deeply touched by this show of genuine affection and appreciation, and deeply humbled as well. He had to blink rapidly against the sting of unwelcome tears, feeling ashamed at his loss of control. His people needed to see a man of strength, not a sniveling weakling.

Meggie appeared as if by magic at his back. Her hand lightly reached up to rest on his shoulder, almost as if she had sensed his need. He turned to wrap his arm around her slender shoulders, to bring her forward so that the crowd might see her, too, and be glad.

Although when he saw how she was dressed, he was concerned that the crowd might see just a little too much of his wife.

Barefooted Meggie wore only a night shift and a shawl, and her hair streamed loose over her shoulders and back. The rising moon showered golden light down over her, streaming over her flaxen hair, catching in the fibers of her white shawl and shift, once again creating the perfect illusion of an angel.

As he moved her around to his side, she glanced up at him. Her lips curved in a joyous smile, her eyes filled with love.

Hugo's heart nearly stopped. *Love?*

Oh, God—oh, God. It was bad enough that she thought he loved her, but now Meggie thought she loved him? What in hell was he going to do?

The deafening cry that went up as Meggie came into view distracted him from his panic. He'd deal with it later. That was the answer. He'd deal with it much, much later.

Meggie slipped her arm around his waist, pulling her shawl close with her free hand. "Hello," she called, as if she were perfectly accustomed to dealing with huge crowds come to sing her praises. "Did you have a lovely party?"

A shouted chorus of "ayes" and "yasses," came back.

"Good," she called again. "My husband is a very kind and generous man, is he not?"

The shouts became a roar. Meggie laughed and turned to Hugo. "I think they like you."

He could only shake his head in amazement. He swallowed hard, then raised his hand, waiting for the noise to die down. "Thank you all," he shouted. "You are very kind to come and wish my wife and myself happiness on this special day. I wish the same back to you, and prosperity for us all." Another pause for the cries of approval. "And now that you have had your fun, perhaps you'd be so kind as to allow me to get back to mine."

Shrieks of laughter and more catcalls and a few ribald comments came back to him. He pulled Meggie hard against his side and waved.

"Right hew are, yer lordship," shouted Cookie. "I dessay it's time to be findin' our beds and hew be goin' back to yers. 'Struth, looks unto to me like a tempest be brewing this night."

This last statement brought screams of delight from the crowd, who slowly began to dissipate. They broke into drunken ditties to help them on their way, and old Jimmy was hoisted up on one shoulder to be carried away.

Hugo held Meggie tightly as he watched the last of them melt away into the night, their singing becoming fainter and fainter until all that could be heard was the low sighing of the wind in the trees and the distant trilling of a nightingale.

Meggie pressed her head back against his shoulder. "That was wonderful. Truly wonderful."

He lightly stroked her hair. "How did you know?" he asked.

She tilted her head and gazed up at him, her gray eyes full of sharp question. "How did I know it was wonderful? Hugo, really—sometimes I wonder if you think I have no brain at all."

"Don't be stupid," he said abruptly, for lack of a better response. He'd conveniently forgotten she didn't perceive the simplest of statements in a normal fashion.

Almost as if to prove his point she threw her head back and crowed with laughter. "There you are. You cannot have it both ways, dear man. Either I am to be stupid or I am not. You must tell me which you prefer, for the way you constantly change your mind will surely scramble my already confused wits."

"If you honestly wish to know," he said as casually as he could manage, wishing she hadn't reminded him of her scrambled wits, "I prefer you exactly as you are." There. That was tactful.

"Exactly as I am? Really? Do you really mean it?" she

asked, her eyes shining with that inner light that made his heart turn over.

"I really mean it," he said truthfully. "You are beautiful to me, Meggie. Beautiful and sweet and incredibly innocent."

"Not so innocent anymore," she replied, a wicked, entirely earthly gleam creeping into those ethereal eyes. "And if we hadn't been interrupted, I do believe I'd be even less so."

"Never fear, I left a place-marker. I believe it was just about here," he said, lowering his mouth and capturing her smiling lips under his own, running his tongue along their honeyed outline before parting them and gently invading her soft inner recesses.

"Mmmm." Meggie sighed in contentment as he finally lifted his head. "I could easily become accustomed to this."

"Oh, you will become very, very accustomed," he said, smoothing his hands over her soft hair. Everything about Meggie was soft. Her skin, her breath, her eyes, her touch. And oh, how soft was the feel of her inner flesh, so hot and slick and giving around him. The thought alone intensified his arousal.

"It's so beautiful out here," Meggie said, leaning against him, oblivious to his swiftly growing need. "I think I can smell the sea, Hugo. And if you listen very carefully, you can hear the cry of a shore bird every now and then. Isn't it lovely?"

"Lovely," he said, not referring to the shore birds.

"There's a full moon tonight," she said, gazing up at the brilliant golden circle that hung halfway between the black outline of the lightly swaying treetops and the silver glitter of the stars. "The light makes the birds and animals restless."

Hugo dropped a kiss on the top of her head. Not just the animals are restless. But he told himself firmly that he could wait. Meggie was happy in the moment, rhapsodizing away. Surely she couldn't rhapsodize for very much longer?

"Hadrian's always been partial to full moons," Meggie continued, showing no signs of stopping her soliloquy on nature and its virtues. "I'm so glad Cookie brought him along."

"If I didn't know better, I'd say Hadrian had been drinking with the best of them, given the amount of noise he was making," Hugo answered, making a concerted effort to indulge her.

"Oh, that was just Hadrian calling down the moon," she said.

"Calling down the moon?" Hugo said, still not accustomed to Meggie's odd way of phrasing things. "What the devil is that supposed to mean?"

Meggie slanted a look up at him from over her shoulder. "Well, he sings to the moon with his soul."

"You think that wolf has a *soul*?" Hugo said incredulously.

"Of course he does," she said seriously. "Every creature has a soul, and every soul has a unique voice. The problem is that most of us—humans, that is—forget to use it; we're afraid of unleashing the force of our inner natures. But Hadrian has no such fear—he celebrates his wildness, and he honors creation and the natural cycles of life when he offers up his song."

Hugo just looked at her. She really was gone, poor girl.

"Really." She flashed a grin at him. "You should try howling at the moon sometime. It feels wonderful."

No wonder they were called lunatics, Hugo thought, if they stood around baying at the moon. Oh, well. As long as she didn't do it around him—or anyone else for that matter—he could safely ignore this latest aberration.

"Howling is also part of pack behavior," she said,

oblivious to his extended silence. "Hadrian sees us as his pack, or his family, and I imagine he perceives your tenants as part of his extended pack, so he was happy to join his song with theirs. They certainly made him welcome, didn't they?"

"They did indeed, and I've been meaning to ask. Why *do* you think that people seem to have no fear of him? Wolves are considered to be dangerous predators, you know."

She looked back out over the lawn to where the silver moonlight danced on the river's surface. "Maybe people aren't afraid because he doesn't behave like a dangerous predator," she replied. "He's sweet and gentle and generally courteous, and he conducts himself like an overgrown dog, which is what most people think he is. If it wasn't for the color of his eyes, I'm sure no one would ever guess he really was anything but a dog. Anyway, he *likes* people, so they tend to like him." She looked back up at the sky as if that explained everything.

Hugo rubbed his chin over the top of her head. "You must be right, although I don't think you realize how very strange their blind acceptance is. Any sensible farmer should be up in arms. In fact for one awful moment, I thought maybe the mob had descended on us because they'd seen Hadrian out running with the horses today and had come to demand his hide. And mine." He neglected to mention any of the other scenarios he'd come up with in those first chaotic seconds.

"I cannot understand why you thought for a minute they wanted anything but to honor you. Here you are, a savior to your tenants. A man who, on his own wedding day, took the time to visit them with reassurances and arranged a feast for them for no other reason than he thought it would boost their morale and fill their hungry bellies."

"I wouldn't paint me in quite such a generous light,"

he said, wishing like hell that his motivation had been that selfless, wishing like hell that he could be the man she'd just described.

She turned in his arms to face him and rested her slim, fine-boned hands on his shoulders, her expression grave. "Hugo, you are a good and caring man. Not many would have been so generous or so quick to show that generosity. Believe me when I tell you that every last person here tonight came with the utmost gratitude and a sincere desire to give you their thanks, and why shouldn't they? They have all been deeply worried since Lord Eliot died, watching Lyden slowly creeping downhill and driving them all into debt."

Hugo, feeling more guilty by the moment, thought he'd better set Meggie a little bit straight before she convinced herself that he was a knight in shining armor—his mission in life to rescue everyone and everything he possibly could.

He could imagine what the result of that misguided assumption would be: He'd find himself not just with Gypsies and thieves and batty old maids on his hands, but taking in stray guttersnipes and one-legged widow-women with Meggie's heartfelt urging.

"Wait," he said, forcing himself to tell her at least a small part of the truth, and God knew, it was only a small part. "I should explain something to you about—"

"No, please listen to me," she said, refusing to be interrupted. "I know it embarrasses you to hear this, as you are a very modest man, but you have to understand why you are such a hero to them. Just think of it from their point of view: Any sort of idle person might have bought Lyden, not caring anything more about the tenants' welfare than those greedy trustees did. *Of course* they feared terribly that they'd be left to rot, and *of course* they see you as their savior."

Hugo looked down at her, a slight frown on his face.

His earlier objection was forgotten in his bewilderment at her wealth of incredibly accurate information on a situation even he hadn't been aware of until that morning. "How in the name of heaven do you know all of that?" he demanded. "About the tenants and the trustees, I mean—I surely didn't tell you."

"You didn't have to." She dropped her gaze abruptly, a faint blush staining her cheeks. "I put the pieces together from everything . . . everything I heard."

"Aha," he said in relief, seeing the answer straight in front of him. "The Mabey women. They've been chattering away, is that it?"

"They told me a little," she agreed in a small voice, "and then the vicar said his piece after the wedding, and Mr. Coldsnap, too, and the tenants told me themselves—I . . . I mean just now, when I heard what they said to you."

Her shoulders hunched under his hands as if she was suddenly afraid, as if she thought she had said too much. "I am sorry. You have made it clear that you do not wish me to interfere in your affairs in any way, or even to speak of—of anything much at all."

"Meggie, I was not chastising you. Why would you even think it?" he asked, and in the asking already knew the answer for himself. His own words, delivered only a day before with an overbearing arrogance, had already come back to haunt him.

All I require of you is to do as I tell you to do and to speak as little as possible.

Only now was he coming to realize how precious so many of her words were to him and how much her unique perspective affected his. It gave him an entirely different—and extraordinarily gratifying—outlook on his life. "Tell me, sweetheart, please. I do want to hear what you think. Truly I do."

She gave him a sidelong look from under her lashes,

her eyes uncertain. "Well, there's really not anything more. I just thought you needed to hear why everyone thinks so highly of you, since you are too noble and humble to see it for yourself. You have given so many people happiness this day, Hugo, myself included, and I, for one, will spend the rest of my life counting my blessings."

Hugo didn't know what to say. No one had ever accused him of humility before. Nobility, maybe, but never in that sense, either. If anything, he had gone through life behaving with a distinct lack of nobility, in spite of the blueness of the blood that ran through his veins. For the first time in his life, he felt ashamed of himself.

Here was Meggie who came from the simplest of stock and yet had the most generous of natures, as well as a graciousness that he was only beginning to recognize. Where most people chose to take, Meggie chose to give, where most people chose to judge, Meggie chose to accept.

What right then did he have to judge her? None whatsoever that he could see. It was he who was fortunate, he who should be counting his blessings. He wasn't entirely sure how it had happened, but Meggie had slowly crept into his heart and taken up a solid residence there.

He found that he didn't really want to disillusion her about him after all, but he knew he should give it one last try if he was to live with his newfound conscience.

"Meggie—I'm not any of those things," he forced himself to say, the words grating in his throat. "I am not noble, not humble, not even particularly decent. Believe me, I'm not."

In answer she simply reached a hand up and touched her fingertips to his cheek in infinite tenderness. And then, after a moment, she spoke, her voice carrying the same heartbreaking tenderness in it.

"Oh, but I know you are all of those things and more," she said, her eyes shining with such translucence that Hugo's breath left him altogether. "So does everyone else. You are the only one who does not count your worth as you should."

Hugo struggled for an answer, his concentration blown all to hell by her touch and the starlight in her eyes. Her shawl had slid off her shoulders and drifted to the ground. A trick of the shifting shadows somehow turned her night shift from white into dusky lavender, and Meggie was seductively backlit by the moon as she stood facing him, the curve of her spine leaning against the railing.

He couldn't help but notice the silhouette of her slender figure, any more than he could ignore the one long, shapely thigh and calf that showed through the open seam, any more than he could help noticing the rosy points of her nipples standing out through the thin fabric.

"That's because if I counted my worth, I'd come up impoverished," he only just managed to say, remembering belatedly that he owed her a reply of some kind.

Meggie shook her head with a smile. "Maybe that's the trouble—maybe you really don't know your own worth, and maybe I should be pleased because it means that at least there is *something* I can teach you." Her smile widened into the grin he so loved. "I do know I have much to give you."

So saying, she feathered her fingers down to his mouth and traced over the line of his lips, and then she reached up on tiptoe and kissed him lightly, softly, where her fingers had just been.

Hugo's arms tightened around her back, holding her close. But he let her lead him, handing himself over to her in a way he had never before done with a woman.

He shivered in surprise and delight as she took the

initiative—her tongue slipping into his mouth and delicately touching his tongue, lightly circling it. Unable to resist, he bit down very gently on the tip of her tongue, then pulled it between his teeth, sucking. He coaxed her into his own mouth in an intimate dance that Meggie instantly recognized and responded to and imitated, until he wanted to take her right there on the floor.

She surprised him again. As he was still lost in the frenzied kiss, her hands trailed down to his chest and stroked over his half-open shirt. Slipping inside the cloth, her thumbs circled his nipples, caressing them just as he had earlier done to hers.

He gasped sharply as she applied a steady pressure, pinching and rolling his nipples until he gritted his teeth against the intense pleasure.

Much to his regret she took her hands away. But he didn't mind at all when they landed on the lower buttons of his shirt, the only ones he had managed to fasten in his haste. She undid them, drawing his shirt out of his trousers and pushing it away. Her mouth slid down over his hot skin and closed over his erect nipples, sucking and pulling on them until he had trouble drawing breath into his body.

"Meggie," he groaned, his hands twining in her hair, his thighs shaking with the effort of keeping control. "Meggie . . ."

She didn't answer. Instead, her nimble fingers went to the waistband of his trousers and undid those buttons as well.

Hugo was in agony as her fingertips pressed against his aching erection with every tiny movement.

She pulled the fabric away and freed him, but not for long.

Just when he thought she might succumb to a post-virginal shyness, her fingers closed over and around his exposed and excruciatingly engorged shaft.

Hugo clenched his teeth, his breath coming in rough pants as she lightly stroked. She outlined his dimensions with no sign of inhibition at all. No, not a single sign, he thought through the frantic pounding in his head. The pounding echoed twice-fold in his groin, and his legs were about to give way as she decided to run the palm of her hand over his exquisitely sensitive tip, stroking downward, then squeezing.

His hands wrapped even more tightly in her hair and he gave a strangled gasp. His back arched and his hips could not help from thrusting forward into her cupped hand. A big mistake.

"Sweetheart, I warn you, if you go on like this," he croaked, his chest heaving, "my pleasure will be too great and . . . and I will not be able to pleasure you."

He gently wrapped his hand around her wrist and forcibly drew it back to his chest, pressing it flat against his skin. At the same time, he slid his other hand down over the firm, lush curve of her buttocks and slipped the cotton of her shift up over her thighs to her waist. Fair was fair, after all.

A fiery hunger curled in his gut as she gave a little whimper of excitement. His hand slid down to the soft, curling down of her mound brushing against his throbbing arousal. Then he touched her between her trembling thighs, his fingers seeking and finding the parting of her hot cleft, so wet, so slippery. The scent of her own musky, sweet arousal inflamed him even more as he stroked just between the petals of her outer lips and then moved deeper still, into her inner flesh.

Meggie shook like a leaf in a wind gone wild—her arms holding hard around his neck, her legs parting for him, her hips thrusting against his hand, her inner muscles pulling him into her even more deeply. Sharp little cries and gasps tore from her throat and quavered against his shoulder where she tried to smother them, her mouth open against his skin.

He knew he should take her inside to bed immediately, but it was no use. Stripped of every last vestige of control, he also knew he'd never make it, not with Meggie on the very edge of explosion, and him so close as well.

"Meggie—sweet girl," he panted heavily, lifting her up against him. He pulled her back into the shadows and found the support of the wall.

With another swift lift, he picked her up and wrapped her legs around his waist, then eased her bared thighs down upon him. His pulsing tip found her entrance as unerringly as a compass found true North, with no hesitation, with a simple, absolute knowing.

That was it, Meggie was his North, he thought through a mindless daze, pushing slowly into her. This time her flesh yielded readily to his, embracing him, welcoming his penetration, pushing upward into his demand.

He thrust hard and strong, answering her invitation. And he thrust again and again, taking full possession of her. His hands guided and supported her hips, pulling her down on him in potent demand, wanting her pleasure even more than he sought his own.

Despite his many years of sexual experience, not one woman had ever responded to him as quickly and furiously and fully as Meggie had. Nor had he ever before given so much of himself—always holding back a measure of control, always holding back his heart. No longer. Not with Meggie. It just wasn't possible.

Even now he felt the deep gathering of her internal muscles starting. A wave drew back and under before curling over the top, unleashing the full strength and thunder of its power as it surged back down.

"Hugo," Meggie gasped, her arms grasping even more

feverishly around his neck, her throat working hard, her head thrown back, and her eyes closed. "Hugo, it's going to happen again—oh, I can't bear it . . ."

"Let it, my love, my darling, let it come," he said, burying his mouth against her glistening neck. He tried to contain his own fevered excitement, knowing damned well that once her wave crested and released, he'd be lost. Her tight muscles tensed, pulling him upward toward the beginning of her swell, squeezing hard on him, so hard he thought he might die.

He took everything left in him, every last shred of control, and with one last surge, one great drive upward, he held deep within her, and willed her to ride the surf of her beloved sea home to shore. Home to him.

Meggie sobbed, her wave of ecstasy peaking and breaking. Her contractions fiercely throbbed around him until he shuddered, with every muscle in his body clenching and then frantically, furiously, as he crested on his own ecstasy, releasing to find his own pounding waves home. Home to her.

Home at last.

19

6 June 1822
Lyden Hall, nr. Orford
Suffolk

Dear Messrs. Gostrain, Jenkins, and Waterville:

I write to inform you of my marriage. The happy event took place yesterday here at Lyden Hall by special license.

As I recently explained to Mister Gostrain, my wife, nee Madrigal Anna Bloom, is a local Suffolk woman of no social consequence. Her mother, Margaret, died at Meggie's birth, leaving her a penniless orphan. I know nothing of her father, nor does she, only that he predeceased his wife by some months. She spent the next nine years in the care of a widow, and upon that woman's death, she was sent to the Ipswich Orphanage where she lived under the care of the nuns.

My wife is now twenty-three years of age, well above the age of consent, so I assure you that there is no impediment to the legality of our marriage, should anyone think to challenge it.

Hugo read over what he'd just written, then threw down his pen in disgust at what he was doing—what he had already done.

God, how he hated himself. No matter how hard he tried to justify his actions, he still felt like a complete cad.

Oh, yes—Meggie's money would have come to him anyway once they were married, and true, Meggie would have had no use for the money had she stayed locked up in an asylum. She certainly wouldn't be as happy as she was now if he hadn't taken her away and made her his wife.

Why then, did he feel like such a black-hearted swindler?

He shoved his forehead into his hands, knowing the answer. Because he would never in a million years have asked Meggie to marry him if she hadn't come with four hundred thousand pounds. So to all intents and purposes, he had stolen—or was about to steal—what she didn't even know was hers.

Even worse than that, he had lied to her. He had told her he wanted to marry her because he loved her, that he had loved her for weeks—a blatant falsehood she had believed, and believing it, had accepted his hand in marriage.

The biggest absurdity of the whole situation was that it was no longer a lie. He did love her, and with all his heart. Which, of course, made him as mad as Meggie.

Hugo groaned. How it had happened, and when, were questions he couldn't answer. He only knew that at some point between marrying her and finally falling asleep at dawn with Meggie wrapped tightly in his arms he had come to the realization that she was all he'd ever wanted. If that was madness, so be it. He wouldn't trade what he felt for her for an entire lifetime of sanity.

Lifting his head, he rubbed one hand over his eyes and smiled. Thinking back over the long, private hours of the night, he had been astonished by Meggie, with her unflagging enthusiasm and infinite capacity for learning. She had matched him at every turn, with her finely tuned body in perfect pitch with his.

As, it seemed, was her soul. He'd never in his life felt so connected to another person, as if he had no need to hide any part of himself from her.

Except, of course, his lies.

He shook his head, knowing that nothing could diminish his shame. Loving Meggie only made him feel worse, for he had no choice but to continue to deceive her. She would never understand his treachery or his reasons for it.

Her heart was too good, too pure, too innocent, and her mind was too simple to grasp the reality of the world and the deceptions it sometimes necessitated.

He supposed he'd have to live with his lies for the rest of his life, not a pleasant prospect. The only saving grace of the entire mess was that if he hadn't behaved like such a damned idiot and lost all his money, he never would have gone to the solicitors' office, never would have heard about Meggie's fortune, never would have married her. He never would have known such happiness.

It was small comfort to a guilty conscience, but he'd take any comfort he could find. He also had another small balm to his conscience, which would not only make him feel better, but also give Meggie guaranteed security no matter what might befall him.

He picked up the quill again and dipped it into the inkstand, applying it to the paper with renewed determination.

I mention my wife's less-than-illustrious background only to inform you of the truth, for you are bound to hear various versions. Meggie is not interested in going about in society; she is happy to live quietly here at Lyden. Inevitably though, there will be talk, probably much of it malicious, given the difference in our social stations.

I also mention these few details of her background so that you understand that my wife brings no dowry to the marriage, which will explain the following request.

I ask you to attend me at Lyden at your convenience in order that we may discuss drawing up a legal document providing my wife with a jointure in the event of my death. I would also like to establish portions for any children we might have, as well as arranging for a sum of money to be made available for my wife's personal use during my lifetime.

"Yours, etc., and so on," Hugo mumbled, finishing the obligatory salutations and signing the letter with a flourish.

He blotted the paper, then picked it up and read it through in entirety. He was satisfied that he'd said what he wanted to say and laid the appropriate groundwork. He'd included enough detail about Meggie to pique the solicitors' interest, but he'd also left out enough detail to make himself appear entirely innocent of any foreknowledge of Meggie's inheritance. He'd certainly given them enough leads, and with any luck, they would scramble to confirm the facts and discover the other pertinent details on their own.

He gave them about a fortnight before appearing on his doorstep.

Now he could only pray that James Gostrain would forget Hugo had been in his office at the time that the discussion about Margaret Bloom and her offspring had taken place. Mr. Gostrain hopefully would remember only that Hugo had spoken in glowing terms of the impoverished woman he loved and had decided to marry.

He folded the paper, sealed it with wax, and addressed it. That done, he put it to one side of the desk to be posted, and started on the next arduous and far more difficult task—that of writing to his mother.

"Good heavens. Good gracious heavens above." Eleanor, Dowager Duchess of Southwell, removed her reading glasses and stared down at the letter in her hands, sure she couldn't possibly have read it correctly.

"What is it, Mama?" Rafe looked up from his breakfast, an eyebrow raised in question. "You are not usually so vociferous about your correspondence. What has happened? Perhaps Hermione Horsley finally expired, leaving the throne of the *ton* empty at last? Or perhaps Lady Stanhope launched yet another mysterious debutante and made the match of the Season two years in a row."

Eleanor looked up at her elder son with exasperation. "If you refer to your own match, dear boy, you might consider who was responsible for that, and it certainly was *not* Sarah Stanhope. She was merely an accessory to my plan. However, if I were you I would wipe that ridiculous smirk from your face, or you will be feeling very foolish in another moment. This is news indeed, and it concerns you as well as me."

"Well?" Rafe said, leaning his cheek on his fist. "Have out with it, then. I want to get back upstairs to Lucy and our son."

"Besotted, that's what you are. I've never seen a father make such a fuss over a newborn," she said with a wave of her hand that hid her own very great pride in her infant grandson. He had been born only two days before and with a minimum of fuss. "Very well, I will tell you. This letter is from your brother."

The amused smile faded from Rafe's face. "I see. What has Hugo gone and done now? The last I heard he was playing at gentleman around town, attending all the fashionable events in an effort to attain a respectable reputation. I suppose he's fallen foul and reverted to his old bad habits?" He rubbed the space between his eyebrows as if developing a headache. "I will *not* bail him out again, not this time, not after he promised me that he would reform."

"You are too quick to judge your brother, darling. He

did indeed promise to reform, and it appears he has, in a way I never expected." She passed the first page of the letter over to her son, allowing him to read the astonishing news for himself.

Rafe read in silence, his mouth dropping open. "What in the name of God . . ." He looked up at his mother. "*Married?* Hugo? To a penniless orphan from *where*? Isn't Woodbridge the name of the town where Eunice Kincaid's asylum is?"

"Yes, that's right, although Woodbridge Sanitarium is three miles outside of the town itself," the duchess answered absently. "No, what is particularly interesting is that Hugo has married not just a penniless orphan, but Meggie Bloom of all people. This is extraordinary news."

Rafe regarded her as if she had a screw loose, which she found rather amusing under the circumstances.

"I think," he said slowly, "that you had better explain. Who the devil is Meggie Bloom? You obviously know something about her, and since you don't tend to spend your time in the company of penniless orphans, I have to wonder what you have been up to and why you have mentioned nothing to me."

She graced her son with an indulgent smile. "Really, my dear boy, you cannot think I tell you every last detail of my busy life? You would be bored to tears if I attempted such foolishness."

"Have you been matchmaking again?" Rafe said, one eyebrow raised.

"Not in the least. This news comes as great a surprise to me as it does to you. I don't know what to make of it."

"Get on with it, Mama," Rafe said, his eyes glittering.

"Very well," she said. "I can only think that Hugo met Meggie Bloom last March when I sent him to the Woodbridge Sanitarium in my place. I had the most dreadful cold, and since Hugo was going out that way, I thought he could do my business for me."

"You sent *Hugo* to visit that madwoman?" Rafe said, looking appalled. "Mama, what were you thinking?"

"Don't be absurd, Raphael. I sent Hugo to speak to the director and deliver a bank draft and a letter."

"But my solicitors already pay a small fortune for Eunice Kincaid's upkeep—why would you be sending the place money?" Rafe said, scratching his golden head. "Forgive me, but none of this makes any sense. Would you care to elaborate?"

"Well . . ." the duchess said, not entirely sure how her son was going to react to the entire truth. "You already know that the Woodbridge Sanitarium is a quiet home near the coast in Suffolk, a soothing setting for people who suffer from mental disturbances. What I haven't told you is that the sanitarium is one of my most cherished charities. I am a patroness."

Rafe stared at her. "A patroness. How long have you been a patroness of this—this sanitarium?"

"Since you were a boy."

"Since I was a boy. Yet you said nothing even when you had Eunice committed."

"I saw no need. You have never been interested in my charities, Rafe. Why should you be?"

"I suddenly find myself mightily interested," he replied, throwing Hugo's letter down on the table and regarding her with unsettling intensity. "Do go on. How did you come to be a patroness of a lunatic asylum?"

"A sanitarium, dear. I think 'lunatic asylum' is a bit harsh."

"I don't care what you call the damned place. I want to know how you became involved and why."

"Well, let me see," the duchess said gingerly, knowing that she was treading on dangerous ground. "I helped to found the sanitarium as it happens, not too long after your dear father died, and I have been keeping an eye on it ever since. It's really a very lovely place," she said, taking a large sip of coffee, trying to maintain her equilibrium in the face of Rafe's relentless interrogation.

"You founded the sanitarium after my father died," he said, turning his knife over and over in his hand. "Why, exactly?"

"I—I wanted to ensure that people who needed help would receive it when their families could not look after them properly, see to their safety." Oh, dear. She hadn't thought Raphael would be this displeased. The subject was sensitive and not one he was inclined to discuss, which made her wonder why he was pursuing it with such determination.

"I see," he said. "I suppose I can guess at your interest, given Papa's frequent bouts of melancholia."

"Yes. Yes, that is it exactly," she said, relieved that he had brought it up himself. In the year since she had told him the truth about his father's illness, he hadn't mentioned it once. "You see," she continued, trying to help him understand her motives, "there were times when I thought your father might be better off under professional care, but at the time no place existed that would not have been a dreadful experience for him."

"Hmm," Rafe said, raising his inscrutable gaze from the knife to her face. "I also suppose you hoped that by establishing a place for others like him that you could keep them safe from their own destructive acts."

It was her turn to stare. Surely Raphael had not guessed at the rest of the truth—but how could he have? She'd been so careful, so very careful to protect him from it.

Oh, dear Lord, let it not be so, she prayed. Let him at least have that one small piece of innocence left to him—the memory of his father?

"I—I am not sure I understand you," she said, trying very hard to keep her face composed as her heart fluttered with panic.

"No? Let me be clearer. I suddenly suspect you know far more about the manner of Papa's death than I previously thought."

"What do you mean?" she said, still praying that he knew nothing more than that his father had died in a terrible accident. "What more could I know? You were the one who discovered his body after the accident, darling. You told me everything you saw, right after it happened."

"Not everything. Not everything, Mama." He stood and turned away, walking over to the window, his back to her. "I don't think you've told me everything either, and I wonder if we should not finally be honest with each other. I find my taste for keeping painful secrets has diminished since marrying Lucy, and quite frankly, I would far rather have truth between us than a pack of half-lies and evasions."

He turned abruptly and looked at her from across the room. He met her gaze squarely, his gray eyes clear and full of question. "I will not press you, but I would like an answer."

She saw it then, saw that he knew, and had known all along. A part of her wanted to curl up and die, for she'd tried so hard to protect him, to protect both her sons from the grim reality of their father's suicide. She hadn't wanted either of them to carry an untenable burden.

Now she knew she had failed and failed badly. Because of her silence, she had forced Raphael not only to carry that burden, but to carry it by himself. So he had, keeping his own silence, becoming a controlled, responsible nine-year-old boy who had grown into a controlled, responsible man. He had given away nothing of himself or of his feelings until he'd finally found his Lucy and a measure of peace.

"Very well," she said, summoning up her courage. She knew she owed him not just an answer, but the full truth he had asked for. "I established the sanitarium because I could think of no other way to absolve my conscience," she said, meeting his gaze equally squarely. "I did it because I had no other way to deal with the pain and the guilt I felt over your father's death. I did it because I wanted to keep other wives from needlessly losing their husbands, husbands from needlessly losing their wives, and children needlessly losing their parents. Do you understand, Raphael? Need I be more clear than that?"

"Thank you, Mama," he said raggedly, staring at the floor. "Thank you. I know the admission was difficult, but you have no idea what a relief it is to have the truth out in the open, to finally be able to speak of what really happened. All these years I thought I had to protect you, to keep you safe."

"To keep *me* safe? But my dearest, that was what I was trying to do for you. That is why I said nothing."

Rafe raised his head. "You said nothing, but you knew his death was no accident; you knew that he deliberately put the gun to his throat and pulled the trigger. Given what I've just told you, you must realize that I saw it all happen."

The duchess pressed shaking hands to her temples. "No," she whispered. "Oh, no. Not that. Not that . . . I didn't know. Oh, Raphael, I didn't know."

"How could you know? I didn't tell you," he said bluntly. "I will tell you this now, though, and I apologize if I cause you pain, but you have a right to hear. I saw him go out with the gun, and I thought he'd forgotten to call me. I chased after him, taking the shortcut through the woods. Just as I broke through the last copse he fired. There was no mistaking his intent."

"My darling boy—what can I say to you other than I am sorry, so terribly, terribly sorry," she choked, reaching up to wipe away the tears that had sprung to her eyes. "You said only that you'd found his body in the field. Since you never mentioned another word about it, I believed you didn't want to bring up bad memories. I never imagined—truly, I never imagined there was anything more to your silence than that."

"Mama, please do not upset yourself, not over me. I put the worst of the pain to rest some time ago, with Lucy's help, and although the scars may never go away, they do heal cleanly. Tell me this, though. Since you weren't there, how did you know the truth?"

She shook her head back and forth, the tears slipping down her cheeks. Her memory flooded back as clearly as if it were only yesterday. "I—I just knew. There were things he'd say in a fit of despair, things he'd threaten that scared the life out of me because I knew he half-meant them," she said, blotting her cheeks with her napkin. "That last morning he went into his library in a terrible state, ranting and raving." She closed her eyes.

"Please, you don't need to speak of it," Rafe said gently. "You are upsetting yourself, Mama, and that was not my intention."

"No," she said, cutting him off. "It is long past time that I spoke, and you, too, have a right to know." She drew in a deep breath, steeling herself to continue. "I never got over the fear of what he might do, but since nothing ever came of his threats, I tried to make myself believe it was only the darkness talking. He always recovered and then life went on—and happily, Raphael. We were always so happy until the next time."

"So you decided to leave him alone when he retreated into the library in another one of his dark spells," Rafe said.

She nodded, seeing that morning so clearly. The bright sunlight had glanced off the walls in defiance of the darkness in the house. "I never knew how long they would last. Sometimes he would be better in hours, sometimes it took weeks. I found it best to let him be.

This time, he'd been drinking heavily for days. He closed the door and locked it, and I thought he would sleep it off as he often did and eventually come out feeling better. That was the pattern, you see, but this time he slipped out of the house, and—and he finally did what he always said he would do."

She pressed her forehead hard into her hand as if she could push away her guilt and regret.

Rafe crossed the room and knelt in front of her, covering her free hand with his own. "It wasn't your fault any more than it was mine, Mama, although it took me years to understand that. We can torture ourselves with all the things we might have done, should have done, and none of it does any good, none of it will bring him back. We have to absolve ourselves and go on."

"You are wise, Raphael," the duchess said, laying a hand on his shoulder. "Very wise to realize that."

"As I said, it took time before I learned to stop torturing myself. At least you did something productive in founding the sanitarium. I only wish we had been able . . ."

"That we had been able to do what, darling?"

He paused, then gently smiled at her. "Able to talk about this when it happened. I lied to protect you and Hugo, and you lied to protect us. It's been one large parcel of lies, designed to protect each other, and all you and I managed to do was to lock ourselves out alone in the cold, and I suppose we locked Hugo out there, too."

"Darling," she said uncertainly, lifting her head, determined to have it all out, now that they'd come this far. "Your brother—does he know that his father's death was self-inflicted?"

Rafe pushed his other hand through his hair and sighed heavily. "No. I don't think he even suspects, and I hope to God it stays that way. He's been through enough, losing Papa when he was only five. At least I had a few more years of maturity to help me deal with the shock, but he was just a baby." He shook his head. "I remember—I remember how devastated he was, how worried I was for him. He'd always been such a sunny, happy lad, full of nonsense, making everyone laugh, and then that terrible day happened, and all the light went out of his eyes. I'm not sure it ever came back, not really, despite the act he puts on."

"I do know," the duchess said in a low voice. "I have been gravely concerned about him for the longest time—not just because of the gambling and all the other pieces of nonsense he gets up to, but because I don't think Hugo knows who he really is. I feel I must be at fault, that I wasn't a good enough mother to him, that I should have done something different or better." She wiped away a fresh rush of tears with shaking fingers.

"Please do not blame yourself. You have been a wonderful mother to us both," Rafe said, handing her his handkerchief. "I've blamed myself for his troubles as well, but to tell you the truth, I've always thought that the real Hugo disappeared after Papa's death. Do you remember? He shut himself away in the nursery and refused to come out for weeks, and when he finally did emerge, he was a different child, difficult and rebellious, jumpy as could be, lashing out at everything and everyone."

"Yes . . . I do remember," she said with a frown, thinking back to those dreadful months after her husband's death. "I was so caught up in my own grief that I wasn't paying proper attention to either of you, I suppose, but I do remember thinking that he wasn't himself. I put the change down to shock and unhappiness, but he never grew out of his difficulties, did he?"

"No, although I have seen a few small glimpses of the old Hugo in the last year, enough to give me hope . . . Good Lord, Mama," he said with a choked laugh, standing and picking up the letter. "What are we doing hashing over the past when it's the present we should be thinking about—Hugo's gone and gotten himself married."

Eleanor's voice caught on a half-laugh, half-sob. "So he has. So he has. I can't quite believe it."

"I am knocked flat, myself. So please enlighten me—who is this Meggie Bloom? You never did say, except that you thought Hugo met her when he visited your sanitarium." Rafe froze, his eyes filled with sudden horror. "No—oh no, don't tell me. She's not . . . is she? Please tell me there's another explanation? I couldn't bear for Hugo to make such a terrible mistake—not that one, Mama." Rafe winced. "Here I thought he had managed to perpetrate nearly every scandal in the book . . . Wait—surely he wouldn't have been *allowed* to marry her? Or would he have been, if she was lucid at the time? Dear God. Oh, dear, dear God, what has he gone and done now?"

Eleanor laughed merrily, a cleansing relief from the intense emotions of the last half hour. "No cause for worry," she said. "There is another explanation, thank goodness. Meggie Bloom works—or worked—at the sanitarium, and although I have never met her, from all accounts she is a lovely girl, very compassionate, and truly gifted with those who are troubled."

Rafe snorted. "I doubt Hugo was interested in those sort of gifts. Is the girl a striking beauty?"

The duchess searched her brain, but came up blank. "I don't really know. Sister Agnes, the nun who runs the sanitarium, never gave me any details other than that, but why would she? She knows I am concerned only with the level of care the patients receive. She mentioned Meggie Bloom merely in the context of her excellent work."

"Odd, Hugo doesn't say anything about the sanitarium. He says he met her in Woodbridge."

"Yes, dear, but then he doesn't go into much detail about anything. I suppose he didn't think the actual location important, and it is certainly possible that he met her in the town. She's not confined, after all, and Woodbridge would be the largest village near Lyden."

Rafe rubbed his thumb over his bottom lip. "Mama, do you suppose it's possible that this girl, being without family or money, decided that Hugo would make a nice catch and set her cap at him in the most obvious way? The marriage does seem rather precipitous, after all, and given the difference in their social rank she would have a very great deal to gain if she did the time-honored thing."

The duchess gasped. "Do you mean you think he got her—oh, dear. I hadn't thought of that, although I suppose I should have, knowing your brother. Oh, that would be unfortunate."

"Mmm," Rafe replied, rereading the page. "On the other hand he says that he loves her very much and is happier than he's ever been. He would have to love her if he decided to marry a penniless girl with no breeding to speak of, although I confess to true astonishment if that really is the case. It seems a hell of a selfless act to take on a girl of no consequence, and Hugo has never been known for his selflessness."

"It is true that he tends toward self-indulgence," the duchess agreed unhappily.

"Anyway, Hugo would say he loved her, wouldn't he, if he was going to put a good face on the matter, and you know how he is about trying to gloss over his mistakes."

"People do grow up, dear," she said in her younger son's defense. "Not everyone comes to responsibility as early as you did."

"Mama," Rafe said with obvious exasperation, "I am

not trying to be hard on Hugo or paint him as a devil, I am only trying to make sense of this. As much as I love my brother, I have no intention of letting him pull the wool over my eyes, not if he's done something that might seriously compromise the family."

"Such as what?" the duchess asked sharply. "He's only married the girl, Raphael, he hasn't committed a crime. The match might be inappropriate, but it's done, and we will just have to put the best face on it we can."

"I have no trouble with that," Rafe replied, "as long as Hugo does love her and she loves him in return—Lord knows, anyone who can bring my brother real happiness has my blessing, and I don't give a fig about her background. No, my problem is that we know very little about Miss Bloom's strengths and a great deal about Hugo's weaknesses. I am only looking for the truth, whatever it may be—forewarned is forearmed." He cocked his head and looked at his mother in an appraising fashion. "Can *you* think of anything else, anything else at all that might logically explain this sudden and highly surprising marriage?"

"Well, I did broach the subject of marriage to Hugo," the duchess said, tapping one finger against her mouth. "He had just bought Lyden Hall and said he intended to settle there. He told me he would consider the idea, and he did go to London for the Season, after all."

"Which in itself is not normal behavior for Hugo," Rafe pointed out. "I can only think that he must have taken your words to heart and been looking for a wife, as bizarre as the idea is."

"Yes . . . and I've heard from more than one person that he had his eye on that awful Amelia Langford with the intention of making a match, although I never believed it for a moment, despite the size of her fortune."

"Amelia Langford?" Rafe closed his eyes for a brief moment as if pained at the very idea. "I should think not. If there is one thing I can say for my brother, his taste has always been impeccable—not necessarily correct, but impeccable no matter what he was getting up to. Which brings me back to my original point. If Hugo was so busy looking for a socially respectable wife in London, then when would he have had time to court this Meggie Bloom all the way out in Suffolk? And why?"

"I cannot think. My sources place him at nearly every important event in London since April. I can't imagine his driving back and forth in between social engagements."

"Precisely. Which indicates to me that if he did get up to mischief with Miss Bloom, it was back in March, as you said. He married her at the end of the first week in June. Need I be more clear?"

The duchess frowned. "I just don't know, darling. Even if he had put her in the family way, who would have forced him to marry her? She has no influence, certainly no relatives to hold a gun to his head, and even if she had, Hugo is a duke's son. He wouldn't be expected to marry a girl of no consequence—these unfortunate things happen all the time, and a tidy sum of money usually takes care of the problem."

"How worldly you are," Rafe said dryly.

"One needs to be, especially with a son like Hugo," the duchess replied, picking up Hugo's letter again. "I would like to think that we are wrong, that he does love her. It is not outside the realm of possibility. As I said, I've been told that she is full of compassion, acutely sensitive, and . . . and I can only think that your brother must have seen all of those qualities in her," she finished lamely, scanning the rest of the letter. "Maybe he really has changed. According to this, he is deeply involved in seeing to Lyden business."

"Let me see," Rafe demanded, holding out his hand.

"Yes, of course, although it doesn't seem to say anything more about the marriage." She handed the next page to him.

Rafe read carefully, rubbing the back of his neck. "He says that there have been some sort of misdoings involving previous trustees." He looked up. "What previous trustees? Does he refer to Linus Eliot's time? Who managed the estate?"

"I have no idea, dear. Hugo told me very little when we last spoke, although he did say there was a steward."

"Hmm. He says he is trying to straighten all of that out." Rafe sucked in a breath of astonishment. "He *says* he intends to write me for advice when he has more details in hand, as he is deeply concerned about his tenants and their ongoing welfare." Rafe looked up at his mother. "He intends to consult me? Hugo has never consulted me about anything, ever, unless it was over how I was going to bail him out of trouble."

"As I said, people grow up, dear."

Rafe's voice became even more incredulous. "He says that he is presently making certain his tenants are looked after until he can sort out the problems, but wants to be sure of their future security no matter the cost."

The paper fluttered from between his fingers and floated down to the tabletop, landing halfway between the butter dish and the marmalade pot.

"Mama? I think you had better dispatch yourself to England immediately and see just what is going on. I'd go myself if I didn't have a wife and infant son who need me."

"I think I had best do exactly that," the duchess agreed, "and I believe I know exactly where to start."

"With our esteemed firm of solicitors?" Rafe replied, shooting her a look of wry amusement.

"No. With Sister Agnes, director of the Woodbridge Sanitarium. If anyone has answers, it will be she. Who would know better what went on between Meggie Bloom and Hugo?"

Rafe's face split in a broad grin. "Oh, good idea, Mama. You go and ask a nun all about it. Do be sure to write and give me the details."

"Dreadful child," the duchess said fondly, rising to drop a kiss on her son's head before going to make her travel arrangements.

20

"Such lovely stitchery, child, simply lovely. Did the nuns teach you?"

Ottoline hung over Meggie's shoulder, watching as she placed the finishing touches on Eve. "Mmm," Meggie replied absently, sitting back and appraising her work, now stretched on a proper frame that Dorelia had produced from some corner of the house. She continued to produce all sorts of Lally treasures that she'd been saving over the years.

Silver-backed hairbrushes, tortoiseshell combs, beautiful crystal bottles full of creams and lotions that Dorelia had made up herself all appeared as if by magic in her room. Dresses for all times of the day and night, cleverly altered by Dorelia to fit the present styles, began to fill the cavernous wardrobe. Shawls and delicate chemises, gossamer-thin night shifts, retrimmed hats, marched along side by side with shoes and boots and gloves.

Meggie felt as if Dorelia and Ottoline expected her to waltz about like an overdone fashion plate, but she had no place to wear most of the beautiful clothes—let alone any time or inclination to change seven times a day. A day dress, a riding habit, and a dinner dress were good enough for her, even if the aunties didn't approve of her lack of attention to fashion.

The afternoon sunshine poured through the windows of Meggie's very own sitting room, a luxury she never would have dreamed of three weeks before, and lit up the tapestry in a brilliant display of colors. Meggie's embroidered Garden of Eden looked as fresh and dazzling as her new life.

She'd had hardly any time to devote to her stitching in the last three weeks, far too busy with Hugo and her work on the estate. What few moments of solitude she could snatch she did, wanting the time to think and reflect on what had been done, what needed to be done, what might be done down the road.

She began to better understand why Sister Agnes considered deep silences and long contemplations essential. Before Lyden, Meggie's responsibilities had been confined to the management of patients and gardens. Now she had so many more obligations. The tenants and their welfare needed attention, from the health of their children to the state of their drains.

Mr. Coldsnap, of whom she had become very fond, was a godsend, taking her around and introducing her to the various families. He carefully answered any questions Meggie asked and explained all sorts of other things he thought she needed to know as Hugo's wife. He made her feel like a proper lady—and Meggie found to her delight that she didn't have to alter her behavior one iota to have him treat her like one. As far as he was concerned, she was Lady Hugo, and that was that.

Lyden Hall itself needed managing, too, for the more staff Hugo hired, the more people she had to oversee. Much to her surprise, the Mabey sisters had stepped back, professing themselves overjoyed to be relieved of responsibility, but gently nudging and instructing whenever they felt it necessary.

Two footmen had replaced Roberto, who had been elevated to butler. Meggie now had a housekeeper, a gentle soul named Mrs. Hitchcock who thankfully got along with everyone, including Cookie.

Meggie even had her own personal maid, Daisy, whom she'd brought over from Snape, just as she'd promised Rose—and thank the good Lord, Daisy was proving a great deal more intelligent and efficient than her younger sister.

"Where's the apple, dear?"

"I beg your pardon?" Meggie asked.

"I said, where's the apple? Shouldn't Eve be holding out an apple to tempt the poor boy?"

Meggie looked up at her dear adopted auntie, who sometimes tried her patience, but whom Meggie valued highly. "No, she should not. I've always thought the notion that woman was responsible for corrupting man rather depressing and ill-spirited. Anyway, Adam took the apple, didn't he, but that was never made much of at all."

Ottoline cackled. "Good for you, child, good for you. Right you are, too. Where is Adam in the scheme of things? I presume he comes next?"

"Yes, he does." Meggie grinned up at Ottoline. "I didn't have a proper model before now. I think if I'd tried to depict him, I would have ended up with a Jasper Oddbins, who is not very inspirational, being barrel-chested, knock-kneed, and nearly bald."

Ottoline nearly collapsed in giggles. "My, no. That would be no good at all. Now dear Hugo, he's another story, eh? He would grace your tapestry nicely, with that fine masculine figure and a head of hair any girl would be happy to sink her fingers into."

"Auntie, sometimes I think you have no shame," Meggie said, knowing perfectly well it was the truth. She'd long since intuited all the details of Ottoline and Dorelia's extraordinary relationship with Linus Eliot, and in her secret heart she thought it wonderful, even if wildly eccentric.

At least they'd all been very happy together for well over forty years from everything she'd gathered. She still wondered exactly how they'd managed their unique arrangement, but given that the aunties seemed to operate as one voice, she couldn't be surprised that they'd made it work to everyone's benefit.

Both sisters certainly had a lusty approach to the physical aspects of life, which they made no attempt to stifle in Meggie's presence now that she was a married woman.

"Madrigal, dearest? Do you attend me? Sometimes I do wonder if you haven't Lally's tendency to drift off when one is speaking."

"I am listening," Meggie answered, digging in her satchel for another skein of thread. "You were speaking of Hugo's hair. It does need cutting, I agree," she said, hiding her smile. "I wonder if he ever is going to summon his valet—he keeps saying he will, and then nothing comes of it."

"That comes as no surprise, dear girl. Use your brain. Why would your husband want to introduce a blatant reminder of his past life into the idyllic situation he has here? He's learning to manage on his own, and if you ask me, he likes it, or at least he likes it for the moment."

Meggie sat up, the thread forgotten. "What do you mean he likes it for the moment? Are you saying that he will not like it for very much longer?"

"I am saying that he is a man. Men become restless very easily. He might decide that he has had his immediate fill of the splendor of marriage and the simplicity of country life that goes along with it."

"I don't—what do you mean, auntie?" Meggie asked, concerned. She felt a strange, nervous energy coming from Ottoline, most unusual in the usually ebullient and outspoken woman, and it worried her.

"I only mean that he will most probably vanish shortly to London and places beyond before eventually returning and picking up the pieces," Ottoline said abruptly. "That *is* what men of his station do, you know."

Meggies mouth went dry. She didn't believe it. She wouldn't believe it. Hugo wouldn't do that to her. She knew he wouldn't. "I think you are mistaken about him," she whispered.

Ottoline moved around to Meggie's front. "I do not mean to distress you, child, only to warn you," she said, taking Meggie's hand. "That is how life goes. If left to their own devices, men will stray, so they will. They bore easily and are always on the lookout for new sexual conquests, especially once they think they have you in hand. You need to keep them where they belong, or go where they go. One trick is to keep the bed as welcoming as you can, and your tongue between your teeth if that doesn't suffice, but I personally recommend staying close by their sides so as to forestall temptation."

Meggie blindly nodded at this unsolicited and unwelcome piece of advice.

Ottoline patted her hand and placed it back on Meggie's lap. "You're a good girl, Madrigal, that you are."

She then proceeded to trot out of the room as if she'd said nothing more remarkable than that the habit of eating three meals a day was to be recommended.

Meggie sat frozen. The idea of Hugo seeking out another woman made her heart contract painfully. Being told that it was an inevitability, and told from someone who would know how these things went, made her want to die.

Made her want to die? She brought herself up short. Absolute nonsense. She'd survived far too much to let herself be brought low by the base assumptions of an old woman who hardly even knew Hugo.

Meggie took a deep breath and raised her chin defiantly. She wouldn't believe it of Hugo, she just wouldn't. It didn't matter what other gentlemen of quality did, Hugo wasn't anything like them.

He cared nothing for their empty values. He'd said as

much, lying in her arms, murmuring countless times to her how happy he was to be away from that world, how none of it meant anything to him. He'd had his fill and had no intention of going back to that sort of life.

Meggie believed him.

He loved Lyden. He loved his work, his people, he loved her, or at least everything he knew about her. She was still very careful to keep her education to herself, since she didn't want to upset him in any way, and she certainly took care to keep her gift to herself, but in all other things they were in accord with each other.

Hugo was even in accord with Hadrian . . . well, in a manner of speaking, she amended. They put up with each other. Hugo allowed Hadrian to come along when he and Meggie went walking or riding together. He made no objections to Hadrian's presence in the house, but the bedroom was firmly off limits. Hadrian slept in the kitchen, and that was that.

For his part, Hadrian made it clear that Hugo was no foe, but he wasn't exactly a friend, either. Hugo never received the licks that Hadrian lavished on everyone else, nor did Hadrian ever invite him to a playful game of tag. He tolerated Hugo, no more, and Meggie understood. For so long it had just been the two of them, and she had bestowed all of her love and her affection on Hadrian. Now Hadrian had to share Meggie with someone else, and that someone happened to be a man who did not hold Hadrian in the same high regard that he was accustomed to.

She shook her head with a laugh. Dorelia had been right about that—the two of them were engaged in a struggle over territorial rights, and they were still coming to terms.

Glancing up at the clock on the mantelpiece, she realized that if she didn't hurry, she'd be late for her meeting with the vicar. He wanted to organize a Ladies Aid Society, with Meggie as chairwoman and patroness.

She felt rather odd about the idea of being a patroness of anything, but she certainly saw the worth in the idea. It had also occurred to her that this might be a good venue for showing people that Hugo's interest in good works went beyond the boundaries of Lyden Hall. She thought she'd keep the proposition to herself though, until she had something concrete with which to present Hugo.

He tended to be very protective of her, worried that she might be overcome by the pressures and demands of the outside world, given her previously sheltered environment.

Unfortunately, to Hugo the outside world included not just London and all that it entailed, to which she readily admitted a fear of, but also the tiny hamlet of Orford.

Really, as much as she loved him, sometimes Hugo could be very silly.

"Tell me, Mr. Coldsnap," Hugo said, riding out on the daily afternoon rounds that he enjoyed immensely, "seeing as it is only mid-June, if we planted the southerly fields with hay, and plowed up the northerly fields, leaving them fallow until the autumn, would we not be able to plant a winter crop in the latter and still make next spring's schedule for crop rotation?"

"Indeed we would, and very good of you to see it," Coldsnap said, his voice filled with approval.

"Not at all. It is you who provided me with the books and charts and suggestions. I only wish to implement them in the wisest way possible, and this occurred to me as an interesting option."

"A fine one, too, the more I consider it," Coldsnap

said. "I daresay, Lord Hugo, you have learned an extraordinary amount in hardly any time at all, and absorbed it better than I ever would have imagined. It takes imagination to see beyond the obvious, and you have plenty of that."

Hugo glanced over at him. "So I've been told," he replied wryly.

He didn't add that for once in his life he was putting that imagination to good use. Oh, how he liked the feeling of being truly productive, of having each day count for something, of seeing even in this short time his efforts make a difference. The satisfaction that he had when he went to sleep at night, Meggie wrapped up in his arms after a rewarding session of lovemaking was far beyond anything he'd ever expected when he'd taken on Lyden—and Meggie.

Life was good. Hugo felt blessed far beyond anything he deserved, and he couldn't help questioning the gifts bestowed on him out of nowhere.

"I cannot tell you what pleasure I take from working alongside you, just as it was in the old days," Coldsnap said, rambling on. "The tenants, they feel just the same, my yes, for they've said as much over and over again, and none of them can say enough about your dear wife, either. She seems to know just what they need to hear, and her manner is so easy, so natural, and charming that they light right up when she goes to visit." He nodded. "A lovely woman, Lord Hugo. You could not have chosen better."

Hugo personally agreed with him, but he only inclined his head and smiled. It didn't do to say too much about Meggie, just in case she should have a relapse. He prayed that would not happen.

She had made such improvement in only two weeks that he had actually begun to believe that Meggie's mental condition had been caused only by a severe lack of love, coupled with the lack of stimulation endemic to institutional life.

He'd once seen the same phenomenon occur in a horse who had been locked away and badly neglected. Destined to be shot, at the last moment it had been sold for a song to a new and caring owner and had flourished, its nervous habits and peculiarities disappearing as if they'd never been.

Once released from confinement, Meggie had flowered at Lyden. Her brain appeared to heal from its dysfunction with every hour, every day that passed—and with each of those hours and days he loved her more. True, she still had her odd moments when she'd come out with the most bizarre statements and observations, but he now barely noticed them at all. Or maybe he was simply becoming inured to them.

He did worry that she had yet to tell him she loved him, even though he was nearly certain that she did, but he could only think that she was not capable of understanding the fullness of her feelings, never having loved a man before.

For the first time in his life, he truly blessed his family, and the love that had been freely given to him. The reason that he had not freely or readily received it still escaped his understanding.

He supposed part of his reticence stemmed from being a second son, another part from losing his father before he had a chance to know him. His memories of the man were mere vestiges of light and shadow that still played tricks with him—sometimes ringing with the faint recollection of laughter, of being tossed high in the air, of sunshine that trickled down through every day.

Then there were the other memories—dark and oppressive, fearful, times when the sun ceased to exist. He remembered finding places to hide, keeping well out of sound and reach, although he couldn't remember why.

It was probably best he didn't, best he kept that part of his life tucked well away. Some things didn't bear too close an inspection. In any case, his childhood was not important. He'd survived it well enough, his mind intact. Meggie was his concern now. Meggie had not so well survived the ravages of her own childhood.

He wished he had full confidence that she would heal completely, but something deep inside him refused to believe that he might be so lucky. A nagging voice persistently told him that just when all appeared well, disaster would strike. Meggie would fall back to pieces, and his world would come crashing down around him.

"Yes, indeed," Coldsnap continued, ignoring Hugo's protracted silence, not needing anyone's conversation but his own. "It is a shame that not all marriages are so happily made." He pointed toward a cottage that sat close to the road, with a neat fence surrounding a front garden filled with vegetables. "For example, that place over there is Johnnie Jaffrey's place. Johnnie works out at the landing dock, and a good, hard-working man he is, but broken in heart and spirit."

"Why is that?" Hugo asked, not at all sure he wanted to hear; he had enough concerns on that subject as it was.

"It's a sad story, my lord, and one I wish I didn't have to tell. You see, some twenty years ago, Johnnie married a girl from Thorpeness, some distance up the coast, so he knew nothing of her family or her history. They'd met at one of the annual markets and fallen in love. Not more than six weeks later they wed, and if you ask me, Johnnie should have asked the girl's family why they were in such a rush to have her off their hands."

He took off his hat and scratched his balding scalp. "Turned out not a month after the marriage that the girl—Stella Goring was her maiden name—was right out of her mind. She tried to stab Johnnie to death one night. Sadly, he couldn't prove she was mad at the time of the wedding, which would have invalidated it. The law forbids marriage to a lunatic."

All the blood drained from Hugo's face as Reginald Coldsnap's words sank in. *Dear God,* "Are you sure?"

"Indeed, my lord," Coldsnap said, shooting a look of surprise over at Hugo. "I daresay you're a good and caring man to be touched by old Johnnie's plight, though I'm sorry to tell you that the story is not over."

Hugo barely heard Coldsnap. He thought he'd covered all contingencies, but this one remote detail of the law had completely slipped by him. He should have thought of such an obvious point, but in his anxiety and haste to marry Meggie, he'd overlooked the most pertinent detail—her sanity, or lack thereof.

He wiped his hand over his brow, where a fine film of cold sweat had beaded. Think, man, think, he told himself. If anyone should discover Meggie's mental state at the time of their marriage, he had to be able to challenge it.

"Lord Hugo? Do you not wish to hear the rest of the story?"

"Oh, yes. I beg your pardon. Please continue," Hugo said, only half-listening, the other part of his brain racing to find some sort of plausible solution to the new, horrifying possibility that his marriage to Meggie might not be legal.

"You see," Coldsnap said, "the other tragedy was that no one from her family or even from her village would testify that she'd actually been mad at the time of her marriage. Before, indeed so, and after, without question, but not during that particular period, so old Johnnie could do nothing to free himself from the bonds of matrimony."

"I don't understand," Hugo croaked. "You just said a lunatic cannot marry."

"Ah, but here lies the rub, and old Johnnie's tragedy, my lord. The law says that as long as a lunatic is in a lucid interval and fully understands the import of the contract, then the marriage is legal."

Wait, Hugo told himself—that might be it! Sister Agnes. She had given her blessing to the marriage, hadn't she? She'd actually said that Meggie had to use her own judgment; he remembered that clearly enough, since he'd wondered at her particular use of the words at the time. The statement alone surely would show that Sister Agnes thought Meggie sane enough for marriage, and what court of law would argue with a nun?

"I can't say, of course," Coldsnap continued blithely, "that Johnnie had the right of it and that Stella really was mad when she married him, but the end result was that the girl was shipped off to an asylum where she lives to this day, and poor old Johnnie Jaffrey is condemned to live his life out alone."

Coldsnap settled his hat back on his head.

Hugo rubbed the back of his neck. "Mmm," he said. "A pity indeed." On the other hand, he thought, the very fact that Meggie had consented to marry him while locked up in a mental asylum could go against him, as well as the fact that they had been wed less than twenty-four hours later. A court of law might rule against Sister Agnes's judgment, based on that alone—if Meggie had been sane at the time, then why had she still been incarcerated?

He tried to steady his breathing, deciding that he was looking for trouble where there was none, or at least not yet. The trick was to keep Meggie's incarceration a secret.

Anyway, who would think to question her sanity now when she behaved in as normal a fashion as could be hoped? He knew some eccentrics who acted more lunatic than she did. The Mabey sisters were a classic example, and no one had ever locked them up.

Best not to think about it, he told himself firmly. Meggie would stay healthy and semi-sane, and they would live out the rest of their lives in a state of happy matrimony. He would accept nothing less: if he had to, he would fight to the death for Meggie and his marriage, and that was all there was to that.

"I believe our scheme worked, Sister, although I am not entirely sure," Ottoline said, handing Dorelia a bottle. "I cannot help but feel I was a little cruel to the poor child."

"Thank you, dearest," Dorelia said, taking the bottle and inserting a funnel into the top. "Never mind being cruel, you said you thought it imperative that Madrigal go to London with dear Hugo when he suddenly ups and leaves. I wish I understood better the reason why he would do such a thing, though, and this urgency you feel about the situation."

"If I knew myself, I'd tell you," Ottoline said with irritation. "All I saw was trouble if he went on his own—he needs Madrigal there at his side. Betrayal. That was the word, clear as day. Betrayal, linked right up with Hugo."

"Hmm. Hmmm. I don't know," Dorelia said, frowning in concentration as she carefully poured her herbal oil into the bottle and wiped the neck with a cloth. "Hypericum perforatum," she mumbled, writing on a label. "Lovely healing stuff—never known anything to penetrate the tissues as fast as Saint John's Wort. What were you saying? Oh, yes. Betrayal. It seems very early in the marriage for Hugo to be taking up with another woman. Look at the way he is with the girl—he can't keep his eyes or his hands off her."

"I didn't *say* the betrayal would be infidelity, although I believe a woman is somehow involved. I *said* the best way to get Madrigal off to London with him was to put the thought in her mind that dear Hugo might stray if she didn't go." Ottoline took the full bottle back and stoppered it. "She's made it perfectly clear that she dreads the very idea of London, and why shouldn't she, poor angel? She's convinced she will embarrass her husband, not knowing anything about the ways of the *ton*. Absolute nonsense, of course, but she's not to know that."

"All she needs is a little confidence," Dorelia said, holding out her hand for another bottle.

"Yes, but I still think it cruel to imply that her husband is going to go dashing off to bed with another woman the first chance he gets. You should have seen the expression on her dear face. Crushed, she was, and rightly so."

"Well, you didn't come up with anything better," Dorelia snapped. "When needs must and all that."

"I was only saying that I hated to upset her," Ottoline snapped back. "Dear me, I do wish I knew what this is all about, but never mind. We'll find out soon enough." She leaned her elbows on the table, watching her sister pour the next batch of herb-infused oil. "Dorelia, dearest, what about finding a solicitor? Do you think it is time to approach Hugo on the subject of arranging Madrigal's dowry? We've already waited three weeks."

"Hmm. Perhaps, Sister, perhaps. I confess that I have been trying to build up my courage. One slip of the tongue to the dear boy and we could do some real damage."

"Yes indeed," Ottoline agreed, "although we still don't know how much he realizes about Madrigal. Suppose he's aware of the entire story and we're fussing over nothing?"

"Dear, oh dear. I just don't know." Dorelia clucked her tongue. "Doesn't your B.G. tell you anything?"

"Nothing, although my common sense tells me that we should be doing something more than praying for a Sign."

"Speak for yourself. Praying for a Sign has never failed us yet. I do think you are lacking in patience, beloved." She started to hum as she removed the funnel from the next filled bottle.

"Miss Ottoline, Miss Dorelia?" Roberto appeared in the stillroom door, dressed in his fine new blue and gold livery.

"Yes, dear?" they said in unison, beaming fondly at him.

"A Mr. Gostrain has just arrived with urgent business for Lord Hugo, who is not yet returned. Mr. Gostrain says he is with the legal firm of . . ." Roberto consulted the snowy card in his hand, "of Gostrain, Jenkins, and Waterville. What would you like—"

He didn't manage to finish. The Mabey sisters shrieked in tandem and streaked past him out the door, nearly knocking him flat in their headlong rush for the house.

21

Hugo, who had come in the back way and gone upstairs to change out of his riding clothes, stopped dead in his tracks at the sound of frantic female twittering coming from the hall below. In between shrieks of delight he could make out an equally frantic and alarmingly familiar male voice.

Hugo made his way over to the railing with trepidation, terrified he might be right about the identity behind that familiar voice.

He looked down, then closed his eyes and slid a hand over his face.

Not only had James Gostrain arrived with no warning, but the damned Mabey sisters were attempting to hold him up as if they were elderly female highwaymen.

"Mr. Gostrain, you dear, dear man, what an absolute marvel that you've come just when you did," Dorelia cooed, her hand clamped like a vise on the startled solicitor's arm. She glared at her sister. "What did I tell you, Ottoline? One asks and one receives and patience is the key. Is this not a Sign?"

Hugo groaned. This was *not* the dignified welcome he'd had in mind for his solicitor. God only knew what Gostrain could be thinking—or why the Mabey sisters had assaulted him. He couldn't imagine what they wanted from the poor man, unless it was to denounce Hugo for some crime he hadn't committed.

Ottoline grabbed Mr. Gostrain's other arm. "So it is, Sister, so it is. Now, dear Mr. Gostrain, since darling Hugo is not in at the moment and you have nothing better to do, perhaps you would like to hear what we have to say."

So would Hugo. He'd have their scrawny necks if they turned out to be up to no good after all he'd done for them, and by God he'd silence them if they even tried to pollute Gostrain's ears with a pack of lies.

"Begging your pardon, but who are you?" the startled man asked, looking from one to the other of the bony hands that held him captive.

"Why we are Dorelia and Ottoline Mabey," Dorelia chirped. "Hugo's beloved aunties. Has he not mentioned us to you?"

"Ah—ah yes, the late Lord Eliot's leavings—er, that is to say, his bequest."

Hugo smothered a laugh. So Gostrain hadn't forgotten Hugo's own description of the Mabey women.

"Precisely. And since you mention it, bequest is exactly the point, since we would like to make one to darling Madrigal. We need some advice, my dear man, and the sooner we receive it the better . . ."

A *bequest*? Hugo had heard enough. Since the old bats had nothing to bequeath but their furbelows, he didn't intend to have Gostrain waste any more of his time on their silly prattling.

He tore down the staircase, forcing a smile to his lips.

"Mr. Gostrain. What a very pleasant surprise," he said, slowing his pace to a dignified walk halfway down. "I see you have met Miss Ottoline and Miss Dorelia Mabey, my, er, aunts. Aunties, do unhand Mr. Gostrain, won't you? I think he values not just the sleeves of his coat, but his limbs as well."

Their faces fell as if they'd had a delicious sweet yanked straight out of their fingers. "Very well, Hugo dear, but we do wish you would listen."

"Later," he said, meaning most likely never. "I have

business with Mr. Gostrain, and I would be most grateful if you would allow us to get on with it."

"Yes, of course." Ottoline—or was it Dorelia? He still couldn't tell which was which—scuffed the toe of her slipper against the floor. "Later, then." She dropped Gostrain's arm and grabbed her sister's instead, tugging on it. "Ottoline, dearest, let us leave the men to their work and get on with our own."

As if functioning with one shared brain, they both turned around at exactly the same moment and slipped out the front door.

Hugo smiled weakly. "I apologize," he said. "Please, do come into my study where we will be undisturbed. As you have most likely perceived, Lyden is not yet functioning as smoothly as it might."

"No need for apologies, Lord Hugo. It is I who should apologize for not having written to inform you of my arrival, but you will shortly understand my reasons. I thought you would be happy to wave the formalities in light of the news I have come to deliver."

"Oh? Good news I hope?" Hugo said in polite inquiry, but inside he was in knots. Either Gostrain had come to tell him about Meggie's fortune, or else he had somehow discovered about Meggie's years in the asylum. One way led to victory, the other to certain disaster.

"I can only say that it is astonishing news, my lord. Astonishing. I do not know how you will receive it. I must warn you, I received a great shock upon hearing it."

Hugo wasn't sure if he liked the sound of that at all. He drew on all the lessons of his gambling days and smiled easily, despite the sick twisting in his stomach.

"Nothing could be more astonishing than the happy turn my life has taken recently," he bluffed. "I cannot tell you what joy my wife has brought me, Mr. Gostrain, and I am most sensible of my debt to you. My present happiness would not have been possible had you not steered me straight with your sage advice."

"I do not recall exactly what I said, but I am gratified that my words served you well." Gostrain took the chair Hugo indicated on the opposite side of his desk.

"I hope your partners share the same generosity of sentiment," Hugo said dryly, relaxing a bit. "It is not every day that a man of my position chooses to marry a woman of Meggie's station."

"Indeed not, sir. I—er, that is mostly what I have come to discuss with you."

"I see." Hugo steeled himself, folding his hands together on the desktop. "I assume you refer to the marriage contract I asked you to draw up? I warn you, Gostrain, I will hear no argument against my wishes."

"I will give you none. I have, in fact, brought you far more than a marriage contract, my lord. Before I go into details, however, I am first obliged to ask you some pertinent questions regarding your wife's past."

Oh, dear God, let him not be referring to Meggie's most recent past, he prayed, working hard to keep the impassive expression on his face.

"Ask away, although I have told you what I know of my wife. She is an honest, decent woman who bears no responsibility for the harshness of her life."

"I am sure you are correct, my lord. However, these questions are directed not at your wife's character, but rather at her parentage."

Hugo nearly keeled over in relief—Gostrain didn't know about the asylum after all. "Her parentage?" he managed to say in an even voice. "I told you, I only know that Meggie's mother died in childbirth."

"Yes," Gostrain said, producing a document from his case, then reaching into his pocket for a pair of glasses. He placed them on his nose, and peered down at the sheaf of papers. "You said, my lord, that your wife's mother was named Margaret. That would be Margaret Bloom, correct?"

"Yes . . ." Hugo said warily. "Why do you ask?"

"Allow me to continue. You said your wife was a local woman, but do you have any idea where her mother came from?"

"Ramsholt, I believe, although that is not where Meggie was born. Again, why do you ask?" Oh yes, it was all going exactly to plan, he thought gleefully.

"Bear with me, if you will. In your letter you mentioned that after her birth your wife had been taken in by a widow. Do you have any idea of the name of that widow, or where she lived?"

Hugo adopted a puzzled frown. "I do. Her name was Emily Crewe and she lived in Bury St. Edmunds, where Margaret Bloom also lived. See here, Gostrain, where is all this going?"

"Patience, my lord. You also mentioned that your wife's father had died prior to her birth. Who gave you that notion?"

"My wife did," Hugo said, thanking his lucky stars that Meggie had told him what she had. "Although the information she has about her parents came from Mrs. Crewe and is cursory at best. Again, I ask you why this is of any importance? I only wish to draw up a marriage contract, sir, not a genealogical chart."

"Yes, quite. I think that is enough confirmation." Mr. Gostrain scratched his head. "Lord Hugo, you are under the impression that your wife is penniless. I am pleased to tell you that is not the case. Your wife is, in fact, a very wealthy woman."

At those words a flood of relief swept through Hugo, leaving him weak. Done. It was done. Lyden was safe, and he and Meggie were home free. All he had to do now was to play out the rest of his hand without tripping himself up.

He summoned up an expression of incredulity. "Mr. Gostrain, I beg your pardon, but I believe you have not been listening. I thought I made the situation perfectly clear—Meggie has no family, no roots. She lived in an orphanage from the age of nine, for the love of God."

"Yes, and everything you have just told me explains why no one was able to find her before this. You see, my lord, your wife's father, a Mr. David Russell, did not die before her birth. He sailed to India, leaving behind Margaret Bloom and their unborn child. Mr. Russell later tried to locate Margaret and the child but with no success, but still he left the enormous fortune he'd made in the East India Company to Margaret Bloom and their child, in the hope that they would eventually be found. We were asked to act as executors of his will."

Hugo didn't have to pretend a thing. He stared at Gostrain as if the man had lost his mind. "What—what are you saying? Are you implying that . . ." He swallowed hard. Gostrain wasn't implying a thing, he was giving Hugo the facts outright. Meggie was base-born.

What an idiot he'd been—he'd assumed when he'd overheard his solicitors speaking about David Russell that the man was a distant relative of Meggie's, given the difference in surnames. It had never occurred to him that he might be her father. Why would it?

Oh, *God.* Meggie was illegitimate. How was he going to explain this to his mother on top of everything else?

He rubbed his hands over his face, trying to recover from his shock. "I—forgive me. I need just a moment."

Mr. Gostrain smiled broadly. "I understand perfectly. As I said, my lord, the news is astonishing. The wife you thought penniless has brought a dowry of four hundred thousand pounds to the marriage, which will be yours upon signing some simple documents."

Hugo just nodded. Meggie . . . poor Meggie. How was she going to take the news about her parentage?

He'd have to break it very, very gently, assure her that he didn't mind at all. He frowned as a realization hit him. He really *didn't* mind, or at least not for himself. Meggie was Meggie, and whatever her parents had gotten up to was no responsibility of hers. Why should he care if her parents had been married or not?

The real shame was the miserable childhood she'd been condemned to live, just because her reprobate father hadn't stood by the woman he'd impregnated. Hugo's blood boiled with anger. If he'd *really* wanted to find his child, he could have, and Meggie might have been spared all those years in institutions.

"Lord Hugo, you are very quiet. Do you not have any questions? Four hundred thousand pounds is a great deal of money."

Hugo looked up. "Yes. Yes, I do have a question. What do you know of this David Russell? What sort of a man was he?"

"Oh, joy! Sister, did you hear that? All our worries were for nothing!"

Hugo spun around in his chair to see the Mabey sisters barging into the room with a tea tray. "What the devil?" he sputtered. "What do you think you are doing, interrupting a private meeting?"

"We thought you needed nourishment, and a good thing we came in when we did, or we never would have heard you ask about dear David."

Hugo slammed his hands down on his desk. "That's it!" he roared. "I will not tolerate any of your foolishness when I am trying to sort through a very sticky problem. Out with both of you!"

"But you wanted to know about David Russell, and who better to tell you than us, isn't that right, Dorelia?" Ottoline put the tea tray on the low table in front of the sofa. "Milk or sugar, Mr. Gostrain? Neither? Good, much better for the digestion."

Hugo groaned. "Please forgive them," he murmured to the solicitor, who was looking back and forth from one twin to the other, his eyes blinking rapidly. "It is their advanced age . . ."

"Age has not affected my brain, and there's nothing wrong with my hearing either," Dorelia snapped. "Do you or do you not wish to hear about Madrigal's father and what happened between him and Meg Bloom that summer of 1799?"

"Do you—do you mean to say that you actually *know* something?" Hugo said, gripping the edge of his desk so hard that his knuckles showed white. "You know something about Meggie's parents and neither of you has bothered to speak up before this? What in God's name is the matter with you?"

Ottoline pushed a cup of tea at him. "There's no need to work yourself up, dear. We were only waiting to discover how much you knew, if you knew anything at all. We didn't want to say anything that might alarm you or Madrigal. Why, was there something important?"

"Oh, only a small matter of four hundred thousand pounds that David Russell left to the daughter no one could find," Hugo said dryly.

"Goodness gracious." Dorelia clapped a hand to her cheek. "Cousin David did make a success of himself after all. I always hoped he might."

Hugo stared at her. "Cousin David?" he said faintly.

"Yes, dear. Lally's brother. He was a clever boy, if a bit impetuous." She plopped onto the sofa. "A good nose for business does run in the family, if I do say so myself."

Hugo's mouth opened, but nothing came out except a strangled choke. Meggie was actually related to the crazy old bats? Well, he knew of one thing that really did run in the family. Poor Meggie—no wonder she had ended up at Woodbridge Sanitarium. Between her miserable upbringing and the family tendency, he was amazed she coped as well as she did.

"Why don't you calm down, dear?" Ottoline said to Hugo as she handed a cup to Mr. Gostrain. "We'll have a nice little chat after we've had our tea. In the meantime, we can discuss that bequest we mentioned."

"The bequest," Hugo said, rubbing his finger hard over the space between his eyebrows where a vein pulsed rhythmically.

"Exactly, the bequest," Dorelia said. "We have a little money in a trust that we'd like to give to darling Madrigal as a part of her dowry."

Hugo picked up his cup and looked down at the dark liquid. If anyone belonged in an asylum it was the two of them.

"Yes, but there is a little problem," Dorelia added, "and that is that the trustees are perfectly dreadful, and we were hoping that nice Mr. Gostrain could fix them for us."

Mr. Gostrain raised his eyebrows at Hugo, and Hugo shrugged. "Oh, do go ahead," he said. "Why not waste your valuable time? Otherwise we'll never hear the end of it."

"Very well," the solicitor said, taking his cup and saucer and moving over to an armchair next to the sofa where the Mabey twins perched. "Tell me, who established this trust?"

"Well, dearest Linus—that's the late Lord Eliot—willed us everything he had, as he had no heirs," Dorelia replied cheerfully. "He told us to do with it as we wished, since he knew how much we enjoyed investing his money. Ottoline is particularly good at foreseeing events on the 'Change."

Hugo closed his eyes. So Coldsnap had been right about that. No wonder Linus Eliot had been nearly bankrupt when he died.

"Sister is absolutely correct," Ottoline said, looking extremely pleased with herself. "But you see, the trustees have no idea how clever we are, and because we are aged females they do not think us responsible. They refuse to do anything but dole out handfuls of pennies to us—really, they are so aggravating. They continue to put all the income except for our handful of pennies back into investments, thinking they can increase the principal better than we can. Ha!"

"I see," Gostrain said, tapping the ends of his fingers together. "I can certainly look into the matter of the administration of the trust; you are entitled to the full income to use as you please. If the trustees have been legally amiss in their duties, they can and should be replaced."

"I told you so, Sister," Ottoline said gleefully.

"It was *I* who told *you*," Dorelia retorted. "Or have you forgotten?"

"Don't be absurd, Dorelia. I never forget anything, and if you do not mind, I would like Mr. Gostrain to get on with the matter at hand, and so should you, seeing as our Sign is sitting right in front of us."

Hugo shuddered. If Meggie ever turned into one of the Mabey sisters, he was going to personally escort her back to the Woodbridge Sanitarium.

"I must tell you, however," Mr. Gostrain continued, "that although you may will the money to whomever you please, you may not dispose of the principal unless Lord Eliot made a highly unusual stipulation, and I very much doubt that, given what you've said."

"Never mind, never mind," Dorelia said, waving her hand. "It is not a crushing blow. All that matters is that Madrigal receives the money in the end, seeing as it does come from her family. In the meantime, I am sure dear Hugo will find the income useful, if you are able to arrange the correct dispersal."

"I will do my best. Ah, how large is the trust, if you don't mind my asking?"

"Not at all," Ottoline chirped. "The last accounting put it at three hundred fifty thousand pounds."

Hugo dropped his teacup.

22

Meggie came in from the garden with a basket full of roses, delighted with the way her meeting with the vicar had gone and even more pleased because he'd been delighted about it, too. She hadn't needed her gift to know that, although the waves of approbation that had come from him made her feel particularly happy.

She thought she was beginning to do quite well at behaving like a lady, which was exactly what Hugo had hoped for. Meggie had worked hard to learn, observing everything around her and tucking away the smallest details. She was determined to make Hugo proud. Since he'd stopped criticizing every move she made and every word that came out of her mouth, she thought she must be doing an adequate job.

"Hello, Cookie," she said merrily, putting the basket down on the kitchen table. "It's a lovely day, isn't it?"

"There hew be, yer ladyship, and owd dog, too. Saved a nice bit o' bone for him, I did, full 'o juice an' marrow."

"Cookie, you do spoil him," Meggie said with a smile. "It's a good thing Hadrian is getting so much exercise these days, or he'd develop a paunch."

"Aye, like this 'un," Cookie replied, cheerfully patting his stomach. "Took me years to grow."

"You did a magnificent job, Cookie." Meggie fetched a vase and began to arrange the roses. "Do you know if my husband has returned yet?"

"Aye, thass right, an' he be takin' tea in the study wi' a strange gentl'man and the misses, and them two in a proper frap ower suffin'."

"Oh, dear," Meggie said, pulling off her gardening

gloves and apron. "That's interesting—we weren't expecting anyone. I'd better go see what it's all about."

She quickly set off for the study, knowing that Hugo found the aunties very trying when they were in a flap.

She stopped abruptly in the open door, taking in the scene before her.

The shattered remains of a teacup lay on the desk. Hugo was hopping up and down, cursing as he swatted at the dark wet patches on his coat and trousers. Dorelia and Ottoline both hopped around him, jabbering and flapping their arms as they were wont to do when overexcited. Only the man sitting in one of the armchairs next to the sofa appeared relatively composed.

He immediately stood as he saw her. "Lady Hugo, I presume?" he said, crossing the room.

"Yes," she replied, wondering at the combination of anxiety, agitation, and anticipation that emanated from the stranger and belied his calm exterior.

"I am James Gostrain, Lord Hugo's solicitor," he said bowing over her hand. "I am delighted to make your acquaintance."

"Thank you," she said absently, looking back over at Hugo. "Is everything all right? My husband does not look quite himself."

Mr. Gostrain smiled at her. "I daresay your husband is not feeling quite himself, either. He has just received some extraordinary news. If you would care to sit down, I imagine he will want me to share it with you when he recovers his composure."

Meggie nodded, thoroughly baffled. She took a chair, folded her hands in her lap, and prepared to wait. She didn't have to wait long. Hugo spotted her almost instantly.

"Meggie—ah, sweetheart, thank God you're here. You won't believe what's happened. I've had the shock of my life, and so will you when you hear what Mr. Gostrain has come to say."

She regarded him neutrally, unable to tell if the news was very good, very bad, or somewhere in between. She couldn't even sense anything helpful from the aunties, since they were in such a twitter. "Perhaps you had better tell me," she said, squeezing her hands together hard, praying that whatever the news was, it would not affect the happiness that she and Hugo had found together. That she truly couldn't bear.

"Well. I hardly know where to begin. Mr. Gostrain—oh, I beg your pardon, Meggie. You have been introduced?"

Meggie nodded again, wishing Hugo would get on with whatever he had to say. She'd never seen him so rattled, and she was beginning to feel exactly the same. Her heart pounded painfully hard in her chest and she had to fight to appear calm.

"Yes, well, you see, Mr. Gostrain is the senior partner in the legal firm that looks after my family's affairs. I wrote to the firm after our wedding to request that a marriage settlement be made for you, to protect you and our future children."

"A settlement?" she repeated, relaxing slightly to hear the problem was nothing worse. "But you needn't give me anything, Hugo. I have everything I need—more than I need. You have already been overly generous."

"Never mind that, just listen, Meggie," he said, his voice quick with impatience. "I included a few details about you in my letter so that—well, never mind why, but it seemed a good idea."

All the blood drained from Meggie's face. She'd known her marriage was too good to be true, that she didn't deserve such happiness. Mr. Gostrain had found a loophole, a reason that the marriage was not valid and thereby saved Hugo the humiliation of having a base-born social outcast for a wife. "What sort of details?" she asked in a near whisper.

"Just the basics," he said in an offhand manner. "Who your mother was and how she'd died, what happened to you after that. Mr. Gostrain put the rest together."

Meggie wanted to die of mortification. What must Mr. Gostrain think of her? What must the aunties think? No wonder they were in such a tizzy. Their dear little Madrigal Montagu, who was supposed to be a replacement for Lally in every way, including respectability, was a bastard.

"The rest?" she asked, wondering how long it would be before the rest of the world knew the truth about the unfortunate wife poor Lord Hugo Montagu had taken—and discarded.

"Yes, sweetheart." Hugo said very gently. "He made some inquiries and discovered who your father was, which is the crux of the matter."

Meggie stared down at her hands. A marriage couldn't be invalidated just because one of the parties had been born out of wedlock, could it? She didn't think so. There had to be something else, something really terrible—something to do with her father, maybe a terrible crime he'd committed. "Oh," she said, feeling sick to her stomach. No wonder no one had ever told her anything; the truth was too awful, even more awful than leaving her mother unmarried and pregnant.

"He didn't die as you thought, sweetheart." Hugo crossed the room and knelt by her chair, taking her hand in his. "I'm sorry. You are going to find this difficult to hear."

Meggie squeezed her eyes shut. It really was bad. The only thing she could think of was that her father had committed murder and received the ultimate punishment.

"Was he hanged?" she asked, trying very hard not to cry.

"Hanged?" Hugo stared at her. "Where on earth did you get an idea like that?"

"You said—you said that I wouldn't like it. That he didn't die the way I thought." Meggie pressed a shaking hand against her mouth. "If he didn't hang, then what happened to him?"

"Darling Madrigal is not so far off, you know," Dorelia said, speaking up for the first time. "David *was* a wanted man. That is why he had to leave the country as quickly as he did, poor boy—such a shame he had to spend all those years in exile, but never mind, at least he made a fortune, which is all he ever wanted to do."

Meggie, stunned, clenched her fingers on the arms of her chair. "Do you mean he *didn't* die before I was born?"

"Certainly not. He was much too clever for that," Dorelia said, looking smug as could be.

"Wanted for what?" Hugo demanded, his eyes blazing. "By God, I could throttle the two of you for keeping this to yourselves."

"Temper, temper," Ottoline said. "You won't hear another word if you don't keep a civil tongue in your head."

"Don't you threaten me," Hugo snapped. "Get on with it, woman. What was David Russell wanted for?"

"He was a smuggler, dear," Ottoline said. "He was a dashing smuggler, but a smuggler nevertheless, and His Majesty's excise men knew all about his activities. The very night they were going to apprehend him he escaped, and by the skin of his teeth, I might add."

"Oh, marvelous," Hugo said, pressing his index fingers against the corners of his eyes. "Simply marvelous."

Meggie leaned her head against the back of the chair, her hands over her face. Her father had been a smuggler wanted by His Majesty's government. Perfect. Mr. Gostrain must be thrilled by that additional tidbit about her unsavory background. She couldn't even begin to imagine what Hugo was going to have to say about it later, but given the thunderous expression on his face, quite a lot.

"You cannot leave them hanging there, Sister," Dorelia said. "Madrigal will want to know why her father left the country without her mother."

"I was going to tell her, Dorelia. I do wish you would stop rushing me." Ottoline settled her skirts and placed her hands together in her lap, making Meggie want to scream with impatience. "Now then," she continued, "the truth of the matter is that Cousin David knew Meg Bloom was with child and he intended to marry her, only Meg's parents interfered."

"What?" Meggie's hands dropped and she sat up very straight, glaring at both Dorelia and Ottoline. "Aunties, just what have you been keeping from me? You both said that you didn't know a thing about my mother—and what is this nonsense about 'Cousin David'?"

Hugo took her hand again and held it tightly, as if he could check her shock. "It transpires that your father, David Russell, was Lally's brother."

"He was *who*?" Meggie croaked in disbelief. She already thought the circumstances of her new life impossible, but this information went beyond anything plausible, beyond any reasonable bounds.

"Meggie, love, I know the story must sound outrageous, but I've only just learned of the connection myself," Hugo said very gently. "It is the truth, however."

"Oh, aunties, how could you lie to me so thoroughly?" Meggie said, so outraged that she shook from head to foot. "My father was Lally's brother? Did you not think that worthy of mention, given that you knew all about it, especially when I asked most specifically if you knew my mother? How could this be? How could this *possibly* be?"

"Now, Madrigal, do not fly into the boughs," Dorelia said in a soothing voice. "We *didn't* know your mother; we didn't even know about her, not until much later. We certainly didn't know what David had been up to, naughty boy, not until after he'd left the country. If I'd known he was smuggling, I'd have walloped his bottom, grown man or no. Imagine such nonsense—and getting an innocent village girl with child? Well. He might have thought to marry her before bedding her if he wanted her so badly."

Meggie felt like wringing both their necks for keeping such important information from her. "I think," she said slowly, her eyes narrowed on the aunties, "that you had better come out with all of it, every last detail, no matter how dreadful. I have a right to know, and so does Hugo. He was good enough to marry me even though I was illegitimate, but this—this is beyond anything he could have anticipated, and I won't have him kept in the dark."

Hugo's hand froze hard on hers and she looked at him in startled question. "You didn't know?" she asked. "Sister Agnes made it clear that you were aware of the circumstances of my birth and that you didn't mind."

He nodded, but he looked miserable. She couldn't blame him, given what else he'd just discovered about her. "I told her I understood," he said, his voice shaking slightly. "I did. I do. Meggie, listen to me sweetheart. None of this is your fault. It is your story, but not your fault."

"Madrigal's fault indeed," Dorelia said with a sniff. "As if anyone said it was. I lay all the blame at David's door, since he should have had the good sense to keep his nose clean. His problem was a need for high adventure and an endless supply of money—that's what led to all the smuggling trouble, and to the tragic ending."

Ottoline nodded vigorously. "Tragic. Truly tragic.

Poor young Meg, thinking him shot dead when he actually made it away safely."

"Shot—shot dead?" Meggie said, her head reeling with each new revelation. For twenty-three years she'd lived with no answers at all, and now she was getting more answers than she'd ever imagined existed—and so far each one was progressively more awful.

"Shot dead. That was what the poor girl's parents told her, the meddlesome fools," Dorelia said. "They didn't approve of their daughter's involvement with David, and little wonder, given his unsuitable occupation, never mind his high social rank. Most liaisons like that end up with the girl ruined and the man off willy-nilly after another conquest; your poor mother was certainly ruined, even if that hadn't been David's intention."

"Oh . . . oh, how awful for her," Meggie said, trying to imagine how her mother must have felt, alone and pregnant, believing her lover dead.

"I can understand the Blooms' concern when they found out about their daughter's attachment," Ottoline hastened to add. "But what they did was unconscionable. Truly unconscionable." She shook her head, sending her white puff of hair bounding from side to side. "Of course, they didn't know she was with child, since she hadn't bothered to tell them. If only she had, it all might have ended differently, but you know how foolish young girls can be about that sort of thing."

Hugo wrapped an arm around Meggie's shoulder, as if to give her comfort. "We know that Margaret Bloom ended up alone in Bury St. Edmunds," he said. "I can only think she must have gone where she could be certain no one would know her."

"Oh, dear," Dorelia said, dabbing at her eyes with a handkerchief. "So very, very tragic. If we'd only known, we would have taken dearest Madrigal to our bosom in an instant, isn't that right, Sister?"

"Oh, yes indeed. Family is family, no matter which side of the blanket it comes from, but you see, we didn't know. No one knew that there was a child at all. We didn't even know that David had been carrying on with Meg until he wrote a long time later, once he'd settled in India, and asked us to find Meg and her child."

"He did?" Meggie frowned. "Why? Why did he bother to do that when he'd abandoned us?"

"Because he wanted to bring you both to India, now that he had enough money to support you and a place to live. Did I not mention that theirs was a true love match?"

Meggie drew in a deep breath, then released it. "No. No, you didn't mention it. That's one piece of good news in this whole mess, I suppose."

"Oh, child," Ottoline said, "I do apologize. You were very much wanted by your mother and your father, who loved each other to distraction."

Meggie didn't know why, given the rest of the story, but she gained great comfort from the knowledge that her parents had at least loved each other. She'd always wondered about that, always hoped it had been so, and now she knew they had. "What else did he say in his letter?" she asked, suddenly desperate to know what her father had thought, what he'd felt after it all had gone wrong.

"Well, he explained that he'd already planned to go into exile, knowing that he couldn't carry on smuggling for very much longer, not with the excise men getting closer all the time," Ottoline said. He told us that he'd written to Meg in Ramsholt, where she lived with her parents, telling her to meet him at Bawdsey at eleven o'clock the night of June 24th. He'd moored his ship, the *Hope,* there, and he intended to take Meg away with him." She sighed heavily, then pulled a handkerchief from her left sleeve and pressed it against her mouth, smothering a sob. "I cannot bear to go on."

Dorelia, her own tears flowing freely, snatched the handkerchief from her sister's grasp and blew her nose with vigor. "Oh, dear. Dear me, the tragedy. And that is *my* handkerchief, Sister."

"Nonsense," Ottoline barked. "I took it from the laundry pile myself this very morning."

"Please," Meggie begged, "don't stop now, Aunt Ottoline. What happened? What went wrong?"

"Yes, and there lies the rub, child," Ottoline said, glowering darkly at her sister, "for nothing would have gone wrong at all if it hadn't been for those interfering idiot Blooms. They intercepted the letter, you see, before poor Meg could read it, and they tipped off the excise men as to where dear David would be that night, and exactly when."

"No . . . oh, no," Meggie said, her hand slipping to her throat in real dismay. "How *could* they do something so dreadful—and to their own daughter? Then to tell her he'd been killed. . . . But are you sure that's what happened? Are you absolutely sure? How could my father possibly have known that the Blooms were responsible for setting the excise men on him?"

"He didn't know, not until two years later, when we replied to his inquiry and gave him all the details," Ottoline said. "Oh, the blow he was dealt. I don't know that he ever recovered." She dug a second handkerchief out of her other sleeve and mopped at her eyes. "To have to tell him that his true love and their child had disappeared without a trace . . ."

"You see, we investigated the matter, dear," Dorelia said, while her sister recuperated from her surfeit of emotion. "We found the Blooms and we asked them of Meg's whereabouts. They said they didn't know and didn't care, that she had left without a word after they had told her of David's death. They called her an ungrateful baggage, only not in such polite terminology."

"Oh," Ottoline chimed in, "and you should have heard what they said when we told them she'd been carrying David's child! Terrible things. Just terrible. That's when they told us what they'd done—they even went so far as to tell poor Meg that they'd taken her letter and used it to betray David. No wonder Meg ran away."

"No wonder," Meggie echoed. "No wonder at all . . ."

"They said they had only one regret," Dorelia sniffed, "and that was that dear Cousin David had survived."

"A miracle that he did," Ottoline added in a thick voice, sweeping her handkerchief around her entire face, "given that he waited and waited for her until the last possible moment, he and his crew fighting it out until he was forced to set sail without her. Broke his heart, it did, but he had no choice. To learn she'd never received his letter, that only deepened his wound . . ."

Meggie thought her own heart might break. As the story unfolded, she'd received the first real picture of her mother and father that she'd ever had. She sat very still, trying to absorb everything she'd learned.

They had loved and loved truly. Her mother in her grief had left everything she'd ever known behind and set off on her own to bear her child. Meggie couldn't help wondering if in the end her mother hadn't lost her will to live and died once she'd safely brought Meggie into the world. Her last act was to name her infant daughter. Which led her to another question.

"Aunties," she asked hesitantly, "do you have any idea why my mother named me Madrigal? My aunt Emily told me those were her last words—that I be named Madrigal Anna. She said my mother was insistent about it."

Dorelia and Ottoline both dried their eyes in the same moment and beamed at her. "Dear Madrigal," Dorelia said fondly.

"Dear, dear Madrigal," Ottoline agreed. "A lovely woman she was, our first cousin, and David and Lally's mother, which makes her your paternal grandmother. Your mother named you after her, and also after your father's grandmother. Anna was her name. Remind me to show you the inscriptions in our family Bible."

Meggie drew in a sharp breath. She'd been named after her grandmother . . . and her great-grandmother.

"Oh," she said, her voice choked. "Oh, my." She hadn't really taken in the connection until now, not fully. She had roots, real roots, a father she could finally name—and a real resemblance to her father's sister Lally, not just an imagined one the aunties had been trying to recreate. She *did* look like the portrait on the stairs.

Family. Her family. Which made Ottoline and Dorelia actual cousins of a sort—second cousins three times removed, if she wasn't mistaken. All her life she'd been without any relatives at all, and now she found herself living under the same roof with two people she shared actual blood with.

Overwhelmed, she couldn't find a word to say, not a single word.

She pressed her hands to her eyes, fighting back tears.

"Sweetheart?" Hugo spoke softly against her ear, his breath warm against her cheek, the pressure of his arm reassuring around her shoulder. "Are you overwhelmed? Do you need to be alone?"

Meggie stifled a half-laugh, half-sob. "No. I've been alone all my life," she said, wiping her eyes with the back of her hand. "Until you came along, I had no family except Hadrian. Now I have a husband and aunties, and—oh, Hugo! I actually belong to a pack of my own! I cannot believe it—I feel like howling." She looked at him and laughed in real joy.

Hugo abruptly released her and moved to face her, looking into her eyes, his hands gripping hers tightly. "Meggie. Meggie, listen to me. I know you've had a series of shocks, but you must concentrate," he said in a voice so low she could barely hear it. "You don't want Mr. Gostrain to think there is anything amiss with you."

Her eyes clouded over. She'd forgotten all about Mr. Gostrain, who had discreetly retreated out of her line of sight, although not earshot. "I don't think I could do anything at this point to persuade him otherwise," she said just as softly. "He has obviously come to dissuade you against our marriage, and everything he has heard this afternoon can only strengthen his case. He must see I am not fit to be your wife."

"No—no, my love," Hugo said, wrapping his arms around her and drawing her close against his chest. "He does not see that at all, and you must not give him any reason to think that is the case. Please, if only for my sake, pull yourself together. Please."

"Forgive me," she said, feeling dreadful for letting him down. She had committed the unforgivable error of showing emotion in public. "I will behave, I promise."

"Good girl. Now try to compose yourself, for there is more, and you need to appear as calm as possible. Can you do that for me?"

"For you I think I can do just about anything," she said as bravely as she could. "Just tell me now if Mr. Gostrain is going to try to dissolve our marriage. I am not sure that I can be calm about that unless I have advance warning, and possibly not even then."

"He is not going to do anything of the sort," Hugo said, kissing her hand. "The exact opposite is true. You only have to listen carefully to him and sign whatever he asks you to sign, as I will also do. Do you think you can manage that, Meggie? Be calm, listen quietly, and sign some papers?"

"Yes, of course," she said, supposing she deserved to be spoken to like an imbecile, given the undignified way she'd just behaved. "I am perfectly prepared."

"Good. Excellent." He wrapped his warm fingers around hers, gently squeezing them to reassure her. "Mr. Gostrain. I think my wife is now ready to hear the full extent of what you have to tell her. I would, however, appreciate brevity on your part, as she is already exhausted from the revelations of this day."

"As you wish, my lord. I will be as quick as possible." He cleared his throat. "We first begin with David Russell's legacy to his immediate lineal descendant, Madrigal Anna Bloom . . ."

23

All in all, Meggie thought she'd behaved reasonably well. She hadn't screamed, or fainted, or really done much of anything except nearly break Hugo's fingers.

He hadn't seemed to mind, or at least not about his fingers.

Something was very wrong, though. Hugo had not been himself ever since Mr. Gostrain and the aunties had delivered the news not only about her inheritance, but also the truth about her parents. His mood had been distant and abstracted. He'd been perfectly kind and polite, but he'd barely met her gaze during dinner, nor spoken much at all.

She took a deep breath of the night air, watching as a barn owl floated silently across the river and disappeared into a thicket of trees on the opposite bank. The rain that had fallen earlier had left a crystal sheen on the grass, and the light from the crescent moon glittered on the droplets like tiny stars.

The outer world went on just as it always did, with no indication that everything in Meggie's inner world had been turned topsy-turvy. She was not the same woman who had awakened that morning and gone about her day. The boundaries of her life had been redefined; her existence had been given a shape and substance it had lacked before.

She was utterly miserable.

Through the clamor of her thoughts she heard Hugo walk through the open door onto the balcony, felt his hands rest lightly on her shoulders.

"Meggie? Come to bed, sweetheart. You'll catch a chill standing out here in nothing but your night shift."

She turned into the circle of his arms and gazed up at him, her heart aching. She was sure she knew what troubled him. "Hugo, you have always been honest with me, haven't you?"

His arms tightened slightly around her back. "Why would you ask me that?" he said, two furrows marking the space between his brow.

"I—I want to be sure that you are telling me the truth when you say that you really don't mind about my father."

Hugo's face instantly cleared. "How can I possibly mind about a man who left you a fortune? I don't think I even mind about the Mabey sisters since they plan on leaving you another one."

She smiled uncertainly. "Yes, they are very generous—but that's different, Hugo. They're not criminals."

"I don't know if you can really call your father a criminal, sweetheart. He may have broken some laws, but in this part of the world, smuggling is a time-honored profession."

"That may be so, but it certainly got him into a lot of trouble. Look what came out of it—he lost the woman he loved, he had to leave his family and his country behind, he never even met his own child. The aunties said his heart was broken."

Instead of answering, Hugo bent down, scooped her up in his arms, and carried her inside. He kicked the glass door closed with his foot, then deposited her in their bed, and pulled the covers up around her.

"All right," he said, sitting down beside her and taking her hand. "What is this really about? I don't think you're cast down over your wayward father's broken heart. You've been unusually quiet ever since James Gostrain emptied the bag, and you hardly ate anything at dinner—oyster stew, one of your favorites. Most people would be jumping up and down with joy at being told that they've inherited four hundred thousand pounds, with another three hundred and fifty thousand coming to them."

She'd been unusually quiet? Hugo must think her completely oblivious to his behavior. Either that, or he was oblivious to it himself, which wouldn't surprise her. She pulled her knees up and wrapped her arms around them, trying to think how to get him to tell her the truth. Her last attempt had been entirely unsuccessful, and she was certain he was evading the issue in order to protect her.

"Meggie? Are you worried about the money for some reason?"

"Oh, no—I'm sure the inheritance will be very useful," she said, wanting to reassure him on that point, "and I am happy that after all you've done for me I can give you something back. I don't really understand about money, since I've never had any, but you understand all about it, so you'll know just what to do with it. It's yours now anyway, so I don't have to worry about it, do I?"

"Then what is the problem?" Hugo asked, pulling off his shirt and tossing it over a chair. "Something is wrong, Meggie, and I'd rather you tell me what is worrying you instead of holding it inside and making yourself miserable."

She swallowed hard, summoning up her courage. "I—I always want to have truth between us; nothing is more important to me than that. The only way our marriage can flourish is if it is based on trust and honesty."

He nodded, looking down at the floor, his hand rubbing the back of his neck. "And?" he said.

"And I can't help but feel that it is you who are keeping something from me."

At that his gaze flashed back to her face, his eyes

narrowed. "Why would you think something ridiculous like that?"

"Because I know you, Hugo, and I can tell when you're hiding something. I also think I know what it is."

"Do you?" Hugo said in a biting tone, his eyes suddenly going cold. He stood and crossed over to the fireplace, then turned to face her, his arms folded across his chest. "Then why don't you tell me what you think I'm hiding, clever Meggie, if you know me so well?"

Meggie sank back against the pillows, surprised and hurt by his anger. "I think you really do mind about my being illegitimate," she said in a small voice. "I think that being the generous man you are, you've tried very hard to tell yourself it's not important, and you found that easier to do when you didn't have any real details. Now that you know everything, though, you can't help but be repulsed by the truth and by me, as hard as you try not to be. That's it, isn't it?"

To her astonishment, Hugo threw his head back with a shout of laughter. "You are a little fool, aren't you?" he said, looking at her with a shake of his head, and then another.

Devastated by his cavalier attitude when she'd just poured her heart out to him, Meggie glared at him, her temper rising fast. "Think what you will, but please do not laugh at me. That wasn't easy to say, and the least you can do is respect my sensibilities, no matter how stupid you think I am." Her eyes filled with tears and she turned her head to one side, furiously brushing them away with the back of her hand.

The next thing she knew, Hugo was beside her on the bed, holding her, her face pressed against his bare chest. "I'm sorry, Meggie," he said, stroking her hair, his voice rough against her temple. "I didn't mean to upset you."

"Well, you did," she said furiously, somehow managing to bring her hands up between his body and hers and forcibly shoving him away.

"What—what the devil did you do that for?" he asked indignantly.

She rose to her knees, hot anger surging through her veins, the blood pounding so hard in her head that she could scarcely see, let alone think straight. "You can't just go saying whatever you like with no thought to the consequences, and then presume a quick apology will fix everything," she said, her entire body shaking with emotion. "Some people have feelings, even if you don't!"

He looked at her in bewilderment. "What is that supposed to mean?"

"Just what I said," she replied curtly, swiping impatiently at her face again, cursing the tears that ran down her cheeks. "If you do have feelings, God only knows what they are, because *you* certainly don't have any idea, and neither do I. I've never known a person to blow hot and cold the way you do, one moment kind and considerate, and the next acting like a bully, when you're not being altogether indifferent. You may be a duke's son, Hugo Montagu, but that's no excuse for your boorish behavior, and it is no excuse at all for lying to me!"

"Lying to you? What the hell do you think I've lied to you about?" he demanded, glaring right back at her, his blazing blue eyes only inches from hers. "I told you I don't give a damn about your bloody father, and I don't, except to think him an unprincipled idiot who ought to have married your mother and stood by you both, but that's neither here nor there. What I do give a damn about is you, Meggie. I am outraged that you were abandoned when you might have had a perfectly decent upbringing, and now that you don't need him or his money, your father finally provides for you."

He raked one hand through his hair, his self-control as shredded as hers. "I could happily murder him for that alone, since it seems to me that if he'd wanted to find you badly enough, he could have managed it, and when it might have meant something to you."

"Oh," she said foolishly, her anger instantly draining away. She sat back on her heels, thinking that Hugo looked anything but indifferent.

" 'Oh?' Is that all you bloody well have to say?" he roared. "You accuse me of—of lying, not to mention telling me I'm a bully with an entire lack of feelings. I suppose that means loving you more than life itself doesn't count for anything with you, but why should it? Why the hell should it?"

"Wh-what?" she said, so stunned by that bald statement that she could hardly draw breath. "What did you say?"

"You heard exactly what I said." He moved quickly off the bed, walking over to the French doors. Instead of going outside, he leaned one hand against the glass, his back to her, the muscles in his shoulders taut, his head bent.

Meggie shot bolt upright, her hands over her mouth. She was more disconcerted by the revelation that she could shake him so deeply than she was by any other of that day's alarming disclosures.

That he'd been so badly shaken as to break every one of his rules and actually tell her that he loved her showed the depth of his hurt, and she was responsible.

She climbed out of bed and padded across the floor, slipping her arms around his waist, holding him close against her. "Forgive me," she whispered against his back, abandoning all pride. "I let my temper get away from me, and you didn't deserve the tongue-lashing I gave you. I—I have no excuse other than being easily wounded because I love you, too, so very much."

He stiffened, then turned abruptly, his eyes glittering like cold blue starlight and looking just as distant. "Ah.

You say the words so easily, Meggie, and yet this is the first time I've heard you use them. I wonder why you choose to speak them now?"

Meggie blinked, backing away from him, his anger palpable. "But—but I thought . . ." She bit her lip, completely confused.

"You thought what?" he said bitterly. "That I am indifferent to your feelings in that direction as well? That I don't care whether you love me as long as I can take you to bed and have my boorish way with you? I suppose you also think that since I am such an unfeeling man I am incapable of loving you, no matter what I say."

"N-no," she stammered. "I know you loved me, because you told me so when you asked me to marry you, but since you haven't mentioned anything about it since then, I thought—well, I thought it must be an improper subject."

Hugo stared at her. "An improper subject? Where the hell did you—oh, never mind. Never bloody mind." He shoved both hands through his hair, then looked down at the floor, his mouth compressed in a tight white line.

"Please don't be angry with me," she said, flushing and feeling like a complete idiot. "I don't know the first thing about the rules and regulations that govern love in the upper classes, except that you told me I don't have to behave like a lady in bed."

He lifted his head and gazed at her with absolutely no expression, one finger stroking the corner of his mouth.

"So I thought that in bed I could show you that I love you, but that I had better not actually *say* anything," she said, fumbling for an explanation he would understand. "You hate it when I speak out of turn or say things I oughtn't, and I've been trying so hard to be the sort of wife you want."

He still didn't say a word.

Meggie wanted to curl up and die—he'd probably

never forgive her, he might not even speak to her ever again, and she probably deserved it. "I suppose the only thing left to say is that I'm sorry I accused you of having no feelings, and I'm sorry if I hurt you," she said miserably. "I told you that I can be perfectly awful when I lose my temper—I was caned more times than I can remember for that single fault alone."

"Were you?" he said, raising one eyebrow. "By Sister Luke of Mercy, I suppose?"

She nodded, clutching her hands together, relieved that at least he had finally said something. "I expect you feel like caning me yourself."

"Not exactly," he murmured.

"No?" she asked nervously. She didn't have the first idea what he was thinking, for he was regarding her in a most peculiar, speculative fashion. At least he didn't look murderously angry anymore. "Are you sure?"

"Quite sure," he replied, the shadow of a smile crossing his face. "Beating my wife is not the first thought that comes to mind when she finally tells me she loves me."

"Oh, *Hugo*," she said, the tight knot in the pit of her stomach beginning to uncurl. "Do you mean it is not an improper subject after all?"

"If you are referring to the badly misnamed Sister Luke of Mercy and her proclivity to cane you, I would say that is a highly improper subject. If, on the other hand, you are referring to loving me even half as much as I love you, then no. That is a subject I could listen to all night."

Meggie released a huge breath of relief. "And I could tell you all night—I've been wanting to say it to you for ages, and now I feel very silly that I haven't before this." She paused, an obvious question occurring to her. "I was just wondering . . . is there a reason you didn't—well, that you never mentioned anything again about being in love with me?" she finished awkwardly.

He sighed, looking at some point over her right shoulder. "I suppose I thought it best not to push you. You never pretended to marry me for love, Meggie, and although I had strong suspicions that your feelings had changed, I reckoned you would tell me in your own good time. I confess, I was growing concerned that I'd been mistaken."

"Oh, Hugo—Hugo, I'm so sorry," she said, filled with remorse. "Please forgive me for being so obtuse?"

"It is not your fault," he said gently. "You weren't to know what I was thinking."

"Maybe not," she said with a wobbly smile as the paradox of his statement struck her, "but I certainly should never have lost my temper and said all those dreadful things to you. Will you forgive me for that at least?"

"There is nothing to forgive," he said, closing the distance between them and running his knuckles down her cheek. "We had a misunderstanding, no more than that."

"Thank goodness," she said, her eyes welling with a fresh rush of tears. "I didn't know what to think. I honestly believed that you'd decided I wasn't a suitable or worthy wife, and you didn't really want me anymore, and then when you became so angry when I asked—"

He pressed his mouth against hers, cutting her off and kissing her long and hard, leaving her in no doubt of the strength of his feelings.

Releasing her, he took her face in his hands and looked down at her, his expression fierce. "You are mine," he said, his voice low and ragged. "Now and always. Do not mistake that, Meggie, or ever doubt my love."

Her vision blurred from the tears that wouldn't stop, she shook her head in the cup of his hands. "I won't, but don't you doubt mine either, Hugo Montagu. I might not have married you for love as you did me, but I swear to you that I have loved you since the day we were married, when you took me to the sea and gave me some of the happiest hours of my life."

"Don't—don't cry, my love, my darling," he whispered, kissing her eyelids. "It doesn't matter when it happened, only that it did."

"No—please let me finish. This is important." Her tears ran down her face and collected in his palms, as if they were all the words she'd held back for so long, finally released and given up to him in humble offering. "You have to know that when you took me to bed on our wedding night my vows were true. I gave you not just my body but my whole heart and soul, and they are yours forever."

"And mine yours, Meggie, and mine yours." He ran his wet hands up her back with a strangled groan, then pushed her night shift up and pulled it over her head, throwing it to one side.

He struggled briefly with his trousers before those went the way of her shift. His mouth fastened hot and hungry on hers as he abruptly pulled her with him to the floor. His weight pressed her flat against the rug, the heat of his body burning into her bare breasts. "Now," he said, his breath coming in short gasps as he thrust his hips against her thighs, and his engorged shaft pressed hard against her belly. "Let me love you now, Meggie. God help me, but I can't wait."

"Yes, oh yes," she cried, feeling his urgency, willingly opening her thighs to him. She sucked her breath in as he drove into her wet, ready flesh in one deep, powerful stroke that sheathed him completely and forced the breath straight out of her body.

"You are mine." He pulled back and pounded into her again. His fingers gripping her hair, he held her head tight in his hands. "My body, my blood," he said with another ruthless thrust so deep that she cried out. "My heart, my soul, my very life, Meggie."

"Yes," she sobbed, meeting each powerful thrust fully. Her hips arched up in complete surrender to his hard masculine penetration, and in her surrender, she claimed him every bit as much.

"I love you—God, how I love you," he groaned, taking her mouth in a kiss that bruised her lips and left her with the coppery taste of blood—hers or his she didn't know or care.

Her fingers raked over his back, slippery with sweat. Her hands clutched his hair, pulling his mouth down to hers again. Driven beyond thought to a blind, desperate need that came from her heart as much as it did from her body, Meggie needed to be filled, to be completed, made one with him.

She shook with the intensity of his assault. She felt the gathering tension deep in her belly—the escalation of exquisite sensation that built and built until it threatened to sweep her away altogether. She reached toward the peak, her hips straining up against him, her hands desperately grasping his buttocks, drawing him closer yet.

He answered her silent plea, pushing into her hard. His final deep thrust drove her into a shattering release, with the force of her body's spasms leaving her helpless to do anything but sob over and over.

She felt him shudder in her arms. His teeth bit into her shoulder as he anchored her against her body's tempest and surrendered to his own. A cry ripped from his throat as he spilled his seed into her—the molten heat of his ejaculation searing them both, binding flesh to flesh, heart to heart, soul to soul, the vow sealed.

Hugo desperately needed to sleep, but sleep continued to elude him, and he knew exactly why. A guilty conscience could do that to a man, and God knew, his conscience was as guilty as it could be. If he'd been ashamed of himself before, that was nothing compared to the burden of shame he carried now.

He looked down at Meggie sleeping peacefully in the curve of his arm, a slight smile turning up the corners of her mouth. She was truly remarkable, he thought, his heart aching. Honest to the core, her every feeling freely given without reservation or subterfuge—she was everything he was not. He knew perfectly damned well he didn't deserve her.

She loved him—and oh, how those words had gladdened his heart. The problem was that she loved him because she thought him perfectly wonderful in nearly every way, brave and strong and moral, a paragon of virtue. The irony was that since marrying her, he'd tried to become exactly that, but his past sins kept getting in his way.

For with every word of love Meggie had spoken, she'd also unwittingly driven a dagger into his guts. He had fashioned that dagger entirely from lies—the handle crafted by corruption, the blade honed by deceit.

For one truly dreadful moment he'd thought she'd somehow guessed the truth, that she knew him and loathed him for the reprobate he was. When he'd realized that her distress was caused because she thought herself unworthy to be his wife, he'd felt completely sick.

If anyone was unworthy, it was he. He'd married Meggie with the sole intention of getting his hands on her inheritance and engineered the situation to perfection. That was criminal enough, but along had come the Mabey sisters, who sweetened the pot with nearly half of that again. This gave Hugo a sum total of seven hundred fifty thousand pounds, not a penny of which he deserved.

Oh, he was now a rich man indeed, and he felt as if

he'd taken blood money from a complete innocent, who would surely hate him if she ever learned the truth. The very thought made his blood run cold. If she ever learned why he'd really married her, she'd never trust him again, let alone believe that he truly had fallen in love with her.

Why should she? Why should she ever believe anything he said again? Even Meggie would never be that forgiving or understanding. She had been completely truthful with him that night and he had been forced to give her his own truth sprinkled with damnable omissions and evasions.

He rubbed his free hand over his aching brow, wishing he'd been able to unburden himself, to tell her everything, for only then would his conscience be clear.

He hoped that she would know from the way he'd made love to her that he had meant every word of what he had said. She was part of him, the fabric of her being woven into his. From the moment Meggie had entered his life, she had entwined herself around his heart, and that heart had opened and grown and learned to embrace, just as she had taught his spirit to fly.

No amount of money in the world meant anything next to those precious gifts she'd given him, and none of those gifts was more precious than her love.

He released a heavy breath. Maybe the best thing to do was to go straight to London and pay off his debt to Waldock, erasing that problem. Now that the documents releasing Meggie's inheritance had been signed, he was free and clear to do so, and the sooner he put that chapter of his life behind him, the better. The guilt would always be with him as well as a lingering fear that one day the truth would come out and his life would come crashing down.

He didn't really see how that could happen. The debt was between Waldock and himself, the only other witness to his stupidity being Foxlane. Foxlane had no interest in how Hugo got in or out of trouble—he only cared about the thrill of the play and securing his own fortune.

Meggie stirred against his shoulder and sleepily opened her eyes. "Mmm," she said, pressing her mouth to his shoulder in a soft kiss. "What are you thinking about? You look terribly preoccupied." She smoothed a hand over his chest.

He covered her fingers, then pulled her closer against him. "I'm thinking I should go to London tomorrow," he said. "I have some business I've been putting off, and James Gostrain's visit reminded me that I shouldn't neglect my other duties."

Meggie struggled upright and wiped the sleep out of her eyes, oblivious to the sheet that had fallen down around her waist, exposing her high, creamy breasts. "London? Tomorrow?"

"Yes," he said, lazily stroking one of those lovely soft mounds of firm flesh, the pink nipple standing hard against his palm. "London. Would you like to come?"

The idea suddenly seemed brilliant. He didn't know why he hadn't thought of it before: he didn't want to be without Meggie for an instant, and she might like London if he kept her out of the fray of society. A few cozy walks, a great deal of time in bed, maybe some light entertainment that didn't involve anyone else—yes. It was an excellent idea.

"But—but Hugo . . ." she said, frowning. "I thought you didn't think me suited for life in the outside world. Are you just being polite?"

He grinned. "When have I ever been polite to you? Anyway, I think you'll do just fine. I've been meaning to see to a proper wardrobe for you and this is the perfect opportunity. You can't go about in Lally's castoffs for the rest of your life."

She tilted her head and gave him a searching look. "Are you asking me because you truly want me to come, or are you asking me because you're expecting me to refuse and you'd rather not hurt my feelings by neglecting to ask me at all?"

Hugo squinted, trying to make sense out of Meggie's skewed logic. As much as he loved her, deciphering her haphazard statements did sometimes give him a headache. "I'm asking you because I'd truly like you to come," he said, grasping at the obvious answer and hoping it would suffice.

Meggie nodded. "Why?"

Hugo groaned. "Meggie, did I not just finish showing you how I feel about you?"

She colored, a lovely flush that ran from her high breasts all the way up over her neck into her cheeks. "Aunt Ottoline said you'd suddenly want to go to London, that men become easily bored and like to go off and conquer new territory."

He sat up abruptly. "She told you *what*?" he said, his blood starting to boil. "The damned witch, how dare she imply I would do such a thing! Meggie, when are you going to stop listening to those silly old women, who wouldn't know a cock from a—from a cockatoo, or what to do with one!"

Meggie tapped her finger against her mouth. "I believe you are very much mistaken," she said.

"What? You don't mean to tell me you think those two old bags are anything less than frustrated virgins who like nothing more than to dispense bad advice? Meggie, come now."

Meggie slipped out of bed and marched across to the wardrobe. "Did you ever wonder why our rooms don't have a connecting door?" she asked, hands resting on her gently rounded and very naked hips. "I believe it is usual in the upper class for the husband and wife to have an easy passage through to each other so as to conduct their marital affairs discreetly. Or at least that is what Mrs. Lindsay told me."

Hugo watched her with amusement. She had no idea what effect she was having on him, standing there without a stitch on, conducting a lecture on proper aristocratic bedroom etiquette, courtesy of mad Mrs. Lindsay of all people.

"There is a connecting balcony," he pointed out.

"Which in the freezing middle of winter would be an enormous deterrent, I believe. Do you also know that this room once used to be Aunt Ottoline's? Aunt Dorelia's was on the far side of yours. That was while Lord Eliot was alive, before they moved into the suite of rooms down the hallway."

"And?" he said, wondering what convoluted mental path she was traveling now.

"Observe. I always wondered why this wardrobe was so huge, and I also wondered how it was that Aunt Dorelia vanished so quickly my first night here after she'd finished dressing me. I knew she hadn't used the bedroom door, and I would have seen her leave through the balcony door."

"What do you mean, she vanished?" Hugo said, seizing on the most salient point.

"Like so. I only discovered this by accident this morning when I was looking for a missing shoe." Meggie swung the wardrobe door open and pushed aside the dresses, then stepped inside and clicked a latch. To Hugo's astonishment, the back panel slipped away, revealing another panel. Meggie turned another latch and pushed back the panel. Through the opening Hugo could clearly see his own bed—in which he'd slept precisely one night. Meggie went through, and turned, waving at him through the open space.

"Good God," he said. "Do you mean to tell me that

wretched biddy hopped from your room into mine? I never heard a thing! Why didn't she just use the damned door like everyone else?"

"Force of habit?" Meggie grinned. "Or maybe she was curious about what sort of a man had moved into her dear Linus's bedroom. I don't know. You should count yourself lucky that Aunt Ottoline didn't pull the same trick from the other side."

Meggie's meaning finally dawned on him. "Are you saying that you think the aunties and Linus Eliot . . . no. No, I refuse to believe it."

"Fine," she said, re-emerging from the wardrobe and beaming at him triumphantly. "Believe what you want to believe, but I've heard enough to make me quite sure they had a very satisfactory arrangement among the three of them after Lally died. I think it makes perfect sense that they had these wardrobes made so that the proprieties would appear to be observed. No connecting doors, no indiscretions—if you look closely enough, you can see that they went so far as to have railings built to separate the balconies, railings which have only recently been removed."

Hugo fell back against the pillows, clutching his stomach. "Ah, no," he howled. "Oh, God—it's too good to be true."

Meggie burst into laughter. "It is, isn't it? Actually, I think it's rather touching. No wonder Lord Eliot left them all his money—probably in payment for devoted services rendered twofold over the years."

Hugo wiped tears of laughter from his eyes. "Meggie—oh, Meggie, your relatives. What am I to think?" He buried his face in the pillows with a snort.

"You are to think that irrepressible sexual desire runs in the family," she said, climbing back onto the bed and rubbing her cheek against his back. "My mother clearly had a passionate nature, and so must have my father, and now the two aunties. Poor Hugo. What *are* you going to do?"

He rolled over onto his back and pulled her down on top of him. "It is a foolish man who does not turn weakness into strength," he said, his already swollen penis growing stiff and ready against her belly. "The question is what you are going to do." He reached up and ran his finger over one of the puckered tips of the breasts that hovered just above him and lightly pinched.

Meggie shivered, her head arched slightly back, and a sigh eased from her throat. "Oh, I don't know . . . ah!"

He pinched a little harder, twisting the erect nub back and forth. "Are you absolutely sure?"

Meggie gasped, her knees parting slightly over his hips. Hugo shifted to take full advantage of the situation. He lifted his head to take her breast in his mouth, tasting her, suckling on her, his tongue working circles around her sensitive flesh. He loved the way she squirmed on top of him, although he wished the sheet weren't in the way.

Meggie slipped her hands behind his head and pulled him closer still. "Don't stop," she whispered. "Please don't stop."

He had no intention of stopping, shifting again to press his stiff shaft against her parted thighs. But the damned sheet still impeded him. Impatient, he took her by the waist and flipped her over, kicking the sheet half off the bed. He had a mission in mind and he needed her free and clear and on her back.

Kissing the hollow between her breasts, he slid his face down her soft belly, cupping her hips and nuzzling his face into the damp musky curls that smelled of them both from their last bout of lovemaking.

He lapped at her soft plump folds, drawing a gasp from her, then slid the tip of his tongue between her cleft and stroked leisurely from bottom to top.

"H-Hugo? What are you doing?" she said shakily.

"I've decided that the only way to convince you to come to London with me," he said, briefly lifting his head, "is to appeal to the insatiable family proclivity for sex. You clearly will not survive a week without it."

Meggie laughed breathlessly. "I don't know whether you mean to compliment or insult me," she said, running her fingers through his hair, her parted thighs shaking.

"I do nothing but compliment you, madam. I wouldn't survive a week either." Taking his thumbs, he parted her swollen lips and lowered his mouth, and sucked her tiny, sensitive nub in between his lips, using his tongue to draw delicate circles around it.

Meggie's hips bucked under his and her fingers clutched in his hair as her cries echoed above his head. "Hugo—it's too much—oh, oh *Hugo,* I can't take any more!"

So saying, she pushed herself even closer against his mouth, twisting and turning as if she could draw him into her.

Hugo, shaking with his own desire, thrust his stiffened tongue into her entrance, then plunged deep and hard. He relished her salty taste—the slick moisture that poured into his mouth like sea nectar. He felt her trembling, knew she was on the edge, and instantly rose over her, pinning her shoulders down against the bed.

"Come with me, Meggie. Come to London. Say you will."

She gasped and bucked again as he probed her this time with the turgid head of his penis. He pushed it just inside her entrance and then withdrew, deliberately teasing her, rocking shallowly back and forth, then pulling out and rubbing between her distended flesh. He sat up, holding his shaft in his hand and circling the blunt tip over her erect nub. "Say you will, Meggie."

She cried out, her eyes squeezed shut, with a fine film of moisture covering her face. "Hugo, please," she begged. "Oh, please?"

"You only have to say the word and I will give you everything you want," he replied, positioning himself back at her entrance, desperately trying to hang on to his own control.

"Yes," she cried, grabbing his buttocks and pushing him home. "Yes, whatever you like, just make love to me!"

He only had to stroke three more times before she went over the edge into a climax that threatened to undo them both. Her mouth opened in a silent scream, her internal muscles convulsing so fiercely that he nearly screamed himself. He climaxed in a split second, with his guts practically wrenched from his body with the force of his ejaculation.

He collapsed onto his side, struggling to pull breath into his body. How did Meggie manage to shatter him every single time they made love?

She pushed her forehead against the side of his neck, and her arm fell over his waist. "Don't you ever—ever do that to me again," she said between pants. "All you had to do was ask nicely."

Hugo turned his head with a smothered laugh and kissed her damp hair. "I thought that was exactly what I did."

"Beast," she said, lovingly stroking his back. "I would have come anyway."

"Do you mean I didn't have to exert my full powers of persuasion? Oh, well. Had I only known I could have saved my strength."

Meggie lightly bit his ear. "When do we leave?"

"As soon as you can pack in the morning," he said with a yawn. "There are some things best done quickly."

"What about Hadrian?" she asked sleepily, snuggling

up against his side, her body curved into his. "You will let him inside the carriage for part of such a long journey, won't you?"

"No. Oh, no—you can't possibly think you're bringing him to London," Hugo said, his eyes shooting wide open.

"I don't see why not," Meggie said reasonably. "I can't leave him behind, so if you won't let him come along, I suppose I'll have to stay here after all."

Hugo groaned, having already been through the Hadrian argument with Meggie and losing soundly. In any case, he was far too tired to argue.

"Very well," he said, "as long as you clearly understand that Hadrian is not to leave the confines of the property. The garden is large enough to keep him happy, and I will not have the ladies of London shrieking to the constabulary that there is a wolf in their midst."

Meggie chuckled against his shoulder. "From what I hear, Hadrian would not be the first."

"And I thought you were supposed to be sheltered," Hugo said, turning his head to kiss her temple.

Meggie murmured something indistinct, and her breathing gradually slowed into sleep.

Hugo sighed heavily, hoping for both their sakes that he had made the right decision and not just the selfish one.

24

Meggie stretched her arm over her head and tossed the ball as far as she could. Then she watched with a smile as Hadrian bounded after it, disappearing into the trees that bordered the far wall of the enormous garden.

She'd never realized that London had such huge houses, or that magnificent parks came attached to them. When Hugo had told her Hadrian would have a garden to play in, she'd imagined something more like a fenced-in area of grass with a few flowers, not this sweep of lawn and trees with landscaped beds interspersed around and between. Hadrian was content enough with his lot, spending most of his time basking in the sun in between bouts of wild frolic. If Meggie had known how dirty the London air was, though, she'd have left him at Lyden.

She wondered if she might not have been wiser to leave herself there, too. Although she'd had a week to adjust to London life, she still couldn't believe the size and scope of Southwell House. A beautiful white granite building, it sat in the middle of Hanover Square and took up a good portion of it. The interior, as impressive as the exterior, was filled with exquisite paintings and furniture, and a collection of tapestries that Meggie had spent hours poring over and admiring the fine work.

Above all the things that took her breath away though was the library. It was three times the size of the library at Lyden which she'd already thought extraordinary and packed with precious volume on top of precious volume of the great masterpieces.

Her hands itched to read Sophocles and Euripides and Callimachus, all in the original text. Milton and Donne, two of her favorite poets, also graced the shelves with their complete works. So much to absorb, to take joy from, and yet, just as at Lyden, she couldn't possibly afford to have Hugo catch her with her nose in a book.

Some things she was certain he'd never understand or accept, and the discovery that she was a secret bluestocking was one of them.

She'd had to bite her tongue over and over again as he'd taken her around London to show her the sights. She'd found the British Museum particularly difficult to keep her silence in, since nearly every room contained something wondrous that she longed to exclaim over or comment on. Madame Tussaud's Waxworks had created the same problem: she'd been thrilled to see the astonishingly accurate depictions of historical figures, but had to pretend to ignorance of the history itself.

Sister Agnes had recommended that Meggie see Miss Linwood's needlepoint at Leicester Square and Meggie had persuaded Hugo to take her there. She'd been able to exclaim all she liked without fear of revealing anything more than an appreciation of skilled stitch work and a love of pretty pictures.

She smiled, remembering how Hugo had been bored to tears and dragged her off for ices as soon as he feasibly could.

Hadrian brought her the ball again, dropping it at her feet. His golden eyes sparkled in invitation. She obliged him and picked it up, winging it in the opposite direction.

Wiping her fingers on her handkerchief, she settled on a bench under a shady elm and gazed out over the ornamental pond filled with goldfish, resting her cheek on her hand. Despite how much she was enjoying herself, she had a niggling concern at the back of her mind that would not go away as much as she tried to ignore it.

Hugo. Something weighed on his mind, and she hoped to heaven it wasn't her. As attentive as he'd been, he'd been careful to keep her away from places where he might run into any of his acquaintances. Not that she minded. London itself was enough to cope with without worrying about embarrassing him in front of his friends, but she didn't want him to be ashamed of her either.

She still couldn't help but wonder if he'd really wanted her to accompany him. Although he had been most persuasive at the time, every now and then she did feel as if she'd intruded into his private world.

Here he was accustomed to being waited on hand and foot by proper butlers and proper footmen and a valet who had been with him for fourteen years and knew his habits, his likes and dislikes better than Meggie did. Mallard, like the rest of the staff, treated her with a reserved formality that made her suspect they thought Hugo had lost his mind in marrying her. She definitely sensed their bewilderment, as if Hugo had grown another head where the original, familiar one had been. Hugo didn't appear aware of their bafflement though, so he couldn't be troubled about that.

The only other reason she could think of for Hugo's preoccupation was the business he'd mentioned the night before they'd left Lyden. He'd been busy all week, mostly with James Gostrain, finalizing the marriage settlement he'd insisted on. He seemed pleased with whatever he'd done. He had, however, said that a person he'd particularly wanted to see was unexpectedly out of town, and they'd have to wait until his return before they could return to Lyden. Maybe that was all he was concerned about, and she worried for nothing.

He certainly gave her no reason to worry about his chasing after other women. In the close privacy of the nights, he always loved her fully, sometimes with passionate intensity, sometimes with simple tenderness, but never leaving her in doubt of the nature of his feelings. Both of them reveled in the joy of their mutual love.

Against all probability, she had found her Adam and he his Eve, and the two of them reigned in an Eden, just as she'd always envisioned.

" 'These two imparadised in one another's arms,' " she murmured, " 'the happier Eden, shall enjoy their fill of bliss on bliss.' "

"Milton's *Paradise Lost,* I believe? An excellent piece of work, and one of my personal favorites."

Meggie, who hadn't had her usual warning that anyone was close by, started violently at the unfamiliar female voice that spoke from behind her. Jumping to her feet, she spun around to see an elegant older woman regarding her with clear gray eyes and a smile on her lips.

Meggie opened her mouth, but no sound came out. She was as much taken aback by the complete silence that emanated from this stranger as she was by her sudden appearance. Only once before in her life had Meggie experienced such a phenomenon. It didn't take anything more than simple deduction to put the pieces together.

She pressed her hand to her throat as she realized with horror just whom she must be facing.

"Y-Your Grace?" she said. "Is that you? I—I mean, you must be Hugo's mother." She colored furiously. "That's the only person who could . . . that is I—I mean we—did not expect you."

She raised her hands over her face, knowing she'd already made the worst impression possible. Not only was she babbling like an idiot, but her hair was falling all over the place, and her dress was dirty from playing with Hadrian.

The dowager duchess, on the other hand, looked perfectly immaculate and completely composed.

Meggie, in the midst of wishing herself to the very center of the earth, found her hands taken between the duchess's, gently pulled down, and held in a warm and firm grip. She risked a tentative sideways look up at the Dowager Duchess of Southwell.

"How could you expect me when I did not write?" the duchess asked cheerfully. "I came immediately upon learning you and Hugo were in London, my desire to meet you far greater than my concern over intruding on your privacy."

"Oh, but it is your house, Your Grace," Meggie said quickly. "Surely I am the intruder here. That is to say, I know I am. It is your home, not mine."

"My dear child," the duchess said, smiling at her with unexpected warmth, "you are absolutely charming, even more charming than I had been led to believe. How Hugo ever was so clever as to fall in love with you I cannot imagine, but I am delighted that he did."

"You—you are?" Meggie stared at her in complete disbelief. Hugo had obviously not told her the full truth, or anything close to it, or his mother would never be so warm and welcoming to her most unsuitable daughter-in-law.

"Naturally I am, my dear. Hugo made his feelings clear when he wrote to me in Ireland, and from what I have heard since my return, he is a very happy man. I have only you to thank."

Meggie's mouth fell open in astonishment. She had been dreading the reaction of Hugo's family to their marriage, and now she was being *thanked* for marrying him? Someone had better tell the poor woman the truth, or at least part of it, before she received the shock of her life.

"No—no, you mustn't thank me," Meggie managed to

say. "It is Hugo who has made me happy, really, but perhaps he hasn't told you about me properly . . ."

The duchess chuckled. "He told me enough, although being Hugo, he only gave me the barest details, the most important being that he was head over heels in love with the woman he'd married. The rest I had to discover on my own. I've just come from Suffolk."

Meggie blanched. "Oh," she said in a small voice. "Oh, dear. Then you do know about me."

"Let me sit beside you, Meggie, for we have much to discuss," the duchess said, arranging herself on the bench. "Isn't it interesting, I first became acquainted with my elder son's wife on a bench in a London garden. Dear Lucy looked just as nonplussed as you do. I must make a terrible first impression," she added with a mischievous smile.

"No—oh, not at all, Your Grace. It is just that I have been terribly concerned that you would not approve at all of me, not when you found out about my background." She stared down at her hands. "I suppose Sister Agnes must have told you everything, then."

"Sister Agnes told me great deal," the duchess agreed. "As did Dorelia and Ottoline Mabey. What a pretty place Lyden Hall is. I understand that Hugo has made great strides with it in a short amount of time."

"Oh, he has, Your Grace. He is doing a magnificent job, and his tenants think the world of him. Everyone does. Your son is the most responsible, caring man—his first concern always for others and never himself."

"Yes," the duchess said thoughtfully. "I heard about that, too. The Mabey sisters were most informative in every regard."

"They told you that we are related?" Meggie asked, biting her lip. She doubted that the aunties had spared the duchess a single detail.

"Yes, and such an extraordinary story," the duchess

said, shaking her head. "So very tragic, and yet look at how well it has all turned out. I am so happy for you, my dear. Not only have you found your family after all those lonely years, but you've found Hugo as well. It only goes to show that God does look after us." She laughed. "Heavens, in your case, not only did He guide you home, but He made sure you were very well provided for when you got there."

Meggie gazed at the duchess, dazed by her complete acceptance. What had she ever done to deserve such incredible good fortune? "You are saying that you honestly do not disapprove, despite—despite everything?"

"How could I possibly disapprove, my dear child, when you have everyone singing your praises to high heaven, Hugo included? Dorelia and Ottoline Mabey went on with such enthusiasm that I thought I'd never be allowed to leave!"

Meggie smiled. "They do have a way about them, the dear old aunties. They have a tendency to drive Hugo to distraction, but I think he's secretly rather fond of them."

The duchess chuckled. "They haven't changed a bit, not a bit, even though I haven't seen them for ages. The last time must have been oh, twenty-five years ago when they appeared in London with Linus Eliot—that caused quite a stir, I can tell you, the speculation flying about what was going on among the three of them."

"Oh, dear," Meggie said, not referring to the aunties and their questionable behavior, but to Hadrian who was making a beeline for them, the ball clamped between his jaws.

"Goodness, this must be Hadrian," the duchess said as Hadrian drew to a halt at her feet and dropped the ball, cocking his head at her in curiosity. "What a handsome fellow he is." She reached out and stroked his head as comfortably as if she had wolves drooling on her lap every day of the week.

Meggie grinned with delight. If she'd had any doubts about the duchess being as relaxed as Hugo had implied, they vanished with this one easy gesture. "He's been a wonderful friend to me," she said.

"Yes, Sister Agnes told me how you raised him from a tiny pup. I can see how devoted he is to you. Apparently he is missed almost as much as you are at the sanitarium. Which reminds me—tell me, Meggie dear, how did you find Eunice Kincaid's state of mind before you left? I understand that you were largely responsible for her care, poor woman. Such a pity that she ended up as she did, although she really was rather dreadful. But you probably know the entire story."

"Not really. I know she is connected to you in some way, but Sister Agnes never went into details."

"No? Oh, my *dear*," the duchess said, settling in for a good gossip. "Let me tell you, for it is quite a story. You see, my dear son Raphael rescued his wife from Eunice Kincaid's cruel clutches. She is Lucy's stepmother, you see, and was perfectly dreadful to the poor girl for years. And then a year ago last spring, Raphael went to Ireland to see to a property he'd come into, and there he first spotted Lucy, walking on a cliff . . ."

"My wife is *where*?" Hugo said to the old butler, sure he hadn't heard correctly. "With *whom*?"

The butler cleared his throat. "Lady Hugo is in the garden with your mother, my lord."

Hugo shook his head. "No. Not possible. Your eyesight must be going, Loring, as well as your hearing. My mother is in Ireland."

Loring drew himself up. "Begging your pardon, my lord, but there is not a thing wrong with my eyes or my hearing. Her Grace arrived not an hour ago, and her very first request was to be directed to your wife."

Hugo's mood, which had been excellent when he'd walked in the door, plummeted to the depths of despair. He'd known that the moment of confrontation would have to come eventually, but he'd planned it later rather than sooner, and he had counted on a well-orchestrated introduction with himself there to carefully supervise the proceedings.

The very last thing he'd anticipated was for his mother and Meggie to end up alone, with Meggie helpless to deflect the subtle but relentless questioning his mother was a genius at.

"Dear heaven," he murmured, his blood running cold as ice. He calculated the chances that Meggie would keep her wits about her at about zero. "Where exactly in the garden are they?" he asked, trying to keep a level head. Someone had to present the voice of reason.

"I couldn't say, my lord," Loring replied, his face impassive. "Her ladyship went out to play with her ah, dog, and when Her Grace went out to find her ladyship, she asked that they not be disturbed, so they might be anywhere."

Hugo cringed. Marvelous. Just marvelous. His mother had been faced not just with Meggie for the last hour, but her damned wolf as well.

Well, there was nothing to be done but face the consequences and put as bold a face on the matter as possible.

He strode through the house and out onto the terrace, stopping to scan the vast park for a sign of his mother and his wife. It was the wolf who finally tipped him off. Hadrian leapt around the ornamental pond, tail high, nose low, eyes fixed on the water, no doubt planning a light repast of goldfish.

Hadrian could have the whole damned pond, for all Hugo cared. Meggie and his mother sat on one of the nearby benches, their backs to him, and their heads turned to each other in conversation.

He didn't waste another moment. He ran down one side of the double staircase that led to the garden and walked briskly across the lawn, slowing his stride just long enough to put on an appearance of composure.

That concerted effort went wasted, for as he approached, he heard the murmur of Meggie's voice, followed by a burst of hilarity from his mother and then another. He'd never heard his mother laugh in such a way before, and the shock nearly sent him to his knees. She must be finding Meggie a proper sideshow.

Oh, God. Oh God, oh God, oh God. Help me now in my hour of need. Please help my mother understand, let her at least see that I love Meggie.

He still didn't have much faith that God ever listened, but Hugo sent the prayer up with more sincerity than he ever had before.

Swallowing against the knot of terror in his throat, he casually approached. "Mama," he said, walking around the side of the bench and dropping a kiss on her cheek. "This is a wonderful surprise."

He straightened, anxiously examining Meggie's face, but to his relief, she seemed relaxed and untroubled. "Hello, sweetheart. I see you and my mother are becoming acquainted."

The duchess wiped her eyes with her handkerchief. "Hugo, darling. How—how lovely to see you. Oh—oh, dear." She burst into laughter again. "Forgive me, your wife has just been telling me a story about . . ." she covered her mouth and muffled a highly unladylike snort before continuing, "about a certain Martha Lindsay and her *difficulties*."

Hugo's knees nearly buckled. "Meggie?" he said, shooting her a questioning look.

"Don't look so worried, Hugo," his wife said merrily. "Your mother knows all about my time at Woodbridge Sanitarium, and she doesn't mind in the least. What she didn't know about, because Sister Agnes didn't like to tell her, was Mrs. Lindsay's particular type of obsession. We were discussing the aunties and Linus Eliot and *that* arrangement, and that of course led to Mrs. Lindsay and—well, you know."

"Dear Sister Agnes," his mother said just as merrily, her eyes still streaming. "I think she likes to protect me from what she considers to be the more unsavory forms of mental illness."

Meggie grinned. "Don't you ever repeat this to Sister Agnes, Your Grace, but personally, I think that if Mrs. Lindsay had to be ill, she chose one of the more pleasant afflictions."

The duchess doubled over. "Oh, my dear, you will be the end of me, you really will," she gasped. "No wonder you are so sorely missed at the sanitarium. I think you must have been a ray of sunshine to everyone."

Hugo passed a hand over his face. His mother knew that Meggie had been living in an asylum, and she was behaving as if nothing could possibly be more delightful. Meggie's affliction was contagious, that was the only explanation.

"Hugo, darling, whatever is the matter?" the duchess asked, sobering abruptly. "You look positively ashen. You are not unwell, are you?"

"Never better," he said helplessly.

Meggie caught her bottom lip in her teeth, looking guilty as could be. "Hugo, I'm sorry. I know you do not like me to speak of the sanitarium, but your mother had already been to see Sister Agnes, so there didn't seem to be any point in dissembling. You did say that you were going to tell her everything anyway." She regarded him uncertainly. "You were, weren't you?"

Hugo looked over at her, a flicker of anger sparking in his gut, not at her but at his mother. "Meggie, my love, you have nothing to be sorry for, and yes, of course I was going to tell my mother everything. However, I would appreciate it if you would do me a very great favor and leave us to have a word in private. I will join you in just a few minutes."

Meggie nodded and stood, but a slight frown of worry marked her usually smooth brow and her clear gray eyes held a guarded expression of alarm.

"It's nothing, sweetheart, just some family business," he said, trying to reassure her. "I really won't be long."

She gave him one of the wobbly smiles he so loved, then called Hadrian, curtsied to his mother, and left without another word.

"Meggie is a lovely girl," his mother said, after she'd gone. "So sweet and pretty and such an original. I can see why you must have been instantly attracted to her. Sister Agnes told me the whole story, and I thought it most touching."

Hugo ignored her. "Checking up on me, were you, Mama?"

She tilted her head. "I confess, when I received your letter, I was concerned that you might have done something ill-advised, and so I decided I'd best return to England and see what I could find out."

"Why am I not surprised?" he said bitterly, although he knew deep down inside that he deserved her mistrust.

"Do not be unreasonable, darling. I am your mother, after all, and it is only natural that I would be interested in your welfare. I wanted to be sure that you had made a wise marriage and not just an impulsive one, and I must tell you that after speaking both to Sister Agnes and Ottoline and Dorelia Mabey, my heart could not be happier for you."

"Oh, and why is that? I suppose you heard about Meggie's newly acquired fortune, is that it? That makes everything perfectly acceptable, does it, her past wiped clean?" He really couldn't think of another explanation for his mother's astonishing acceptance of not only Meggie's illegitimacy, but her history of mental instability.

His mother regarded him with surprise. "Darling, do you have so little faith in me that you believe I would cavil at a marriage made for love? All I ever wished for you was happiness, Hugo, that and a productive life, and you have managed to find both with Meggie."

Hugo opened his mouth, then closed it, finding absolutely nothing to say. He was beginning to think he was the one who was out of his mind.

"To address your question, dear Meggie might not have the most splendid past," his mother continued, "but you are right, that is behind her, and she is your wife now." She lifted a hand to forestall him. "Yes, extraordinarily enough, she has also turned out to be an heiress who will eventually make you one of the richer men in England, but I would say that is beside the point."

"*Beside* the point?" Hugo said in disbelief. "Mama, I cannot think that you are serious. Since when do you ignore the import of sizable fortunes?"

"I am perfectly serious as far as your happiness with Meggie is concerned—money has nothing to do with it. As for the rest of the world, I think that Meggie's dowry will be a most useful decoy. I intend to spread word around London of your fortuitous marriage immediately, with a slight rearrangement of the details for the curious—I worked them out on my way, and I think my plan is completely feasible."

Hugo stared down at the ground. So. She was going to take care of it all was she? Make a few choice amendments and purge Meggie of her past?

He knew he should be grateful—grateful for her blanket acceptance of their marriage, of Meggie, and for her offer to help deflect any hint of scandal. A month ago he would have been grateful himself, but now . . . now he didn't know how he felt, only that he wanted his mother to accept Meggie as she was, not as she thought Meggie should be.

"Hugo, darling, please do not look so downcast. I do not in any way criticize your dear wife, I only mean to make her way easier. You know how cruel society can be about one they perceive to be—well, *different,* if you understand my meaning."

"What an interesting euphemism you use, Mama."

"My dear boy, I know that you love your wife and you are therefore understandably sensitive about her, but you surely wish to protect her from scorn, do you not? I cannot see what purpose would be served by having all the *ton* know that Meggie is illegitimate."

"No," he said, digging the heel of his boot into the grass. "There would be no purpose served in that."

"Good. So I thought we would say that Meggie, orphaned when young, grew up very quietly and simply in Suffolk, that she is connected to both the Aldeburgh Russells and the Southwold Mabeys, and that being the only surviving relative on both sides, is beneficiary of both fortunes—all of it true. How is that, darling?"

"Well enough," he said tonelessly. "What are you planning to say to explain away her six-year stay at the Woodbridge Sanitarium? Or perhaps you intend to delete that part of her life entirely."

"I cannot think why it should ever come up, Hugo. Not that there is any shame in Meggie's time at Woodbridge. Sister Agnes could not say enough about her work—how brilliant Meggie was with the patients—but people can be terrible snobs about that sort of thing."

Hugo's head shot up. He had to force himself to keep a neutral expression as his mother's words echoed around and around in his head like a roulette ball endlessly spinning, finding no place to land.

Meggie had *worked* at the sanitarium? She had looked after the patients, not been one herself?

"Sister Agnes said Meggie's work was brilliant?" he repeated, so stunned it was a miracle he could speak at all.

"Yes, darling. Did Sister Agnes not tell you? Meggie was her right hand, a true godsend from the time those awful nuns at the orphanage sent her over as punishment for some imagined sin or other. I think the only reason Sister Agnes let Meggie leave with you so easily was because she loved Meggie and wanted her to be happy, and she saw that you also loved her, too."

Hugo turned his back and walked over to the pond. He sat down on the very edge and stared down at the water. The distorted reflection of his face stared back at him in mockery.

Every presumption he'd ever made about Meggie stemmed from his belief that she had been an inmate, someone who had been confined because her mind was unbalanced. He had accepted her despite it, loved her despite it, thought that maybe she'd healed to a large degree, and worried in equal measure that she might revert to her previous condition.

Only there was no previous condition. Had he been mad, completely mad himself to see an illness in her that had never existed? Had he because of one huge and erroneous assumption interpreted everything she'd said and done through a distorted filter?

He tried to go back to the beginning and reinterpret all that had passed between them from the very first. His mind raced furiously. Incredibly, as he ran through the details he really could see Meggie as a woman who was absolutely normal and had been sane all along.

He'd assumed her mad on first sight simply because she'd been present in the asylum, and because no sane person could possibly possess such translucent, untroubled eyes, and such an otherworldly presence. He'd assumed her mad because it suited him at the time and it suited him even better when he'd had need of her money.

He'd assumed her mad because when he had gone to propose to her out of the clear blue sky she had laughed in his face and called him mad himself. What he'd mistaken for lunacy had only been rattled nerves and a healthy suspicion of a man from a completely different station in life—a man who had appeared out of nowhere with a proposition that must have seemed outrageous to her. He wondered now why she had accepted him at all, considering the way he'd behaved.

When he'd taken her to the sea on the day they were wed she had frolicked there with an unlimited joy. Later when she had given herself to him without reservation and not a hint of shyness, he'd assumed her mad for her complete lack of inhibition.

For every last one of her virtues he had judged her deranged, and Meggie had never realized it for an instant.

Why should she have, even though he'd treated her like a complete idiot for the first twenty-four hours of their relationship and not given her much more credit since? He was the true idiot, having made it perfectly clear to her from the first how he expected her to behave. She'd only done her best to oblige him.

He pressed the back of his hand hard across his mouth, too shaken to speak. The profusion of emotions sweeping through him was too raw, too profound for coherent thought.

Meggie was sane. Beautifully, perfectly, brilliantly sane. Their marriage was safe, their future children without potential threat. He loved her with all his being. She loved him in the same way. Somewhere a miracle had happened, although he vaguely registered through his shock and confusion that the miracle had happened a long time before and he was the last one to see it.

Meggie. Oh, Meggie. Has there ever been anyone more sane than you in your honesty? Anyone more direct, more free of guile, more uncaring about what the material world might give you, yet more caring about what beauty the world's natural bounties hold? Anyone ever more willing to love with no conditions attached?

He bowed his forehead into the palm of his hands, tears stinging at his eyes. Meggie, his dear, sweet Meggie, unique among women. What the hell had he done? What the *hell* had he done?

"Hugo, what on earth is the matter with you?" his mother said impatiently. "The way you are behaving, one would think you were hearing all this for the first time."

He quickly wiped his eyes. The last thing in the world he wanted was his mother, let alone Meggie, to think that he had ever considered her anything less than perfectly sane.

"I beg your pardon," he murmured, standing and turning around to face his mother. The guilt he now carried was nearly enough to crush him, as if it hadn't been bad enough before. "I cannot—I cannot express to you the strength of my feelings. You have accepted my wife so readily, trusted my judgment when I have given you no reason to do anything but doubt me. I couldn't at first believe your generosity toward Meggie, but I see now that you really do understand."

"Hugo, my dear, but how could I not?" she replied gently. "I wonder if you think me such a dried-up old woman that I have forgotten the wonders of love?"

"Mama," he replied, coloring at her unabashed candor, "I would never think such a thing. To tell you the truth, I—well, I haven't considered you in that light at all. How could I? You are my mother."

She laughed. "So I am. Has it not occurred to you that

you would not be here at all if I had not at one time felt the same way toward your father as you feel toward your Meggie? Really, Hugo, you cannot be so lacking in imagination."

"I can honestly say that there is absolutely nothing amiss with my imagination," he said dryly.

"You were certainly imaginative enough to see beyond the limitations society places upon us and marry a woman for love rather than position and fortune. As for doubting you, I can see for myself the changes your marriage has made in you, never mind all the wonderful testimonials I heard when I was briefly at Lyden. I believe you have finally come into your own, my darling child, and I could not be happier about anything. You have learned your lessons well."

What could he possibly say to that? Actually, Mama, I'm a far bigger bounder than you ever imagined. He thought not. "Meggie is an excellent teacher," he said instead and with complete honesty. "I learn something new every day." That also was entirely true.

"Meggie said much the same thing about you," his mother replied. "You may not have had similar upbringings, but you do have so many other things in common. I shudder to think how quickly you would have become bored had you married only a pretty face."

Hugo braced himself, something telling him he was about to receive another shock. "Meggie is far more than a pretty face," he agreed cautiously, not having any idea what direction his mother might be going in.

"Indeed, yes. If I can approve of nothing else those dreadful nuns at the orphanage did, at least they recognized your wife's intellect and made good use of it, training her to be a teacher."

"Mmm, hmm," he murmured, feeling as if a bucket of cold water had just been dumped over his head.

"Sister Agnes told me Meggie was already fluent in

Latin, Greek, and French when she arrived at the sanitarium, and once there she continued to study everything she could. I find that so commendable, but of course you know how strongly I feel about women being properly educated."

Hugo rubbed the lobe of his ear very, very hard. "Yes, you've mentioned it often."

"For good reason, darling. We females are encouraged to be flaccid of thought, interested only in the mundane occurrences in our daily lives and the equally mundane lives of those around us, but in my opinion nothing compares to the richness of one's inner life. Some might scoff, but I think you are truly blessed to have married an educated woman, especially given your own interest in the classics."

Hugo thought he might very well wring Meggie's neck. An intellectual was she, masquerading all this time as an ignoramus? No wonder she'd so easily trotted out a Greek name for her mare. No wonder she'd belatedly tried to disguise her knowledge, making up some idiotic excuse. He supposed that he was responsible for that subterfuge on top of everything else. When had he ever given her an indication that he expected anything of her but ignorance?

"Mama," he said, suddenly in desperate need of setting his wife straight on a few vital points, "would you mind terribly if I take my leave of you? I promised Meggie I wouldn't be long."

"Darling, do go to your dear wife. In all truth I am rather tired. I have been traveling for what seems like weeks and would be happy to disappear to my rooms and sleep, although I do think I can manage to have dinner with you tonight. Tomorrow I will rise and descend upon London Society, singing Meggie's praises and yours." She stood and kissed his cheek. "Your brother will be so pleased to hear the good news—oh!

Oh, good *heavens,* what was I thinking? Hugo, darling, you are an uncle! You have a beautiful little nephew, the most adorable infant, born three weeks ago. I think he looks very like his father at that age, although they are so small and red in the beginning that it is always hard to tell exactly."

Hugo grinned, filled with real happiness for his brother. "Rafe must be over the moon. I will write him immediately with my congratulations—and I will give him the details of my own marriage at the same time."

"He would like that," the duchess said solemnly. "I do believe that next to having his wife safely delivered of a healthy newborn son, nothing could give him more joy than to hear that you are as happily wed as he is."

Hugo found Meggie in the library, head bent over a catalogue of old manuscripts, so focused that she didn't even hear him come in.

"Hello, Meggie. What are you reading?" he asked wickedly, watching her jump six inches off the ground.

"N-nothing," she said, stuffing the catalogue into a drawer of the desk she was standing in front of.

"Nothing?"

"Well, er, Madame DeChaille told me that she thought I ought to educate myself about the latest fashions before our next appointment." She blushed furiously.

"Meggie, you clever girl. I think I am only beginning to see how you've been getting around the truth without ever actually telling me an outright lie."

"What do you mean?" she asked, her hand creeping to her flushed cheek.

"I mean that you have been pulling the wool over my eyes for a good month now, and I would like to know why, my little scholar. *Altissima quaeque flumina minimo sono labi.* Translation, please?"

"The deepest rivers flow with the least sound," she whispered, her face frozen, her eyes huge and hollow. "Oh, *Hugo.* Do you hate me for deceiving you?"

"Hate you? Meggie, in this moment I love you more than ever, but you do baffle me. Why—*why* did you not simply tell me the truth from the start?"

"I thought you wanted a stupid wife," she said, her head bowed.

Hugo's gaze fixed on the exposed nape of her neck that looked absurdly fragile, little wisps of flaxen hair curling about it like dandelion fluff. He wanted to press a kiss just there, but knew that if he did he'd quickly be pressing kisses elsewhere, and they would never complete the conversation. "You thought I wanted a stupid wife," he repeated. "Why? Did you think me so stupid that I couldn't bear the thought of intelligent conversation?"

"No! Oh, Hugo, never that. It was just that you didn't seem to want a smart wife, and since you were so kind as to fall in love with me the way you thought I was and take me away from Woodbridge, I thought I should oblige you as best I could—or at least until I could adjust you to the idea that I was educated." She lifted her hands in a gesture of helplessness. "Then the first night at Lyden, Aunt Dorelia told me in no uncertain terms that no man ever wanted an educated wife, and I should keep my silence. She said that men didn't want to hear women's opinions, that they didn't like women to be clever, that all they wanted was a pretty face and a pleasing manner."

Hugo rubbed his hand back and forth over his mouth. "I see," he said after a moment. "You believed the silly old bats, naturally, since you've never had anyone else to instruct you in what men wish and don't wish from their wives."

"You did treat me as if I was simpleminded, Hugo," Meggie pointed out miserably. "So yes, I believed them."

Hugo stared up at the ceiling. He didn't have a leg to stand on and he knew it. "I am entirely at fault," he said, having no way to explain his original assumption. "Looking back, I can see that I behaved badly in any number of ways, and for that I am sorry. I—well. I never thought that you might have been given any kind of education, and I suppose I acted on that misguided premise."

"Do you mean you really don't mind?" Meggie said, her beautiful eyes filling with starlight. Her joy and relief were so clear and strong that Hugo's breath left his body.

"Meggie—Meggie," he groaned, closing the distance between them and pulling her tight against his chest. His arms wrapped about her as if he could draw her into his soul. "There is so much I feel a fool for, so much. *Mea maxima culpa,* my darling. It is for you to forgive me."

"There is nothing to forgive," she said, tilting her head back and looking up at him, her eyes filling with tears that only made their starlight dance brighter. "Nothing. You have never been anything but loving and good to me. You took me on sheer faith, married me when you knew all I wanted was an escape from my life." She shuddered in his arms. "You took an enormous risk, Hugo, believing that you loved a stranger, and yet your faith proved true, for I love you more than I can ever say. I will never be able to express my gratitude enough, or my love. The very idea that you are willing to accept this part of me as well brings me to my knees."

He buried his mouth and his hands in her hair, drinking in her sweet fragrance. His fingers traced the delicate shape of her skull, and his eyes closed. His heart was beating so fast he could scarcely contain it—not from passion, but from fear.

"Meggie," he murmured, some final barrier in him

crumbling. A realization swept through him that if he didn't tell her the absolute truth and tell it to her now, he would never be redeemed. His life would always be a lie, and their marriage would never be fully realized.

He understood in the deepest part of himself the risk he took, that he might lose everything, that this was his last and the most desperate gamble he had ever made. This gamble was for Meggie, for their life, their future together, and the die he cast could only come up one way. Meggie would have to call it.

He drew in the deepest breath he'd ever taken. "My love, I have not been entirely honest with you. Will you hear me out, try to forgive me for the transgressions I have made?"

Meggie placed her hands on either side of his face. "How could you possibly have transgressed against me?" she asked with a tender smile. "You are the very best of men."

"But I'm not, my love, I'm not. This is what I need to tell you. I pray that you will somehow find a way to understand." He gently took her hands in his, intending to sit her down and confess all, whatever the consequences.

He nearly screamed with frustration when a knock came at the door. "Yes, what is it?" he snapped, stepping away from Meggie as the door opened and Loring appeared.

"Lord Waldock to see you, my lord. He says he is here at your urgent request."

Hugo swore silently. Of all times that Waldock might have appeared, this was the worst possible moment. On the other hand, he couldn't possibly refuse the man.

"Meggie—may we continue this later? This is the man I have been waiting to see for the last week."

She nodded, then walked to the door. "We will talk later." She hesitated, her hand on the doorknob. "Hugo, whatever is on your mind, please do not be troubled. You really are the best of men, even if you refuse to believe it."

He tried to smile at her, then turned away, steeling himself to face his past and his future all at once.

25

For the life of her, Meggie could not work out why Hugo thought he required forgiveness. He'd looked so pale, so troubled, his deep blue eyes haunted with remorse.

It was typical of Hugo to take the blame for thinking her dim-witted, as if it was any fault of his. She had been the one to give him that impression, or at least to encourage it once she thought it was what he wanted. It was she who ought to be asking his forgiveness for having misled him in the first place—hadn't she been the one who had insisted on honesty between them?

She pulled the catalogue out of the desk drawer and replaced it on the shelf, no longer in a mood to pore over it. She'd been reading it only as a distraction.

"It's been quite a day so far, hasn't it, Hadrian?" she murmured, looking at the wolf who had made a comfortable bed for himself under the desk.

He lifted his head and gazed at her, his yellow eyes blinking once as if in agreement.

"Imagine Hugo's mother appearing just like that, and what a wonderful woman she is, so open-minded and such a generous nature. No wonder Hugo turned into such a fine man."

Hadrian put his head straight back on his paws and closed his eyes.

"Oh, very well," Meggie said with a smile. "Be like that, but one of these days you will come around to my way of thinking. You're just jealous."

Hadrian continued to ignore her.

"Silly wolf. I'm going upstairs to change for dinner.

You can stay here and sulk, but I think you might try to be a little more open-minded yourself."

Bending down, she gave him a scratch behind his ears. He grunted but showed no interest in vacating his position, so she left him where he was and softly closed the door.

She stopped abruptly as she strongly sensed a stranger's presence in the entrance hall, a presence that emanated murderous fury. That fury was directed straight toward Hugo—Hugo, and less so toward a man named Waldock . . . Waldock, whom Hugo had been anxiously waiting to see all week.

Meggie couldn't imagine what reason this person would have to be so dangerously angry, or even what he was doing in the house at all. Loring had not announced anyone else to Hugo, and Loring was the grand master of butlers.

She tried to stanch her apprehension, determined to find out more, for if Hugo was in any sort of trouble she wanted to know about it.

Drawing on all her strength, she summoned up a poise she certainly didn't feel, then walked into the huge hall where a well-dressed man of about Hugo's age paced. His handsome face was drawn into an ugly frown.

"Good afternoon," she said, trying to sound perfectly casual. "I am Lady Hugo Montagu. May I help you in some way?"

He started at the sound of her voice, and his expression instantly smoothed into one of pleasant greeting.

"Lady Hugo—this is a surprise," he said, walking directly over to her and bowing over her hand. "Allow me to present myself. I am Michael Foxlane, an old friend of your husband's."

Meggie had to suppress a shudder. She found it hard to believe this man was any friend of Hugo's. There was something repulsive about him, something dark and twisted in his heart that his false joviality tried to hide.

"How do you do?" she said, quickly removing her hand from his grasp. "If you have come to see my husband, he is occupied at the moment, but Loring must have already told you." She knew the polite thing would be to offer him refreshment, but she wasn't about to give a man who held such hatred toward Hugo a single crumb.

"Actually, I only wait for my companion to finish his business. We are on our way to a pre-dinner engagement, and I grew weary of waiting in the carriage. I thought to greet your husband briefly, not having seen him for some time, but meeting you is an unexpected bonus, Lady Hugo."

A pretty little bitch, aren't you? I wonder just what the real story behind this marriage is—God knows, Montagu needed an heiress after I was finished with him. But odd how this one popped out of the woodwork just in time to save his cursed neck from ruin.

Meggie practically gasped as the horrifying words drilled straight into her head, clear as day. She only rarely perceived someone else's thoughts as fully and lucidly as if she'd formulated them herself, and the few people whose thoughts she had perceived in that way had usually been unbalanced. She couldn't help but wonder if that wasn't the case with Michael Foxlane, despite his urbane, self-possessed appearance.

She forced herself to smile, determined to get to the root of this man's enmity. For once she was truly grateful for her talent. "You said you and my husband were old friends. Have you known him many years, Mr. Foxlane?"

"We were at school together," he replied, looking her up and down with an insulting smile that made her stomach turn over. "And you, Lady Hugo? How long have you known your husband? I never heard mention of you or your marriage to Montagu until this very day when our mutual friend Lord Waldock returned to town and received your husband's letter."

And gave me the shock of my life—I could murder Montagu with my bare hands. Seventy-five thousand pounds straight into the sewer on that damned wager at White's, and damn Cousin Amelia to hell anyway for swearing Montagu was as good as leg-shackled to her. She'll pitch the fit of her life when she hears the news, and serves her right, the stupid bitch.

Still, I'll somehow see that Montagu pays for my loss, and he'll pay in a way that really hurts—first with his pride, and later with his reputation. And maybe, just maybe, when he's suffered as much as possible, I'll have him finished off for good, the smug bastard.

"I have known my husband for some months," Meggie said, trying to hide her shock, acutely aware that she needed to tread very, very carefully, that she couldn't afford to make a single mistake if she was to help Hugo. "I wonder that he has never mentioned you to me, given that you are such old friends."

Foxlane shrugged nonchalantly. "I am sure there are many things your husband has neglected to tell you. For example, did he think to inform you that he lost not only his estate but his last penny to Arthur Waldock in an evening of gambling only days before your marriage? Waldock has come to collect."

Silly cow. Of course he didn't tell you. How does it feel to know your husband married you only for your money? I'll wager he swore it was all for love, and you believed him, you little fool.

Meggie couldn't help paling. "Yes, I knew," she lied, trying desperately to keep her composure in place, a nearly impossible task. Hugo had married her for her *money*? But that was impossible—neither of them had known anything about her inheritance until a week ago.

Yet she knew that Foxlane spoke the truth about Hugo's losses. The images crowded into her head, just as if she had been there herself that night. Hugo drunk and despondent, Foxlane dealing the cards.

Meggie sucked in her breath. Marked cards. Foxlane had cheated, and he'd had an accomplice, a footman at a place called Boodle's, where Hugo and Foxlane had been that night . . .

Her hand crept over her mouth and she stared at Foxlane, horrified. She envisioned it all as if she were looking through his eyes, thinking the thoughts inside his head. He was a monster, a true monster.

"He didn't tell you a thing, did he?" Foxlane said triumphantly. "I suppose he also didn't tell you that he is an inveterate gambler whose own brother exiled him to the continent for three years, tired of his debts and the constant scandals."

Meggie clenched her hands together behind her back, her nails digging into her palms. She forced herself to concentrate, to pull every last detail that she could from Foxlane's vile mind.

"Yes, he told me all about that, too," she said, absorbing another painful rush of images. "He returned last year, after making a great deal of money in Paris at the gambling tables, and then he lost it all a month ago to Lord Waldock at Boodle's. Lord Waldock gave him ninety days to repay the debt in full so that Hugo wouldn't lose Lyden."

Meggie felt sick at heart as the truth came pounding home to her. Hugo had lied to her, over and over again, about so many things. She pressed her shaking hands even harder together, thinking that the one thing he hadn't lied to her about was loving her because he couldn't have known about her money. At least there was that. At least there was that.

She wouldn't let Foxlane destroy him, destroy what

they had together just because of Hugo's past mistakes. She had to protect him against this vicious man, would protect him, no matter the cost.

"Ah," Foxlane said, looking mightily disappointed. "So you do know all about it. I confess to surprise. Most men do not want their wives to know about their past sins, and your husband has so many I am sure even he has lost count."

"My husband's past is no concern of mine," Meggie retorted, raising her chin. "I care only about the man of honor that he is now." She desperately wanted to believe that was true, but she didn't know what to think anymore. Her brain was so numbed by Foxlane's series of devastating revelations that she could hardly think at all.

"A man of *honor*? Oh, my dear Lady Hugo, you have been hoodwinked, haven't you?" he said with a nasty smile. "My friend must make you very, very happy in bed, but then he always did have quite a reputation with the, ah . . . ladies."

Meggie lost her fight for self-control. She wasn't going to listen to any more vicious slurs about Hugo, even if some of them were true. "Tell me, Mr. Foxlane," she said coldly, "why are you so eager to tell me all about my husband's past? Were you hoping to destroy the love and the trust that exists between us? If that is the case, and I can think of no other, you surely have a strange notion of friendship."

He flushed a dark red, his eyes narrowing dangerously. "So, the sweet little wife has claws, has she? Careful, she-cat. You do not wish to cross me."

"Don't I indeed?" Meggie replied, her temper about to erupt. Oh, she'd cross him all right. He'd be sorry he'd ever thought to hurt Hugo.

At that moment the door to the study swung open and Hugo appeared with a tall, pleasant-looking man at his side. Hugo spotted Meggie and Foxlane instantly, and a look of guarded surprise crossed his face.

"Foxlane—I hadn't realized you were here. I see you have met my wife."

"A charming woman," Foxlane drawled. "May I wish you every happiness, Montagu?"

Meggie practically choked. It was everything she could do to keep her mouth from falling open.

"Thank you," Hugo said, crossing the room, his hand outstretched. "You are kind to wish us well."

That was it. She couldn't bear the idea of Hugo being so deceived, of his even touching Foxlane's treacherous hand. She didn't stop to think about the consequences, just knew that Hugo had to learn the truth then and there. "No—don't believe anything he says! He is no friend to you, Hugo. He's betrayed you horribly!"

Hugo stopped mid-stride, staring at her in astonishment. "Meggie . . . what is this?" he said slowly.

"He cheated at cards," she said, realizing she must sound a complete fool, but not caring. Foxlane couldn't be allowed to get away with his treachery. "It happened the night he took you to Boodle's."

"How dare you accuse me of such a thing?" Foxlane bellowed, his face turning red. "Montagu, silence your wife before I silence her myself! Is she mad?"

"I suggest you keep your own silence," Hugo said, shooting Foxlane a look of cold fury. He walked straight over to Meggie and took her by the shoulders. "What in the name of God has gotten into you?" he demanded in a low voice.

"It's true," she insisted, not knowing how she was going to make him believe her. She'd only realized belatedly that if she told him the entire truth, she would have to give away the entire truth about herself, too. She'd just have to find another way to force him to listen.

"Meggie—I don't know what you think you're doing

or why, but you had damned well explain yourself and quickly," he said, his hands holding her shoulders firmly.

"I'm trying," she said, looking directly into his eyes, silently pleading with him to hear her. "Mr. Foxlane made a wager for seventy-five thousand pounds in White's betting book that you would marry Amelia Langford before the end of the Season, and when he found out that you had no intention of doing any such thing, he set out to make sure you lost everything and would be forced to marry her anyway."

"How could you *possibly* know anything about that?" Hugo demanded, looking as shaken as she felt.

Tears started to Meggie's eyes, partly from the pain his fingers were inflicting, but more from the sudden terror that he was going to despise her forever no matter what happened. If he didn't believe her, he'd despise her forever for thinking she'd lied to him, and if he did believe her, he'd despise her even longer than that for her freakish aberration. "I—I overheard it," she stammered, praying that sounded believable.

"You overheard a piece of gossip, you took it for gospel without ever thinking to ask me if it was true, and then you accuse my friend to his face of the worst sin a gentleman can commit?" he said, anger shaking his voice.

"Hugo, you must believe me. Please. He meant you ill then, and he means you ill now."

"Montagu, I warn you now—either your wife retracts her insulting accusations or I will call you out," Foxlane said from behind her, his voice cold as ice.

"Stubble it, Foxlane," Lord Waldock said, speaking up for the first time. "Let Lady Hugo finish. I am curious to hear what more she has to say, for she would have no reason to make such a drastic accusation unless she believed it to be true. I confess I did wonder why you were so upset this afternoon when you learned from me that Montagu had not only married, but could repay his debt."

"You were mistaken in my reaction," Foxlane said smoothly. "I was surprised, no more. Obscure heiresses do not grow on trees, and I could not think where Montagu had found one with so little trouble just when he was most in need."

Hugo rubbed the corner of his mouth. "That, my friend, is none of your damned business. Is my wife correct about your wager at White's?"

"Yes, but wagers at White's are general knowledge," Foxlane said with a shrug, as if Hugo was a fool for asking. "Any number of people could have seen my entry in the book—in any case, what does that prove? You know yourself how many people were betting on your making a match with Amelia. That most certainly doesn't make me a cheat at cards." He spread his hands out. "What would be my motive? I only learned about your marriage today. Naturally I was slightly upset to learn I had just lost a large wager, but who wouldn't be?"

"True enough," Waldock said with a curt nod. "Lady Hugo, forgive me for questioning you so closely when we are not even acquainted, but your allegation is a serious matter. Is there anything else you can tell us about what you overheard and from whom you overheard it?"

"I cannot tell you from whom I heard it, my lord," she said, turning to face him, "but I can tell you that Mr. Foxlane took my husband around the clubs that night with the deliberate intention of getting him intoxicated so that he would lose his judgment. He also deliberately ended up at Boodle's, knowing my husband would not be able to resist the deep play."

Foxlane snorted. "What is that supposed to prove? We went together to the clubs, yes. Do you say I forced him to come along, Lady Hugo, that I forced the drink down his throat? Or perhaps you are saying that once at Boodle's, I forced him to play hand after hand, staking large amounts of money on each, and then forced him to lose each hand?" He turned to Hugo, his eyes glittering. "If you recall anything at all about that evening, Montagu, you might recollect that I wasn't even playing."

"I remember well enough." Hugo wearily rubbed two fingers over his forehead. "Meggie, put an end to this, if you please. You can have nothing else to say, so apologize to Mr. Foxlane for misinterpreting a piece of gossip. If we are fortunate, he will understand that you are not accustomed to London and know nothing of its entertainments, and that you were overset to hear that I engaged in some ill-advised card-playing and lost a great deal of money."

Foxlane laughed, the sound so sinister that it sent chills down Meggie's spine. "Don't be absurd, Montagu. Do you think you can bamboozle me into accepting an apology because your wife is a complete innocent?" He tilted his chin in Meggie's direction. "She already informed me that she knew not only about your wayward past, but also about your most recent fiasco in all its glorious detail, and she saw fit to inform me of the facts with no prompting on my part."

Hugo's hands fell away from Meggie's shoulders, and he stepped away from her as if she were a pariah. He clearly thought that she'd somehow learned the truth and had been playing at some awful game designed to shame him. His extended silence only confirmed her fear.

She drew in a deep breath, seeing that there was nothing else to do but expose Foxlane completely and in exact detail, no matter the cost to herself. She fixed her gaze on the man who was now every bit as much her enemy as he was Hugo's.

"You speak of facts, Mr. Foxlane. I wonder if the name

Joseph Potter means anything to you. He has been employed at Boodle's for the last eighteen months, his wages generously supplemented by your monthly bonuses."

To her immense satisfaction, Foxlane turned white as a sheet. Stretched to the breaking point, his thoughts were in chaos, blind panic obscuring his reason. "Who—what the devil are you talking about?" he sputtered. "I know nothing of a Joseph Potter."

"How odd," Meggie said coolly, reeling him like a hooked fish, "since he is the footman who supplies you with the decks of cards you like so well." She took advantage of the stunned silence that came from all three men. "You may not have been playing that particular night, Mr. Foxlane, but you were dealing," she continued, watching him cautiously, knowing that he might do anything once cornered. "Marked cards make such a difference in the outcome of play, do they not, especially when one has a vested interest in the result of that play? What *was* the winning hand that you intentionally dealt Lord Waldock . . . let me see. I believe it was the six of spades down, ace of diamonds up, finally crowned by the four of clubs? Would that be right?"

"You—you must have paid Potter a small fortune for that information! I'll kill you, you little bitch!" Foxlane made a lunge for her, but Hugo caught him before he reached her, holding him in a viselike grip, one arm across his throat.

"What is this?" Hugo hissed from between his teeth. "Have we been misbehaving ourselves, Foxlane?"

Foxlane gasped for breath and Hugo abruptly released him, throwing him to the floor. "She's lying," Foxlane choked. "Lying through her accursed teeth."

Meggie stepped away and moved into the shadows, trying to make herself invisible as Waldock strode up to

Foxlane. He bent down, taking a fistful of Foxlane's coat in a tight grip and hauled him to his feet.

"I wonder who is lying through his accursed teeth, my dear friend? My God, there were times I wondered at your runs of luck, especially at Boodle's, but I never went so far as to imagine you would stoop so low. To learn that you deliberately went about ruining Montagu for your own gain and used me as your pawn, to accuse his wife of lying about it—I should kill you."

He pulled back his fist and delivered a punch to Foxlane's jaw that cracked across the hall, then violently shoved him back onto the floor.

Foxlane skidded across the marble, with his hand to his bloodied mouth, and his feet scrambling to get a grip. He pushed himself to his knees. His head lowered, and his breath coming hard.

"Damn you all to hell," he spat. "Damn you! You've always thought yourselves better than me with your titles, your inherited wealth—what did I ever have except a useless pedigree and my wits? Answer me that! You try being a fourth son in a family that could barely afford to keep its head above water but insisted on image and respectability at all cost. What was I supposed to do, get a job in the city like a plebeian? Or maybe I should have become an accountant and worked for one of you."

He raised his head and glared at them. "You would have liked that, wouldn't you, like to see me degraded, humiliated by my betters? You've always looked down at me, both of you, ever since our days at Harrow. Well, I made you sit up and pay attention, didn't I? I made my fortune, I kept up with the best of you after all, despite my disadvantages."

Meggie couldn't bear to look at him, couldn't bear the self-pity that emanated from him. He made her feel dirty, invaded. She was infinitely grateful when Hugo moved over to him and took him by the elbow.

"Get up," he said quietly. "Get up and stop behaving in such a pathetic fashion. You might not have any morals, but show a little self-respect, man."

Foxlane did as Hugo commanded as if automatically responding to the voice of authority. He stood, brushing himself off, then straightened his shoulders. "What do you intend to do now?" he asked through a swollen lip, assuming an air of bravado that fell flat.

"Quite obviously you are finished here," Waldock said. "If I were you, I'd take myself out of the country as quickly as possible and not make any plans to return."

Hugo raised one eyebrow. "Did Waldock say quickly? I'd amend that to instantly, if you value your life."

Foxlane smiled sardonically. "Odd hearing that threat coming from you, Montagu. As I recall, you were the one whose life was forever at risk for your depraved deeds. Of course, you always had an influential brother to bail you out."

"I doubt even my sainted brother would have come to my rescue had I done what you have. I have no leg to stand on when it comes to my past sins, but I can at least say that I have never cheated anyone." He suddenly looked over at Meggie. "At least never at cards," he added in a low voice.

Meggie could only stare at him, stunned. She didn't need her gift to know the truth; she could see it in his eyes. He'd married her only for the money—it had always been about the money. Somehow he'd found out about her inheritance, and he had come to claim her not for love, but from necessity. Love had never entered his mind.

She wanted to die right there on the spot.

"Please, just leave, Foxlane," Hugo said with a weary sigh. "Do me the extreme favor of never showing your face to me again, and I will do my best to forget not only your crime to me, but also the insults you paid my wife."

"Never fear, Hugo, I will see this piece of filth out of the country personally," Waldock said, taking Foxlane by the arm and jerking him around to face the door. "By the by, that bank draft you signed today? I'll tear it up. Consider it null and void. As far as I am concerned, the evening never took place. We, at least, are men of honor."

Hugo nodded without a word. He looked more exhausted than Meggie had ever seen him before. Oddly, she found she didn't care. She didn't care about much of anything.

"My apologies, Lady Hugo," Waldock said, noticing her for the first time in the shadow of the column where she'd stepped back from the fray. "I hope you can find it in your heart to forgive me for doubting you, if only briefly. I also hope we can be friends in the future. You were very brave to speak up as you did, and I admire you for discovering the truth on your husband's behalf."

Meggie did her best to smile at him. She wanted nothing more than to be away from all of them, Hugo included. Hugo especially.

The second the door had closed behind Waldock and Foxlane, Meggie made a move for the staircase, praying Hugo would let her pass in peace. She was too filled with the confusion of her own thoughts to be able to deal with his.

"Meggie—Meggie, stop," he said, catching her arm as she hurried by. "We must talk. I have a hundred questions to ask you, and you must have a hundred questions also."

She couldn't meet his eyes. "I do not wish to talk," she said, disengaging her arm. "In all honesty, I wish to be left alone."

"My love—I'm sorry for everything that just happened, even sorrier for what you learned about me, about my past, but for God's sake, please don't walk away from me. Tell me how you discovered everything that you did about Foxlane, why you even thought to try to discover it? I cannot understand how you would have had the first inkling about what happened."

For the first time, Meggie looked directly at him. "I read Foxlane's mind."

"I suppose I deserved that," he said, rubbing his finger against the corner of his mouth. "Your anger is completely understandable, but at least will you tell me the truth?"

"You've told so many lies that you can't recognize the truth when you hear it," she said quietly. "Anyway, does it really matter? You betrayed me. You married me not for love, but for the money that you knew I had coming to me."

He lowered his gaze. "I did. I betrayed you and lied to you, Meggie, I fully admit it, and you know the reason why. You seem to be aware of a great number of my transgressions. But please, give me a chance to explain?"

She turned her head away. Those transgressions were far too enormous for her to absorb just now. Everything was too much. She felt as if every last nerve in her body had been rubbed raw, every last emotion stretched so far that she was beyond feeling anything. She could only reach for a quietude she desperately needed. It was then, with an enormous sense of relief, that she knew exactly what she had to do.

Home. She needed to go home.

"I don't want explanations. I want to leave, Hugo. I'm going back to where I belong."

He stared at her, his face turning as white as Foxlane's had been only minutes before. "You can't be serious."

"Perfectly serious," she replied with as much dignity as she could muster. "Your life is very full here, and you have no need of me that I can see. I would ask only that you not try to dissuade me, as it will do no good. I won't change my mind."

"I see. There is no way I can convince you to reconsider?" he asked, looking as if she'd struck him just as hard as Waldock had struck Foxlane.

"There is nothing to reconsider," she replied. The pain in her heart tightened into an unbearable knot. "I need to go. Would you be so kind as to give me the use of one of the carriages?"

He inclined his head in assent. She couldn't see the expression in his eyes, but she didn't wish to. She was in enough pain as it was.

"As you wish, Meggie," he said softly.

She heard the heavy irony in his voice and it nearly undid her, but she steeled her resolve. "Thank you. I will leave tonight as soon as I am packed. You needn't worry, I will take Hadrian with me."

"Take anything you wish," he said, and then he was gone.

26

"Meggie did *what*? And you let her go, just like that?" The dowager duchess looked at her son as if he'd lost his mind.

"Yes, just like that," he replied, turning his back and gazing out the window of the drawing room. He was so tired from battling with himself that he could hardly think, let alone speak. He certainly didn't want to go into a long explanation of why Meggie had left him. His mother would only agree with her decision.

"Darling, when I left you earlier, all was perfect, and this evening I come downstairs for dinner only to discover your wife gone, you looking like something the cat dragged in, and the staff all tiptoeing around with long faces as if it were the end of the world. What on earth did you do to chase her away?"

Hugo just shook his head. What he'd done, he'd done in what seemed like a lifetime ago. His crime had caught up to him, as he'd always knew it would. Really, it was a miracle he'd managed to fool Meggie as long as he had.

"You might find it helps to talk about it," his mother said.

He turned back to face his mother, but found the sympathetic look on her face almost too much to bear. "Leave it alone, Mama," he said, his voice hoarse. "There's nothing to be done, nothing to be said. Meggie made her position perfectly clear: she wants nothing more to do with me, and I can't say I blame her."

"Don't be absurd," the dowager said firmly. "I have to assume this is your first marital tiff from the way you are behaving, so let me give you a piece of unsolicited advice. Whatever you did to upset Meggie can most likely be mended with a few well-chosen words of apology, and the sooner you make them the better. It doesn't do to let these things drag on."

"The only apology I can see Meggie accepting would be one in which I put a gun to my head and pull the trigger," he said bitterly.

"Hugo!" his mother cried, jumping up from her chair, her lips and cheeks suddenly bloodless. "Don't ever say such a thing—not *ever,* do you hear me?"

Hugo, who had never seen his mother so visibly upset, stared at her in astonishment. "I was only speaking metaphorically," he said, wondering if she'd actually thought him serious. "I'm not so despondent as to want to take my life, Mama, although right now I feel as if it might be a great deal easier to be dead. Dead men can't feel."

The duchess slowly sat down again, her hands gripping the sides of her chair. "Nevertheless, I would rather you not say such things," she said in a nearly inaudible voice. She cleared her throat, pressed her hands flat on her knees, then raised her head and looked at him, perfectly composed again. "Now, back to the business of patching up your quarrel with Meggie. I presume she has gone back to Lyden, which would be the sensible thing to do, and Meggie strikes me as being a sensible girl."

"Infinitely sensible," Hugo replied. "She also has a remarkable sense of self-preservation. Look, Mama, to save you wasting your breath, the truth of the matter is that Meggie discovered some unsavory things about me that I'd rather not go into. My past, shall we say, is rearing its ugly head."

"Oh, is *that* all? Well, really, darling, what else did you expect?"

Hugo very nearly laughed. "I have no idea. I suppose I expected nothing less. As I said, I deserved what I had coming. Meggie would be ma—Meggie has no reason to take me back."

"Save that she loves you," his mother pointed out. "Hugo, it is not like you to sit back and lick your wounds. You have always been a fighter, so I suggest that you fight. You love Meggie—that is obvious."

Hugo bowed his head. "That is also the point. I love her more than I can say, and because I love her, I wish only for her happiness. Unfortunately, now that she knows the ugly truth about me, all I am able to give her is what she asked for—a life at Lyden free of me."

"My dear child, you seem to think that by sacrificing yourself on this ridiculous pyre of nobility you have built that you can atone for all of your past mistakes. I am afraid it is far too late for that."

"Thank you so much for your words of comfort," Hugo said caustically. "And here I was thinking you were trying to help."

"You really can be a silly boy," his mother said, ignoring the acute pain he was in. "My point is that mistakes are to be learned from. The way you are going about matters, you are only going to compound your mistakes tenfold. You are under the impression that the past is the issue, when the issue really is the future." She waved her hand at him. "Now go and order a carriage and be on your way. By now Meggie must be wondering where you are."

Hugo, already exhausted and pushed to the limit of his emotional endurance, snapped. "I don't think you've heard a bloody word I said," he roared. "Meggie doesn't *want* me!"

"That's perfectly ridiculous. Of course Meggie wants you. She's just upset, and when women are upset, they like to make a statement. She's made hers, and now it's time for you to make yours. Really, Hugo, sometimes I wonder if you understand the first thing about human nature."

"I am trying," he said tightly. "I have not had much practice to date."

She smiled at him fondly. "If you remember nothing else, remember that you are no longer that foolish, rebellious boy who so liked to get into trouble. You are a responsible married man who is devoted to his wife, his land, and his tenants." She chuckled. "I've often thought it peculiar that men govern entire countries but never seem to understand what is going on right under their noses."

She pushed herself to her feet, marched over to the window, and gave him a peck on the cheek. "Do let me know how it all turns out. I will be here in London for at least the next fortnight, spreading the good tidings about your marriage. Yes, and I think a wedding announcement in the papers would be a good idea . . ."

Hugo shook his head in exasperation. "You really haven't been listening. Still, if you wish to embarrass yourself, go right ahead."

"I do love you, darling," she said, not looking the least bit concerned. "Loring, order up a carriage for Lord Hugo," she called as she vanished through the doorway. "He needs to depart for Suffolk immediately."

Hugo stared after her, his eyes narrowed in thought. Exactly fifteen seconds later he bolted out of the room and commanded Mallard to pack his case.

"My dear girl, as lovely and unexpected as it is to see you, I can also see that you are distressed," Sister Agnes said, looking unperturbed by Meggie's dawn arrival. "I think what you need is food and sleep in that order, and then we will talk about what troubles you."

For some ridiculous reason, Meggie felt vastly relieved

and reassured by Sister Agnes's matter-of-fact control of the situation. She was right. Meggie was deeply distraught, exhausted, and hungry, and the latter two problems were the first that needed fixing. The most important issue could wait. Meggie knew she wouldn't make much sense right now anyway.

She'd ended up at the Woodbridge Sanitarium rather than at Lyden because she'd felt the deep necessity to search her soul, and Sister Agnes was the only person she knew who could help her in that quest. Sister Agnes was also the only person who could help her with the answers she needed about Hugo.

She did exactly as Sister Agnes suggested, eating an early breakfast, then curling up in the bed of her old room. Hadrian rested in his accustomed place on the floor next to her. She closed her weary eyes and finally slept.

"Hugo, darling boy! How wonderful to have you back!"

Dorelia and Ottoline had come rushing out of the house the instant they'd heard the carriage and were now jumping up and down in tandem, their hands flapping wildly in the air.

"Why, where's Madrigal?" Ottoline asked, peering inside the carriage.

"Hugo . . . what have you done with her?" Dorelia demanded, turning to him, her eyes filled with deep suspicion.

Hugo's heart sank. "Do you mean she's not here? She should have arrived at least three hours ago."

"No, she's not here, and I would like to know why you think she should be," Dorelia retorted, her eyes flashing. "Since when does darling Madrigal leave London without you and drive through the night, may I ask?"

"The Betrayal!" Ottoline gasped. "Oh, Sister, it is the Betrayal to be sure!"

Dorelia's eyes grew huge. "Ottoline, I do believe you must be correct. Oh, dear. What are we to do now? Does your B.G. tell you anything, anything at all? Poor Madrigal, the dear, darling angel. She must be in a terrible way. Quickly, beloved, you must see what you can see."

Hugo, who had been on the road for eleven hours with no sleep, a stomach knotted with anxiety, and a guilty conscience screaming at him the entire ninety miles, bellowed, "What the *bloody* hell are you two jabbering about?"

"Hush," Dorelia snapped. "Ottoline is working."

Hugo stared at the other auntie, who had closed her eyes and was swaying back and forth, while her sister started to hum and sway along. "Oh, dear God," he muttered. "They're mad. Utterly gone. Lunatic."

"If anyone is lunatic, it is you," Dorelia said, pinching his arm hard. "We should never have let you go off to London, not with the Betrayal waiting in the wings, and now you've gone and lost Madrigal, so shut your trap while Ottoline tries to find her. The B.G. does *not* like to be interrupted."

"What the devil is the B.G.?" he demanded, rubbing his bruised bicep.

"The Blessed Gift, you idiot. All the women in the family have it one way or the other, your wife included." Dorelia stomped on his foot, and he yelped in surprise. "Now be quiet!"

Hugo glowered at her, then at her undulating sister, who looked as if she thought she were about to receive the Word of God directly from heaven. The Blessed Gift? What the hell was that? "What do you mean, Meggie has it, too?" he hissed in Dorelia's ear. "Explain yourself, woman!"

"Oh, for heaven's sake," Dorelia whispered back. "Ottoline has the Sight of the Future, I have the Healing Power, and Madrigal has the ability to Read Minds. If I didn't know better, I'd think that she'd read yours and run away, which would make perfect sense, but she says you are the only person she can't access at all. You're a blank to her, always have been."

Hugo peered down at her in disbelief. "You're trying to make me believe that Meggie really *can* read minds?"

"I'm not trying to make you believe anything. I am simply stating the facts as they exist. She thought her B.G. was a curse instead of a blessing, the little lamb, until she came here and discovered that she was perfectly normal, just like us. Now stop interrupting."

Hugo didn't know what to think. He didn't believe in that sort of hocus pocus at all. Yet for the first time he had an explanation of how Meggie might have learned not only the truth about Foxlane, but also the intricate details of that night, when there had only been the three of them to see the cards dealt in that last hand. He'd been puzzling over it ever since.

He'd been puzzling over so much. She had given no indication that anything was amiss until she'd run into Foxlane in the entrance hall and suddenly—too suddenly—she'd been a mine of information, information that Foxlane most certainly hadn't handed her. Furthermore, as far as he knew, Meggie hadn't even heard of Boodle's, let alone been aware of what it was and what went on there.

And since when did she know anything about vingt-et-un? The nuns surely hadn't taught her. They'd been too busy teaching her Latin and Greek.

The nuns . . . of course. Sister Agnes.

Hugo's head shot up. *I'm going back to where I belong.*

Oh, God. Oh, dear, dear God. That was what she'd meant, that was why she hadn't come home. She really had left him.

"Never mind," he said to Ottoline, who was now weaving her hands back and forth in front of her face. "I know exactly where Meggie is."

Ottoline's eyes snapped open. "Well, if you know so much about it, what are you standing around for, pray tell? All *I* can see is something that looks remarkably like a penguin, which makes no sense at all to me."

"That would be Madrigal's Sister Agnes, dearest," Dorelia said triumphantly. "Quick, Roberto," she called to the butler who had been standing close by, listening to every scintillating word, "launch the barouche!"

"You will launch nothing," Hugo said, shoving both hands through his already disheveled hair. "Roberto, if you wish to make yourself useful, saddle up one of my geldings and bring it around instantly. You, aunties, will both stay here and out of trouble, do you understand?"

They both nodded, looking extremely pleased with themselves.

"Very good." He turned to go up into the house to splash some water on his face before setting off again.

"Yes, but Hugo, dear," Dorelia said, poking him on the arm, "what are you going to do about the Betrayal?"

"What betrayal?" he replied, wishing she'd stop abusing his person.

"How am I supposed to know? *The* Betrayal. Ottoline said there would be one, and it would all come out in London, and Madrigal had to be there at your side or else, and it must have come to pass, or why would Madrigal have run back to the sanitarium?"

Hugo gave her a long, hard look, wondering if there really wasn't something to this B.G. nonsense after all. "Never mind about that. I need to talk to Meggie and the sooner the better."

He had no idea what possessed him, but he leaned down and kissed Dorelia's cheek. "Don't worry," he said. "I'll find a way to bring her home."

"As Virgil said, *'Amor vincit omnia,'* " she replied, to Hugo's blank astonishment.

" *'Et nos cedamus amori,'* " Ottoline added, standing up on tiptoe for a kiss of her own. "Remember it, Hugo dearest."

"I'll remember," he said, gently brushing her soft, wrinkled cheek with his lips. "I will remember."

Love conquers all, and let us yield to love.

"Meggie dear, I have no trouble at all understanding why you are upset," Sister Agnes said when Meggie had finally finished. "What I cannot understand is why you feel that your marriage is compromised." She folded her hands in front of her on the desk and regarded Meggie impassively.

Meggie wanted to scream with frustration. She'd spent the last hour explaining everything to Sister Agnes in great detail. Still, there was no point getting herself more upset than she already was. She took a deep breath and released it.

"Hugo lied to me, Sister. He lied from the very beginning about why he wanted to marry me. He didn't love me in the least, he wanted my inheritance. It is no wonder he didn't care about my background—he needed the money too badly to have time to worry about that. How am I *supposed* to feel?"

"As you said, betrayed," Sister Agnes said calmly. "But isn't the point that *you* agreed to marry *him*? You didn't love him in the least, which you made perfectly clear to me as well as to him, I believe. You wanted your freedom, as I recall."

"Yes, Sister, but at least I was honest with him and

with you. I didn't make up a huge story about love at first sight and all that other drivel he fobbed off on me, not to mention everyone else, including his mother."

"Do not be so sure it was all drivel," Sister Agnes said with a smile. "You forget that I was right here the very first time he saw you, and if ever there was a man who looked as if he'd been struck by lightning, it was he. That was one reason why I believed him to be a man who thought himself in love when he came to ask for your hand. I do not believe you were indifferent, either."

Meggie colored hotly and looked down. Her feelings had been caused by sheer lust, it was true, but she could not say that she'd ever been indifferent to him, nor he to her in that way.

"Meggie. Your husband may have deceived you, and for that sin he will have to ask God's forgiveness as well as yours. But does God Himself not give us chance after chance to redeem ourselves? None of us is perfect, after all."

"I wasn't asking for perfection," Meggie replied, hot tears filling her eyes. "I was only asking for honesty. Hugo had chance after chance to tell me the truth, and yet he chose to continue to lie to me. How am I supposed to believe that he ever loved me, given that?"

"Has it not occurred to you that after you were married he really did fall as much in love with you as you did with him, that he was afraid of losing you if he told you the truth? Think, Meggie. Search your mind for signs that he felt remorse and your heart for the compassion to understand and forgive him."

Meggie did as she was asked, looking for something, anything that told her Hugo had at least not lied to her about his feelings, and that he fully regretted what he'd done. She'd been so overwhelmed since Foxlane's revelations, so hurt and distraught and angry, that she hadn't been able to think with any coherence at all. Now Sister

Agnes's clarity of vision helped to clear her own, and forced her to look even deeper, beyond her confusion to the wellspring of her heart.

Words came drifting back to her, spoken in those last moments of trust between them before the cataclysm tore their lives apart.

Mea maxima culpa . . . I have not been entirely honest with you. Will you hear me out, try to forgive me for the transgressions I have made? My love . . . my love . . .

They echoed over and over again in her head, reminding her of his tenderness. She remembered the haunted look in his eyes as he'd tried to make a beginning at confessing, for surely that was what he'd intended to do?

"I—I do remember something," she whispered. "He was going to tell me the truth, but we were interrupted. I'd forgotten until just now."

"I wonder what else you have forgotten, my child. You have spoken freely of your disappointment to learn of your husband's past behavior, your disappointment that he is not the man you thought him, and yet you have also spoken about the happiness you have experienced with him. Is it not possible that he has changed since marrying you, that he really is the person you thought him? Love can work miracles."

"It is possible, I suppose." With her whole heart she wanted to believe Sister Agnes.

"I should think it is more than possible. Think about the woman you have become, about how love and completion have changed you for the better. Why would they not do the same for your husband?"

"I—I don't know. I understand what you mean, but I cannot seem to move beyond the lies, the real reason Hugo married me. Shouldn't that be important?"

"Tell me this, child. Have you examined your own conscience to see if there are not perhaps things you have kept from your husband, small untruths you might have told him for reasons of your own?"

Meggie bowed her head. Sister Agnes was right. Meggie had allowed Hugo to think her stupid, uneducated. Worse, she had never told him about her gift, and why? Because she'd feared that he'd be disgusted if he knew the truth, that he would cease to love her. "Yes," she said in a small voice. "There are things I have kept from him because I was afraid he would turn away from me."

"Hmm. 'He that is without sin among you, let him first cast a stone,' " Sister Agnes said. She touched her fingers to her cross in the involuntary gesture Meggie had seen her make so many times before when reaching for wisdom.

"Do you have so little faith in God's plan for you both that you can think only of what brought about this marriage, rather than seeing what you have received from it, what you are destined to receive in the future? God must enact His divine plan in some earthly way, and I see no flaw in how cleverly He managed to bring you and your husband together."

Meggie covered her face with her hands, trying to stifle a sob of infinite relief as Sister Agnes's words sank in.

She didn't know what to say. She really didn't. She felt the biggest fool, for Sister Agnes was right, of course. If Hugo hadn't gambled away his money, he never would have wanted to marry Meggie for her money. She would still be living an empty life, and Hugo would not have Lyden, nor would the tenants have him to see to their safe future. The aunties would have nobody to brighten their days, and all in all, everyone would still be miserable. God must have had a plan, after all. Who was she to argue with Him?

Meggie looked up, wiping the tears from her cheeks. "I suppose I've been very silly."

"My dear, dear child, you have not been silly in the least. We are all entitled to our feelings, good and bad, and we are equally entitled to our doubts and disappointments. The trick is to relinquish those feelings and disappointments when they do us no good. We are responsible to ourselves and others for getting on with life, and that is what I believe you must do."

Meggie nodded. "I do love Hugo," she said, gulping back another sob. "I just wish I understood him better. I seem to understand everyone else too well, and him not at all. I thought he was so responsible, so caring about everyone, but then to learn about all his past misdeeds . . ."

"Meggie, have we not just been through all of this?" Sister Agnes said sternly.

Meggie nodded sheepishly. "It is just that everything was in that dreadful Foxlane's mind, you see, and oh, Sister—the images were so *awful*."

To her enormous surprise, Sister Agnes burst into peals of laughter. "That is what you get for nosing around in other people's heads," she said, wiping her eyes. "Oh, dear me, oh my goodness gracious. I am grateful I am not saddled with your gift, Meggie dear." She wiped her eyes again. "Poor, poor Lord Hugo, defenseless to protect himself."

"I don't know what you find so amusing," Meggie said, annoyed. Of all people, Meggie expected the nun to take Hugo's wayward behavior seriously.

Sister Agnes sobered abruptly. "Meggie. My dear child. Forgive me, for I think I have been insensitive. The truth is that you are yet young and you have much to learn. You might be able to read other people's thoughts, but that does not mean that you always have the wisdom to interpret correctly what you discover. First, you must remember the source from which you took your information, and second, you must remember that you do *not* know all there is to know about your husband's past."

She sighed, fingering her cross again. "I wonder if I should not tell you something most pertinent that I learned when the dowager duchess last came to see me. I hope I am not speaking out of turn, but I do believe you might understand your husband's behavior much better if you know what he suffered as a child."

"Please, Sister, anything you can tell me would be truly helpful."

"Very well, but you must agree that this information stays strictly between us, because your husband has no knowledge of the actual facts that surround his father's unfortunate death. His mother and brother would like to keep it that way."

Meggie knew only that Hugo's father had died in an accident when Hugo was a young child. Hugo had also made it clear to her that the subject was not open for discussion. "I will keep my silence," she said with alacrity.

"It all begins with an unfortunate mental illness the duke suffered from, a severe melancholia that came and went and created a terrible chaos when it exhibited itself—he had severe mood swings, and his behavior was unpredictable. Oh, dear. This is not easy to speak of."

She looked at Meggie with a sadness coupled with a hesitation that made Meggie sit up straight and clench her hands together. "Go on, Sister. Please." She tried to steady herself, sensing something truly awful coming. She could feel the dread inside Sister Agnes, the deep distress. "Please go on," she urged, knowing neither of them could leave it there, not now that the story had begun.

"Yes. Yes, of course I must." Sister Agnes drew in a deep breath. "The truth is that the duke committed suicide, Meggie. The poor dear man took his own life."

Meggie, taken completely aback, stared at Sister Agnes. "Hugo's father *killed* himself?"

"I am sorry to say he did, my child. Let me tell you a bit more about it though, so you can better understand exactly how it all came to pass . . ."

27

Hugo didn't even bother to tie up his horse. He threw the reins over its neck and dismounted, running straight for the door of the sanitarium. His only intention was to find Meggie and drag her out of there before she could draw another breath.

He'd spent the entire journey between Orford and Woodbridge praying—not a behavior he was accustomed to indulging in, but praying nonetheless and with the utmost sincerity. If he'd thought God wanted his firstborn child, he would have happily handed it over in exchange for Meggie and her forgiveness.

Anything—he'd do anything to get her back, anything to regain the peace he'd found with her, the fulfillment, the simple happiness.

The trouble was that he'd already bartered his soul to the devil a long time before, so it wasn't his to barter again to God. His heart, yes. He could still barter away his heart as he pleased, and a great aching bleeding miserable heart it was, belonging entirely to Meggie, whether she wanted it or not.

He knew that the likelihood of her wanting it was slim, but he still had to let her know it was hers. She could roast it for breakfast if she so chose. He couldn't bear the idea that she thought he didn't love her, that he had lied about that, too.

No one was in the hall, so he took himself straight to Sister Agnes's office, reasoning that she would know where on the grounds Meggie was.

The door was slightly ajar, and he was just about to knock when he heard the sound of Meggie's voice. His knees nearly collapsed as relief flooded through him. She was there. Safe. Thank the good Lord above, Meggie was safe.

"Go on, Sister, please. Please go on," she was saying, a note of urgency in her voice.

Hugo dropped his hand, not sure whether he ought to interrupt at this point. Perhaps it would be wiser to wait. And if he was to be perfectly honest with himself, he wanted to hear exactly what was on her mind. . . .

"Yes," Sister Agnes replied, her voice low and heavy with some strong regret, "yes, of course I must. The truth is that the duke committed suicide, Meggie. The poor dear man took his own life."

Hugo's heart nearly stopped. *What poor man—what duke were they talking about, for the love of God? Not his* father? *Never his father. It had to be someone else, some other duke.*

"Hugo's father *killed* himself?" Meggie said, her voice filled with shock.

"I'm sorry to say he did, my child . . ."

Hugo reeled back against the wall, his hands pressed hard over his temples as if he could block out what he'd just heard. No. Oh, God no. It couldn't be. Couldn't be. Someone would have said something—his mother, Rafe? Surely someone would have told him? The nun was wrong, that was all there was to it. She had to be wrong . . . his father had been a good man, a strong man. A sane man.

Oh, please God, please show some mercy. Tell me it's all a mistake.

But God had no mercy. None at all.

"Apparently the duke had been suffering from one of his unbalanced incidents, and he took his gun out into the field and . . . well, the painful fact is that he shot himself in the head," Sister Agnes relentlessly continued.

Each word pounded just as relentlessly into Hugo's

head. Each one ripped at his heart, shredded his very soul. His father had died of a shooting accident. A shooting *accident*.

"The most tragic thing was that the elder son witnessed his death. The duchess had no idea until recently, as he never spoke of it. She has suffered terribly from guilt for all these years, but now she struggles with the knowledge that she could not protect her child . . ."

Hugo couldn't bear to hear another word. He stumbled sightlessly down the corridor, fighting to pull air into his lungs. Somehow he made his way outside where he was immediately sick, heaving over and over although there was nothing in his stomach.

Trembling violently, he finally straightened and leaned back against the wall, with his head resting on the cool stone and tears pouring down his cheeks, blinding his vision.

His poor mother. She'd known the truth and suffered from it, carried a mountain of guilt. No wonder she'd gone white in the face when he'd made that stupid comment about putting a gun to his head and shooting himself . . .

And Rafe, Rafe had seen it all. . . . Dear Lord in heaven, Rafe had witnessed the whole damned thing and never said a word to anyone. He'd probably wanted their father to have a Christian burial instead of being interred at a crossroad with a stake through his heart, for committing suicide.

Suicide.

I cannot go on, it is all too much. . . . Best to finish myself . . .

Hugo shook his head over and over again, trying to block out the images that crowded into his brain—memories hidden so deep so long ago, when he'd been only five, that they had ceased to exist for him. But now, like a dam unstopped, they came pouring forth unchecked.

Each nightmare moment was as clear as if it had all happened yesterday.

The library, the forbidden room. He'd been playing, that was it. Playing soldiers, lost in an imaginary world where everything was safe, where nothing could harm him, where he could control events and their outcome, where fathers didn't shout and mothers didn't cry.

Then he'd heard his father coming and he'd run to hide behind the curtains of the window seat. Oh, *God,* he remembered it all now—how his father had come in and locked the door behind him, and he'd started to pace and rage, saying things Hugo couldn't fully understand, but which terrified him anyway. And then, while Hugo cowered silent as a mouse behind the curtains, his eyes squeezed shut, barely daring to breathe, his father had stopped raging and begun to weep.

It is all too much, I cannot go on. Best to end it quickly. Best to finish myself, put this misery to rest. Eleanor, the children, they'll be better off without me—I am no good for them, no good for anyone. I'll do it. This time I'll do it.

A long silence had followed, and then the sound of the door finally unlocking, his father's footsteps going out, and the door softly closing behind him.

Hugo hadn't been able to bear locked doors ever since.

Or the hoot of the owl. He suddenly remembered why. That was how his father used to say good night to him, softly imitating the owl's plaintive call. *Hoo hoo-hoo, hoo hoo-hoo, time for all little boys to go to bed.*

And then he'd kiss Hugo, give him a pat on his bottom, and send him upstairs to the nursery.

Hugo groaned, feeling as if his belly had just been sliced open. He blindly started to run, desperate to get away from the memories, as if he could outdistance them if he went far enough, fast enough.

The next awareness he had was being in a copse. He

had no idea how much time had passed or exactly where he was, only that he was doubled over on the ground, with his arms wrapped around his waist as if he could keep his guts from spilling out.

Something cold and wet poked into his neck, and he reached his hand out to push it away. His fingers encountered warm fur.

Hadrian, he vaguely registered through the tempest that tore through him, threatening to destroy his very foundation. It was Meggie's wolf Hadrian, a solid reminder of reality, enough to shock him back to the present.

He wrapped his arms around the animal, burying his face in the soft, sweet-smelling fur as if the wolf could somehow anchor him, save him from destruction. But he knew in the deepest part of his heart that he needed more than Hadrian if he was going to survive. He needed his wife.

"Meggie," he cried, lifting his head to the heavens and releasing a keening wail that came from the deepest part of his soul, "oh God, Meggie, my love, I need you . . . please, come to me? Please—please come to me . . ."

Meggie lifted her head in the middle of Sister Agnes's sentence, listening. She was aware only of the slightest whisper inside her head, no more than a rustle, but she felt a desperation behind it. It was a call from somewhere that she couldn't place. She frowned.

"Meggie, what is it, child? You look preoccupied."

"Forgive me, Sister. I was paying attention, really I was—it's just that something . . . well, something interrupted. I don't know what exactly." She rubbed her fingers against the sides of her head.

"Never mind, my dear. I was only saying that in the course of my work here I have observed that very often people are deeply influenced by events in their past that they might not even be aware of, but which still exert a strong influence on them. Do you understand what I am saying?"

Meggie nodded, trying to concentrate despite her distraction. "Are you saying that because Hugo lost his father in a tragic fashion when he was very young, he felt angry and abandoned and decided to misbehave as a result?"

"In a way. Your husband might not remember very much at all about his father, but he is bound to have been affected by his father's irrational behavior, as well as his untimely death. Meggie, for goodness sake, what has gotten into you? You look as if your chair is on fire."

"I—I don't know," she replied. "I feel as if there's something very important I should be doing, but I cannot think what it is. . . ."

As the words came out of her mouth, Hadrian came tearing through the door and jumped up on her. With paws on her shoulders and yellow eyes boring into hers, he communicated every bit of urgency that she'd been feeling.

"What—Hadrian, what on earth is it?" she asked, fully focused on him. "Tell me. I'm listening."

He gently took her sleeve in his teeth and pulled, insisting she come with him.

"I have to go," she said to Sister Agnes. "I don't know what's happened, but I have to go now." Without waiting for a reply, she leapt up and tore out after Hadrian who had already turned and run out of the room.

He didn't stop, loping out of the house and across the lawn, heading directly for the woods. As Meggie followed, she saw Hugo's horse grazing freely, Hugo nowhere in sight.

Meggie, my love, I need you . . . come to me . . . please, come to me?

She didn't stop to think, even to wonder why Hugo was at the sanitarium. She knew now with absolute certainty that he was in terrible trouble and needed her. She ran faster than she ever had in her life, praying he wasn't injured, that his life was not in danger.

"I'm coming, Hugo," she cried when she was forced to stop, nearly doubled over from the stitch that grabbed at her side. Hadrian paused and looked back at her impatiently, his burning golden gaze demanding that she hurry. "I'm coming, just wait, you have to wait for me," she panted, then took a few deep, steadying breaths and hurried on.

In the end she spotted Hugo easily, even before Hadrian reached him. He sat with his back huddled against a beech tree, his knees pulled up, his forehead lowered on them, his shoulders hunched and shaking. Thank God, she sobbed in relief when she saw that he was physically in one piece. But relief was instantly replaced by fear. It was not his body that was in danger but his mind. Hugo was in terrible emotional pain. Some dreadful torment was tearing him to pieces.

She ran to his side, dropping to her knees and wrapping her arms as tightly around him as she could, pulling him close against her.

"I'm here, my beloved, I am here," she whispered against his cheek. "You are safe. Safe, my love, my darling. Safe with me."

His arms went hard around her back, practically crushing the breath out of her. "Meggie," he said, his voice barely audible. "Meggie, my Meggie. You came. You really came."

"Yes, of course I came. What else would I do, Hugo? I love you."

He moved his hands up her back and buried them in her hair with a groan. "Thank God for that," he said, his voice ragged. "Thank God at least for that."

"What is it? What happened?" she asked, trying to sound calm despite her panic. She pressed her cheek against his, trying to sense something, anything that might give her a clue, but all she could feel was his desperate unhappiness. He'd had a terrible shock, that much was clear.

"Did Mr. Foxlane come back after I left?" she asked tentatively feeling him out. "Or Lord Waldock, perhaps? Did you receive bad news of some kind?"

He muffled an acerbic laugh against her neck. "Bad news? I suppose you might say that. I just learned that my father killed himself, that every last damned glorious thing I've ever believed in my life about him was a pack of lies, Meggie. A pack of lies."

"You overheard Sister Agnes and myself," she said, her blood turning to ice. She couldn't believe it. Of all the dreadful things that might have happened, that had to be the worst.

"Yes," he said tonelessly. "I came to find you, to talk to you, tell you how much I love you and how much I regret your learning the truth the way you did. Instead I discovered that for the last twenty-one years I've been laboring under a gross misapprehension." He shuddered heavily. "I can't—I can't somehow seem to take it in properly."

"Hugo—oh, Hugo, I am so sorry, so very, very sorry," she murmured, kissing his cheek, his hair, and smoothing her hands over his back. She tried to somehow draw him close enough to protect him from the savage pain that rocked him.

"I'm sorry," he said, his voice cracking. "I don't think I'm entirely in my right mind, Meggie. Perhaps I take after my father after all."

She felt the tears on his face where her cheek pressed against his, felt the anguish in his heart where her love claimed its own part. "You are entirely in your right mind," she said softly. "You always have been. How can you possibly expect to take such news with equanimity? No one could."

He released a broken sigh. "No. I suppose not. Memories—I have so many damned memories that have come out of nowhere, like one giant nightmare that wants to suck me under with it."

He shakily recounted what he'd remembered, Meggie listening carefully. When necessary, she added details she'd learned from Sister Agnes in order to help him complete the picture of what had happened that terrible day.

Nearly as shaken as he by the time they'd finished, she kissed his hair, then both his eyelids, tasted the salt of his tears. "The nightmare is in the past, my darling. Now that you've finally remembered you can wake up, wake up and be free. Please believe me when I tell you that it is not your burden to carry—you told me much the same thing when I learned the truth about my parents. You said it was my story but not my fault, and surely the same holds true for you?"

"How did you ever become so wise?" he said, pressing his mouth to her forehead. "Meggie, my blessing from God."

"We have both been blessed by God," she said. "I think that was His great lesson to me, that faith must guide us, faith and trust that He gives us what we need. It is up to us to open our arms to His gifts and His grace. I forgot that yesterday when I left London."

"Forgive me, my love," he said, running his hands over his face. "Forgive me for that, for all manner of things, but at this moment forgive me for being such a pathetic excuse for a man. I came to try to make things right between us, and all I seem to be able to do is show you what a weak character I really am."

"No, Hugo. There is nothing weak about you—you

are fine and strong, a survivor despite the difficulties of your childhood. I do think you are too harsh on yourself."

He shook his head against hers. "Look what I've done to you, you, who had a far more difficult childhood. I saddled you with a marriage contracted under pretense, swore that I loved you before I actually did, I lied to you about your inheritance. I pretended complete innocence about it when Gostrain came calling—when it was Gostrain whom I inadvertently heard talking about the inheritance in his office when he was looking for the missing heir. That was what led me to you. I already knew your name and a few details of your life from Sister Agnes, enough to make me certain you were the person he sought." He sighed heavily. "I'm sure I've left out a large number of my other sins, but no matter just now. You have no reason to forgive me for anything, and yet you think I'm being harsh on myself. My generous Meggie."

Meggie hiccupped against his neck, her heart bursting with love for him. "I have no reason not to forgive you," she said, struggling for coherent speech herself and not making a very good job of it. "I have every reason to ask for your own forgiveness."

"My forgiveness?" he said, raising his head with a choked attempt at a laugh. "Pray tell, my love. What do you imagine I have to forgive you for?"

Meggie sucked in a deep breath and summoned up every last ounce of courage she had. "I haven't told you the truth about me. About a part of me." She scrunched up her face and forced the words out. "About my aberration."

He burst into laughter so unrestrained that Meggie did have to wonder if he was in his right mind. His entire body shook with hilarity. "Do—do you mean about your . . . about your B.G.?" he gasped, wiping at his tears, this time ones of laughter.

Meggie stared at him, appalled. How could he possibly know about it—unless . . . unless Ottoline and Dorelia had told him? Who else used that expression?

She saw it all in a flash, Hugo going back to Lyden to find her, the sisters spilling the truth in a misguided attempt to smooth things over. "Oh, those wicked, wicked aunties—they *did* tell you," she said accusingly. "I really will murder them!"

"What, murder those adorable aunties? Over my dead body," he said, taking her face between his hands. "We need them, Meggie. Or at least, we will if you agree to come back to me. Will you, sweetheart? Will you come home?"

"I was never *not* coming home, I only needed some time with Sister Agnes to clear my thoughts and gain some perspective."

He smiled. "Do you mean I really didn't have to come chasing after you in a horrific panic that I'd lost you forever?"

"No, but I'm amazed you did after what the aunties told you about me. Are you *sure* you really don't mind about my being a freak?" she said, smiling back at him.

"A freak? Heavens, no. Look what good use you've already put your talents to, uncovering Foxlane's nefarious deeds and saving us two hundred thousand pounds in the bargain. I call that a boon. Anyway, since I understand from the aunties that you find me entirely inscrutable, why should I have anything to fear from your gift?"

"I do love you," she said, wrapping her arms around his neck. "I will love you forever. And yes, I will come home."

" 'Flesh of flesh, bone of my bone thou art, and from

thy state mine never shall be parted, bliss or woe,' " he murmured against her cheek.

"John Milton, *Paradise Lost*," she said happily, reaching up to kiss him.

He returned her kiss in full measure, and Meggie could feel all the love in his heart pouring into hers, filling her, completing her, making her finally whole. He loved her just as she was, just as God had made her, complete with strengths and flaws, and she loved him in the same way.

God really had blessed them with each other.

"Come, sweetheart," he said when he eventually stopped kissing her. "Let's you, Hadrian, and I go home. I promised the aunties that I'd return you safe and sound."

He stood, reaching down a hand to help her up, then whistled for Hadrian, who had taken up a watchful position under a nearby gorse bush. Hadrian immediately jumped to his feet and padded over to Hugo's side as if he'd always belonged there.

Meggie smiled to herself. More than one issue had been resolved that day.

"By the by," Hugo said casually, his arm wrapped around her waist, "I was thinking . . . between your B.G. and the aunties', we really could make a killing on the 'Change, don't you think?"

"Hugo!" Meggie said, looking over at him in mock horror.

He laughed. "Don't worry, my love, my gambling days really are over. You are the rest and the best of my life. . . ."